YOU and the PIRATES

Cover design and illustration by Jade Ratcliffe
Editing by Vivienne Jones

Library and Archives Canada Cataloguing in Publication

Allen, Jocelyne, 1974-
You and the pirates / Jocelyne Allen.

ISBN 978-0-9812612-0-1

I. Title.

PS8601.L4453Y69 2009   C813'.6   C2009-903335-6

The Workhorsery
132 Heward Avenue
Toronto, ON
M4M 2T7
www.theworkhorsery.ca

10 9 8 7 6 5 4 3 2 1

YOU and the PIRATES

jocelyne allen

THE WORKHORSERY

You

You don't think anyone was expecting the Honda building to explode.

Of course, you were hoping it would, but only idly, in that way you used to hope that the car behind you would explode when you tossed your cigarette out the window. You never actually expected that the car behind you would really somehow catch fire from the smouldering remains of your cigarette as the butt flew beneath its tires. You just tore your eyes from the road long enough to follow the arc of your cigarette in the rear view mirror and verify the lack of explosions or fires behind you. A way to pass the time on long drives across the prairies where the best you can hope for is a cigarette-induced explosion.

You were just standing there, distractedly playing with your mobile phone, watching the rush-hour stragglers make their way down those steps that always stink of urine. You had decided that meeting here would be easier than a station closer to where you would end up. Less crowded, easier to find each other. Plus, it was looking to be a nice evening and the walk would do you good. You swear you can feel your ass spreading in your soft office chair as the days slip by.

A flash like lightening, but the thunder is accompanied by dirt and glass and crap flying through the sky and hitting you in the face, on the head, your hand still typing in a message to your date sitting on a train. You look up just at the tail end, when it's almost over and it's the Honda building. The crap is flying out of the Honda building directly across the street from you, from one of the top floors. You wonder if that's the president's office, if someone finally took that guy out. Bombing him seems extreme, though.

Around you, the rush-hour suits are throwing themselves to the ground mostly. A few are standing like you, mouths half-open, staring up at the fire burning on the thirteenth or fourteenth floor across the street. Seeing them, you close your own mouth. A lot of the debris and glass seems to be headed for mouths.

Across the other street from you, the three police officers from the police box have rushed out onto the corner to join you and the rush-hour people in staring. Two of them just stand and stare, like all you yahoos on the street, but the third one, the younger one that directs traffic in the morning, despite the traffic lights which function perfectly, starts yelling and pointing. You listen hard and think you can hear him shouting, "Terrorists! Terrorists!" Which is a perfectly natural reaction since these days, the whole city is on 'high alert', as the signs all over the train stations tell you. Although 'high alert' seems to mostly consist of taking the garbage cans out of the stations.

But when you follow the line of his pointing finger, you see what he's talking about. The terrorists. Who appear to be four or five people, you can't quite make them out, shimmying down the side of the building. You have half a mind to shake your head cartoon-style and rub your eyes in disbelief. Instead, you squint and try to move closer, as if walking those three steps to the edge of the sidewalk will help you see into the evening sky better. There are actually people sliding down the side of the Honda building. They seem to have ropes, or you hope they do anyway, but still, what the hell is going on? If they're really terrorists, why would they blow up one floor of the Honda building? Don't terrorists have better targets?

Walking too close to the edge of the sidewalk in your attempt to see into the sky demonstrates to you in a very real way that the traffic is still moving, surprisingly. A lot of cars just don't seem to care that something exploded. You guess that they just want to get home or whatever, which you can understand. If you had been at work today, you'd want to get home too. But the heavy traffic on this street makes it practically impossible for the police or anyone to get here, other than the three officers manning the police box across the street. But those are the guys you ask for directions to the nearest Indian restaurant; they're not exactly equipped to handle explosions. Traffic Director thinks this is his chance to shine, though. He's jumped out into traffic and, with his flag in one hand and whistle in the other, is bringing traffic to a halt, clearing the way for the fire engines and ambulances and police cars sirening their way to the scene.

No one seems to be hurt. Not seriously at least. Most everyone dropped to the ground or covered their heads to protect themselves, and their clothing took the rest of the blow. And was the explosion even that big to begin with? Feeling like it wasn't. You take a look at the backs of your hands and see a piece of glass stuck in the one, not so deep, but other than that, no real damage. You pull the shard out and wish you had a mirror to check your face.

Slowly, emergency vehicles are arriving. You remember the high speed of ambulances you saw arriving on the scene when you were in Canada and have to smile a little at the toy truck speed of these ambulances. You can walk faster than that. But at least now, thanks to Traffic Director, you can cross the street and get a better look at those guys coming down the side of the building. Who are almost down at this point. Shit, they're fast.

But on your way across, a paramedic accosts you and drags you to a nearby ambulance. It seems that you are bleeding in an ugly way and this guy will not take no for an answer. Looking up, you see that the terrorists or whoever they were have disappeared, so either they got down to the ground and made their getaway or they got down to the ground and got arrested. Either way, you'll have to wait to hear about it on the news. You submit to the persistent paramedic and allow your minor wounds to be treated.

You're following Persistent Paramedic's finger with your eyes, just your eyes, since you've been chided at least twice now for moving your head, when you hear your name and look up.

"Shit hell, here you are!" The boy, the one you were waiting for when this all started, the one you totally forgot about once shit started falling from the sky on your head, runs up to you and bends over, hands on his knees, panting. He still smokes. He pushes his hood back and looks at you. "Are you okay? I mean, really. You look like hell."

"Gee, thanks." You remind yourself that he's good in bed.

He stands up straighter now, still panting a little, but back under control for the most part. Runs a hand through his short hair. "No, c'mon, you know what I mean. You have dust or some crap all over you, there's blood on your face. You don't look so okay. Are you okay?"

Persistent Paramedic eyes him suspiciously and answers for you. "Just some scratches and cuts from the debris from the explosion. Nothing serious." He turns to you. "In fact, you can go now. I think the police will want to talk to you, though, so you had better stay nearby for a while. You seem okay, but if you start feeling strange in any way, like suddenly being extremely drowsy or having trouble swallowing or hearing, please go to the nearest hospital and see a doctor. Or come see me again." He smiles winningly and you suddenly understand what the suspicious look to the boy was about. Persistent here was hoping for a little more than tending your wounds. Does he always look for his next date at the scene of an emergency? If so, what kind of relationships does he end up having? You half-consider giving him your number, just to find out. But the boy is standing right there and he wouldn't understand where you were coming from on that, so you return Persistent's smile and thank him, then allow Boy to lead you away from the ambulance, the street, the scene.

"What the hell happened here?" he asks, holding your hand, walking you to the sidewalk where you started the evening.

You glance up. The fire coming from the top floors is smaller, it's obvious the firefighters are on the scene and soon enough, there will be no fire at all. "It exploded."

He follows your gaze and his eyebrows slide up his forehead. "That? The Honda building? Someone blew up the Honda building?"

You pull your hand free of his and lean back against the window of a shop. Nod. "Yeah. I was standing here waiting for you and it exploded. Bam. Nuts."

The eyebrows slide back down and pull in towards the centre of his face. "It just exploded? Shit. Are you sure you're okay?" He starts to move towards you, but is pushed back by a salaryman stumbling by. Drunk? Injured by the explosion? Somehow, you feel sure it's the former. He probably doesn't even notice all the sirens and flashing lights.

You're thinking this and suddenly he's grabbing you. Not in the way the salarymen on the train grab you, but his hand is on the ribbed collar of the shirt you bedazzled yourself and he's yanking it up and towards him with all his might, you with it, some comic strip come to life, so hard that your breath jumps out of your chest. The shirt pulls up into your armpits and the fake jewels on the sleeves dig into your arms until you think they will draw blood from you. His face in yours and there's no alcohol on his breath when he hisses, "There was no one on the side of the building." His eyebrows are pulled to the centre of his face in a completely different way than Boy's. There's no mistaking the intent behind his words. He has you pulled so close, your nose actually bumps his. His face fills your field of vision, but too close so that you can't make out any features except the stray hairs in the space between his eyebrows. "Right?"

Although you live in one of the largest cities in the world in a country with a ridiculously high population density, you have never before come close to being threatened with real injury or face-to-face with any kind of crime other than the petty kind. Scamming the train, gropers and panty thieves, that's about all you know of the seedy underbelly. So you're scared now and all you can think to do is to kick this guy in the balls. But even that you think of too slowly, too late, and he gives you a shake.

"There was an explosion and a fire, but there were no people on the side of the building." His voice is barely a whisper, but it reaches your ears like he was yelling.

And you actually feel yourself gulp. Not only feel it, but hear it and you want to bust out laughing at how stereotyped and cartoonish this situation is. Only it's real and you are scared, so you keep your gulp-related laughter to yourself and nod, force your voice out of your throat. "Yeah, there was just that explosion."

Sweet release. He drops you the way a real salaryman drops the end of a cigarette on his way back to the office after lunch and lurches away, not even pausing to look at Boy, who has barely had a chance to realize what's going on.

And he didn't even. "Did that guy just grab at your chest? How much has he had to drink? Should we get the police? Are you okay?" He didn't see anything and you realize it was not so long, this time with your shirt in your armpits.

You turn your head to watch Salaryman walk away, but he's already gone. What you want to know is how did he know that you saw the guys on the side of the building? Everyone saw it. Was he just standing somewhere watching you in particular? You suddenly wish you had taken some kind of self-defence course so that you could at least pretend you could protect yourself. You've let the surface safety of this city lull you.

"No, there's no point. He's already gone."

"Man, what the hell is going on?" He sounds as bewildered as you feel. Which is odd since you are the one that all the crazy shit is happening to. You want nothing more than a stiff drink right now.

"Fucked if I know. C'mon, buy me a drink." You slip your arm through the crook of his.

"Don't you have to stick around and talk to the police?" He is concerned about illegalities, but it is clear that he wants to get out of here. He looks like he needs a stiff drink too.

You shake your head. "Why? I saw what any of the other hundred people here saw. Maybe less. I saw a flash, looked up, saw some fire, had some glass fall on my head. What's to tell?"

One stiff drink turns into you stopped counting hours ago. Through your vodka-stained eyes, Boy is charming and entertaining and you can't imagine what you would do without him. When you wake up the next morning, though, you find yourself wondering if he really stuck that *edamame* up his nose and if he did, what does that mean for your relationship with him? He may charm you after several stiff drinks, but really. Are you looking for a man who will stuff beans up his nose in a sad attempt to entertain you?

Praying to any deities that may exist, you clutch your head and push the heavy blankets off you. It's silly the number of blankets you need to keep warm at night. Once again, you long for the central heating you enjoyed in North America or even the radiator of your crappy apartment in Europe. Anything besides the frozen morning air that greets you now.

You curse as you realize your slippers are lost to you somewhere in your tiny flat, and stumble to the washroom, find that you have the strength and coordination to make toothpaste and toothbrush come together. And to bring the whole combination to your mouth. Your prayers have not gone unanswered. You ask yourself if you shouldn't have prayed for something better than the ability to drag your gigantic, pounding head out of bed.

Enduring the back-and-forth scritch-scratch of your toothbrush, you remember the explosion. Oh yeah, the explosion. And Salaryman. What the hell? You leave your toothbrush hanging out of your mouth to stand there scratching your head and your ass simultaneously.

You're not the only one who saw the terrorists or whoever they were coming down the side of the building. Hell, it was Traffic Director crying out and pointing that made you look up in the first place. Practically everyone on the street must have seen what you saw. And it's not like Salaryman could go round and pick everyone there up by their collars and give them all a good shake. No matter how strong that forearm of his was, there's just the physical impossibility of getting to all those people in the limited time before the police really made a strong showing.

You grab the dangling toothbrush and wincingly resume brushing, decide to give it up and cut the whole thing short, to make spitting and rinsing as quick and pain-free as possible. Wipe your mouth on the towel that smells like old closet and curse the humid air that makes everything mold in seconds. Everything in your house smells like old washcloths and unwashed grandfathers.

Explosion, right. Stay on track. You're a little freaked out by the whole accosted by Salaryman thing. And the worst part is you couldn't identify him if you tried since all you really saw of him was his nose and his pants that were too short and kind of pulled up his ass a little. But you seriously can't deny how scared you were when he had you by the collar. And although you didn't say anything to the police — hence, the previous night's heavy drinking and your current aching head — you're still afraid that he'll—what? Come back? How would he find you? He didn't steal your wallet. A quick glance at the contents of your bag somehow spread all over the sofa is proof of that. It's true that you're often in that area, since you work there, but doubtful that he is really going to be hanging around. So what are you feeling so freaked out about?

The coffee percs while you stand in front of the machine.

It's doesn't make any sense at all for him to threaten you. If you could feasibly reveal something unknown to anyone but you, then you could feel safe by keeping your mouth shut. It's not like you're in love with Honda. You have no real reason to see the bombers behind bars. If you knew something, you could keep it to yourself and protect yourself. It would be that simple. But the fact is, all you know is what everyone else knows. The cops don't need to talk to you to know what you know. They're the ones who showed it to you in the first place.

Pour coffee, drink coffee, hold head.

You should just forget the whole thing. Those guys coming down the side of the building are no concern of yours. Salaryman obviously has no real interest in you. Probably just some drunk trying to make you shit your pants. Forget it. Drink your coffee, take a shower, spend some time with Boy. His solicitousness always makes you feel secure.

Beans? He really stuck *edamame* up his nose?

Boy is not meeting your eyes for some reason and you have a bad feeling about what's coming. You just want to hang out, have him soothe you and maybe make you forget about the whole explosion yesterday. And have sex. You confess to yourself that you would also like to be having sex with him at some point today. Instead, you are in a 'family restaurant', one of the millions of peculiarly Japanese chain restaurants filled with uncomfortable vinyl booths, all serving the same 'hamburg steak' and salads covered in seaweed. The only good thing that can be said about the family restaurant is that there is a drink bar supplying endless free refills. And even that happiness is tainted by the low quality of the drinks. After two cups of that coffee, it no longer matters if it's free; you don't want to force any more of it down your gullet.

However, Boy enjoys watered-down soft drinks, hamburg steak smothered in ketchup and chain-smoking, so he is quite at home in any family restaurant. Which is why you are stuck here. Today, though, he is nursing that soda and smoking even more heavily than usual, all the while boring you to tears with detailed descriptions of his colleagues at the tire company where he works. (He's a salaryman in training.) Boring you to tears without meeting your eyes.

"So I was thinking," he starts, lighting another cigarette when the carcass of his last one is still smouldering in the ashtray.

Here it comes, the emotional confession. Will it be break up talk or I love you talk? You are not especially eager to hear either. Why can't you just go back to your place and have sex?

You can almost see him mustering his courage. Slowly, it moves up his body, he leans forward, his eyebrows slide up, he takes a quick and forceful drag off his cigarette, raises his eyes to yours and then blurts, "What do you think about moving in together?" Spent, he leans back, exhales smokes, looks away.

You can't stop your own eyebrows from jumping up. Not quite a confession of love. Not a break-up. Moving in together. This is something new. "Moving in together?"

He nods, sucks at smoke again, puffs it out. "I mean, we've been seeing each other for a while and it seems like the next step."

"The next step?" Has he been reading one of those women's magazines? Does he know now one hundred and one ways to please his man? Where is this coming from?

He places his cigarette carelessly on the ashtray and it rolls off onto the table. You reach over, put it back on the ashtray so that it stays and when you go to pull your hand back, he stops you by placing his own hand on top. Looks meaningfully into your eyes. You glance involuntarily at the speakers in the ceiling. This is where the strings should come in. You're not sure whether it is good or bad that the nasal whining of the J-pop artist du jour continues.

"I just was thinking that you're someone I want to have in my life." He says this with a straight face, so sincere, so oblivious.

You have never had any intention of getting seriously involved with this boy. Let's be honest, he's a salaryman. True, he just started out, so he doesn't have the rotting teeth and the questionable personal odour yet, but you have caught him once or twice snorting for all he's worth and then spitting whatever appeared in his mouth out into the sink. It's only a matter of time before the long hours and societal pressure catch up with him. It's his destiny. But right now, he's still young, extremely good-looking, good at sex and even fun to hang out with at times. But not forever. Living together is out of the question. There's a good chance you would catch him hawking shit up into the sink again and all your stuff would stink of cigarettes. That smell already lingers for days after he has stayed at your place. Imagine it smelling like that all the time.

"Look, are you sure about this?" You try to get him talking so that you can have a moment to figure out how to deal with this.

He nods vigorously. "Totally. I've really been thinking about it, but especially since yesterday. Seeing you in the middle of all the ambulances and the fire and the police and I didn't know what the hell had happened. All I could think about was whether or not you were okay. When I thought that something might have happened to you..." He allows himself to trail off and again you find yourself looking at those speakers.

"I'm just not sure it's the best idea right now. I mean, you're going through a lot at work and I did just get exploded on yesterday. Maybe we should, you know, just kind of let things be for a while, settle down."

"But I really think this is right for us. We both work so much that I hardly get to see you. If we lived together, we could see each other every day." You try to not let your wincing be seen. "I think it would be so great for both of us and we could really get to know

— 11 —

each other better. Hell, I just want to be with you."

Reaching, reaching, scrabbling around in your head for a way to get away from this. Finding his habit. "I hate to bring this up, since you know I used to smoke and it mostly doesn't bother me that you do. I mean, you're free to do whatever you want. But I don't think I can live with that. You know, it would be kind of difficult for me to stay a non-smoker if I was living in a smoking house." An escape! You feel triumphant. There's no way he can get around that one.

He frowns slightly as he crushes his cigarette into the ashtray. "I hadn't thought of that. You're right." He leans forward, rests his head in the palm of one hand, drums the table with the fingers of his other hand.

You sit back, allow yourself to relax. Safe from salaryman spousehood.

After more finger drumming and frowning, he pulls head up off his hand. "I'll just have to quit then," he declares, and you can see that he's serious.

What? "No, no, that's not what I meant. I mean, I don't think you should quit smoking for me or what."

"No, that's what I'll do. Smoking's not good for me anyway and the laws are starting to get kind of tight. I can't even smoke in the office anymore, I have to go into the parking garage. It's inconvenient and expensive too. It just makes sense. I don't want cigarettes to keep us apart."

Fuck. You glance down at your watch, don a concerned face. "Shit, I have a dentist appointment. I have to go."

"You have a dentist appointment today?" He is startled by your abrupt declaration.

"Yeah, didn't I tell you?" you say as you push your arms through the sleeves of your corduroy jacket. "For that tooth, you know, the one that's been bothering me?"

"I guess I must have forgot." You can see that he's digging through the storage shelves in his head, searching for this crucial piece of information and coming back with nothing but a vague feeling that it never existed.

You slide out of the booth, stand up, lean down and kiss him quickly. "I'll call you tomorrow, we'll talk about this more."

"Okay, I'll see you later."

You force yourself not to run out the restaurant.

Burying your hands in your pockets to protect against the autumn chill in the air, head down against the wind, trying to put a lot of steps between you and Boy. Move in together? Have you both been having totally different relationships with each other? Is this the point where they collide and worlds end?

Overheard conversation between a middle-aged couple, while waiting for the light to change:

"What are you talking about? Up is up." The husband.

"'Up is up,' you say. Which way is that? That's what she asked me. That's what I'm saying." Frustration in the wife's voice.

The light changes and you walk away from them, not wanting to hear the end of the conversation. Just the fact that someone else out there is wondering which way is up is enough for you.

"It's a good question," a familiar voice remarks and you see a pair of legs fall into step next to you. A pair of legs in a suit and ending in shiny dress shoes. The legs of a salaryman, you realize and start to bring your head up for a look at the face.

His hand forces your head back down. "No need for that. Let's just keep walking, shall we? It's such a lovely day."

You stare at his feet then your own feet as you move forward and wonder if the situation looks odd to anyone around you. Do you look like father and child? Lovers? How old is he? Does he look threatening? If he does, you hope some passerby you notices and is concerned about you. "What do you want? I told you I didn't see anything but the explosion. I didn't even see the explosion really, just the tail end."

You feel his hand come to rest on your shoulder. "You see, what you say now implies that there might have been something else to see, something you deny seeing, something that may give someone reason to investigate further." His voice is smooth, the same quiet dagger as yesterday.

"Look, I don't know what you're thinking, but I mean, I'm not the only person who saw those people on the side of the building. It was the police shouting about it that made me look in the first place." Without him pulling you by the armpits, you feel a little braver.

The hand on your shoulder squeezes hard and fast and you gasp in pain. "At this point, you would do well to remember the lady's question. You may think you know which way is up, but clearly you do not. You were heard last night to be discussing this very situation which you say you did not see. How can I believe that you saw only an explosion when I hear you questioning the motives of the people sliding down the side of the building?"

At this, you jerk your head up involuntarily, but his hand is still there to keep you looking down. "I was talking about this last night?" You're surprised. Even when you're drunk, you're not the chatty type. Plus, Salaryman scared the hell out of you. You had no intention of going back on your word and having to deal with him again. You are horrified to realize that he must have been following you all night. He probably followed you home. He probably knows where you live. "I was really drunk last night. Anyone who heard me saying anything would know that I was totally hammered and was talking shit."

"Your companion seemed charmed by the 'shit' you were talking." The hand tightens a little on the back of your neck. "A very nice-looking young man."

So now he's threatening Boy. Great. "He never takes anything I say seriously. We're just together for the sex."

"It seems that's not what he thinks. I'll be interested in seeing if he will really be able to give up cigarettes for you."

There's that comic-style gulp again. Have you been away from Salaryman for one second since yesterday? And has it only been since yesterday?

"You shouldn't be so quick to turn him down. You two make a lovely couple."

"What do you want?" You're breathing hard, heart racing, the whole deal. You're a B movie.

"I'll get back to you on that." The hand slides off your neck and the feet you've been staring at fall behind you.

You jerk your head up, whirl around and slam into a tanned girl in panda make-up. She teeters unsteadily on pencil-thin heels. Gravity wins and she falls back on her ass with a thump, legs pinned together by a tight leopard-print mini-skirt. She glares at you.

By the time you help her up and apologize for knocking her down in the first place, the whole time trying not to stare too much at her bleached hair and white-ringed eyes, Salaryman is long gone. Or at least, he's out of your sight.

Shaken, you head home quickly. Even if he knows where you live, with a locked door between you and him, you'll feel a little better.

On the train, you alternate between looking out the window at the landscape of power lines and rooftop machinery and at the uniformed high school girl sitting across from you. Your gaze rests a little too long on the girl as you notice the pattern pushed into her knees and realize it's carpet and suddenly you know how she spent the last few hours. A glance at her dyed red hair mussed into a halo around her head and smeared make-up confirms your thinking. Does she have a boyfriend or is this the 'compensated dating' you've been reading about in the papers?

She meets your eyes and sticks out her tongue. You dip your head in apology and look away.

When the train is pulling into your stop, one of your fellow passengers, a balding man with a backpack worn on his chest instead of his back, jumps up and literally runs to the door. Even though the door is not open and in fact, the train has not even stopped at the station yet. He pushes his face up against the window and presses his hands against the door on either side of the window, butt arching out behind him thanks to the bulge of his backpack in front. He even hops from foot to foot. You can't keep yourself from staring, half-grinning but trying not to let it show. The train stops and he pushes his fingers into the crack, trying to get the door open. He squeezes through as soon as the doors are open wide enough for him to do so. You detrain less eagerly.

It's already getting dark, you notice as you slip your train pass into the slot of the gate and walk through to grab it as it pops out the other side. You turn the corner to leave the station, thinking that you will stop by the grocery store on your way home, pick up some stuff for those delicious bean burritos for dinner and you are exploded on again. But more than just the glass falling on your head that you enjoyed yesterday. You are thrown into the street from the force of the blast. As are several other people on the sidewalk around you. You hear cars braking hard to avoid you, feel the debris tapping you on the head and you take a minute to just lie there. Close your eyes and think about which way is up.

You struggle to push yourself up on your elbows, feel dirt and glass crunching under your weight, wonder if your jacket is protection enough. Other than feeling like someone punched you really hard in the face, you feel okay and you don't think anything is broken. Opening your eyes, you look into flames where the Buddhist religious stuff store used to be. You have often stopped in front of their big window to admire the prayer beads and contemplate the uses of the assorted Buddhist paraphernalia. You see that some of that paraphernalia is now resting on your chest. You sit up all the way and the lacquered altar drawer slides down into your lap. Some prayer beads that have lost their elastic roll by. On the sidewalk, what appears to be Buddha's head is on fire. Someone is going to be spending some time in the Hell of No Interval for this. You're pretty sure that's the hell for anyone who tries to hurt the Buddhist community. Not that atheist you cares.

Then the hell-bound walk out through the glass-less window. All three of them dressed head-to-toe in black, complete with the head gear that the Kuroko in kabuki wear, which kind of looks like those scarves that some Middle Eastern women have to cover their heads with, so that only their eyes are visible. The littlest one kicks the burning Buddha head as she? he? steps onto the sidewalk. You see that the tallest one is carrying a black sack, not so big, and then they're off running down the street before you can get any more details or even confirm in your mind that they were really there.

Hey, you try to say, but your voice does not come out. You try again and end up coughing your lungs out. What you wouldn't give for a glass of water right now.

Over the sound of flames and approaching sirens, you hear a moan and turn to see an old woman in a kimono next to you. Her feet have lost their zari sandals and looking at those little white cotton socks with the big toe kept apart from the other toes, a special kind of outcast, you feel disoriented, like you're seeing someone walk down the street naked. You think you remember seeing her in the Buddhist shop and think she is the owner. Was she in there when they blew it up? She doesn't look too good. You hope the sirens get here soon.

And then they're here. You're lying flat on the ground again somehow. Maybe you blacked out a little? Can you black out a little? You are forced to admit that you blacked out. Period. No qualifiers for that.

Not for too long, though. The sky is darker than before, but not dead of night dark.

A silhouette leans over you, blocking the street lamp that you were staring up at. "Miss, can you hear me?" You've heard that voice before. You squint, but the head and torso remain a silhouette.

You try your voice again and manage a squeaky "Yeah." You slowly sit up and the silhouette backs off.

"You again!" he exclaims and now with the light on his face, you see that it is Persistent Paramedic. "You certainly get to all the explosions!"

You nod weakly and his grin fades.

"You seem a bit worse off today. Let's get you checked out." As he pokes at you and holds fingers up for you to count, he sucks air through his teeth. "I think you may have a concussion. You'll definitely need to get to the hospital." He turns away from you and calls out to his fellow paramedics. And then two more of them are at your side bearing a stretcher between them.

It's lowered to the ground and you are one-two-three-ed onto it and wheeled hurriedly to the ambulance. Despite your throbbing head, you are amused by the total TV-style of the whole thing. You wait for the theme song to start. Would it be a comedy-style hospital show you're in or the more serious kind? You hope for the comedy-style, not only for the inevitable laugh track, but also because then you can't possibly be seriously injured. You have a feeling it's a comedy. The Buddhist beads rolling down the street couldn't possibly fit into a serious drama. Unless someone died. Then they'd be some kind of symbolism from a director who usually makes movies starring dogs. But you're pretty sure no one's died. It's a comedy. You can practically hear the jokes of your slightly incompetent doctor.

Clearly, you have a concussion.

You must have passed out again on the way to the hospital because when you open your eyes, you are faced with white. Such a complete, featureless white that your eyes refuse to focus and you are forced to turn your head away or go mad.

Or be showered with kisses. You can't see what the new direction of your head reveals thanks to lips falling on your forehead, your lips, your eyebrows. You protest, but it seems that you still have not gotten that glass of water. Your voice is stuck in your throat and the only audible noise is a faint wheezing. You used to wheeze like this when you smoked too much in one evening. For a brief moment, you wonder if all the time since you quit smoking has been nothing but illusion. That would certainly explain all the explosions.

"You're awake!" More kisses from above. "Christ, I was so worried about you."

It's Boy. Why is Boy raining kisses on you? How did he get here? Where is here? Attempting to voice these questions causing another coughing fit.

Which leads to a gentle hand on your forehead and soft, shooshy noises from Boy. "Hey, don't try to talk. You've been through a lot. Just rest now." He strokes your head and begins to hum softly. He's humming softly as if he were your mother or some other maternal figure. How can you ever have sex with him again?

Bypassing your vocal cords, you use your breath to convey a message. "Can I have some water?"

You are reminded of an excitable dog from your childhood, the one that used to wag its hind end all the way to its head whenever you spoke to it. Boy's ass practically touches his head as he leaps up to do your bidding. "Yeah, water. Of course, coming right up." He rushes out of the room, presumably to fetch water, although if he's anything like that dog, he'll forget what it is he went off for and end up bringing back a dead gopher.

And now that he's gone, with your head still turned to face the chair where he was seated, you can see the tray with the pitcher of water and plastic-covered cups on the little stand next to your bed. You roll your eyes and try to scooch yourself up with your elbows, so that you can get your own damned water.

But before you can get even a little support from your bent limbs, there's a firm hand pushing you back down. For a second, your heart goes double time and you see feet in shiny loafers. Then you tell yourself to quit being such a stupid baby when you notice the distinctly feminine nature of the hand.

"Please don't try to get up. You need to rest." The voice of practically every woman in this country, polite, high-pitched, softly audible.

You accept defeat, look up at her to confirm that she is in fact a nurse and dressed in the unflattering white uniform, complete with paper cap, to prove it, and then cast your eyes pleadingly to your side, the side with the water pitcher. Boy still has not returned and you are starting to fear that you may expire of dehydration, regardless of the damage your head and other parts suffered in the explosion.

She smiles and her whole face lights up. She's kind of pretty, despite the paper hat, you think, until her smile grows a little wider and her teeth start showing. Her brown and yellow, jutting-out-at-odd-angles teeth, topped off by brown gums. You wince in your head. Brown gums. "Would you like some water?" she asks gently, leaning towards the water pitcher.

You nod. At least her brain is better formed than her teeth.

She pours about a thimbleful of water into a glass, puts one hand behind your head and gives your head a tilt up so that she can pour some water down your throat. You try to protest this infantile treatment, but she's already got the glass to your lips and you're too thirsty to fight. The thimbleful is gone before you can even taste it. She eases your head back onto the pillow and puts the glass down.

You clear your throat and she smiles again. "You shouldn't have too much to drink right now."

"But why?" Forcing your breath through your parched desert of a throat, you manage to form some words. If you could just get more water, you could talk again. You feel like slapping the nurse.

Nurse smiles again. Despite her youth, she has the same life-is-grand, I'm-enjoying smile of the middle-aged women you see on the street and on television with their young grandchildren. The smile that says, 'I've stopped hoping. This is good enough for me.' You feel that Nurse is too young to be wearing that smile. "You'll have to wait until the doctor sees you."

Huh? You just hit your head. You didn't have surgery. There's no possibility of extra fluid collecting anywhere in your body. Unless you were well salted in the explosion. But you feel like that's the sort of thing you would have noticed.

Nurse pulls the sheets up around your shoulders, actually picking up the hand that has escaped from under the sheet and tucking it back in. From the slight furrow of her forehead as she noticed your loose hand, it is clear that she has a whole set of tucking-in rules in her head that she is following.

When she bids you once more to rest and then turns to leave the room, you pull the hand free. In fact, you pull both hands free. You're too crazy for this hospital. But more than that, you are determined to get the dust out of your throat.

As you are pulling yourself into a sitting position, Boy returns empty-handed and apologetic. "They said you can't have any water." He slumps down in the chair from whence he departed.

You gasp and point towards the door.

Boy whirls around. "What? What is it?"

You grab the water pitcher from the nightstand and take a long drink from the side, where the spout isn't. Boy is a salaryman in training and good at obeying the rules. If the nurses say you can't have any water, you could cry your eyes out and start gnawing on your arm to drink your own blood, but he would not pour you a glass of water. Or allow you to get it yourself.

And of course, when he turns to you again, the question of what you saw on the tip of his tongue, the confusion falls off his face and he scowls a little as he takes the pitcher from you. "I just said that they said you can't have any water."

You lean back and roll your eyes. Cough tentatively. Hum a little. "What's going on?" Huzzah! A voice! Still kind of scratchy and you could do with another drink, of something stronger than water perhaps. But you can talk again without choking on dust and gravel and possibly Buddhist religious goods debris.

"You don't remember?" His scowl slips into something more serious. You think you could call it consternation. Or maybe just Concerned Big Daddy. "You were in another explosion."

"I know that. I saw the little altar roll down my chest."

The Big Daddy look gets more serious.

You shake your head a little to blow off your remarks and his concern and end up wincing. You guess Persistent was right. If you don't have a concussion, you at least have some kind of head injury.

Boy's Big Daddy mask is slipped into his pocket and he reaches forward to rest a loving hand on your shoulder. Oh, so loving. Maybe you're in the serious hospital show after all. The doctor will come in any minute to tell you that you have a very rare and life-threatening disease. Then it will be time for poignant piano sonatas with the tenderest hint of violin as you meet Boy's eyes, which will be quickly filling with tears. And he'll clasp your hand and promise to take care of you. And you'll be meant to cry at that point, only that's not your style—

Fortunately, the doctor, the real doctor, not the stereotypically handsome male lead in your concussed imaginings, walks in and pulls you out of your hospital drama. The fact that he wears glasses and is not stereotypically handsome, but not too ugly for TV bodes well for comedy-style hospital show. You listen hard for the laugh track.

"Well, that's quite a blow to the head you took." His tone is jocular and you swear, his words are from an actual sitcom you saw about hospitals many years ago. You suppress a giggle.

He frowns. "We're going to have to keep you overnight for observation, possibly longer. We took some head x-rays and it seems like nothing is broken, no permanent damage, but with head injuries, it's always difficult to tell."

The urge to giggle is still there, but abating, so you can speak. "Is it all right for me to have water?"

He shakes his head a little, a startled pull-back. "Well, yes, of course, if you're thirsty."

You smile sweetly at Boy.

"If you feel dizzy or anything out of the ordinary, tell one of the nurses. Now I suggest you get some rest." Nurse hands him a clipboard and he glances at it briefly, nods, hands it back. She bows slightly and leaves the room with it. "Any questions?"

"No, I'm fine. I was mostly concerned about the water." You realize once you say this that you're starting to sound like a crazy person. First the bit with Boy about the altar rolling down your chest, now fixated on water. You hope it's not being chalked up to the head injury.

His eyebrows go up as if he's not sure what it is he's looking at, then drop back down as he automatically tosses out the usual "Get well soon" and leaves the room.

Now it's just you and Boy.

You and Boy.

You wait for a lightening strike. You're not ready to deal with him yet.

He is more solicitous than usual, due to the head injury and the hospital and all this, you suppose. "When they called me, I thought my heart would drop out of my chest," he confides, while stroking your hair softly, leaning his head in close, so that it almost rests on your chest. "When they told me that you had been in another explosion and you were in the hospital, I couldn't get here fast enough. Seriously. I took a cab, paid him extra to speed."

You push his head up a little so you can look him in the eyes. His shiny brown orbs like marbles you used to have. "How did you know I was here? I mean, how did you find out about the explosion?" Your voice trails away and cracks at the end of that, so you have to cough for a while again.

Boy leans back and pours some water for you, waits for the coughing to subside, passes it to your outstretched hand. "They called me. Don't you remember? I'm on your insurance as the contact person."

You frown as you place the empty glass on the side table. "You're my contact person? I don't remember that." Would you do that? It doesn't sound like you. Too much of an invitation to Boy to stay.

"Yeah, when you got this job and you got insurance again. Remember? I think my phone number was the only one you had on you when you had to fill out all the papers at work." He resumes the hair stroking, hums a little and you lean back again.

Oh yeah. You did do that for exactly that reason. "Anyway, you don't have to stay. I'm fine."

"No, I'm staying. I was so worried about you. I'm still worried about you. Christ, there was another explosion right where you were. What the hell is going on? This city is fucked." He starts to sound more like himself and less like humming, concerned Big Daddy. You feel comforted. "We should move away from here." The comfort instantly evaporates.

Frozen, you hope again for the lightening strike.

Welcome, Nurse! "I'm terribly sorry, sir, but I'm afraid I'll have to ask you to leave now." She is half-bowing the entire time she says this, so great is her apologetic urge.

He turns on his little bedside chair to face her. "What? Why?"

"Visiting hours are ending, sir." As she says that, the loudspeakers make the very same announcement. With the addition of a soothing statement that everyone is welcome to come back again in the morning after eight. "You are very welcome to come back in the morning after eight o'clock." You wonder if she is the voice in the loudspeaker. Or if the voice in the loudspeaker is her. Dizzied by the philosophical implications.

You are showered with kisses again, hugs, promises to return as early as possible, he'll take the day off work call them tell them what happened he'll be back don't worry you won't be alone for long. You sigh, hope he's lying. You need some time to figure out what is going on and you're starting to realize that the hospital is about the safest place right now. Unless the Kuroko come and blow this place up too.

You slide back down to a more horizontal position. You're sleepy, but not overwhelmingly so. Even still, you're afraid to sleep. You have seen enough of the hospital dramas to have the unreliable knowledge that if you're concussed, you shouldn't sleep since you might not wake up. You have the feeling that this is just TV medicine, much like the law practiced on law shows. Plus, if you shouldn't sleep, the doctor would have told you, right? You're doing a good job of convincing yourself that it's okay to sleep, but a less great job of actually sleeping. The lights being still on doesn't help.

You consider pushing the button near your head to bring Nurse running to your side. But then she comes on her own.

If by on her own, you mean with two other nurses pushing a bed with a person on it.

There is much cooing and tucking of blankets as the bed is wheeled to the right of yours. You should have expected this. The room remaining yours and yours alone would be too much to hope for. In this land of no space, there's no way they would let you be in here without another person jamming their elbow into your chest.

Once Team Nurse disperses, you turn to take a look at the body on the bed. Before you can get the best look, a member of Team Nurse — possibly Nurse herself, it's hard to tell when they are all wearing the same clothes with the same apologetic attitude and hair pulled back in ponytails — turns out the lights and you are left bathed in the glow of the floorboard nightlights. Your eyes take a moment to adjust and refocus in the hospital dusk.

It's the lady in the kimono from the Buddhist store. At least, she is if you were right in assuming that the lady on the sidewalk next to you with the naked big-toe socked feet is the Buddhist store lady. You feel confident that you were. It's not like you can ask her in any case. She seems to be out like your grandpa after too much Scotch.

Staring at her from your bed, which is not so cozy, but the pillows certainly are comfortable, and the sound of her regular deep breaths fills the room and you start to feel like that sleep you were thinking about earlier might not be so far away after all. Breathe in, breathe out. She doesn't even have that annoying nose whistling thing going on that you can barely stand and the rhythm of her lungs flows over you. Your own breathing falls in step with hers. You don't think it's on purpose, but then, you don't really understand yourself that well.

You're almost asleep when she starts coughing up both of her lungs. You are close to jumping out of your skin.

Her hacking just keeps going. You think about Nurse or any member of Team Nurse and wonder if you should push your button on Kimono Lady's behalf. You decide instead to offer her some of the slightly stale water on your bedside table.

You have to get out of bed to bring her the glass and the floor is cold on your bare feet. You realize at last that you are only wearing a hospital gown. It is firmly secured in the back, but you can't help but question where your clothes are and who put you in this gown in the first place. You touch your bum with the hand not holding the water glass and feel a small relief upon discovering that your underpants, at least, have not gone anywhere.

"Ma'am," you say, the politest expression you can come up with at this late hour with your concussed head and your generally poor manners. "Would you like some water? Are you all right, ma'am?" You suppose that you should probably be referring to her as 'Old Mother' or some other stereotypical Asian address, but this is no samurai movie and 'ma'am' is about as polite as you get.

bullying.

She nods. "Oh yes. They dragged me out of the back and then they pushed me out the window. Awful people." She rubs her head again. "Now, dear, you must let me sleep. I feel so tired after this terrible day. I can't even pray to my ancestors since our family shrine was in the shop. It's probably been destroyed. This is so terrible, just terrible. "

She seems about to cry. Is she going to cry? You don't think you can handle elderly tears right now. She better not cry.

You stand up. "I'm sorry. I shouldn't be keeping you up like this. Please go to sleep. I'm sure everything will seem so much better in the morning." A breeze wafts up the bottom of your gown and you feel grateful for the underpants keeping your bottom warm.

She sighs, rubs her temples with the tips of her index fingers. "Good night, dear." How can she keep referring to you as 'dear' when she holds you responsible for the destruction of everything she's ever had? She reaches over the edge of her bed to push the button that sends the bed sliding back down. "Could you pull the curtain shut?"

"Of course." You grab the edge of the curtain that separates your beds and pull it round hers. It gets stuck on the curve and there is an awkward moment as she watches you trying to free it. You want to be free of those accusing, yet gentle eyes.

You let your breath out as it finally comes unstuck and you can pull it all the way closed. You can't see her anymore, but you have a feeling that her gaze has not shifted off you. You tiptoe back to your own bed. If she can't hear you, her eyes can't follow you from behind the curtain. You crawl into your bed and pull the thin blankets up to your ears. When you were small, you had this fear of things crawling into your ears in the night while you were sleeping, so you used to pull the blankets all the way up to your ears and then hold them over your ears until you fell asleep. Each morning, you were distressed to see that your hands had fallen away during your sleep and the blankets always ended up somewhere around your stomach, but when you were trying to fall asleep, covering your ears made you feel so safe. You do it now, an unconscious search for security that doesn't seem to exist anymore.

And it works. You sleep. In your dreams, strangers in a variety of scenes and situations ask you which way is up. It seems to be the only thing your dream brain can create, variations on this one theme. One of them is so casual, so real. Sitting on the window ledge of your hospital room, one leg bent at the knee, foot up on the ledge, the other dangling off the edge, she snaps her gum loudly and considers all the directions, not just up. "It's all the directions that are going to go wrong," she tells you off-handedly. "You think it's just up, but down is getting all twisted up too. Not to mention left and right. Someone opened the stupid door." Holding up her left then right hands to inspect her long red nails as she says this. "When you ask yourself which way is up, don't stop there. Really think about left especially. What's left?" She runs the inspected left hand through pink hair, short and looking like she slept on it, pieces standing up here and there.

You find your voice. "What the hell are you talking about?" That sounds too much like your awake self. You're not usually so straightforward in your dreams. You have a tendency to talk in riddles and rhymes, an aspect of your dreams that you've always enjoyed. "Who are you?"

She laughs, leans back, her swinging leg reaching ever greater heights. "Look, I'm just here because I worry, you know. I know it's only just started, but I don't think you realize what's at stake here. "

"I don't. What is at stake here? What is going on? Who is Salaryman?"

The gum-snapping stops as she frowns, brightly painted red lips turned down. "He's making his own rules. The time's not right."

You feel too exasperated to be sleeping. You want to ask her to pinch you to check if you're awake, but you're pretty sure that she wouldn't. Besides, her long nails are like claws and would probably hurt way too much if she did pinch you. "So what is the right time? Can you just tell me something?"

Still frowning, she brings a nail-claw to her lips thoughtfully. "Just be careful, okay? And if you see any cats, it wouldn't hurt to give them a good rubbing behind the ears."

Metal clattering and banging slaps you awake. "Aah!" you cry out involuntarily.

A paper-hatted member of Team Nurse looks up from where she is crouched on the floor, picking up cutlery. "I'm so sorry," she says smoothly. "I was bringing your breakfast and I dropped the tray. Please forgive me."

Your heart is beating its way out of your chest. You look down, convinced that any second now you will be able to see it burst its way out and if that's the way you're going to go, you want that to be the last thing you see. But the pounding lessens and you realize that today is not the day. You're not sure if you're relieved or not. You'll probably get exploded on again soon.

You turn your head, remembering Kimono Lady, but the curtain is still drawn. You wonder if she's awake yet, if she's staring at you with those accusing eyes again. You have to get out of this hospital. "So I can go home now, right?"

Nurse smiles indulgently. Is it the same nurse as yesterday? Or a different member of Team Nurse? You seriously can't tell. They all look the same somehow. You decide to act as if she is yesterday's Nurse. "You have to wait until the doctor comes by. He'll decide if you are well enough to leave." The look on her face is saying, 'No way in hell are you leaving here today'. She seems to relish the thought of keeping you in her care. These nurse drones kind of freak you out. "I'll have to get you a new breakfast. I'll be right back." Another one of those creepily smooth, settling smiles as she leaves the room with the mess of cutlery and food collected on the tray that she dropped.

The morning slides by. Breakfast is brought, eaten, taken away. Boy comes, talks, goes to the bathroom, comes back, peppers you and Nurse with questions, seems unsatisfied with all answers. The highlight is the visit from the police. A man with no defining features, so that you have a hard time keeping his face in your mind when you close your eyes, who talks exclusively to Boy, waits for Boy to repeat his questions to you.

"But I speak Japanese," you protest in fluent Japanese.

The man drops his notebook in his lap to throw up protesting hands. "No English!" he cries in English.

"But—"

"No English!"

You give up. You've come across this before. You know you can protest all you want, but this man's ears can only hear English when you open your mouth. Your foreign face betrays you yet again. You let Boy repeat questions and answers to you and to him as if he were an interpreter, as if you weren't all speaking the same language. When he leaves, satisfied that you are not responsible for what happened to the Buddhist shop, you drag your hand across your forehead, roll your eyes.

Kimono Lady remains silent behind the drawn curtain. From time to time, you wonder if she's dead. You almost get up to pull the curtain back a few times, but each time you are stopped by the memory of her weirdly accusative eyes boring holes into you. You can't really handle being responsible for the destruction of her shop. If it is, in fact, your fault and she is not just telling stories that match her own versions of reality. She is pretty old, after all.

Waiting for the doctor to show up and set you free, you are drifting about in your head, while Boy sits next to you, going on about whatever he goes on about. For a while, he was talking about work again, so you turned him off and have yet to turn him back on. Until he mentions the Buddhist shop and yanks you out of your own head. "What? What did you say? Say that again."

He looks startled. "Huh? You mean about talking to the police?"

"Yeah, about the Buddhist thing."

"There's nothing extra to say. I mean, it's just that. I was talking to the cops in front of the shop before I came here today." As always, he is perplexed. And surprisingly fidgety. He usually sits still so nicely.

"Why didn't you say that before? Why are you waiting to tell me that until now? And why are you jumping about in your chair so much?" You know that he can't read your mind, but you think it doesn't take a mind reader to figure out that you would want to hear about anything to do with the explosion. At the very least, it should be obvious that you would rather hear about the explosion than about what his intensely dull colleagues discussed at their intensely dull meeting about an intensely dull business matter that doesn't concern you at all.

"Am I jumping about in my chair?" He looks down at himself, kind of pained. "I didn't realize, sorry. I haven't had a cigarette since I saw you yesterday. I thought I was okay with it, but I guess I'm a little jumpy." He smiles self-consciously, with a bit of apologetic thrown in for good measure.

A bit incredulous. "You're really quitting?"

He nods. "I told you yesterday, I don't want smoking to come between us." He seems so firm and suddenly you are more freaked out by this than by the explosions or Salaryman's threats. He's serious. He really wants to move in with you or you to move in with him, whatever, the two of you living together somehow. He thinks that much of you. It isn't just up that's gone astray; you realize the truth of your dream that may not have been a dream. You have the sudden urge to let your jaw drop and your voice flood out freely.

Change the topic quick. "So what about the cops? What did they say?"

He shrugs, picks at his hair, the back of his hand, forces both hands under his ass, sits on them. "Well, it's not like they're going to be telling me so much. I mean, who am I, right? But I told the one cop that you were involved in the explosion and he was pretty sympathetic and kind of chatted with me for a while. He was the guy directing pedestrians off the sidewalk and around the shop, I guess it's not like he had anything better to do." He cuts himself off. "Hey, can I have some of your water?"

You wave your hand dismissively. "Yeah, sure, go ahead. So what did he tell you?"

Gulping down half the glass, then slipping his hands back under his ass. "He said that it looked like the bombs were set up so that they blew out onto the street. It was like they were just trying to get the explosion out of the shop, rather than blowing up anything inside the shop. I guess that's kind of weird since usually, people try to explode things inside or something."

"He really said that? That the bombs were meant for the street?" Kimono Lady is right. They were trying to blow you up.

More shrugging. Why can't he ever just be certain? The frustration you feel over this is nothing new. "I guess. I mean, he said that they were set to blow out. I don't know if they were 'meant' for the street or anything." You roll your eyes. "The other thing was, he said there were some special sutra things, books or whatever you call them that the owner's son says were kept in the back of the shop, but they're not there now."

"You mean they were stolen?"

"I guess. And that's about the only thing that wasn't where it was supposed to be. In the back, I mean. The whole front was gone, so you know..." He trails off.

"Do you think they blew up the place just to get the sutras?" Your brain is whirring. Maybe it's all a coincidence. Maybe Salaryman's got the wrong girl. Maybe some crazy people are blowing up stuff to find rare Buddhist scripture. Although that makes about as much sense as people trying to blow you up.

Before Boy can answer, the doctor walks in, the same jovial, spectacled man as last night and you feel kind of reassured as you flashback to your concussion-induced hospital sitcom imaginings. "And how are we feeling today?" He's looking over the chart Nurse handed him. "I see your blood work has come back clean."

You are not sure whether or not to smile, cheer, or boo. Does your blood have anything to do with you hitting your head? And when did they take your blood? Scanning your arms for needle marks.

The doctor plunks his soft ass down on the edge of your bed and pummels you with questions about your specific feelings, the number of fingers and more, followed by a whole lot of poking and requests for certain movements. Until finally, it seems that he has also had his fill of you and pronounces you free to go. "But of course, if you start to feel ill or dizzy, you must come back immediately." Said with a Big Daddy sternness and you almost drift back into your hospital sitcom fantasy. But you want to go. No time for raising questions about your sanity in the minds of hospital staff.

Someone from Team Nurse brings you your clothes. You feel satisfied that at least one mystery has been solved. Where your clothes went was not the greatest of the mysteries in your world lately, but you'll take what you can get.

You head into the tiny washroom down the hall to change. You could just pull your own curtain shut, but that curtain seems like too small a barrier between you and the total strangers of the hospital. If you can see their feet, then they can see yours. There's something discomfiting about that when you're naked.

Boy greets your return with hugs and kisses. "Ready to go?"

You start to nod, then look at the still-drawn curtain separating you from Kimono Lady. Should you say good-bye or something? Apologize? Beg her to not sic her ancestors on you? You decide that you should say something at least, so you extend a hand.

And are stopped short by Nurse grabbing your wrist. "She's sleeping just now. Please don't disturb her. Trauma like this is very hard on the elderly." Again with the creepy drone smile as she releases your arm.

You let your hand fall back to your side. "Well, could you tell her when she wakes up that I hope she feels better?"

"Of course." The voice is intended to be smooth and reassuring, but only serves to further creep you out.

"Thanks." You tug at Boy's sleeve. "C'mon, let's go."

He takes your hand in his protectively and a little too tightly for your liking and leads you down the hall, the elevator, the doors and the sun is shining on your upturned face. You squint a little, but the warmth feels good. And fresh. Realizing now that someone in that hospital should really open a window.

"Aren't there any bills or anything that I need to take care of?" you ask as the two of you head for the train station.

Boy shakes his head. "No, I took care of everything before."

You feel a shy fondness tug at you. You know that you keep thinking that you are just in this for the sex, nothing serious, but sometimes, he is too sweet. "Hey, thanks."

He tilts his head to smile down at you. "No problem." Just before the station, he suddenly pulls you to a stop. "Hey, are you hungry?"

You hadn't thought about it, but now that he mentions it. "Yeah, actually, I am."

"Let's go get something to eat. There's that Mexican place just over there. They had good bean burritos, didn't they?"

It's a slow day for the Mexican restaurant. Or maybe it's just that you missed the lunch rush, what with being in the hospital and all. In any case, you and Boy are the only two people in the place. Which suits you just fine, except for the fact that the owner/ waitress seems to be eavesdropping on your conversation. Doesn't she have any work to do, you wonder with irritation.

Your irritation is more connected to the conversation itself rather than the eavesdropping staff. Boy has been insisting for the last twenty minutes that you come stay with him, that you shouldn't be alone, that you got hit on the head really hard, something could happen, what if you get exploded on again, is someone targeting you, it's just not safe on your own. And more. He just will not shut up. That shy fondness you felt before has disintegrated.

"Look, I'm going home and that's that. There's nothing to talk about." You try to put a foot down, but you're sitting so they're both already down.

Maybe it's the not having had a cig since yesterday thing, but he is obviously irritated himself and not interested in taking your no for an answer. "Can't you just for once let someone take care of you?"

Do you have hackles? Or is that just cats? You feel pretty sure that yours are standing on end either way. "What does that mean?"

"Exactly what it sounds like. Everyone is always a paper cutout in your life. You act like you don't have a pulse; you have to be tough or something." He sneers the word 'tough'.

You stand up. "Fuck you. Go have a cigarette." You grab your coat from the back of your chair and heavy-foot your way out of the narrow restaurant.

Out on the sidewalk, you half-expect him to come running after you, but he doesn't. You yank your arms angrily through the sleeves of your jacket and head in the direction of the train station again.

The whole train ride, you are thinking of nothing but Boy and the way you stormed out on him. Maybe it was a bit much. It's not like he was crazy to be suggesting that you come stay with him for a while. You have been through some physical trauma the last couple days and it makes sense to have someone around just in case. But him saying that you have no pulse. That kind of stabs at you a little. Are you really that cold? Do people find you unapproachable? Concerns you never had before are pushing their way into your brain. Okay, to be honest, you have had some of these concerns before. You have felt far away from people in your life. You usually just think of it as circumstances, other people, not really coming from you, it's the way things are. But clearly, Boy sees it as coming from you. You sigh and the woman with a pile of grocery bags sitting next to you gives you a funny look. You ignore her.

After a quick train change, you are back on your line, on the train that is nearing your stop and soon you will have to get off, go through the gates, turn the corner and follow the same path as yesterday. Your heart starts to beat a little faster. You rationalize that it's not like there would be another explosion on that street today. That would be a little far-fetched. But you felt like that about the Honda building exploding and look what happened after that.

When the train does pull into your station, you take a deep breath and step through the opening doors, tentatively walk down the stairs to the gate along with several other passengers. You're not alone as you slip your ticket into the slot and that comforts you somehow. You find yourself wishing that you hadn't fought with Boy; you could use the comforting hugs and kisses he's been showering you with since yesterday. You turn the corner and see what Boy was talking about, about the police having marked off the area in front of the Buddhist shop. They're still there. Well, he's still there. Just the one cop, plus a lot of pylons and yellow tape. The scene of the crime.

You slow down as you approach the yellow tape. The police officer sees you and waves his little flag to indicate that you should follow the path marked off by the pylons, an improvised sidewalk. Bowing the whole time. Which you think is funny. But if he didn't bow, you'd be irritated and a little insulted.

"Um, hi," you say. Not the best opening, but you console yourself with the fact that you were in an explosion on this very spot yesterday. You can't be expected to be the most brilliant conversationalist.

He smiles in that trained way. Bows again. "Hello."

"Um, yeah, the thing is, I was here yesterday." You're not exactly sure what you want to say, which could be why it's not coming out so well.

His smile stays on his face as his eyes wait for you to give him some pertinent information. "I see," he says finally.

"No, I mean, I was in the explosion. I was, uh, I don't know really. I guess I was just wondering if you know what happened yet."

Lights go on behind the frozen smile. "Oh, you were injured in the explosion." You can see him make some connections you'd rather he didn't. "Unfortunately, nothing has been discovered in the case yet. We're still looking for the culprits."

"Do you know why they did it?" Are you expecting him to say they were waiting for you, that you are the real cause of the explosion and he hopes you're happy? Or the opposite — that he can somehow clear you, relieve you of this strange guilt you feel?

He shakes his head a little. "It's quite unclear at this point. Nothing much was stolen, so we have ruled out robbery."

"Nothing much was stolen?" You remember the sutras or whatever that Boy told you about.

He nods. "As far as we can tell, the only things missing are some old Buddhist sutras." His trained smile springs to his lips as other pedestrians approach the scene and he waves his flag, ready to guide them through the pylon maze.

You take that as your hint to leave him alone. Thanking him and wondering if he shouldn't maybe keep those loose lips a little tighter since he is a meant to be a cop after all and what if you were really one of the bombers coming back to the scene of the crime, you accept his guidance and, once through the orange outline, you make your way home.

As you unlock your door, Salaryman springs into your brain and you can't push your way inside fast enough. You slam the door behind you and lock all the locks, including the deadbolt that you pretty much never use. You still don't feel safe. You have the feeling that locks are not a serious obstacle for Salaryman. You reach out and flick the lights on.

Your apartment looks the same as ever, which surprises and disappoints you just like every other time you've spent a night or more away from it. Somehow, you expect things to be different. Like the apartment could and should evolve while you are away from it for lengthy periods of time.

You walk through your tiny hallway kitchen to get to the living room. Which is not where you sleep. In your last apartment, it was everything in the main room, which in itself was the size of a large walk-in closet. But now that you are working an ass-spreading office job, you have more money to throw away on rent so you have an apartment with a main room and a bedroom, both of which together are not much larger than a hotel room. And it costs you a fortune. You hate this city. The thought of moving makes a dash from one ear to the other, followed closely by its opponent, the thought of where would you go anyway?

You toss your jacket on the sofa, really the size of a loveseat, but you hate that word. Sit down. Consider what to do now.

You see your work bag, and lights are flipping on all over the place. Your job! You were supposed to work today. And tomorrow. And the day after that. But not the day after that. You do get weekends off. You jump up and grab the phone off the wall. You start to dial, but then realize that you don't know your own office number so you have to rummage through your pockets to find one of your cards. The search reveals one that apparently went through the wash, but the phone number is still legible.

It rings once and that, just barely. The youngest guy in your office works hard to make sure that it never rings more than once.

You think he thinks that this bit of heroic effort might impress your bosses. You, however, know different. You identify yourself to him and he offers his sympathies and wishes for your speedy recovery and then passes you on to your immediate supervisor.

Not only did she read about it in the paper, she tells you, but Boy actually telephoned to fill them in on the whole story. Oh yeah, you say to yourself. He told you that he would. "So please don't worry," she says. "Just take the next week or so off and get better. I'd rather you come back to work when you are completely well again. We'll get a temp to handle things until you can come back."

"Are you sure?" You want to pop about at the thought of a whole week off. Paid. You try to make your voice sick-sounding. "I'm sure I could be back in two days."

"No, no. Please don't overexert yourself." She tells you once again that you should rest and get better, despite the fact that you were in an explosion and unless it was some kind of dirty bomb, you are not ill. You should call next week to let her know how you're feeling. If you're still not well, you should stay home for another few days.

Hanging up, you feel like high-fiving yourself. A whole week off work. You silently thank the Kuroko for blowing so much stuff up. If you're responsible for it, well, at least you're getting something other than guilt out of it now.

Only now that you're free for at least a whole week, you're not exactly sure what to do with yourself. You don't want to admit it, but you really wish Boy was here. Not particularly to entertain you, but just to be his indecisive Boy self. Do you miss him? Is this you missing him? Or are you just freaked out to be alone? You dismiss yourself and sit down on the couch, click on the TV. There must be something there to distract you.

There is nothing.

You suppose you shouldn't be surprised. After all, you've thought too many times that the only thing on in this country is inappropriately subtitled celebrities eating unappetizing food.

Watching a particularly obese celeb chow down some kind of seafood monstrosity, you ponder what to do with yourself. Technically, you've suffered a severe blow to the head and should be resting. But you're not tired and really, you feel fine. No need to spend the evening lying down. Except you can't quite think of anything else. You wonder if you still have that bottle of whiskey under the sink, a gift from a client, but whiskey gives you insomnia so you never got around to drinking it. You thought you never would, because, well, why would you court insomnia? But you couldn't bear to just toss it in the garbage, so you shoved it under your sink with the bathroom cleanser. You hope it's still there. You find yourself unconcerned about the potential insomnia. It's one of those times where you could go for a stiff drink. Is there any Kool-Aid in the fridge?

The whiskey is there, but sadly, the Kool-Aid is not. You are not one for drinking whiskey straight, especially with the insomnia action, but there is nothing else in your fridge. Except the soy milk, but that is for breakfast and not for whiskey. You rummage around in the freezer to discover ice. Ice! All is well!

Four of these on the rocks later and you're starting to feel pleasantly disposed to the celebs downing a variety of soba noodles before your eyes. You even catch yourself hoping that the one eating the crispy soba things wins. Although you're not sure what winning would entail or even if there is a competition to be won. You laugh out loud, then clasp your hand over your mouth. Are you drunk? You thought you were tougher than the whiskey, but maybe not.

When you first hear the insect-style on-off buzzing, you think it's one of the celebrities and lean in for a closer look at the television to see how they are doing that anyway. But as you pour yourself another few fingers of the whiskey, having given up on the ice since heading into the kitchen is just too much hassle, you realize that the buzzing is not coming from the TV.

You smack yourself on the side of the head.

It's not in your head either.

Unless you smacked it out of your head and into reality. You take a moment to savour.

But it keeps going. It's so persistent. You feel compelled to make it stop. You almost pound your head again, but stop short, remembering at last that that solved nothing before.

"The phone!" This exclamation actually escapes your lips and you feel so glad that you are alone. How embarrassing if someone were actually listening to you.

You jump up, then almost fall over. You are too unsteady on your feet. Must be the head trauma. You grab at the phone on the wall and miss. You laugh. It's funny the way your hand reached out and then swung away. You swear you've seen that on some show somewhere.

The buzzing persists. Turns into more like a ringing sound. You chide yourself, focus, focus, your goal is so close. Another swing of the arm yields success.

You have to stop yourself from giggling as you put the mouthpiece to your mouth. Because that's where it goes! you want to cry out. "Hello?" You give yourself a pat on the back for how steady your voice comes out. Although reaching your back in this state is no easy feat.

"Hey, it's me." It's Boy.

You're delighted. It's Boy! You could practically kiss him right now. Only he's not here for kissing. You must rectify this situation. "Hey, honeyhoney." Your voice is melted sugar, sliding through the telephone line.

A pause. "Hey. Look, I need to talk to you."

Talk. You almost snort out loud. You know what he wants. "Why don't you come over, lover?"

Another pause. "Look, are you okay? I just need to talk, but if you're busy or what."

That's your cue to tone it down. Boy is so boring sometimes. But so cute. "No, I'm fine. I think yeah, talking's good. All that's happened, you know. So you should come over and we'll talk."

You swear you can hear his suspicions. "Are you sure you're okay? I mean, I don't have to come over."

"No, no, it's good. I'm good. It's easier to talk in person, just come over." You're growing more and more unsteady on your feet. Those initial wobbles in your steps just keep growing. You are a chaotic dynamical system. You surprise yourself with this bit of forgotten mathematics. Where did it come from? Whiskey gives you insomnia and unearths buried mathematics? You can't decide whether or not that means you should drink more of it.

"Did you hear what I said?"

You are still holding the phone up to your ear. Whoops. Drifted off there. "No, I'm sorry, I must have slipped away for a sec."

"I just said I'll be over in about ten minutes, okay?" There is concern in his voice now and you know he's thinking that it's the bump on the noggin. When he gets here and sees your friend Whiskey-chan, he'll know different.

"Okay, I'll see you soon."

"Okay, see you." You hear the click as he puts the receiver down.

You take the one on your end away from your ear, stare at it a moment, considering how aptly named the entire thing is. You're forced to put it back in its home when the random wobbles grow too large and sweep away from the attractors of your feet. You have to step back to get some balance. And then again to get balance from the balance stepping. And again until you have backed yourself over the arm of the sofa. You're fairly pleased at how that worked out and maybe it was the sofa that was the attractor for your wobbly step system rather than your feet. You have to put a cap on the mathematics freed by the whiskey.

Turning your head a little, you realize you can see the TV

perfectly fine from the side. And everyone on it is sideways. The eating is over and now there is a lot of jumping and running about a contrived set of objects. You feel like you've seen this show before. You also feel like you didn't like it. But you can't remember. You're not sure how you feel about it now. It may still be a shade dumbed down for you.

Now it's some kind of activity where the contestants, who you're pretty sure are actually celebrities of some kind, pull Velcro suits on and then take a running leap at a wall covered in the matching half Velcro. You tilt your head so that it is more upright, but the images on your set still don't make sense to you. You're grateful for the sound of the doorbell so you can walk away from the Velcro jumpers.

You start to unlock the door and yank it open as is your usual style, but seeing the deadbolt closed, you remember why it's closed and you ask who it is.

His voice is muffled through the door. "It's me. What's with you?"

It's Boy. Relief. You quickly pull locks aside and open the door. "Hey." Big smiles.

He comes in, closes the door behind him. Removes shoes and assorted outdoor gear. "I was a little worried the way you drifted away on the phone." He leans in to kiss you, then pulls back abruptly. "Have you been drinking battery acid? What is that smell?"

You grin and allow your random wobbles to send you forward to plant a kiss on his cheek. "It's that whisky that guy gave me. Want some?"

He grabs your shoulders to steady you. "What whiskey from what guy?" You move together into the living room.

"You know." You wave your hand roundabout style. "That guy. The one I used to work with."

He eases you down onto the sofa and raises his eyebrows. "Uh, yeah, okay." He spies the bottle on the floor, grabs it. "Was this full?"

You nod. "Yeah, I don't drink whiskey because it gives me insomnia. But I think it also gives me mathematics, so I don't know what to do." You say this last bit confidingly.

"It gives you math—" He cuts himself off. "Anyway, I don't think you should have any more of this."

You shrug. In your head, you agree with him because you are feeling a little too dizzy and it seems that the whiskey is a late bloomer. You didn't feel so drunk before. Then sitting up bolt straight. "The door! Did you lock the door?"

"I don't know. Does it matter?" His eyebrows are jumping off his forehead; they keep climbing with every strange thing you say. Is it possible for them to escape?

You scramble to stand up, but have some trouble thanks to the softness of the seating. It's holding your ass prisoner. "I have to lock the door."

He holds you down. "I'll lock it. Don't freak out. Just sit there, I'll be back in a sec."

You allow yourself to be pushed down because, frankly, you're not sure how well you could stand.

"Gah!" Accompanied by a thud.

It's Boy. He sounds more panicked than scared, but that doesn't stop you from suddenly feeling ridiculously clear-headed and leaping to your feet. You slam into the wall on your way to the door. You don't think you chipped that tooth, but you might have.

You round the corner and Boy is on his ass on the floor, legs hanging over the little ledge-step to the place where the shoes go and there are two other feet.

"Aah!" you cry out, slightly delayed. Good thing you're not driving. You feel the clouds clearing in your head.

The boy standing in the doorway pushes his asymmetrical, dyed-black hair off his face. "Hey," he greets you, giving a little wave from his free hand.

You put a hand to your chest to stop your heart from jumping out. "What are you doing here?" He seems harmless. Maybe it's just the new wave hair that makes you think so. He looks like he just escaped from an early eighties underground super synth group. Even the clothes. Those tapered pant legs.

He offers a half-smile, well, you can only see half a smile, he may be fully smiling. "Yeah, sorry, uh, didn't mean to scare you or what. Just supposed to like get this uh box to you." He shoves his hair aside again with one hand and thrusts the box in his other hand forward in your general direction. "You know."

The 'you know' tagged onto the end leaves you a little perplexed. "I know what?"

He blinks rapidly with the one eye you can see. "Just you know. Like here's the box. You know." Tosses his head a little, and his other eye is briefly revealed.

You reach forward and take the box from him.

Boy is finally back on his feet, rubbing his elbow. "Don't you know how to knock?" he grumbles.

More rapid eyelash fluttering. "Huh? What, no, man. The door was open, right. Entryway's, uh, you know, public space." Runs his hand through his hair. Reaches in his pocket, pulls out a pack of cigarettes, lights one. The smoke lingers above his head for a moment before being swept away.

"Most people say something." Boy is still grumbling. "You know, 'Hey! Is anybody home?' It's just polite." He pauses, eyes New Wave's cigarette longingly. "Can I have a drag?"

"Huh?" He shrugs. "Yeah, sure, man." He passes Boy the cigarette, pulls the pack out, lights another. "I did call out, uh, said hey, yoo-hoo, but, you know, like, uh, no one came, man."

"I just wanted a drag," Boy says at the same time.

You shush him. "So you're supposed to give me this box?" It's like you drank thirty cups of coffee or maybe just had them injected directly into your bloodstream.

He nods, pushes his hair aside. Inhales from the cig. "Yeah, uh, so freaky, man, this guy, well, uh, he just like came up to me and said, uh, hey, here's 20 000 yen, like, uh, go give this box to the person who like lives in that house. And he like pointed, you know."

"To my place?"

Nod, hair. "Yeah. I mean, I guess so 'cause uh, when I, uh, you know, came to this door, like here you are."

Boy exhales smoke towards the ceiling and you watch the draft coming in through the top of the door catch it and send it flying. "How do you know it's not my place?"

New Wave lifts his shoulders again. "Uh, I mean, saw you come in before, standing at the uh door ringing or what. Figure, like, uh, nobody rings the door to their own place, you know?"

"Well, who is this guy who told you to give this to me?" Talking to this guy is making your head start to spin, mostly because you're not sure if you do know.

"He, uh, he was all suit and tie, man, you know? Like, salaryman all the way. So boring, you know, all uh, shiny shoes and tight tie, that guy like needs to uh, relax or something." He stops, holds up his cigarette, balancing the precariously long ash. "You, like, got an ashtray or what?"

You turn and scowl at Boy, who looks away. He has just been letting his ash fall on the floor. "You're cleaning that up, you jerk." You open the shoe cupboard and pull out the little bowl that you keep meaning to bring back to the kitchen, but the only time you see it is when you take your work shoes out and you don't have the five seconds it takes to toss it in the sink. You push the dish under New Wave's giant ash.

Which promptly topples off and into the dish. "Whoo, just in time, huh?" New Wave grins, shakes his head, sending hair backwards.

"So what about this guy?" You're not especially interested in the mechanics of cigarette ash.

He remembers with his head, moving it up and down. "Yeah, yeah, that guy. Man, at first, I was like, yeah right, you're gonna give me 20 000 yen just to uh, take like a box to uh some person, and he was all, yeah, that's right, man, that's what I'm doing, like you want it, and I was like, well, yeah, you know? I need the uh money, man. Coffee and cigarettes aren't, you know, free. This guy's like crazy, man. The other day, he like uh, gave me 10 000 yen to go talk to some like guys climbing down, you know, the, uh, side of a building." His face lights up suddenly. "Man, that was hot. These, uh, guys or whatever, they're all dressed in like black right and, like, they seriously came down a building, you know?" He shakes his head in disbelief at his own story. "Man."

Boy starts, flashes you the most surprised look you've ever seen on his face, almost drops his cigarette on the floor, catches himself and squashes it in the little dish instead.

A lamp factory exploding in your head. "You talked to some guys coming down the side of a building? Was that after the explosion in Aoyama?"

He bobs his head up and down. "Yeah, yeah, that's it. I didn't, you know, see the explosion since I was, like, around the corner, you know? But my friend, he said it was uh really cool, right." He crushes his stub of a cigarette in the dish still in his hand, then reaches up and pushes that hair off his face again.

Too many dots are connected in this picture. You are suddenly shuddering and shivering at the thought of who this kid has been talking to. Salaryman is definitely still keeping an eye on you. You wish you hadn't drunk all that whiskey. Your head is clearer, but you still have some grey socks tumbling about in there. "What did the guys say?"

He looks startled. "What guys?"

Is he drunk too? "The ones who came down the building, the ones you talked to?"

"Those guys." He reaches in his pocket for his cigarettes again. "Uh, yeah, they like, didn't say anything, I guess. The one like kicked me in the uh nuts, though. Shit, I thought I would, uh, puke, you know?" He sets another stick of tobacco on fire. "Anyway, uh, I better get going right. Lot going on."

You can't even imagine what it is he has going on. You know you're stereotyping here, but the guy can barely string together a comprehensible sentence. "Yeah, well. Thanks for the box."

He opens the door, smiles, brings his cigarette to his lips. "Yeah, you know, it's like no problem. Hope that guy has, like, uh, other boxes for you." As he leaves, he mutters the usual polite phrases of excuse, surprising you. You didn't think he was the type to be remembering old-fashioned courtesies. Maybe he does have a lot going on.

As soon as he's out, you are there, pushing all the locks shut and feeling an unexpected relief. Somewhere in your head, you were expecting New Wave to slip out of that laidback persona and take you out or something.

"Man, I thought that guy was going to kill us or something. There was something kind of creepy about him." Boy is following you back into the living room.

"Totally." You almost mention the cigarette that Boy just smoked in your hallway, but then decide to keep it to yourself. You don't want to be bringing up the quitting thing and then end up making him feel more resolved about the whole issue. After all, he's quitting in order to convince you to move in with him. Which you don't want to deal with. Better if he just takes up the little sticks of smokeable nicotine again.

You sit down on the sofa, box on your knees. Stare at it. Just a box, not so big, can't be too dangerous. Or it could be a bomb. There have been a lot of bombs in your life lately. You feel like smacking yourself on the head for accepting it and not just telling Boy to huck it and New Wave back out the door and duck. But now that it's in your hands, you want to know what's inside. If it's a bomb, at least you'll see it before it goes off. You're very keen on seeing the method of your death.

But it's not a bomb. Or if it is, it's very strangely built. You're not sure what it is, but it seems like there's more than one, so you guess you're not sure what they are. You reach in and grab the end of one to pull it out.

It flip-flops down over your legs and onto the floor. You stare at it. It's one of those accordion-style books or documents or whatever. You've never been too sure how to refer to them, despite having written speeches on them before.

Clearly, Boy has only seen them for the same use. "Is it a speech?"

You pick it up and examine the first page, if you can call the part before a fold a page. The characters are written in that grassy calligraphy style that melts your eyes at the best of times and now with too much whiskey in your gullet is not the best of times. Those clouds are drifting back in with the passing of the moment of tension and your eyes swim as you try to focus and make out some words. Give up, hand it to Boy. "Can you read it? It's that calligraphy style."

He holds it close to his nose, stares intently. "I think this part says 'Kannon'," he says doubtfully.

Kannon, as in member of the Buddhist pantheon Kannon? Connecting to your earlier bombing and the talk with the cop. "Are these sutras?"

Boy jolts his head up from scrutinizing the speech. "Are you thinking the ones stolen yesterday?" He looks down again, more confused than ever. "I don't know. I've never actually seen a sutra, just heard the priests chanting them when my mum took me to the temple when I was little."

The coincidences are too much for you. New Wave said that Salaryman sent him with a box full of old writing. And that he was also sent to talk to the people sliding down the side of the Honda building. By the same guy. So Salaryman is talking to the bombers. And the bombers are the same people who bombed the Buddhist shop. But Salaryman gave the sutras to New Wave to give to you. So the bombers and Salaryman are for sure connected. The room starts spinning. At first, you wonder if all these implications are making your head spin, but then you see the mostly empty bottle on the floor next to the sofa and you realize it's probably just alcohol poisoning.

Boy is studying the slinky characters slipping down the accordion page carefully, really peering and squinting and it crosses your mind that he might need glasses. You should mention that to him.

"I think I can read this bit here."

The sound of Boy's voice startles you. You're getting way too absorbed in your own head. All the nervous excitement of actually getting this box has apparently exhausted your supply of adrenaline, most likely because your poor gland had to overcome so much cloud cover.

"Yeah, this bit here is definitely about Kannon. It's the Kannon with eleven heads. I can't read anything else though. I mean, this thing is seriously old style." He trails off towards the end, more muttering to himself than talking to you.

"Like how do you mean 'old style'?"

"Lots of old words and letters that we don't even use anymore. At least, I think so. I was really bad at classical literature in school." He folds it up again. "It's pointless for me to keep staring at this. I seriously have no idea what it's talking about. All I can read is the name of the goddess of mercy. Everything else is just squiggly lines." He places it gently in the box, almost reverently. You suspect he played down his involvement in the temple. "So why do you think someone paid that creepy kid to bring them to you?"

The room's whirling overtakes your eyes and you can't seem to focus on anything anymore. "Dunno, but I think I need to sleep now." You slump down on the sofa.

"Shit, are you okay?" he asks with concern.

"Yeah, just drank too much an' I have a concussion." And you were exploded on and some crazy salaryman is threatening you and you don't even know why.

He flips the lid of the box shut without another look. Gets up, slips an arm around you, helps you to your feet. "Okay, let's get you to bed."

You let yourself snuggle into his shoulder a little. You love the way he smells, the physical comfort of him at this moment. "You gonna stay?" you say to his armpit.

You feel him turn his neck to look down at you. "If you don't mind. I mean, I don't think you should be alone right now." You hear the tension in his voice and remember that this was why you left him at the Mexican restaurant, which seems like years ago, but must have been just at lunch today. You were fighting with him this afternoon, that's why you ended up drinking all that whiskey tonight. Oh yeah. Oh yeeeeeaaaaaah, you drag it out in your head.

You feel like you definitely want him to stay, you definitely don't want to be alone, especially not after the box o' sutra delivery service boy, who only served to remind you that Salaryman is not just a lie you made up to entertain yourself on the train, the way you sometimes do. But you are not apologizing. Boy gets too needy and girlish about all the relationship issues. Plus, he accused you of having no pulse. "You c'n stay," is all you're saying. Catching a glimpse of the clock on the VCR, you amend your statement. "Plush, think iss too late for you t' go home."

He follows your eyes to the clock and gives a short laugh that sounds like he's not really laughing and you wonder if he's still mad at you. Or mad at you again for some new reason. Or mad at the train. "Yeah, I guess so." He stands up straighter and heaves you up so that most of your weight rests on him. "Well, come on. I'll tuck you in."

Your eyelids keep fluttering shut as you half-walk, half-shuffle to your bedroom, following his lead. He eases you down onto your bed and tries to take off your sweater, but it gets stuck on your head and you have a moment of panic where you can't breathe through the thick knit fabric. Guess you still have some adrenaline leftover, after all.

"Aah! Aah!" you cry out in short repeated bursts as if this will somehow get the sweater off your head.

"Hold on." His voice sounds bemused, but you're glad he's not actually laughing out loud. It's bad enough that you're stuck in your sweater. "Just hold still," he chides as you wriggle about in a futile attempt to get free.

He is an expert at getting your clothes off and the sweater is soon at home on the floor with your other sweaters and laundry that you keep meaning to do, leaving you to breathe easy again.

"Where are your pyjamas?" He casts about the room, expecting to see your familiar striped top and bottoms lying somewhere.

You shake your head. "No, don't need pyjamas. You c'n keep me warm."

"No, seriously, it's freezing tonight. You need some pyjamas." He lifts the blanket to check if they're tucked away in there as they sometimes are and you take the opportunity to flop backwards and let your head hit the pillow.

An involuntary moan escapes your lips. Too much pleasure to be horizontal again. And in a soft bed with piles of heavy blankets. Screw you, hospital. You raise your fist angry old man style in your mind.

You wake up with your head in Boy's armpit. How did that happen? You can't breathe, your nose is pressed flat against his side. You yank yourself free and regret it instantly. Your head starts pounding, throbbing, a nuclear power plant seconds away from total meltdown. The sliver of light seeping in through the crack between the ledge and the metal shutter that pulls down to cover your window at night is shooting across the room to cut your eyeballs out. And Boy's breathy snores are a threat to your sanity.

Then he smacks his lips and that's where the straw is piled too high. You give him a shove. "Shut up," you whimper.

He wakes with a snort. "Huh? Whu?" He lifts himself on his elbows, turns his head from side to side.

"You're snoring." You're almost whispering. Even the sound of your own voice is too much for you to bear. You are a fool for drinking all that whiskey. Possibly a fool in general, but definitely for all that whiskey.

He lies back down, rolls over onto his side, grins at you. "Head hurt?"

You half-open your only defense against the light to glare at him. "Shut up."

He reaches out to stroke your hair softly. You flinch at first, expecting the thudding pain to increase, but it actually kind of soothes you. "I'm sorry, sweetie. Look, I'll get some coffee and painkillers for you, okay?"

You let your lids slide shut again, make the slightest motion with your head, a motion you hope he interprets as a nod.

He stops the head-stroking and pulls back the blankets to get up. The cold air pushes its way in and your skin hurts. Your skin hurts.

All you can do to stop the pain is groan feebly. He covers you with the blankets again, grabs one of the floor sweaters and pulls it over his head. You think it's probably his sweater, but you're not sure. With your eyes only open a tiny slit, it's hard to make out details of anything. But would your sweaters even fit him?

Thankfully, you drift back into a sort of morphine-like half-sleep where the pain is still there, but you can somehow look at it from a distance as some kind of weird object that you're currently in possession of.

When Boy returns, you are in the middle of a half-dream with that pink-haired girl from before. She's talking to the middle-aged couple you overheard at the crosswalk talking about up. And the three of them are arguing about directions. Not like 'which way to the bank', but like 'down is that way' and pointing to the left. All of them so insistent and all of them choosing totally different meanings for each direction. The sound of Boy's footfalls brings you closer to reality than the dream world and the arguing threesome fade away.

"Are you going to sit up?" he asks, setting two mugs down on the bedside table. "The coffee's right here." He sits himself down next to you on the bed.

You will your muscles to work for you now. But despite your exertions, no muscles obey. "Help me," you croak.

He laughs and takes your shoulders, pulls you into a sitting position. You finally gain some control over your body and are able to slide back a little so that you can lean against the wall behind your head. Each movement causes tiny moans to jump from your mouth.

"Here." He is holding one of the mugs up. Your muscle control does not fail you again and you are able to grasp the handle. You would pat yourself on the back if you had the energy or pain threshold for such an effort. Instead, you bring the cup to your lips. The smell of the strong coffee alone clears your head a little. You love coffee. You have small worshipful moments devoted to it. Now is one of those moments. You tentatively take a drink, careful of burning your lips and putting yourself in more pain.

"Is it okay?" When you first met him, he didn't drink coffee, but you didn't know that when you asked him to make some coffee one day. His skills have greatly improved since then.

"Yeah, thanks." Still croaky.

He holds out his palm with two white circles in the centre. "Painkiller?"

You take them thankfully and swallow them with some coffee, which is already working its magic. You feel more alive than dead now. Although it still could go either way. "Thanks."

"How do you feel?" He is actually concerned and not just laughing at your sorry hungover self.

"Am I dead?" you ask in response.

"That bad, huh? I guess you don't want any breakfast, hey?" He is sympathetic, but in that last question, you detect a hint of mockery.

You ignore it. You just can't muster the energy to get angry. "Is there any more coffee?"

He reaches down and picks up the carafe, pours more for both of you. Since he started hanging out with you, he's been drinking coffee. Does that make you a bad influence? He is trying to quit smoking for you, though, so maybe the two cancel out and you become a neutral influence. You try to ignore yourself and just drink the damn coffee. Why do you always have to think so much?

"So that was weird, hey? Last night? That weird creepy kid?" Boy starts and for a second, you have no idea what he's on about.

"Wh—oh, you mean, that new wave kid?"

"Yeah, that and that box of sutras. What was that all about?"

"I don't know." Poor, oblivious Boy. You remember that he knows nothing about Salaryman or the fact that it's all your fault that the shop got blown up in the first place or anything. Of course, he doesn't know because you haven't told him. And you haven't told him, why? Maybe he's right, maybe you are keeping yourself away from people. Then you remind yourself that you only got involved with him because he's cute and he's trying to take this thing in whole new directions and you are not going to let that happen. Just sex is simpler.

But you're sitting here drinking coffee that he made for you, lying in a bed that he put you into. And you remember how glad you were that he was staying over. You tell yourself that it was just because you didn't want to be alone.

He drains his cup, leans in to kiss you and you wonder what your breath must be like. If it smelled like battery acid last night, it has to be even worse this morning. And yet, he kisses you anyway. "Listen, I have to go," he announces and you feel a little panic drift by your heart. "I talked to my manager after they called to tell me you were in the hospital and said that I was taking a few days off. But I still need to go in today and deal with this one client. He's coming from out of town and I really can't change the appointment." He is apologetic.

"No, that's fine," you assure him, trying not to clutch your head as it pounds at each word, while wondering why a person would come from out of town for tires. "I'm just going to go back to sleep anyway. You might as well go earn some money."

He shifts his gaze to the wall beside you. "Can I come back over once I'm done?"

You hesitate. You don't want to be alone, but you don't want to give Boy the idea that the moving in together thing has any chance of actually happening. It seems like it would be better if you tried to spend less time with him for a while. But thinking of the way Salaryman grabbed the back of your neck and all the threats that were implicit in his tone and you cave. "Yeah."

He lights up, kisses you again. "Great. I'll bring something for dinner. Any preferences?"

"Nothing cheesy." Just saying the word 'cheesy' is making you nauseous, all that coffee suddenly sitting less well.

"Can I get you anything before I go?" The usual solicitous Boy you know so well.

The side-to-side movement of your head is slight. "The coffee is right here, right?" He holds the carafe up in response. "That's all I need."

He's off and you're alone in your apartment again. You put your coffee cup on the table and slide back down between the covers.

Pull them up over your ears and snuggle in. Sleep after three cups of coffee is pretty much impossible, but you mostly just want to lie here and feel sorry for yourself. Not just for your pounding head and your queasy stomach, but for all the weird misfortune that's been befalling you. You are one cursed baby.

After spending some time letting out little pathetic moans that make you feel even sorrier for yourself, you realize that you will have to get up unless you have a bedpan tucked away under the covers somewhere. You begin to mentally prepare for the journey, consoling yourself with the thought that your apartment is small so the toilet is only a few steps away and your slippers are right there next to the bed, all you have to do is slip your feet into them, and once you shuffle your way to the toilet, you can come back and curl up in this warm bed again. You're still not quite convinced, but the objections from your bladder are stronger than your doubts. On the count of three, you tell yourself.

On three, you heave yourself up and a strangled cry is wrenched from your gut. You didn't even know you could make a sound like that. You push your bare feet into the slippers that are right where you told yourself they were and shuffle-step as fast as you can to the little toilet room, which actually contains nothing but a toilet. Unless you count the half-sink thing on the back of the toilet as a separate object, in which case, there is also a sink in there. On the way, you notice the stripes covering your body and you suppose that he found your pyjamas after all. You wonder where they were.

You might as well take advantage while you're up. You still feel like hell, but your tummy is more grumbly rumbly than barfing it up, so you figure you could give eating a go and shuffle your way into the kitchen. Where you peer vacantly into the fridge, losing track of what it was you were looking for. Finally, you find an inoffensive-looking orange and decide you could eat an orange.

Without actually lifting your feet, you get into the living room. You have never been more grateful for the lack of carpet in your house. If there was some kind of covering on these floors, you would actually be forced to dig up the energy to lift your feet slightly. Carefully easing yourself down onto the sofa, you feel such relief. No more standing. You are finally closer to the earth, expending less force to hold yourself up against the unending pull of gravity. It's days like this where you wish the laws of nature were different. Not having to hold your head up would be heaven.

You allow yourself to just sit and pull the orange apart slowly, careful to peel all the white off before popping each slice into your mouth. The tanginess is a little overwhelming at first, but the juice flowing down your throat is definitely quenching. You should probably drink some water, but that would mean getting up again. You'll need some time to prepare for that.

You spot the box of mysteries next to the coffee table. Your head thumps once in protest of the thought of trying to sort out the snaky characters covering the pages, but you pick it up anyway. Pop the last of the orange into your mouth and open the box.

It's the same as it was yesterday. Full of the little accordion books and a couple actual scrolls that you failed to notice with your whiskey eyes. You ignore a second thump of protest and take one of the books out. Let it unfold in front of you. It's that same calligraphy. You put it aside, take another one out, same thing. You keep taking them out and checking if they're all the same or if there's something in here you can read without having to get out a classical dictionary. You grab the first of the scrolls and roll it out on the table.

"Boom." is written very clearly in very modern characters.

If your life was a movie, this would be the part where you or the box or something in your house explodes. You look around nervously, your heart threatening yet again to jump out of your chest. So far, nothing is exploding. Your head still feels like it might, but you feel fairly certain that that is merely a metaphor and not a literal possibility. You suppose that this constitutes proof that your life is in fact not a movie.

Clearly, this 'boom' scroll is not part of the original set of sutras. Unless the monks were playing a joke on future monks? But it does seem more likely that this 'boom' is directed at you.

You reach for the other scroll in the box. If all the accordion books have been actual sutras, then maybe all the scrolls are actual threats. You're not sure how you feel about that, but you unroll it anyway.

It's not exactly 'boom', but it's not a sutra either.

"I hope you've been considering the question of direction," it starts. "Regardless of what you may or may not believe, it does matter in a substantial way. I also would be pleased to hear that you are overcoming your relationship troubles with your handsome little friend. He may come in handy. When doors need to be opened, it is so nice to have someone to hold one's hand, to connect one to the door, in a manner of speaking. So many things in this world are uncertain; support is always welcome. There is so much devastation, so much unhappiness, so very little a person can rely on. So many explosions.

"I wish you a speedy recovery from your hangover."

Of course it is unsigned, but your fake brain surgery degree is not required to tease out who it is from. The degree is even less needed in concluding that you are being watched at this very moment as you choke a little on your own saliva. You have an overwhelming urge to lift your head and look around, see if you can see him, but you know that you wouldn't and you know that he would see you lifting your head and looking around and you don't want to give him the pleasure or satisfaction or whatever he is deriving from this sick situation.

So you reread the note. And then again. And again until you have the contents committed to memory. It looks like more explosions ahead for you. What's this about Boy mean though? Boy coming in handy. Are you going to have to sex your way out of some bad situation? Or use dull office talk to put opponents to sleep? And all this crap about which way is up is starting to make you crazy. The pounding in your head starts up again in earnest. Time for more painkillers.

You leave the scrolls and books and everything out of the box scattered on the sofa and unrolled on the coffee table and go into the kitchen. You surprise yourself with your ease of movement; at least, it's ease compared to when you came into the living room. You may yet live through this.

You look up, reaching for a cupboard and find yourself looking at the floor. For a moment, you think that maybe you tilted your head in the wrong direction. After all, you do not have the finest motor control today. But no, your inner ear is telling you that your head is tilted upwards. Your eyes, however, are telling you that you are looking at the floor. Being a logical sort of person, you close your eyes and tilt your head downwards. You are very certain that you are facing the floor now. Your inner ear has never led you astray before. Well, except for those times when you spun yourself around too many times. But there has been no spinning today.

And yet, when you cautiously open your eyes, you are staring down at the ceiling and the cupboards that you were originally attempting to open. There are your feet right next to the top of those cupboards.

Dizzy, dizzy times join in the pounding in your head to create a cacophonous symphony. You close your eyes again and sink to the ground. Rather, you let the force of gravity (the force of up? anti-gravity?) win over the force of your muscles since you're not sure that it is the ground beneath your feet at this moment. You want to open your eyes to check, but you don't dare. If you see the ceiling again, you're not sure what you'll do.

You hear the door behind you open and slam shut. Thump, says your head.

"What are you doing on the floor? Are you okay?" It's Boy. He's back. And he said you were on the floor.

You open your eyes just a slit. The floor greets you. You really are on the floor. You open your eyes all the way, see Boy's concerned face as he squats down next to you.

"Hey, honestly, are you okay?" You can see that if you don't answer him in a second, he will start to freak out and end up taking you to the hospital or some silly thing. Although maybe you should go to the hospital.

"Yeah, I'm fine. I just felt a little dizzy, I guess." And upside down, although you're pretty sure you should keep your mouth shut on that. Did you go crazy for a minute? It was so real, but it must have been you hallucinating. How could you suddenly be on the ceiling? Clearly, that head injury is worse than you thought.

He helps you to your feet. "Why don't I help you to the living room and then I'll make you some tea." His kindness overwhelms you. You know it's just tea and some support to the sofa, but it's so like him to drop everything on his mind to help you out. And right now in freak times central, you need this, his constancy. The same thing that was annoying you not two days ago.

"I just came in here to get more painkillers, actually," you say, while letting him guide you out of the room.

"I'll bring some with the tea." He sees the contents of the box all over the living room. "Wow, you really went to town with those things, huh?" He clears them off the sofa to set you down, sees the scrolls laid out on the table. "Hey, these scrolls are in regular characters."

Crap. Crap, crap, crap. Why didn't you roll those up? You don't want to have to go through the whole story. You know that Boy's protective pants will be pulled all the way up and belted tight if he knows you are being threatened and people are trying to explode you.

But it's too late. He's picked one up and his brow is furrowed so deeply, it may just turn inside out. "'Boom'?" His confusion is clear in his voice, also a little hint of a kind of proto-fear, getting ready to be freaked out. He looks up from the scroll at you. "What does this mean?"

You shrug. "More explosions?" Perhaps your tone is a little too glib, but you really don't want this to turn into what it's bound to turn into. Your previous satisfaction with his kindness is melting back into your usual annoyance.

"'More explosions'?" A little incredulity. "What is that supposed to mean?" He sits down next to you, picks up the other scroll, reads it intently. You look away, waiting for him to finish. You toy with tearing it out of his hands, but that's bound to just make things worse. Seems like it's all coming out now whether you want it to or not. You're not too into the idea of Boy being dragged into this. Even though you're not sure what 'this' is, you feel like it's really about you and Boy is just one of the innocent bystanders, the character who gets written in just to be taken out. You'd rather just handle it on your own.

You feel his eyes boring into the back of your head and you know that that is no longer a possibility. "What the fuck is this?" Is he angry? He sounds angry, which is a surprise. You were expecting more loving concern, more of his awkward comfort, possibly more creepy humming. "What the hell is going on?"

You turn back to him. He is fist-clenchingly rigid. Has he turned to stone? Is that the power of the scroll? Is that his role, how he'll come in handy? But he's still breathing, so whatever he is, it's not stone. You inhale, getting ready to explain, tell the whole story, then exhale abruptly. You have no idea how to tell the whole story. "I don't know," you say honestly. "I'm trying to figure it out."

"But this." He waves the scroll in front of you. "Whoever wrote this, it sounds like they know you. I mean, whoever it is, they know you drank too much whiskey last night."

Seat yourself, lean forward to cradle your heavy head in your hands. "I think who wrote it is this salaryman. I just call him

Salaryman."

"You know this guy?" His voice trembles a little at the end.

"I don't know him, I just—" You cut yourself off. You find yourself wishing that you had managed to get those painkillers before having to deal with this. "Look, you remember when the Honda building exploded?" He nods slowly. "You remember after you came and we were leaving and that salaryman guy bumped into me?"

"The guy who was grabbing your chest?" The trembly wavering note is gone, he's back to plain old confusion.

"Yeah, that guy. He wasn't grabbing my chest, by the way."

"So what was he doing?"

"Threatening me." Now you raise your head from your hands to see his reaction. You want to see if it looks as weird on his face as it sounds inside your head.

It does. "Threatening you? About what? What the hell?"

"I don't know. I mean, he said some shit about how I can't tell anyone about the people coming down the side of the building and he was really—"

He holds up a halting hand. "Whoa, whoa. People coming down the side of the building? You were serious about that? And that new wave kid wasn't high and seeing things?"

You remember what Salaryman said about having overheard you talking about it when you were drunk. Well, at least you know now that he wasn't lying about that. But just as you told him, Boy clearly thought you were talking shit. "Yeah, I was serious about that. Although I don't actually remember talking about it."

"You don't remember?" If his voice goes any higher, he'll go through some kind of second puberty. You would doubt the possibility of that, but you do have in front of you a box of sutras from a shop that was blown up in attempt to get you. Impossible things are seeming a lot more likely to you these days.

You shake your head. "No, I guess I drank too much or something."

He frowns, releasing the furrows in the centre of his forehead and creating new ones with his lips. "You didn't drink that much. I mean, do you remember last night?"

Slow ups and downs with your head. "Yeah," dragging the word out and letting it tilt up towards the end. You're waiting for his conclusion.

"You were waaaaaay drunker last night than you were that night we went out after the explosion. I mean, we only had like four or five beers or something. When I left you at the train, you were fine. I mean, you were kind of giggly, but you weren't hammered or anything."

This is somehow punching you in the gut. "I don't even remember where we went. I remember the first beer we drank, I think." Now that you're forcing yourself to think about it, you realize that it's not just the late evening hours that are lost to you, the way they get lost when you drink too much in a way that you haven't done since you were fifteen. You never get drunk enough to lose time anymore. "What the hell is going on?" You can't keep this exclamation inside.

"I don't know, but you were not that drunk."

"So...what? I mean, I seriously can't remember anything, but I mean, Salaryman said that he heard me talking about the people on the side of the building and that's the only reason I knew I said anything to you at all." You meet his puzzled gaze.

He is scratching his head, very cartoon-style. You half-expect him to stick out his tongue like a character in deep thought. But he doesn't. Which is good, you guess, you need to get more reality-based, not less. Comparing situations to cartoons and TV and movies is just not helping you. "Were you drugged?" he says finally.

"What?"

"I don't know. It's just the only thing that makes sense. I mean, you weren't drunk, but you don't remember anything. And not just the way you wouldn't remember things from a drunken blackout. If you barely remember your first drink, that's weird. And you said that that salaryman guy told you he heard you, which means he was somewhere listening to you, right? Maybe he slipped something in your drink or something. I mean, he was obviously there."

You put both hands in your hair and give it a little tug, regret it when the recently ceased pounding starts up again. "But it doesn't make any sense." Practically a plaintive whine. You're getting to the feeling-sorry-for-yourself stage of things. "Why would he drug me?"

You wonder if Boy's shoulders don't ever get tired from all the ups and downs of his shrugs. And why his neck doesn't get bigger from all the exercise. "Why would he be threatening you?"

You sigh. "Good point."

Boy picks up the scroll from where he dropped it in his lap, reads it again. You can see him committing it to memory, just like you did, looking for clues to tell him which way is up. You want to tell him the answer's not there and spare him the effort. But you leave him to his reading. You need a break from where this conversation is taking you.

Because if Boy's right and Salaryman did drug you, then why? It seems like under the influence of some drug, you'd be more likely to forget his scary threatening self and get a little chatty about the Kuroko. But he's threatening you to keep your mouth shut. Isn't he? If he's doing things to make you talk about what he specifically told you not to talk about, then what the hell does he want? You feel like crying. The combination of frustration and confusion always makes you want to shed tears.

But you hold them in. You're not about to break down in front of Boy.

He finally gives up with the scroll, lays it on the table. "So what else did he say when he said he heard you talking about those people?"

You don't have to think too hard to remember. Salaryman's

— 69 —

words have been echoing around in your head. "Nothing that made any sense. I mean, he said that he heard me talking to you about those people. And then he said something about you and how you seemed all into what I was talking about. It kind of felt like he was threatening you somehow, but it was nothing he said. He was just talking about how he had seen you with me and you seemed nice. Nothing scary, maybe just the way he said it. Or just the fact that he knew who you were and had been watching both of us together."

Boy is visibly upset. "So I'm in on this too and you didn't even tell me?"

You wave your hand in a whoa-slow-down gesture. "No, no, it's not like that. I mean, I don't think you're in on this. I mean, I don't even know what 'this' is, so how can you be in on it?"

"Don't give me that." Nuts to see him angry with you. "All this stuff is going on and you don't even tell me about it, even though it's clear that I'm involved, I mean, someone is watching me and you think I don't need to know?" He stands up, hands clenched into fists at his sides.

His reaction is over the top. You know you probably should have told him about the threats and everything, but you figured that he would want to go to the police or something and in any case, you didn't really take the whole thing too seriously at first. You were sort of hoping that it would all go away. "Hey, slow down. Look, I didn't think you were involved."

He snorts derisively. "How could you not think I was involved?" He grabs the scroll from the table, shakes it at you. "Here I am, written down! I'm involved!"

He makes a good point. Plus, the shaking in your face is kind of unnerving. "Okay, okay, I'm sorry. It was stupid. I just don't know what the hell is going on and I kind of thought it would be better if I—"

"If you what?" He cuts you off. "If you just let me wander around oblivious to any danger I might be in? If you just kept it to yourself so that I couldn't protect you at all?"

Is that what this is about? You have a sneaky feeling that this angry action is more about him freaking out at his inability to keep you safe from explosions and salarymen. Normally, you freak out over this kind of protective thing, but, like the cigarette bummed off New Wave, you figure it's in your own best interests to just let it go, just this once. You stand up. Reach out and put a hand on his arm gently. "You're right. I'm sorry."

He deflates. Sits down. Drops the scroll again. "No, I'm sorry. You're obviously freaked out by this. Me being angry doesn't change anything."

You sit down next to him. "So what does change things?" You're sincerely hoping he can answer that question.

But of course, he's got nothing. Shaking his head. "I have no idea. I don't even know what's already happened."

Right. You barebones it out for him, the Kimono Lady; the people coming down the building, although he's heard most of that, but this time, he's listening and taking you seriously; what Salaryman said to you. You leave out all the direction talk though, mostly because you're not even sure how to put it in words: 'hey, there's a lot of talk about which way is up?' Or: 'people keep talking about directions being different from what I think?' Or: 'I had this dream where a pink-haired girl with nail-claws pondered the true nature of reality and I think it wasn't just a dream?' You keep your mouth shut.

He leans back into the sofa. He seems to be reeling. It's the first time you've ever been able to apply that word to a real world situation. You always thought it was just in books that people reeled. "So the Buddhist shop was blown up to get you?"

You rest an arm on the armrest. Well designed, well named. "That's what Kimono Lady says. But I mean, I don't get it. Don't you think it could have been some other person wearing a corduroy jacket?" You desperately want him to say yes.

He gives you a look that suggests you may have dropped some marbles. "With all the other things, do you really think it's possible that some other person in a corduroy jacket was who they were waiting for?"

You sigh, let go of that hope. "No, I guess not. I just really want it to not be about me. Because if it's about me, what does it mean? Why me?"

Crossing his arms across his chest. "Got me."

The two of you have run out of words. For a few minutes, you sit next to each other on the sofa, not talking, not looking at each other.

Boy clears his throat. You look at him expectantly. He laughs nervously. "I got nothing. I was just going to ask if you're hungry."

Reminding you that you have eaten nothing but that orange all day and your stomach rumbles. Is the evil afterlife of the whiskey finally over? You listen to your stomach, wait for nausea to follow, but none does. "Yes, yes, I am."

"I forgot to pick something up on my way home, so why don't you have a shower and get dressed and we'll go somewhere and get something?" he suggests. "If you're feeling better."

Your head still throbs a little, but the pain is so much less than before. You consider those painkillers again, then decide that you don't really need them after all. You're a tough one. You can handle a little headache. This, after feeling sorry for yourself for most of the day. "Yeah, I think I'll live. Give me twenty minutes." You shuffle off to the shower/bathtub room, which also has a sink that is very convenient for toothbrushing. Which is what you do first. Holding the brush in the 'pen grip' that your dentist lectured you about after the discovery that you had been brushing so forcefully, the enamel on your teeth was being worn down. This discovery having been made by pain suddenly shooting up the side of your head whenever you drank cold beverages.

A brushing style that takes forever, but finally you're rinsing and spitting and showering and drying and underpantsing and pantsing and shirting and all the other million details that go into you being street ready. And then you are. You have to admit, you feel about fifty million times better after that shower.

When you walk rather than shuffle back into the living room, Boy has put all the accordion books back inside the box and rolled the scrolls up and laid them neatly on top of the box. He stands up to kiss your fresh cheek, lays a protective arm over your shoulders. "You ready?"

Nodding. Your belly is emptier than you realized. "Let's move."

It's only when you get to the station that you realize you don't know where you're going. "Hey, where are we going anyway?"

"I have no idea. I never even thought about it. I was just thinking, go to the station." He pulls out his robot voice for the station part.

You laugh with him. "Me, too. But we should probably, you know, decide before we get on any trains."

Further discussion leads to the decision not to get on any trains. There's a place in your neighbourhood that serves this incredible Greek spinach pie and both of you are suddenly drooling at the thought of all that garlic and feta.

The restaurant is not full. It never is and this worries you sometimes. And tonight, it's not just not full, it's actually empty. What if they close down? You really should eat here more often.

While you pour the complementary water down your throat and wait for your dinner to arrive, you want to talk to Boy about this whole thing, but feeling like the walls are just waiting for you to say something juicy. Boy, drumming his fingers on the table and looking intently at each of the crappy paintings on the walls, seems to feel the same way.

You close your eyes to blink and you're looking at everything the wrong way. You can see the top of Boy's head. You look down, or rather, you turn your head so that your inner ear is telling you that you're looking down, but your eyes are once again contradicting that information. Your feet are on the ceiling again. A ceiling that could really use a wash, you note with disgust. It looks like someone left their Greek spinach pie up here once. Down here?

You must be hallucinating. You look down/up. Boy is not reacting weirdly. Of course, he hasn't looked at you. He's too busy trying to avoid talking to you about this mess by looking at the eighties fast food restaurant décor paintings. Has he seen you? Are you really on the ceiling? You feel a little more prepared to deal with it now that the pounding in your head is less, the hangover that paralyzed you all day has finally released you. So it's no hangover hallucination, if there even exists such a thing. It has to be your concussion. Because you're blinking your brains out and you're still on the ceiling. You pinch yourself really hard. So hard that you bruise yourself. And still when you look down, you see what someone threw above their head one night in some kind of drunken revelry. (You are just theorizing on the revelry, but you can't see any other way for dinner to end up on the ceiling.)

You close your eyes. Inhale, exhale, inhale and out, just like on that yoga program you saw on TV a while ago. You were making fun of it then, but the breathing techniques are coming in handy now and you vow to stop laughing at yoga.

You open your eyes. See Boy, still looking away. But not the top of his head, the place where he may bald someday, just the side of his face as he contemplates a woman's wavy outlined portrait. You look up. The pie is there, but your feet are not. Interesting. You're not sure what's going on here and not sure if you should tell Boy. Does this have something to do with everyone telling you to think about the stupid directions? Does everyone else know that you're somehow ending up on the ceiling today?

"Hey there kitty," Boy reaches down and you see a small Persian that's come creeping over to him. It submits at once to his caresses and starts to purr so loudly you wonder if it's really you sitting over there petting it. If you can be on the ceiling, you can be where Boy is sitting, right? Are there rules for this?

Thankfully, your lonely waitress is bringing you your long-awaited dinner so you can finally stop thinking about direction. Although you know your brain will be back at it as soon as you're done eating and there's nothing to distract it anymore. You have the sudden urge to punch yourself in the head. You hold that urge in and grab a fork. You suspect a punch in the head will only exacerbate your troubles.

"Cute cat," Boy comments as the waitress places his pie in front of him. "Does it belong to the shop?"

Cat. Cats. Something about cats. Pink Hair said something about cats. You almost scratch your head with your fork, but remember in the nick of time that you are not in your apartment and scratching your head with your fork is not generally accepted behaviour. Right! You're supposed to be nice to cats. You lean forward under the table, try to reach the fat Persian. Who dips its head to you. Is the cat bowing? Your hangover must still be lingering.

"What cat?" The waitress has clearly never heard of any cat in this shop.

He indicates the Persian to his left with his eyes. "That cat."

Her forehead is wrapped up in consternation. "That's not our cat. How did you get in here?" She uses that mock angry tone that people tend to reserve for mildly misbehaving animals and children and ushers the cat out the door.

Boy digs into his pie. "Huh, weird. I wonder what that cat was doing here."

Is it neurotic couple style for the two of you to have ordered the same thing? You feel like it might be, but it's too late now. The pie in front of you is sending up its garlic scent trails and you are powerless in the face of all that feta. You think they might even put lemon juice in this.

Before long, bellies have been filled and you've almost convinced yourself that the whole flipping upside down thing never happened. After all, you do have such an active imagination. It even gets you into trouble from time to time. No surprise that you would suddenly be seeing yourself on the ceiling. You are so comfortable with your comfortable lies.

"Look," Boy says when the waitress has come and taken away your clean plates. "I want to talk about what's going on."

You really don't. "I don't know if it's such a good idea. I mean, we're in public and all. I know the restaurant is empty—"

He laughs and shakes his head. "No, not that. I mean, I want to talk about that too. I think I just need to think about it for a while and anyway, you're right. Here is not the place for that."

You purse your lips forward. "Well, what then?"

"Just what we were talking about the other day. Have you thought about what I said?" He is shy putting this forward, looking away down at the floor like he wishes the waitress hadn't chased the cat away so he could at least be petting it.

You frantically pull the books off all the shelves and finally, you find the light switch hidden behind the day before yesterday. Appropriately, your stomach drops. "You mean about moving in together?"

He nods, still not looking at you, twirling a straw between his fingers. "I know it's only been a couple days, but I think you've seen the effort I've been making."

The smoking! The quitting! Are you meant to praise him now or something? Alarm bells are sounding and your population is running about without their heads. "Uh, yeah. I mean, you seem like you're really working hard."

He looks up, beaming suddenly. "You noticed? I think I can really do this. The thing is, I really want to do this. The more I think about it, the more I think that you and I should really be together."

Are you worming in your seat? Is that what you can call this creepy crawly kind of feeling of must-escape-somehow? How can he be so great with bringing you painkillers and keeping you warm at night and yet want the Cosmo life that you are not interested in giving him? "I don't know. I mean, I just think with all the shit's that's going on right now, is this really the right time to be thinking about this?"

He gives some chin-jutting nods. "No, you're right. I've really been thinking about that. Even before all the stuff about Salaryman tonight." Seemingly forgetting his professed desire to not mention that in public.

You shush him with your eyes. Frantically glance around the place. Reassure yourself that there is at least no one inside the restaurant who can hear him talk about Salaryman. You feel certain that Salaryman is right outside the door, though. Or under the table.

He continues, oblivious to your frantic eyes. "Even with you being in the hospital—no, especially with you in the hospital and the explosions, I really feel like we should be pulling closer together; like this is the perfect time for us to move closer and really support each other and have that kind of relationship."

If your eyebrow could arch any higher. You pull up images of him kissing various parts of you from your mental archive. Righhht, that's why you're here. You leaf through your library until you are convinced and his meaningful relationship words have less staying power in your head. "I just think that's exactly the reason why we should be backing off a little, you know, take some time to consider. After all, it's pretty traumatic and I don't want you to be deciding anything that you'll regret." That's it, put it on him.

He shakes his head authoritatively. "No, I really think this is right. I've just been thinking about it non-stop. I want to be with you." Suddenly, he's clutching your hand from across the table and trying to look meaningfully into your eyes. You are awash in the desire to look away but you don't want to make everything unbearable, so you force yourself to stay firm. Accept the meaningful gaze.

Clutching at straws. "How about this? How about we just think about it for another few days and make sure that this is something we both want? I want to make sure that you feel okay about quitting smoking and everything. Really think about what you'll be giving up here. I don't want to be the focus of any resentment later. And in any case, I don't think either of us can make proper decisions about anything right now."

He releases your hand, drops his gaze to the floor. "You're right. I feel sure about this, but it has only been a couple days since I quit. If I suddenly started again when we were living together, that would suck."

You almost drag your hand across your forehead in an exaggerated expression of relief. The waitress shows up with the after-dinner coffees and lets you stay silent for a minute or two, get yourself back together. That's what he wants to talk about? He just found out that there is some kind of crazy plot to blow you up and he's obsessed with moving in together? You just do not get him. You blow the steam off your coffee as you bring it to your mouth, take a sip, burn your tongue.

"You have to blow on it for more than a second." In the least told-you-so way possible, but still you resent him for saying it.

Exaggerated blowing before you take another sip, but he seems oblivious to your sarcasm. If you don't get him, he definitely doesn't get you. You wonder if it's time to break up with him, if your time together has stretched itself as far as it's going to. You still like him and you still want to hang out and most of all, you still want to have regular sex. But you're not so much about the forever thing and moving in together is the first step to rocking chairs on the front porch. Plus, if you lived together, you'd never get to run around your house naked playing whatever music you wanted. It would be weird.

"Can I ask you something?" Interrupting your thoughts abruptly, probably for the best. Your thoughts have you romping naked in your living room.

Nodding. "Yeah, of course, what is it?"

He glances around furtively once or twice before leaning in close and you know where this is going. "What does he look like?" Now he remembers it's a secret.

Holding your cup at chest level, café casual. "Who? Salaryman?" You keep your voice low too.

Focused on you. More nods.

"I don't know. I've never seen him."

"What do you mean, you've never seen him? Haven't you 'met' a few times already?"

"Well, yeah, but there was no looking. Just him hissing things at me. All I ever see are his shoes and pants."

Thwarted, he leans back in his chair. Runs his hand through his hair. Looks at the walls, around the room, anywhere but you. You can see the clenched muscles in his jaw and you suddenly get what he was after.

"Look, you can't go after him or anything. I don't think you can make it stop like that. Even if I could tell you who to look for, he'd see you coming. Trust me. I'm pretty sure I haven't been alone since at least when the Honda building exploded, maybe even before." You'd rather not think about when this all started.

His jaw stays clenched. "I can't stand the thought of this creep just watching you all the time."

Now this is the protective Boy you were expecting when he was flipping out angry earlier. Warms you a little and you decide the breaking up thing can wait. You'll find a way out of this moving in together thing. It's funny, you want to be loved in an obvious way, but you'd rather not get caught up in it. Just have it there until it starts to interfere.

You pour the rest of your coffee down your throat. "Are you done?"

"Yeah. You wanna go?"

You let your lids droop a little. "I need some sleep. I've had a rough day."

"So rough, staying home and being hungover all day. How did you manage?" He's put on that boo-boo-baby voice that he uses when he mocks you. A voice which somehow makes you want to say 'muffin' cooingly. You can't explain it.

"Fine, you jerk. I stayed home and was hungover. It sucked the life out of me. I need sleep." You stand and pull your coat on. Your corduroy coat. You'd think after finding out you're being targeted with this coat the thing to identify you by, you'd stop wearing it.

He's in his jacket before you and headed to the cash register to pay the bill. You walk up as he's counting out the thousand-yen bills to cover the cheque. From under a table in front of you, the Persian cat flies out screaming as if she was in labour or being flayed. You have six heart attacks and a stroke. Boy and the waitress at the counter appear to have a similar number of infarctions.

The cat screams its way out the open window and the three of you stare speechlessly after it.

The waitress is the first to work up a feeble grin. "What do you suppose got into him?"

Boy just shakes his head and receives his change.

You unglue your feet from the floor and find that, despite your many heart traumas, you are capable of walking out the door, with Boy not far behind.

"Christ, what got into that cat?" He is shaking his head wonderingly. "Sounded like she was giving birth."

You hook your arm through the crook of his. "I didn't see any baby cat heads coming out."

A little disbelieving. "Did you look?"

You think back to your heart attacks. It's true that you weren't exactly focused on looking at kitty parts. "Well—"

"Hey!" It's the waitress, standing in the door, waving at you.

"You forgot this!"

You jog back to the restaurant, take the small box from her hand, tilt your head like a cocker spaniel hearing things. "I forgot this?"

"Well, it was on the chair next to you and you're the only people who have been in here all night." She shivers a little from the cold. "Anyway, glad I caught you before you got too far. Have a good night."

You wish her the same absent-mindedly, turning the little box over in your hands. Meander back over to Boy.

"What is it?" He's peeking over your shoulder, Christmas-morning style.

"Dunno. It's not mine though." Your heart is still weak from the cat. You don't know how many more trips to the bottom of your stomach it can take.

"Oh." He meets your eyes. "You think...?"

Nodding slowly. "What else?"

"Well, open it," he urges and you can do nothing but stare at him.

"Have you considered what might be inside? There have been a lot of explosions lately."

"Okay, don't exaggerate. There've been two."

"Two is a lot!"

"Anyway. Do you really think there's a bomb in there? I mean, there wasn't in the last box you got."

Now you lower your lids and hope the look you've composed on your face is as menacing as you would like it to be. "No, there was a bomb threat."

There's the sheepish look you were waiting for. "Oh, right." Finds a new line of attack. "Well, that's not a bomb. Open it."

You roll your eyes as you give in to his not-very-persuasive argument. The fact is you want to know what's inside too. Like a ring box, the lid is hinged, so you pull it up.

"What is it?" His eager peering over your shoulder is not bringing the object in the box into his line of sight, despite the little jumps.

You bite your bottom lip as you ponder the contents of the box. "It says 'Push me.'"

"Huh?" Clearly, that's not what he was expecting to hear.

You hold it up high to show him the letters written in sparkly glue pen on a velvet pin cushion. Well, it looks like a velvet pin cushion. You're not sure if that's its actual purpose.

"'Push me.'" He reads it aloud and you roll your eyes again. You've already seen it. You read it out to him. You know what it says. "What does that mean?"

"That we're supposed to push on the pin cushion?"

"I know that. Why? What's pushing this going to do?"

You bring the open box back in front of your face, examine it up close, but you can see nothing else. "I don't know, but I'm not pushing it."

"Do you want me to?" He's stretching out an eager pushing finger and you snatch the box away.

"No! What are you, crazy?" You start walking away from him, towards your apartment building.

He chases after you. "But why not? I want to know what it does."

You walk faster. "Probably blows something up."

"You are just thinking too much about explosions." He is dismissive and you curse his legs that are longer than yours and enabling him to keep up with you no matter how fast you walk.

"Of course I have explosions on the brain! Where have you been? I've been in two explosions in the last three days! That's not normal! A man in a suit is threatening me! That's not normal either!" You know you are going a little over the top in your reaction, but really, what is he thinking?

Holding up defensive hands. "Okay, I'm sorry. But still, I think we should push it."

"We're not pushing it." You snap the box shut, shove it as deep in your pocket as you can.

He is sullen suddenly. "Fine."

"Good." You're not far from sullen either. You turn your head to glare at him, notice the headphones hanging around his neck, get ready to lash out. Are you so boring that he has to bring along electronic entertainment? "What's with the headphones?"

"They keep my neck warm," he snaps.

You hold in the urge to snap back and ask yourself why all of a sudden his neck is cold. He wasn't wearing his headphones in the restaurant. And wouldn't a scarf work better anyway?

You're almost to the corner to turn onto the street where you live. "Look, I don't want you to have to walk all the way back to the station from my house. Why don't you just go now and I'll see you tomorrow?"

Shaking his head. "No. I am definitely not letting you walk home by yourself. A crazy guy is after you."

You stop, take you hands out of your pockets. He stops too, gives you a look you can't interpret. His eyebrows are raised, but at different levels. You didn't know he could do that. You place your hands on his shoulders, square yourself, meet his eyes. "The same crazy guy is after you. If I shouldn't be walking home alone, then neither should you."

"Then I will just have to sleep at your apartment." Ooh, he's smug.

Goddammit! You totally set that one up. You can't stop kicking yourself in the pants. "Fine," you growl through clenched teeth and get back to walking.

Shove your hands in pockets again and the box is gone. The box is not there. You scrabble around in your pockets, but they're just not that big. The box could not be hiding somewhere. You're still scrabbling anyway, when Boy cries out in surprise. "Hey, what is the box doing here?"

It's on the ground where you were standing. Why is it on the ground? That dizzy spinning feeling is slamming into you again. It should be in your pocket. You know you did not drop it.

You can't stop him from picking it up and opening it. He stares at the sparkly letters, are his eyes coming unfocused? Your stomach is a pit of dread.

"Don't press it!" You lunge for it, but he holds it up out of your reach. You see his eyes clearly now and there's no way he's hearing you. He is definitely in some other space place. He starts walking away from you robotically, towards your apartment. Starts running.

"Hey!" you're shouting but he's not responding. You take off after him, but those long legs that you cursed before give him the advantage and despite your better physical condition and non-smoking style, you still have no chance of catching him.

Until he stops abruptly upon rounding the corner. Your apartment building is only a few metres away from the corner; there's just the one house between your place and this corner.

You stop at his side. "Hey! What the hell is wrong with you? Are you even listening to me? Hey!" You're yanking his sleeve as he raises the arm with the box.

And pushes on the cushion with his other hand.

A second passes and nothing happens. Your tension starts to release and you are all set to make fun of yourself for taking that box way too seriously.

And then a fireball comes crashing out of your living room windows.

You're pretty sure that's your place with the fireball. You count up from the bottom just to be sure. Yep, third floor, that's you. Was you.

"Holy shit." You hear a clatter as Boy drops the box. "What the—"

"Um, yeah, you just blew up my house." You feel surprisingly collected. Is it possible that you're getting used to this?

He turns to you, mouth still hanging open. "I what?" There is a note of hysteria in that question that concerns you.

"You blew up my house. Don't you remember pushing the button?" You don't know how to calm him down. You've never been good with the over-the-top emotions. People crying render you helpless.

He slowly moves his head from side to side. "I was looking at the box. I found it on the ground, right? And I was looking at it. And then fire was coming out of your window."

"Really? That's all you remember?" You're digging around in your head for some kind of explanation of this. His eyes did go all wonky there, maybe he was hypnotized. You've seen enough bad television shows with hypnotists to know that there's usually some kind of trigger word or something. Right? Did Salaryman hypnotize Boy to blow your house up?

He can't tear his eyes off the burning wreckage of your home. You hear sirens in the distance and wonder if they're for you or some other disaster. You're pretty sure there's nothing left of your place to save, so you're not too concerned about them arriving quickly in any case. Although maybe your neighbours would like their apartments saved.

"I swear, I—I—I—I don't know, I just—I just." He looks about to collapse and you are quick getting to his side, offering support, even though you are smaller than him and not very strong. He leans on you heavily, heavier than you remember him being, and you think you might both go tumbling down. But you're stronger than you think.

"Hey, just calm down." You try to be soothing or comforting or something. Unfamiliar territory and you're not sure what to say. "It's, uh, I don't know. Maybe you were hypnotized or something. It's not your fault. You were kind of crazy there for a minute."

Your efforts are clearly not enough. He is crumbling fast. "But I—I—I—I blew up your house. I blew up your house. You have no house now."

Oh yeah. Somehow, the fireball bursting through your windows and the fact that you now have nowhere to live did not connect for you. When he says it, it's a slap in the face and a pinch in the butt. You have no house. Everything you owned was in that apartment. Everything. The box with the books, you remember with a jolt. "The box! We have to get that box."

His fear for your apparent insanity gives him new strength. "The box? What box?"

You remove your supporting arms and leave him to stand on his own. Which he does quite well. "The box with the scrolls. We have to get that box." You don't even bother to finish explaining before you start running down the sidewalk towards your flaming apartment building. You're not even sure he heard what little explanation you did give.

People are pouring out of the building onto the street and you're pushing past them to get inside. Several of them try to stop you, which is sensible, since it is clearly insane to run into a burning building. But only part of the building is burning and it's your part so you can do whatever you want. You feel like sticking your tongue out at them.

"Wait! What are you doing?" Boy is calling out and chasing after you, but your neighbours milling about and the arrival of emergency vehicles are slowing him up.

You take the concrete stairs two at a time. When you get to the second floor, smoke is rolling down the stairwell choking you a little, so you cover your face with your sleeve and keep going. On the third floor, you make your way slowly to your apartment. Which no longer has a door. You wonder where it went. There's debris all over the hallway, but the fire seems to be contained in your place. Although it's creeping its way through your kitchen and it won't be too long before it's on its way to your neighbours' apartments.

You start to feel dizzy and remember too late that you have a concussion and smoke is asphyxiating and you probably shouldn't be mixing the two. You want to press on, but you're suddenly terrified that you'll pass out in the middle of the fire and get roasted. You don't want to be cooked alive. And the fire in your kitchen is getting bigger by the second and you remember the gas line and start thinking that there could be more explosions and you should get the hell out of there.

You drag yourself back down the hall towards the stairs and with each step, your feet grow heavier. You start cursing yourself out in the dreamiest way, starting to disconnect and float off. You hear the thudding of boots on the stairs. Firefighters?

When your eyelids flutter open, it's Boy that you see. A grin cracks his face in half and he leans down to kiss you. "You're okay!" He pulls back and the grin turns into a scowl. "What the hell is wrong with you? A burning building is dangerous."

You let one of your eyebrows slide up. Since when does Boy talk like a 1950s educational video? "Thanks, Mr. Safety." You realize that you're lying down and you struggle to sit up.

Boy offers you a hand and pulls you forward. "Honestly, what were you thinking? The firemen found you at the top of the stairs and brought you back down."

You turn your head from side to side, trying to place yourself in the world. "Brought me back down where?"

He indicates behind you with his chin. "The street in front of your building."

You turn around, looking past the fire trucks and police and sure enough, find your house behind you. It's still smoking, but it seems like there's no fire anymore. At least, it's not coming out the windows anymore. You bring your eyes back down to the street around you and see your slippers. Well, one slipper, slightly charred on the edge, but still intact. "My slipper." It slips out. It's patently obvious that it's your slipper and you hate stating the obvious, but it slipped out.

Boy is nodding. "Yeah, your things are all over the street." He holds up a sofa cushion. "This is from your sofa."

You stare at it sadly, take it from him, hug it to your chest. Everything in your house is gone. Your sofa is gone. Your table, your CDs, your chairs, your secret friend, Whiskey-chan. Your life is scattered and charred on the street. Your former collectedness is melting away and you are ready to bust out crying.

Boy rubs your back reassuringly. "Hey, it's okay. I'm sure many of your things survived. The firemen said the damage isn't too bad. Just in the living room. And there's a lot of water damage now from them putting out the fire." He cuts himself off, probably because he realizes that he is not making things sound any better to you. Especially with his new Mr. Safety persona. Too much enunciation.

You sit on the street in front of the wreck of your home, clutching a sofa cushion and you bawl your eyes out. Why is this happening to you? Last week, the worst thing that was going on was Boy was getting too clutch-baby and irritating you because he told you dull stories about his job. You want that back. You want to be irritated by dull office stories. You cry even harder. You don't even have anywhere to live.

Boy leans down and pulls you into a tight hug. "Hey, don't cry. It's okay."

"It's not okay, you jerk." You hate the snuffly, hiccoughy sound of your voice. You try to pull yourself together. "People are trying to kill me. You blew my house up."

That shuts him up. He's been squatting next to you, but he gives that up and sits his ass down on the pavement next to you. You bring your sobs to a hiccoughing, deep breathing, snuffly end. You sit together with the remains of your apartment behind you, listening to the shouts of your neighbours, firefighters, police. "I'm sorry," he says finally. "I didn't know I was blowing your house up."

You wipe your nose on an old tissue you find in your pocket. "I know. It's just that, now I have nowhere to live." You're still hiccupping and occasionally, you suck in a giant gulp of air.

"You'll come live with me." He has it out there almost before you've finished speaking. "I blew up your house. You have to come stay at my house."

You wipe the last of the tears from your face with the back of your hand. Great, you're moving in with him after all. And you have no choice. You have friends, but in this city of miniature housing, no one has space for you. With Boy, you can share a bed. You're pretty sure your friends are not interested in being that close to you. And Boy is close to your job. But maybe you'll never go back to work. Clearly, things are not settling as your boss was anticipating. Maybe the rest of your life will be a continual series of explosions and mishaps and you'll never again be able to hold down a full-time job. You wonder how you'll survive.

Before you can go to your new home, there's police to talk to, firefighters to thank and your possessions to gather up. Your neighbours pitch in on the last one, although when the creepy guy who lives downstairs leeringly hands you a pair of your underpants, you wish they had just left the job to you and Boy. Most of the stuff on the street is ruined anyway—half-melted CDs, your stereo smashed into several pieces, books with pages singed so the last words on the lines of each page are gone, another sofa cushion.

"Hey," You stop one fireman on his way out of the building. "Is it okay for me to go in? It's my place."

He looks you over. "Yeah, go ahead. It's pretty wet, but the fire's out." He heavy-foots it past you to the truck.

So holding Boy's hand, you tentatively make your way up the stairs that a few hours ago you took two at a time. Are you going in to look for the box? You feel now that it's not so important, but you wonder at the sense of urgency that drove you in here to get it before. Maybe you're just distracted by the loss of your worldly possessions to feel too urgent about a stupid box of books.

Finally, you get to the third floor and squish your way down the hall. Enter your apartment and see a pair of shoes swimming in a puddle in your entryway. Stepping past the shoes into the kitchen, parts of which are warped and melted looking. In particular, the red plastic colander that hung on your wall above the sink is now part of the wall above the sink.

In the living room, everything is black. If any of your things are still in here, they are mostly unrecognizable. You expect that the pieces of wood near the wall are what's left of the sofa. The coffee table is gone. You think you might have seen one of its legs outside on the street, but maybe that was one of the sofa legs and the table burned completely. You really have no way of knowing.

Boy squeezes your hand as your eyes wander over the sooty wet mess that is now your living room. You don't see the box, but you figure if the table didn't survive, it's very unlikely that the box on the table did. You sigh.

"You okay?" Another gentle squeeze of the hand and you nod.

"Yeah, just...Well, this was my living room." You sigh again. "Plus, I kind of thought that box might be here."

"You mean the one with the books?" He sounds startled. You suppose that he wasn't expecting you to be thinking about them now. "That's what you were trying to get before?"

More nodding. "Yeah, but the smoke got me before I could get inside."

His brow is so deeply furrowed, he may never be able to smooth it out again. "But they weren't in here."

You drop his hand, turn and stare at him. "Huh?" Your mouth stays open.

He grabs at the bag that he has hung diagonally across his chest, pulls it up, digs around inside. Pulls out the box. Your jaw sinks even lower. "I brought it with us."

Finally, you snap your jaw shut. "But you left them on the table. Didn't you?" You saw them on the table.

"Noooo." He is slow like he's talking to someone with a serious mental disability. You'd be insulted, but you feel like someone with a serious mental disability right now. "I put all the books inside and then I put it in my bag."

"What about the scrolls?" The scroll that foretold this doom, 'Boom'. The scrolls that you saw him place neatly on top of the box. The box you saw him leave on top of the table.

He shakes his head. "Scrolls?" As if he's forgotten what they are. "No, I didn't put those in the box."

Ignore your questions. Ignore what you think you saw and kiss him enthusiastically. You have a concussion. You are not a reliable witness. For some reason, you feel like those books have answers. If you could just read them, maybe they'd tell you what's going on. Or, you're just grabbing for anything now because nothing makes any sense and why should the books in the box be any different?

Pleased to have done something right, he shoves the box back in his bag. "Anyway, we'll read them later. We should try and get some clothes for you, if there are any left that aren't ruined."

The two of you rummage through your bedroom, where there is noticeably less fire damage. But still the floor beneath you is slick with firehose water and everything stinks like smoke, even the stuff way down in the bottom of your dresser drawers, hidden away with dryer sheets to keep them smelling fresh. You drop a sweater on the floor and sigh. "Everything's ruined." You flop down on the edge of the bed. "It all stinks like smoke. Does that smell ever come out?"

He sits down next to you, puts his arm around your shoulders. "I'm sure it does. Why don't we just go back to my apartment and tomorrow we'll come back and try to clean up and rescue some of your things?"

You raise your eyebrows at him. "I don't think clean-up is

possible. Did you see the colander melted into the kitchen wall?"

He pats your shoulder and you wonder if that's to tell you to shut up or to reassure you. Stands up. Offers a hand to help you up. You take it and up you go. "I mean we'll see what we can rescue. Okay?"

"Okay."

The two of you squish your way back out of the apartment, the building. On the street, there are fewer emergency vehicles, but still some linger. You grab Boy's wrist and look at the watch on it. So late. How did it get this late? All you want to do is sleep. One of the firefighters stops you to do a quick health check, which goes something like: "Hey, you okay?"

"Yes, thank you."

"Not dizzy?"

"No."

"Good." And he walks away.

You and Boy, still holding hands, make your way to the train station, but it's too late. The last train has already gone and the station is locked up tight. Fortunately, locked train stations are a natural home to late-night cab drivers and their vehicles. You persuade one of them to take a trip across town to drive you and Boy to his cozy home and soon you are gliding down dark streets to Boy's big bed.

You smell smoke. It's your house, you realize with a start. Your house is in flames and the girl with pink hair is sitting on the window ledge, frowning.

What are you doing there? you cry out, only no words come out of your mouth. Is it only in your head that you're speaking?

But she answers, so you guess not. Trying to save you, she cries back. You can see the way her throat strains to shout it out to you, but nothing reaches your ears.

Save you? You know what she said even though you can't hear it.

Save you? All you can think about is how to save her, get her down. And Salaryman—

You spot him out of the corner of your eye and cease your pleading for the pink-haired girl to come down. What are you doing here? You want to sound brave, but you sound like nothing. There is no sound other than the flames burning your home.

"She can't save you." His voice shattering the emptiness in your ears. Advancing, he's advancing, all the while the same words jumping from his throat to your ears. "She can't save you."

With a glance of apology thrown back to the girl on your window ledge, you start running. I'm sorry, you try to yell.

Is she smiling?

And you are sitting bolt upright in Boy's big bed, breathing hard, recovering from your nighttime marathon. Boy is right there next to you, dead to the world. Some help you are, you grumble in your head, all the while not knowing what kind of help he should be.

The smell of smoke is still filling your nostrils and you are piecing things together. Oh yeah, that wasn't just in your dream, your house really did burn down, it really is gone, you really are homeless. You panic suddenly, flipping through these pages of memories to see if that pink-haired girl really was there. After a minute, you relax feeling certain she was not. But where is she and where is she coming from? The second unrealistically real dream you've had about her and both times, she sits there on the ledge acting like she knows something special.

You push back the covers and with a final glance at your smoke-stink Boy, crawl out of that luxurious bed and head into the kitchen to see if he has any coffee. You know you left some here the other day, but he is always throwing things out without bothering to check if things are still inside. His saving the box last night is practically miraculous.

As you feared, the coffee is gone and you're not sure how to recover from this blow. Toast alone will not sate you and there are so many things coming down on your head that really require caffeine for proper consideration. You make due with a cup of Earl Grey tea made from an old tea bag you find in the back of the cupboard, but only sullenly and with the promise that you will make him go fetch coffee when he awakes.

Which he does and you do.

After he leaves for the coffee, you remember that you wanted to ask him where he put his bag so you can take a look at those stupid little books because that's pretty much all you can think of. But you forgot and the tea is not calming your impatience for his return. So you dig about the apartment and eventually come across the bag on the side of the sofa. Pulling the box out, setting it on the kitchen table before you. You're reluctant to open it, even though it's been opened before and you know that it was Boy and not the box that blew up your apartment. But still, the scaredy-cat part of you is freaking out and you can't seem to actually open the box and take a look inside.

The door slams open and shut. Boy, back. You really need that coffee. You suppose it's too much to hope that he brought it in IV form.

He sets a travel mug in front of you. "Your coffee. I figure you probably need a cup of it right away, no time to wait for me to brew some here."

The precision of his movements, the coffee placed just so, combined with his smarminess irritates you, but you put your annoyance aside and drink the coffee anyway. Now is not the time for coffee issues.

He sits down next to you with his own coffee. "So, you're going to open it?"

You nod, clutching your cup. "Yeah. I mean, eventually." Look up, wonder why he brought music on a coffee run, headphones loose around his neck.

"You want me to?" He's got his therapy voice on.

You are outraged at the implication that you need help. Except, you've been sitting here since he left, practically, staring at this box and unable to open it. Maybe you do need therapy. You give in. "Yeah, would you?"

He reaches over and grabs the box. Lifts the lid. You flinch, not voluntarily, but nothing happens. Nothing explodes. You and Boy are still sitting in his kitchen with coffee.

"So..." he says, finally. "Should we read them?"

"Isn't it more about you reading them? You're the one who actually remembers what he learned in school. That grass calligraphy gives me a headache."

He smiles with you. "So I'll get a dictionary?" Without waiting for your reply, he's off to the living room to find it.

You're left staring at the open box. You reach out and take the top book out of the box, lay it on the table in front of you. How did he think to bring these with him? You can't stop being amazed by this. More amazed by this than your house exploding. It just seems too impossible. You were so sure that you saw them on the table when you left.

He sits down next to you again with the dictionary. "I can't promise we'll be able to understand anything," he warns, taking the book in front of you and opening it in front of himself. "It's been too long since I studied this kind of writing."

"At least you can read something." You can't even pull individual characters off the page. It just looks a long black squiggly line, with breaks from time to time.

He reads and you shut your mouth. Drink coffee. Drum your fingers on your thigh, stop when he gives you a dirty look. Finally, stand up. "Look, why don't I go have a shower? I'm clearly no good to you here." Even though you're dying of curiosity; what's he reading? Why must he be such a silent reader?

He nods, absently. "Yeah, that's a good idea. I'll keep trying here. So far all I can understand is some sizes. Which makes no sense." He's flipping through the dictionary again and you take that as your exit cue.

Head down the hall to the bathroom. Halfway there, you're upside down again and not surprised. Huh, you can get used to anything. It's nice to have concrete proof of that fact and you find yourself wishing that you could somehow record yourself upside down so calm, to remind yourself of the fact that you do get used to everything, because you have doubted it in the past.

Or wait. How about recording it because you're freaking upside down? Which is not normal despite the increasing frequency and you really need to take this seriously and ditch the complacent thing.

Maybe your house being destroyed was the last straw for you, you wonder as you stare at something nasty on Boy's ceiling/your floor. Maybe you're unable to be freaked out anymore. But the sudden rising of your gorge as you contemplate the nasty bit on the ceiling further indicates that you are not as placid as you would like to believe.

You do your yoga breathing again. That helped last time and if nothing else, it'll calm you down. Because now, you're not only upside down, the girl with the pink hair is there with you, also upside down. Is Boy the only one still right side up? You never thought he'd end up being the sane one.

She smiles, runs a clawed hand through her slept-on hair. "No, I'm really here." Answering the question that's on your face.

"Okay, but you're not really, right?" You need her to say yes, because otherwise...otherwise, she's on the ceiling, you're on the ceiling and the world is exploding in your head.

She says, "I am really." Snaps her gum.

"So I'm really upside down? No hallucinations."

"You're really upside down." That same frown as before, biting the lower lip, looking too concerned. "But you have to remember how to turn yourself right side up."

Is the completely uncomprehending way you feel showing on your face?

She seems to get it. "I know all this means nothing to you now, but you have to remember how to turn yourself right side up. It's important. That's the way up is."

The words she's saying are not rhyming, but still it's like some kind of abstract poetry to you. You're expecting her to say something about the structure of concrete and how it relates to who you really are next.

She doesn't. "When you get there, you'll need to be firm. You can't doubt the directions."

"Get where?"

You're staring straight at her, but it's like someone's barbecuing right under her, wavy lines wiggling up, blurring your vision or her, you're not sure which. But being upside down is making you seriously nauseous and you have to close your eyes. Breathe in, breathe out. Using that diaphragm. Everything you've ever learned about yoga right there.

You keep your eyes shut, keep doing the yoga breathing until you hear Boy calling out to you. Is it the Doppler effect that tells you that he's headed your way or is that just the directional ability gained from having two ears? Whatever, you don't want him to find you on the ceiling.

You feel his arms around your waist and his head pressing in against yours, which means that you are not upside down. Or he is. In any case, you both need to be oriented in the same direction for you to be feeling his arms around your waist and his head against yours. You risk opening your eyes.

It's you that is right side up. Relief. Lingering panic at the fact that you were upside down and having a conversation with the pink-haired girl you've been dreaming about. Maybe you should get Boy to take you back to the hospital. No matter how real it seems, you're clearly losing your mind. Or the concussion is worse than you thought. Your brain is definitely physically damaged.

"What are you doing?" he murmurs into your hair. "Didn't you hear me?"

You shake your head, try to stop the rest of you from shaking. You're not very successful. "No, I guess I must have spaced out." There's this part of you screaming, tell him! Tell him about the girl with the pink hair, the upside-down times! But the rest of you is louder, shouting out warnings of potential hospitalization. If you're crazy, you'll become a danger to yourself soon enough and end up in the hospital without even being aware of it. But if you're not crazy, hospitalization is not an option.

He takes you by the shoulders and turns you around to face him. "You're shaking."

"Just cold. I should get to the shower and warm up."

The look on his face is telling you nothing good. "You haven't showered yet?"

"Isn't it obvious?" You're pretty sure your own ripeness is reaching your nose.

"But you left the kitchen an hour ago. That's why I came looking for you." His eyebrows are jumping off his face again and you don't know what to say to bring them back down to forehead land.

An hour? You were upside down with the pink-haired girl for an hour? You have the urge to tear at your hair and beat your breast, Greek tragedy style. He's still staring at you and you can see the commit-you wheels turning in his head. Say something. "Maybe I fell asleep?" you offer lamely. You suck.

"You fell asleep? Standing up in the hall?" There's that voice hitting puberty again.

You bring your shoulders up to your chin, hold them there. "I guess. I mean, I feel like I was asleep. I think I even had this dream." Maybe you're not even lying. Maybe you were asleep. Maybe the concussion is screwing with your sleep patterns. That could happen, right?

He slips an arm over your shoulders, turning you as if to lead you back to the kitchen. "Why don't we go back to the hospital, just get you checked again? That's not normal to fall asleep in the hall."

Again you shrug him off. "I'm sure it's just a weird accident or something. I really feel fine." His doubtful eyes weigh heavily on you and again you're thinking you should just spill it. "Look, if it happens again, I'll go, okay?"

He's reluctant to accept this compromise. "Well, okay. But if it happens again."

You nod. "Totally. Now I'm actually going to have a shower."

The concern will just not leave his face. "Are you sure that it's okay for you to be alone? Maybe you should just leave the showering."

"Or you could shower with me." Remembering that you haven't had sex with him since all this started and now that you're thinking of it, that's not a bad idea at all.

He seems to think so too.

It's worth keeping him around just for this.

Back in the kitchen, with wet hair and snuggly smiles, even though you can't stop yourself from wondering why he would not take off his headphones. Moment of passion or not, a person usually takes off electronic devices.

He pushes a piece of paper towards you. It's covered in his scrawly writing which is almost as illegible to you as the accordion books. "This is what I could get from this book."

You peer at it intently, but all you can make out is 'corduroy'. Not liking the sound of that. You push the paper back to him. "Can you just give me the run-down? Your handwriting is terrible."

"Sorry, I wasn't paying much attention. Basically, there's a corduroy jacket and some Kannon statue in Hase."

"What the—The corduroy bit, is it me?" The way he turns his eyes to the floor is all you need. "What does it say? How do you know it's me?"

"There's practically a description of you in here. There's no way it could be anyone else. I mean, that's what I understand. I couldn't read every word."

"So it's just a description of me?"

Here, he pushes his lips forward, scowls. "It's not so much a description as lots of words that make me think of you somehow. Like bam! There you are in my head. But all the stuff I could read doesn't make any sense."

"Just tell me. Christ."

"Don't freak out. It said some stuff about up, like which way is up or something. And that you are the one who knows the answer."

"I'm the one who knows the answer?" He nods. "What does that even mean?"

"I don't know. That's what I said before. It doesn't make any sense. That way's up." He points at the ceiling. "Everyone knows the answer."

You're actually biting your tongue. Not hard, but hard enough to keep you from moving it. Finally, you set it free. "Is that all it says? Just that I know the answer?"

"There's some other weird stuff about being caught between two places, two people, something. It's not specific. The character they used could mean any object." He grabs the book, opens it, points the character in question out to you. "I mean, if I could read more of the sentence, maybe I could decide what this character is referring to, but I can only make out about half the words." More frowning. "And this stuff about Kannon. It's really specific. Measurements and crap."

"Measurements?"

"Yeah, like here." His finger jabs at a place on the page and if you squint, you can almost make out the character for the number 1000. "It says there's this image of Kannon that's 1018 cm tall. And it has eleven heads. It says something about wood too, so I'm guessing that it's a statue."

Once again, you curse this language that allows one word to mean far too many things. "And it's in Hase?"

"That's what it says. You know anything about Hase?"

Vigorous head-shaking. "I don't even know where it is."

"It's not far. Maybe like an hour from here by train, on the coast." He is really giving you the craziest evil eye. "Are you sure you don't know anything about it?"

"Yeah. What is up with you?"

"It says that this Kannon is where you met someone."

"Huh? I met who?"

"I can't read the name. I'm not even sure if it is a name. It looks like some writing if you look at it through heat waves or something. Kind of blurry and wavy, like it won't come into focus. But it definitely says you met there." He jabs at the page again, but you don't even bother to look. You can't read it anyway.

"I've never been to Hase. I don't even know how to get there. Why would it be written that I met someone in a place I've never even heard of?" It's that spinning feeling again. Maybe you should let Boy take you to the hospital. Maybe you were in Hase and you don't remember. Maybe you haven't been flipping upside down. Maybe you have a brain tumour. Oh god, it's cancer. You have cancer.

Boy is reaching around to rub your back. "Hey, calm down. You're hyperventilating." His rubbing becomes very rhythmic and he chants, "Breathe in, breathe out. In, out. There you go. Relax." Does that humming thing again. Less melodic, more robotic than before.

You drop your head between your knees and follow his instructions, ignoring the creepy tuneless hums, and your breathing gets a little more regular, the spinning slows down. "I think I have a brain tumour," you croak.

The rhythmic rubbing suddenly stops. "What?"

Bringing yourself back upright. "I think I have a brain tumour.

None of this is actually happening. It's the tumour on my brain, squeezing my sanity out."

He laughs loudly, slightly too loud. "You don't have a tumour. You do not have cancer that is squeezing your sanity out. Weird things are happening."

Is that supposed to comfort you? You change the topic. "What about the other books? Can you read anything in them?"

"That's just it." He dumps them out of the box in front of you, flips several of them open. "They're all empty, except for the one I read."

Nothing but white pages looking up at you from the table. You grab a book at random and letting it fall all the way open, seeing nothing but blank paper. "But that's impossible. I looked at them yesterday. They were all filled with writing, the same crazy black squiggles. I mean, I opened every single one of them. Are you sure you put them back in the box, these are them?"

"Yeah, of course." Slightly indignant. "Do you think I would just fill the box with empty books to fuck with you? And where would I get a bunch of these stupid accordion books anyway? The only place I know that sells them is that old man shop down the street. The one with the dusty windows, next to the Family Mart."

"So what? What the hell is going on? What does this mean?" You're ready to stand up and run screaming from the world. If only your sanity would just let go entirely, you could relax and minor details like books with disappearing writing would no longer concern you. "How is this even possible? I know there was writing in all the books."

He is eyeing you suspiciously. He is drawing lines to your concussion, to you 'sleeping' in the hall, to all the stories you told him about Kimono Lady and the Kuroko. You know he is somewhere in his brain reconsidering your sanity-squeezing tumour theory. "I have no idea. Maybe we should ask that salaryman guy."

You jerk your head back. "You want to ask Salaryman?"

You are starting to really hate the way his shoulders look pulled up like that. "He seems to be the only one we know connected to whatever is going on."

You wave your hand in front of his face. "Hello? He's the one that's threatening me and trying to kill me."

"You don't know that he's trying to kill you."

All the warm post-sex fondness that was nestled inside you is fleeing at high speeds. "He blew up my house!"

"Uh, actually, I blew your house up." He's tentative, but still you can't believe he even said that at all.

You shove your chair back, stand up. "We're not asking Salaryman. In fact, we are not doing anything. I am going to go to this Hase place and see what I supposedly saw when I met whoever there."

"Don't freak out. I wasn't trying to say we team up with Salaryman. Just let's try to figure something out."

"You're not even involved in this anyway. I'm the one who's meant to know the answer or whatever." Walking out of the kitchen, thinking you'll put on some clothes instead of this sweater of Boy's which fits you poorly, if by 'poorly' you mean it doesn't fall off you. Then you remember that you have no clothes and all your stuff has been destroyed by smoke and water and fire. You flop down on Boy's bed. What now?

Closing your eyes, Boy's heavy feet coming down the hall hit your ears. You don't want to talk to him, but you have no way of avoiding him. Great. You live here now. You keep your sudden flood of sadness to yourself.

"Look, you don't even have any clothes or anything. Let's hold off on figuring out what is up and see if we can salvage anything from your place." He runs a hand along your bare thigh. Comforting and sexy. If he wasn't so sexy, you could just break up with him and be done with it.

Pushing your lids open. Staring at the ceiling. Pleased to find that it is the ceiling and not the floor. "Yeah, fine. Whatever."

After a hunt for some pants to be belted and rolled up to cover your bottom half, you are out the door and on your way to your wreck of a home with Boy in tow. The crazy jumping guy is on the train again. Wherever he's going, he's pretty eager to get there. But maybe he's just eager to get everywhere. The rest of the train is filled with groups of the elderly replete with backpacks and hiking sticks.

Crazy Jumper gets wildly excited as the train is pulling into your station, even more than the other day. Not content with just jumping and pressing his face up against the door, he is crying out in a freakishly high-pitched voice. You briefly wonder what his problem is, then feel like by wondering that you might be somehow making fun of whatever his problem is, so you flick it away.

Boy grabs your arm suddenly. "Is he saying 'Which way is up'?"

The high-pitch he's shrieking in makes it hard to discern words and you're sure Boy is making it up to freak you out. But if you listen closely, you can hear it and you shiver. Even if it is just a coincidence, it's freaky as hell.

You stand up and move toward him. "Hey." You try to be gentle, take the rough edges out of your voice.

The shrieking stops and he whirls around, stares at you. Jaw drops. The two of you are frozen in some kind of bizarre eye war. Then he starts screaming. And not just that high-pitched freaky chanting or whatever that was, but seriously blood-curdling, like you are coming at him with a knife. "Stay away! Stay away! Stay away! You don't know which way is up! You're wrong! You're wrong!" And then he's off, running down the mostly empty aisle of the carriage, still screaming at the top of his lungs. At the far end, he grabs at the door to the next carriage and pulls with all his might, turning every second or so to check that you aren't following him. Once he manages to yank it open, he is pushing through it and running all the way down the end of the next carriage. You can still hear his screams.

The elderly are staring at you. Boy is doing a staring triangle; first, you, then the elderly, then the direction Crazy Jumper took off in, then back to you.

With all these eyes on you, you feel almost obliged to say something. You open your mouth and of course nothing comes out. Because what would you say? You do too know which way is up? Crazy Jumper is right. You're wrong. You should not be the one who is supposed to know the answer. You hope no one is depending on you. You have the feeling that your own sanity is depending on you, though. You don't want to end up like Crazy Jumper.

Eyes still on you. Murmuring among the elderly. You slink back to your seat next to Boy who, while his head has slowed down, is still doing his triangle dance. Even though Crazy Jumper isn't even visible in the next car anymore. You stare down at your legs in the pants that are too big. If you have to look into accusing eyes, you'll flip. You know everyone is thinking that you were threatening that guy, which automatically makes you pure evil. Threatening a guy with some kind of obvious problem. One of the circles of hell is saved for people who do that.

The train finally stops at your station and you can't get off fast enough. You've almost turned into him, pushing at the doors, too eager for them to open. Boy is right behind you, still casting glances over his shoulder, at the elderly, the way Crazy Jumper ran off. Does he think something more will happen?

"Hey man! Hey!" Followed by slapping footsteps.

"You?"

"Are you following us?" Boy is accusative and sounds ready to punch the boy with the asymmetrical hair.

New Wave catches up to you, bends over, shakes a denying hand without looking up. "No man," he pants. "I, like, you know, saw the guy on the train, uh, whoa, that was so crazy, like, what was his thing?"

You're keeping your suspicious eye on him. "Yeah, pretty crazy. What are you doing here?"

He looks up from his hunched over panting, raises one eyebrow while looking from you to Boy. "Uh, like, can I talk to you?"

"Go ahead."

Another significant glance at Boy. "I mean, like alone, you know?"

Boy is all set to protest and possibly punch New Wave. It's that protective thing that he's not been so good at lately. Maybe he feels guilty for blowing up your house. You stop him before he starts. Too late for his protective guilt. "Yeah, c'mon." You leave Boy to gape at you and you wonder if he's making triangles with his eyes again; you, New Wave, but who would be the third vertex?

New Wave follows you to the end of the platform. "Okay, what?"

He shakes his hair out of his eyes. "Okay, uh, so, like, man." You hope he says something coherent soon. "Your apartment, uh, you know?"

Hairs are jumping to attention on the back of your neck. "What about my apartment?"

Shaking a cigarette out of a box that seems to have appeared from nowhere in his hand, lights it. "Man, it was totally crazy. You know? Uh, like that guy on the train, right? Nuts. I was, you know, hanging, like maybe that, uh, weirdo with, like, those ugly shoes would uh come back, you know? Pay out? 'Cuz like man, I am so broke." Gives his head a shake to indicate the extent of his broke-ness, takes a drag. Exhales. Reaches up with the cig-free hand to push his hair aside lightly. It falls immediately back in front of the one eye. "And uh, you know, like I'm like having a cig, right, and then I see like those dudes in black, man."

It takes you a second to turn 'I see like those dudes in black man' into 'Kuroko!' in your head. "You saw those people who came down the side of the Honda building?"

He nods vigorously, his whole body moving with his head. "Yeah, totally. Totally, man. And I was, like, what the, and uh, then uh they like went in and whatever. I was just standing there, you know? And like, about two cigarettes later, or whatever, they come back out, you know? Crazy. And I'm uh thinking, like, what? But you know, whatever. So then you come around the corner with him, right." He jerks his head in Boy's general direction. "And he's all—" He abruptly pushes his arms straight out in front of him, jerks back and forth from foot to foot robotically. The cigarette dangles between his fingers. Just as abruptly, he stops, pulls the cigarette to his lips. "And you're like, aah! Aaah! And then blam! You know?"

You sincerely hope you did not look like he depicts you with the flailing arms and the whiny cries. "Yeah, I get the idea."

"So, like, I'm looking at you, you know? And then I'm looking over there, like whoa! Flames burning my, uh, eyes, and there he is, you know, that guy, uh, walking down the street, right."

"That guy? You mean Salaryman?" Somehow, you're not surprised. He's probably on the platform right now.

New Wave laughs. "Whoa, you call him 'Salaryman'? Like, uh, I call him 'Ugly Shoes'."

You laugh with him. It's not that funny but you've got a lot of nervous tension right now. "But it was him?"

His hair gets shaken out of its perfect asymmetry as he nods his head, so he is forced to spend several seconds in emergency grooming. When the lines are as straight as he seems to like them, his one visible eye meets one of yours. "Totally. It was, uh, freaky, you know? Like, uh, is he blowing up your house, you know?"

Suddenly, you're frowning. "Okay, but why can't he hear this?" You indicate Boy with your head.

All the laughs are gone from his face and he leans in, his hair leaning in further. Invites you to come closer with a flick of his cigarette. You lean in so that you can smell his styling products, see that he's actually wearing some eyeliner and maybe even mascara.

"Man, like, you know, that guy, I don't uh trust him, right." He's even lowered his voice. Although it seems pointless to lower his voice now after he's already told you what he didn't want Boy to hear.

Just the same, you drop your voice to the same level. "What? Why?" You may not want to move in with Boy, but it's never occurred to you that he can't be trusted. He's too indecisive to doubt.

New Wave rolls an eye. "Man, like, are you uh okay? You know? He uh blew up your house, right, uh."

"But you just said that it was the people in black!" But Boy did push the button.

A toss of the head and then he's back closer than ever, your noses are almost touching. "You know, like, uh, I saw him uh pushing it, right and there's no way he's uh, like, you know." He tosses his cigarette off onto the tracks.

It was bound to happen in any lengthy conversation with this guy. You've lost him. "What?"

He sighs. "I uh, right, saw Ugly Shoes or Salaryman or you know whatever, and like, he was uh, totally uh, what, watching him."

"He watches me. What's your point?" You're starting to feel like walking away if this is all New Wave is going to tell you.

His head shake knocks his hair into your eyes and you pull back, rubbing your eyes, wincing. "No way, man! He had some kind of like I don't know, like connection or something man. You can't trust him, right. Trust me."

"Why should I trust you?"

He shrugs. "I'm here."

You pull yourself up straight. "Look, is that all you have to say? You saw the Kuroko go into my house and Salaryman walking down the street?"

He stands straight too, tosses his head back, sending the hair off to the side and revealing his other eye briefly. "Whatever, man. I'm just you know, uh, trying to like help. All I know is you like need to go to the temple in Hase, right."

Now you're starting to feel a little punched in the stomach again. "How do you know about that?"

Here he smiles in a way that makes you think he's more than a bystander with weird hair. "Trust me, right. I'd uh leave the boy behind, though, you know? Stuff's going, uh, down, right." He's got that pack in his hands again, pulling out another cigarette as he walks away. "I totally gotta get like moving, you know."

You want to chase after him, ask him more questions, make him say a whole sentence without saying 'you know', but you can't seem to impel yourself forward. Watching as he passes Boy on his way to the ticket barrier and then he's out and turning the corner and gone to you. And you still stand there, trying to shove these pieces together and is Boy on someone else's side? How many sides are there?

Walking from the station to your exploded house, you brush off Boy's questions, just telling him the bit about the Kuroko because you have to tell him something. Although you're not even sure you should be telling him that much if you can't trust him. Maybe whoever he's selling you out for didn't know the Kuroko were involved. Is he even selling you out? What did New Wave mean? And really, should you take the word of a guy you can barely understand who can't look you straight in the eye?

More police greet you at your building. They let you in without too much hassle. They seem surprisingly unconcerned about destroying evidence, which makes you think that they're not working too hard to find out who did this. You're beginning to suspect, though, that even if they were sleuthing their butts off, they wouldn't be able to figure it out.

Boy offers to dig around in the living room for anything that may have escaped being blown out onto the street and you squoosh your way down the hall to your room. In this humid country, you know that this hallway may never dry.

The girl with the pink hair is sitting on your bed, snapping her ever-present gum. You're not even surprised. You sit down next to her, hands at your side, palms flat on the bed.

"So I guess you talked to him today."

When she says 'him', the image of New Wave springs fully formed to the front of your brain, so real you almost reach out to touch him. Before you can, the image fades away and you just nod.

She lays a hand on yours. Her hand is warm and you hope that's proof that you're not crazy and you don't have a tumour that is squeezing the sanity out of you. "He's right." And now you're seeing Boy like he was standing in front of you.

"Who is he?" You mean New Wave, not Boy, but you're pretty sure you don't have to tell her that.

She presses her bright red lips together. Crosses her legs, takes her hand from yours, casually reaches down to scratch her ankle. Those painted nails mesmerize you. "He knows some things."

Not really the answer you were looking for. "So you work together?"

She stands up, brushes imaginary lint off her skirt. "Do you have a compass?"

"You mean to tell me which way is magnetic north or like a moral compass?" What are you even talking about?

She takes a moment to fluff her hair, pull out a pin from one place, put it back in in another place and you can't see what difference it makes. Her hair still looks like she slept on it. "Here." In the hand that was grooming, a compass is offered to you.

You can only stare. It's the kind for telling magnetic north, not the moral kind and you're glad for that. Not sure what good a moral compass would actually do you. Or what one would look like. She pushes her hand towards you again and now you reach forward and take it from her, careful not to accidentally cut yourself on her nails. They look razor sharp. Examine it more closely. Instead of north, it says 'UP' but right now the needle is pointing down.

Looking up at her. She's all wavy heat lines and you figure one of you is either being barbecued or on your way somewhere. Hoping it's her. "That should help you get to the temple in Hase."

"But why do I have to go to Hase?"

"What?" It's Boy and he's shaking you. "You don't have to go to Hase. Unless you want to, I guess."

You know that your eyes have been open this whole time. You have not closed them. You have not gone to sleep. You squished down your hall into your room, talked with the girl with pink hair sitting on your bed, she gave you a compass. There's a clear sequence of events, nothing dream-like about it. Except for the part where you're talking to her and then Boy is the one answering you.

"What the hell is going on with you?" Too much frustration in his voice. You don't have to look at him to see his scowl.

Two people today have told you not to trust him. One of those people may or may not be completely in your head. The other one seems about as stable as you feel. And possibly high on something. But he did blow up your house, whether he meant to or not, and if you tell him anything about the girl with the pink hair, he will take you to the hospital. He is a salaryman in training.

You shake your head. "Sorry, I was just thinking out loud." You close your fingers over your palms and feel the cool metal of the compass against the fingers of your left hand. Glad you closed your hand because you don't want him to see and because you have something real. You're not crazy. The compass is in your hand. Pink Hair was here.

He brushes your hair off your forehead, that same protective thing he was doing earlier. "I was starting to wonder. You've been in here for ages." He looks around, sees the same mess that was here when you were here yesterday. "Did you get your things?"

So tempting to ask about how long it's been since you got here, but you know that that is the way to the hospital. Grab about for a reason why you haven't collected anything. "No. I mean, when I saw all this, I just, I don't know." You hope that sounds like a bit of choked sob at the end there. You've never been a very good liar.

But he puts his arm around you and pulls you against his chest, humming that same mechanical tune, so it must have sounded something like you were hoping. "Hey, no, that's cool. Take your time." He kisses you, stands up. "I haven't found anything in the living room other than melted CDs. I think whatever you kept in there is gone. But I'm hoping that some things got scattered into the kitchen or something." He adds this last quickly, as if he is trying to give you some kind of hope. "In fact, I'm going to go back and keep looking. You okay?"

Nodding. Feeling the compass pushing against your palm, the metal staying cool, oddly not warming from the contact with your skin. "Yeah, no. I'm sorry to make you worry. You go ahead. I'll try to be quick in here."

He smiles, looking at you in a way that is more meaningful than you'd like. You can almost see him having babies with you in his head. "Okay, just let me know when you're ready to go."

As soon as he's gone, you're opening your fingers and staring at the cold metal in your hand. The needle is pointing off to the side now and you wonder what that is supposed to mean. You're left of up? How are you supposed to interpret this crazy thing and how is it supposed to help you get to Hase? Even though you still aren't too clear on why everyone's pushing you to some temple in Hase. You want to tell yourself that you won't go, but you already know you will. Somewhere in the back of your head, you are plotting ways to sneak away from Boy and get on a train.

You dig around in your dresser drawers, pull out some sweaters at random, yank pants off their hangers, shove the lot in a bag you found on the floor of your closet. Knowing that the smoke, the stink, the explosion will never come out, but you have to have something to show Boy, prove that this hasn't destroyed you. If you didn't have Pink Hair and New Wave and the trip to Hase, would this have destroyed you? You're not thinking about that.

With all the stuff you shove in the bag, you're careful to keep the compass in your hand.

When you eventually emerge from your bedroom, Boy is sitting on the remains of a chair. You think. It could be the remains of your kitchen table. Everything has a new shape. You're kind of attracted to the unexpected transformation of your apartment and the things inside. It's like the evolution you always hope for when you're away, but hyperaccelerated to the Big Crunch.

He's examining an accordion book, but when he notices your arrival, he closes it, looks up. "You ready?"

"Yeah, I got some stuff. Can we toss it in your machine when we get back?" Didn't you leave those on the table in his kitchen? Has he just taken to bringing them everywhere now?

Standing up, shoving the book in his pocket. The cover is different from the one with words in it. He's reading one of the empty books. You force yourself to act like you didn't just notice that. "I'm sure we can get the smoke smell out." He follows you to the door.

Walking to the station, on the train, the road to his house, it's all you can do to chat with him, act like you didn't notice him reading the empty book, act like no one has been telling you that he can't be trusted, act like your brain is not screaming at you to run! Run already! You squash that last one with: where would you run to?

After supper and Boy is settled on the sofa, a made-for-TV movie gripping him, you're washing the dishes because you'd rather do anything than watch a made-for-TV movie, you consider that last question again. Hase. You're meant to have met someone there. Despite the impossibility of this, the accordion book with visible writing said so. Your gooseflesh indicates that the other accordion books might say something different. What was Boy doing reading an empty book? Put it out of your mind.

So you'll go to Hase, find this temple. Worried that things might just get worse since no one's telling you why you should go and maybe it's just an elaborate scheme to finally blow you up. But you've got nothing else to go on and it seems like you're not walking away anytime soon, so it's just a matter of when. Boy is pretty engrossed in that movie; you're sure he said something once about having a huge crush on the starring actress in junior high school. You could go now, tell him you're going to lie down and read for a while and he wouldn't know the difference. He'd notice in another hour and a half that you're not in the bedroom, but that's good enough for your purposes. You can be at the coast in a couple of hours. The thing that's stopping you is what will you do when you're there. You know this type of tourist town. There's only going to be the traditional style hotels that close early, with futons, and fish for breakfast. Not that you're so concerned with breakfast, but it's this Kannon that you're meant to be seeing and those tourist attractions are never open in the evening. You don't even know where this Kannon is. If Hase is a temple town, there could be hundreds of Kannons.

Rinse the last glass, the water's too hot, burns your hand. Gentle with your wound, cradling your hand, sitting at the table, the TV is yelling in the other room. Should you go? Just slip out the door in these clothes that are not quite falling off you, catch a train and go to that tourist town, find out if you've ever been there? Ignoring your minor dishwater burn, you shove your hand in the pocket of these too big pants, yank out the compass. She said it would help you get to the temple in Hase, maybe it has something to say.

Holding it in the palm of your hand, you stare at it intently. The needle has moved, but it's not giving you any information. Now up is not to the left of you, not completely. It's more left and down of you. Your eyes drop to the floor. Is the compass telling you the way to Hase lies through the floor? You feel confident that that is not the answer.

"Hey! You gotta come watch this!" Boy sounds too eager about his movie. "It's so good! Are you almost done in there?"

"Yeah, almost." You realize that whatever the compass says, you have to leave now. You cannot spend the evening watching something filled with actors washed up from your childhood. You didn't even like them then. "Actually, you know what? I think I'm just going to lie down and read for a while. I'm not in the mood for TV." Your heart starts pounding as this lie runs from your lips to his ears in the living room.

His concern is immediate, but countered by his desire to see the end of the movie. "You okay?"

"Yeah, I just feel like I need a little alone time." Please don't get up, please don't come in here, please love that movie more than me.

"Oh hey, yeah, that's cool." You can hear him rearrange himself on the sofa. He's settling in. You almost high five yourself.

You wish you had some things to collect to make this seem more like a trip to somewhere, but all you have is the bag you always carry, the things inside. Your wallet does not make this seem like any kind of adventurous trip, though, and you are suddenly overcome by the desire to nick something from Boy's house to give your sneaking away more meaning. Your eyes jump around the kitchen and eventually settle on the empty book he was reading before, just laying on top of the microwave where he put it before heading off to watch the movie. Presumably, its back pocket location would interfere with sofa seating. Stealing an empty book seems kind of futile, especially since it's technically yours already, but it's either that or a kitchen knife and the knife does not fit so well in your bag. But thinking it over, you decide you might as well take it too, despite the way it threatens to cut the bottom of your bag open. Considering the threat, you grab the dish towel, wrap the knife in it. Perfect. Your life as a fugitive begins now.

Slip on your shoes and out the door, so quiet the latch doesn't even click when you ease the door shut. You're gone. What do you expect to find? As you make your way to the station, you check the compass. Still to the left, but the downward slope is decreasing. It may actually be on the up side of left soon. Is Hase up? Maybe the temple? Get on a train. Ask yourself again if you're sure that cancer is not squeezing your sanity out. You sincerely hope not, but you are making decisions based on a compass that tells which way is up, given to you by a possibly imaginary woman with pink hair.

It's only when you're on the train that you realize you still have no idea how to get to this place. Of course, you don't have a train map on you. It's probably part of the wreckage in your apartment now. Not knowing which trains to catch to go to Hase certainly poses a problem in getting there.

At the first major connecting station, you get off and go to consult with someone in the know. Who tells you that you actually should have gotten on a train going in the opposite direction at your station. You drag yourself back down to the platform, wondering if you'll just make it back home before Boy notices you missing and thus he'll never know anything about your miniature adventure.

As the train draws near your station, you have almost talked yourself into getting off and just going home because it's the cancer sending you on this ridiculous adventure. Pulling the compass out of your pocket, rubbing the face of it gently with your sleeve. The only proof you have that it's not a tumour. You don't take your eyes off it when the doors open at your stop and the gang of chatty art students get off. Listen for the air swoosh of the doors pushing together. The train lurches forward out of the station and you let your breath out. The needle of the compass jumps up as the train jumps forward and you take that as a good sign.

Your mobile phone starts vibrating in the bottom of your bag as soon as you step onto your next-to-last connecting train, scaring the hell out of you. You completely forgot that you had it with you or that you even had one. Taking it out and seeing Boy's photo on the screen. You wait for the message service to take it. When you hear the muffled beep, you put the palm-sized device to your ear to hear the message he leaves.

"Where are you? Are you okay?" He is frantic and you immediately are overwhelmed with guilt. You caress the compass to remind yourself of your resolve, of your cancer-free brain. "Please call me as soon as you get this."

Almost as soon as he's done speaking, the phone is buzzing again, this time with mail saying the same thing. You wonder if you shouldn't at least mail him and let him know you're not dead. He will worry himself to death and probably call the police.

You tap out a message to him quickly. Not dead, don't worry, have to do this alone. Such a movie-style message that you almost want to add, tell mom I love her. But you don't. That's not going to help anything. You make sure to keep where you're going to yourself. Even though it's not hard to figure out and he'll probably come after you.

His response is quick and in the same frantic tone. You can say nothing else to reassure him without giving everything away and you're not supposed to trust him so you can't do that. So you simply turn off the phone and tuck it away in the bottom of the bag. The vibrating of his constant messages will drive you insane if you don't.

Seems like Hase and the surrounding Kamakura area do not hold any nighttime thrills. Looking around the carriage and seeing only four other people. No surprise really, since the only thing you know about Kamakura is that's where they keep the giant Buddha. And now you know of a temple in a place called Hase with an eleven-headed Kannon. But neither is likely known for its pumping clubs.

Your eyes droop shut as you let your body be rocked back and forth by the gentle motion of the train pushing ahead. It's late and you're tired and you promise yourself that you'll just rest your eyes since the hot air from the heaters under the seats is drying your eyes out, making it hard to keep them propped open.

And then there is gentle but persistent tapping on your shoulder. "Passenger, passenger." So polite, so insistent.

You struggle to force your eyes open, see a man in uniform. For one heart-splitting second, you fear that Salaryman has found some new clothes. But no, it's just the conductor.

Smiling apologetically. "I'm terribly sorry to disturb you, but this is the last stop and this train is going out of service now."

You sit up a little straighter, rub your eyes, wipe the little trail of drool that has been escaping from your mouth during your nap. That's embarrassing. "Last stop? Kamakura?"

Gentle nodding. "Yes, we have stopped at Kamakura station. Are you making a connection here?" He clearly wants you to get off the freaking train already. Beneath that frozen professional smile, you can see his impatience.

Glancing around to check that you haven't left anything on the seat, standing up. "Yeah, I'm trying to go to Hase?"

"You must change to the Enoden Railway to go to Hase." Crisp, like he's got schedules and routes all mapped out in his head. You wonder if he could tell you the departure times of the next five trains, but suspect that he could so you don't ask. He escorts you from the deserted train and sends you in the direction of your next train.

Which is also the last train. Lucky you. What would you do if you got stuck in Kamakura for the night? Although now that you are almost there, you are wondering what are you going to do being stuck in Hase for the night? Boarding the rickety-feeling old train, you cross your fingers that it will actually get you there.

Just as the train is about to pull out, a pretty princess pony girl comes rushing up the platform, teetering on her impossibly high heels, perfectly coiffed hair motionless, and jumps on the train through the closing doors, catching her designer hand bag so that the conductor has to open the doors again and instruct her over the PA system to please pull her bag in and do not run for the trains because it's dangerous.

Her flat-footed prancing pony style of walking hypnotizes you, as it always does when you encounter one of the pretty princess ponies and you are stuck once again contemplating what it is about this country, this city, these people that leads to grown women groomed and prancing like show ponies. She glares at you as she sits down and you finally tear your eyes off her.

Look out the window, but it's dark and all you see are street lamps and cars at intersections, waiting for the slow-moving train to finally pass. Bring your eyes back inside, take the compass out of your pocket. The needle is at about two o'clock and seems to be gradually moving towards UP. Is this what Pink Hair meant about the compass guiding you to Hase? Not much of a guide. If you hadn't asked at the station, you'd still be on the wrong train.

The train trundles to a jerky stop at Hase and you get off. Look around and wonder what you should do now. You're here, but nothing is happening. Although did you expect the world to end because you got off at a small country station? The station master is giving you a dirty look and seems about ready to come over and ask you if there's a problem. You remember that you just got off the last train and this guy probably wants to close up the station and go home already.

The street in front of the station is dark. There's not even a convenience store with people reading magazines in the window. The station master pulls the shutters down over the station entrance behind you and the street gets even darker. You remind yourself that this is a very safe country and even safer way out here in Smalltownland. Your brain believes this, but the gooseflesh you're breaking out in says the rest of you disagrees. You look at the compass and suppose that now is when it will be coming in handy.

It better.

It's closer to one o'clock than two, but still wavering and not straight up. You turn to your left and take a few tentative steps, trying to keep your eyes on the compass, but also wanting to watch for pot holes and roadside ditches so you don't end up breaking an ankle in the middle of the night in this place.

The needle wiggles a little and then starts dropping ever so slightly, so that you need to take another few steps across the tracks to be certain of the downward trend. Once you are, though, you figure that this is not the way and you turn around and walk back the way you came and beyond. The needle responds positively, gradually righting itself. You play this little game of backwards and forwards at every intersection and down a narrow flight of mystery stairs, which cause you to glance about even more nervously. Is this Mugging Alley? This staircase is too out-of-the-way, too secluded and you really feel like a mugger will jump out at any moment to grab your bag and send you tumbling down the stairs and no one will ever hear about it. Shuddering, you don't let your breath out until you are safely at the bottom in the circle of a streetlamp. Then you hold your breath all the way back to the top since the needle has plummeted on your perilous descent and the temple is clearly not at the bottom of these steps. At the top again, you let your breath out in a string of curses.

You are getting closer and closer to the magic twelve o'clock of UP and your gaze is locked on the compass. You almost don't even notice when you walk through the elaborate gates and the sculpted temple protectors. It's even darker on the temple grounds and you slow your pace so that you are barely moving. You can hear koi splashing about somewhere nearby and the last thing you need is to fall into a koi pond in the middle of the night. You have to tilt the compass about above your head to catch the light enough to see the needle.

Eventually, you find yourself at the base of some steps and your cursing begins anew. Temple stairs in the dark. Great. You hope this temple is one of the ones that interprets the necessity of climbing to the gods more figuratively than literally. You remember the one temple you went to with a thousand steps carved into the side of a mountain. The climb almost killed you.

The needle is almost vertical when you reach the top, panting but not dead. There's enough light up here for you to make out the silhouette outlines of several buildings and you head for the biggest one, figuring that they're bound to keep the Kannon in the most impressive building. Unless they use some kind of reverse Buddhist psychology and humbly keep the god in the crappiest building. The needle appears to agree with your choice, wiggling towards UP with every step you take. A few more steps and you are forced to stop, sliding doors preventing your passage. Looking up, you gulp down some air. All your hair stands on your end and you know that this is where it happens. At least, if it doesn't happen, you're going to feel really stupid in the morning. Just in case, you dig out the knife you so carefully wrapped in the towel before you left Boy and his TV movie. Brandish it in the dark, feel a little braver.

You gently push back the sliding door, almost reluctantly. You're scared, but you want this to happen. You want something to happen. You want this to be over so you can go back to your regular life of being annoyed by Boy. Taking a moment to remember fondly; being annoyed with Boy. Shake your head, pull it together, step through the doors.

You don't need to look at the compass you still clutch in your knife-free hand to know that this is the place. The eleven heads of the Kannon overwhelm you, even in the dark. And it is dark. You feel like you can see Kannon, like you are part of that image, but you know it must be all in your head since it's too dark to see anything.

You walk into a large piece of furniture and the knife you had carefully defending your advance gets stuck in the wood. Sigh and give up on it after a feeble attempt to pull it free. You're more likely to stab yourself with it than thwart any menacing dangers anyway. Reach around on top of the wooden structure for a light switch or a candle or anything.

Your fumbling hands come across candles. Of all the times to be a non-smoker. You fish around in your bag, hoping that you did not throw all your lighters out when you quit last year.

Just when you're about to give up and go back outside to look for some sort of flame that you can use, your fingers stumble upon something cold with rounded edges. You grab it and pull a convenience store lighter out. You take a moment to be glad that you never clean your bag.

Fumbling in the dark, it takes several attempts to get a flame to stick to the candles you have felt out, but eventually, you have enough light to see the golden gleam of the polished wood. You look down at the compass and in the light of these candles, you can just make out the needle pointing straight up.

And the shadow in the corner when you look up.

"Just when I was beginning to wonder where you'd gone astray. The boy promised me that you'd be here tonight and yet, the hours kept passing without you. How delightful that you made it after all." He steps forward from the entryway shadows, even though you don't need to see the face to place the voice. Especially since you have never seen the face. But that voice has been giving you nightmares, so smooth and polished and you always feel like he must be examining his fingernails indifferently as he speaks.

Which he's not doing today. His eyes bore a hole through you and although you want to run out of the temple screaming, you are paralyzed. You can only squeeze out his name. "Salaryman?" Dammit, you should have tried harder to get the knife free. You consider whether or not it's too late to turn around and try again, give up, focus on what the straight UP action of the compass needle means.

Pink Hair said the compass would help you find up. The needle pointing up, does that mean this is up? If this is up, what are you supposed to do now? The look on Salaryman's face as he draws closer is telling you nothing good. And still, you cannot move. What is wrong with you? You close your eyes and breathe deeply. Focus, focus.

His sinister, cartoon baddie chuckle makes its way into your ears. "I'm still here even when you close your eyes." He sounds too amused by this, laughing at you and your attempt to make some sense of your world.

Another deep breath and you force your eyes open, ready to confront or attack or maybe run away if your muscles are willing to obey you again.

For the first time ever, you are staring directly into his smirking face. Only it's all wrong and you realize with a start that you are facing the wrong way yet again. He smiles at you, raising his eyes slightly as if to let you know that he knows where you are.

The first outside confirmation of your own upside-down-ness. You can't count Pink Hair since you still doubt her reality, despite the compass cutting new lines into your right palm. So you're really upside down. The crazy man who's been threatening you is raising his eyes to you. "He is probably here to kill you." Muttering it to yourself. The stress has turned you into a crazy bag lady.

Again with the sinister chuckle. "Now that you're here and up can meet up, we can finally put the pieces together and finish this."

Deep breaths. Calm, calm. Remember what Pink Hair said. "You're here to kill me?" Oh god, he's here to kill you. What have you got to do with anything? Keep your panic to yourself.

His snorting laughter is clearly derisive. "Forget what she told you." Did you say that out loud? Is this how bag ladies get their start — unsure of whether they spoke or not and then one day, they're pushing all their worldly possessions before them and hissing at cats? "She really has no idea what she's talking about."

You're getting used to being the wrong way up. At least, you don't feel like barfing when you look at him. "What do you want?" Did he hear that tremble in your voice?

His smile stretches across his face, threatening to rip it in two. "You, of course. Just you." He drops the hand he was examining to reach into his pocket and you're starting to panic in a very serious way.

"But why? What am I?" You throw this out hastily, anything to keep him from pulling that hand out of his pocket. You risk a glance down at the compass. It's still pointing straight UP. How is that possible, when you are upside down and thus holding it upside down? Is up down now? Are you up? Overcome by the urge to rub your temples with your forefingers and sigh.

He seems startled by your question, as though the answer was obvious to anyone paying attention. "You? You're up. You're everything." And from his pocket, he draws a slim knife.

In role-playing games, it's called a dagger.

You tell your nerd brain to shut the hell up.

With your feet on the alcove ceiling and the whole paralysis you've been experiencing, you're finding it hard to run away, despite the dagger coming your way. All you can do is will yourself away, just somehow not be there anymore.

You fall down. Up? You fall and Salaryman's little dagger goes swooshing harmlessly by. You want to jump for joy and relief and yay you're still alive, but you're afraid if you move at all, you'll be right side up again. Being upside down has a real advantage right now. Even if you feel insane to be lying flat on the ceiling.

Your murderer seems unfazed by your escape. Lowering the little knife to his side, he slowly raises his gaze to meet your eyes. "I can wait. You don't know how to stay there forever."

Is this what everyone is going on about how you need to know which way is up? Glancing down to the compass still tightly clutched in your hand, still straight UP. Turning your head, looking the hall over, beyond the little nook you're upside down in, the candles, the sliding doors leading in, the statue of some guy next to the Kannon. If you could just get to the Kannon. That's where you're supposed to have met whoever it was. Maybe it's even up? Although aren't you up? Your head starts to throb again.

"You think you can make it that far before you come crashing down to earth?" So smug and you think once again of kicking him in the nuts, again impossible. Someday.

Let's get some control here. You focus on getting to the Kannon, your limbs no longer so frozen as when you were being lunged at by a knife-wielding nut in a suit. First, you have to stand up. Slowly pressing your hands flat on the ceiling to push yourself into a sitting position, ignoring Salaryman's taunts. Sitting, good. Next, standing. Your body is growing more fluid by the minute, responding to you as long as you don't look up. Seeing the floor and Salaryman standing on it has a dizzying effect.

One foot forward, other foot forward. You are careful to keep your gaze focused on the ceiling. No need to confuse yourself with where you should be walking. Walking on the ceiling is fine if you just accept that it is the floor.

Out of the alcove and walking up the wall to the ceiling of the main hall. Don't look up, don't look up. You know that the ceiling of the main hall is very high up indeed. After all, it has to house about ten meters of Kannon. Ten meters is a long way to fall.

It's not falling you do, but one step you're on the ceiling and the next step, Kannon is right side up in front of you. Crap.

"Told you." Salaryman's creepy smugness is not far behind you and you don't bother to do the classic checking-over-your-shoulder that results in the demise of so many horror movie starlets. Just run.

Running full out, as fast as you possibly can. If you can just get to the Kannon. If nothing happens when you get there, that's it.

There's no way you can get past Salaryman to the sliding doors out. Unless you can get back on the ceiling, but you have no idea how you're doing that.

"You have nowhere to run. You think the statue will save you? It's just a piece of wood, carved in the shape of an idea. Do you really believe that there is something like a goddess of mercy? Someone to help people in distress?"

You hear the heavy falls of Salaryman's shiny footsteps behind you. You're faster than him, but there's altars and fences and accoutrement between you and the statue to climb over and you've got nowhere to go once you reach that statue. And then you're there.

Now what?

Your death is mere seconds away and nothing is happening. Something is supposed to happen. This goddess helping those in the earthly realm is supposed to save you. You're an idiot. You have bought into your cancer-induced mental illness and now you will die.

Those don't sound like Salaryman's shiny feet. Unless Salaryman got some extra feet and is using them in many places.

"You!" Authoritative.

You spin around, wincing in case the dagger is right there in your face. The dagger is in someone else's face, so you're safe. "Me?" You barely squeak this out; surprise is scaring your voice away.

A pony-tailed woman in black stomps over to you. "Of course, you. Do you think I'm speaking to him?" She gestures towards the tumbling mass of Salaryman and Person Fending Off Dagger.

You stare. Dressed in black. They're dressed in black. And there's more of them. A guy is running towards the rolling dagger fight, another woman — this one smaller with shorter hair — is stuffing something from the altars into a black bag.

"You're the Kuroko."

The Pirates

"**Great.** Now we're terrorists."

The boy who is frequently soused rolls his eyes slightly as he says this.

Squatting on the floor, a heavy desk in front offering cover, the four of them keep their gazes focused on the side of the room that isn't there anymore.

"We're not terrorists," protests the smaller of the two girls, without taking her eyes off the flames licking the wall calendar. "We're pirates."

"You tell yourself whatever you want. We blew something up, that makes us terrorists." He reaches into his backpack without taking his eyes off the wreckage in front of him.

"W-we didn't b-blow anything up. Our friend the g-g-genius here did. High f-five, Miss D-dynamite!" Stars in his eyes and smiles on his face as the boy with too much enthusiasm turns to the smaller girl and raises an expectant hand.

She very slowly rotates her head around to meet his eyes. "Did you just call me 'Miss Dynamite'?"

His hand falls down awkwardly to rub his closely shorn head. "Well, uh, y-y-yeah, I mean, yeah. I just thought, y-y-you know, you b-built the bomb and all and it w-worked and it was pretty awesome, y-you know, and w-well, um, 'Miss Bomb' sounds lame, so...uh, Miss

Dynamite!" He tries to end on a triumphant note, ready to raise his hand again for the high five, but clearly the moment is over.

The drunkard catches the end of this exchange and nods approvingly. "Aye, I like it. 'Miss Dynamite'. I think it really works for you. Although maybe it should be 'Dr. Dynamite'. You have the degree, after all."

"Oh, D-doctor Dynamite. I like that."

"Now is not the time." The captain raises a curt hand. "We have to finish our job and get out." She stands up abruptly and crosses the room on long legs. The boy with too much enthusiasm hurries after her.

"Y-You're sure there's no s-s-structural damage?" What was once a wall is now a gaping hole. He fears the abrupt collapse of the ceiling on his head.

"We must trust the engineer." A direct order. "If she says there is no structural damage, then there is no structural damage." The captain steps through the hole.

"Hey, D-Dr. Dynamite, y-you're sure that the ceiling w-won't fall on our heads, right?" He likes to double check. And after actually saying 'Dr. Dynamite' in context, he comes to the conclusion that his original choice was better, decides to use it next time.

"Positive." To the drunken boy at her side: "Can you hand me a belay?"

"A belay? You mean the little doohickey that goes on the ropes, yeah?"

"Are you drunk?"

The dipsomaniac slowly shakes his head. "Why is it when I talk stupid you automatically assume I'm drunk?"

"Look, do you have them or not?" She holds out a demanding hand.

"Hang on. I almost found them before but then Muffin there started talking about you blowing stuff up and I lost them." He digs deep in the bag, frowning and staring off into space. The frown vanishes as the hand is yanked back from the depths. "Yeah, right here!"

"Christ, I thought we planned this. Why is your bag such a disaster?" She snatches the metal pieces from his hand, her short hair swinging forward. "Come on." She heaves her pack up onto her back and follows the other two through the hole in the wall.

He knows they can't get far without him since he's got half the ropes in his bag, but he's in enough trouble with everyone already for sinking the boat. He follows without objection.

Miss Dynamite starts to set up next to the glassless windows, clearing away the shards still stabbing up from the bottom of the frame. The drunk squats next to her and gets to work untangling the heap of rope that has been mating on his back. The bomber rolls her eyes at the brightly coloured snakes coiled together.

The sound of faraway sirens drifts up on the cool evening air, soon drowned out by sudden alarms above their heads.

"Are you almost ready?" The captain peers out the window. "We're falling behind schedule."

The bomber clutches her head. "What's with the alarms? I thought we disabled them."

Muffin grabs a harness and locks himself into it. "I g-guess there w-was one extra and I s-set it off. Oops." He grins in a way he hopes is charming, possibly even coy. It always works with his mom.

Ropes untangled, the drunk gets into his own harness. "No matter. We're almost gone. And the alarms can't give us away now." He makes a grand gesture towards the street below. "I think they already know we're here, yeah?"

"Did you get it?" the bomber asks.

The captain holds up a small black bag before shouldering it and getting ready for the descent.

"We g-got it. B-but all this for a b-book, I think it's k-kind of pointless."

"It's not pointless to the man who is paying us." The captain is always focused, always commanding. Muffin thinks she might be a robot. He hasn't had a chance to check, despite being a member of her crew for almost a year. He hasn't even been out to sea with them. "Double check, people."

Safety checks done, they lower themselves out the window.

Despite her slow and steady style, the girl with the science brain makes it down first. The two boys are too concerned with what's happening below and keep looking to see if they've been spotted and how many people are there and is the media there and will they be on the late news.

"I think we've been spotted!" the drunk shouts out halfway down, jerking his head in the direction of the police box across the street.

Muffin turns his head to look at the three small blue people standing on the corner. "A-are they looking at us?" He squints but can't make out where their eyes are pointing. "A-are they? C-can you see?"

"Aye, look, the little one's pointing at us." The drunk takes his braking hand off the rope to point and suddenly lurches downward.

Miss Dynamite is already coiling her ropes when the drunk hits the ground, having forgotten to knot the ends of his. The ropes ending about a metre above the ground means no serious injuries. He is, however, again accused of being drunk.

More and more sirens are pulling onto the scene and the captain starts to feel uneasy. "We have to get to the car." She shoves her ropes into Miss Dynamite's bag, ignoring the scowls on the bag owner's face.

"Hey, uh, did you guys like just come down the side of uh this building?" A boy with asymmetrical black hair sidles up next to the drunk who is standing idly rubbing the bump on his head. "That is so, you know, awesome, right." He takes a drag off the cigarette in his hand, pushes his new wave hair out of his eyes, slouches forward a little more.

"Aye. Can I have a drag, mate?" The drunk doesn't wait for a reply, just lifts the cig out of the boy's hand as it makes its way to his poised lips.

"That's cool, right." He lights another one from nowhere. "So uh, I'm like supposed to tell you that uh, the cops, right, have like some serious resources on the way, so you guys better you know."

Before the drunk can ask what action is indicated by 'you know', the captain jerks her head up. "You're supposed to tell us? Who instructed you to?"

The boy shrugs. "You know, some uh guy in a suit, right, pair of ugly shoes. I told him like I could uh hook him up, right, but he like loves those uh loafers or some shit, you know. Gave me these uh cigarettes, right, and ten thousand yen, you know. He said, like, talk the uh guys coming down the uh building, right. Which is like you, man. Except you're uh like, a girl."

One long step and the captain is in front of him, bringing her knee to his groin. Muffin and the drunk suck air in through their teeth, wince, turn away. "We do not need your warnings. Tell that to your man in ugly shoes."

"Right, like, okay," New Wave groans and clutches his inguinal region, the straight lines of his hair falling across both eyes.

"C-c-couldn't you have just p-punched him in the face?" Muffin asks, noticeably paler.

"Come on." The captain stalks off towards the car waiting around the corner.

"You guys are late," the driver says evenly as he pulls onto the road. No traffic now that the police are on the scene in full force preventing cars from passing down the main road and turning off onto this side road as wide as a sidewalk; their car just barely fits.

"There was an extra janitor." The captain reaches over her shoulder to pull the seatbelt across her chest.

"Didja get it?" Eyes eternally half-open, the driver looks high or asleep. It doesn't help that his hair often covers the parts of his eyes that are open.

"Yes, it's here." The captain pats the small black bag on her lap.

The driver turns corner after corner onto sidewalk street after sidewalk street to get to a main road, main road to expressway, expressway to another main road, then back to the sidewalk streets. He eases the car around yet another corner, slips it into a parking spot. "We're here."

"W-where is here?" Muffin pipes up from the backseat. "Are we going to d-drop off the 'goods'?" Trying to use the 'lingo', except that he doesn't really know what it is. He hasn't ever heard any of them say 'Arrr'.

"The apartment." The captain opens her door and gets out.

"I thought we had to 'p-pass the package' t-to 'the man'."

"You stupid git! What the hell is wrong with you?" A thump on the back of the head from the drunk. "I thought I told you to quit that movie talk."

Muffin rubs his head, frowns, amends his previous statement. "W-w-we have to deliver, right?"

"I have to deliver. The agreement is that only I am to have any contact with this man." The captain shudders a little thinking of him and that dark room where he sits. "You have to stay here. No one is to go out."

The drunk is not pleased. "But what if some of us want to have a drink? All right if we just stop in at the pub down the road, yeah?"

"There's beer in the refrigerator. Drink that if you have to drink something," she responds, moving swiftly away from the lit parking lot.

The remaining pirates head in the other direction toward the apartment they're renting for their short stay in this overcrowded city. The apartment without parking of its own: the norm rather than the exception here.

Muffin supposes that an apartment is easier to hide out in than a hotel, but he was the one who had to jump through all the hoops with the real estate agent. He's nothing but a glorified concierge. Piracy is less exciting than he was led to believe.

"W-what is with all the c-cats?"

The drunk shrugs, quickens his pace. "Who cares? Let's get back to that beer."

"But w-when was the last t-time you saw this many c-cats?" They are everywhere, sitting on top of short fences, leaning against the curb, sitting on the swings in the small park the pirates pass. Some of the braver ones even come forward and, purring, rub furry bodies against legs. "S-something is very p-p-peculiar here."

"They're just cats. It's night, cats are nocturnal. Probably a load of strays. Nothing to bother about."

"Hey." Miss Dynamite gives his sleeve a tug. "Did you see it?"

"S-see what? Oh, you mean the—n-no, I j-just set off the alarm. The c-captain grabbed it right away. Why?"

"I don't know. Just—I mean, it just seems weird that the captain is the only one talking to this guy and now she's the only one who's even seen the thing." The science girl shifts her shoulders, adjusts the weight of the pack on her back.

She's got the driver's attention. "It's just a book. Who cares? You think the captain is up to something?" The lids of his half-open eyes actually slide up a little.

"No, not at all. I know the captain would never. We're all just trying to get back out to sea." She pauses to glare at the drunk, who pretends to be too far ahead to hear her, but is rolling his eyes and wondering when they'll just let it go already. How many times does he have to apologize for sinking the boat? It wasn't even his fault really. How could he expect that his old crew would break out of jail and come after him?

The engineer pushes her short bangs off her forehead. "But you know, why did we have to set off the bombs just so? There was a door. Couldn't we have just gone through the door?"

"G-g-g-guys, I think the r-real mystery here is w-w-where are all these c-c-cats coming from? T-turn around, look."

The other three stop and turn, the engineer with hand on a hip and eyes ready to roll.

"Fucking hell." The words slip unexpected from the drunk's lips.

"What the—"

The girl just lets her jaw drop.

The cats that lined the street on their passing have grouped up behind them, a cat army filling the narrow street. Stopping as the humans in front of them stop.

Incapable of speech and speechless, felines and pirates stare. The jaws of one cat or another stretch open wide in luxurious yawns. A few cats fall to grooming themselves. At length, a calico comes forward to wrap itself around the legs of the driver.

He looks down and it meets his gaze with several plaintive meows. He squats to run his hand over its head and it immediately drops to the ground, pushing itself to and fro on its back. Her back. "They're friendly at least."

"I-I-I-I think we all know that-that-that is not the big-biggest concern here."

"I think it is." Still petting the cat, much to her delight. "Imagine if all these cats had it in for us."

Miss Dynamite shudders involuntarily. "He's right. Just calm down. They're not going to hurt us."

The drunk takes a few tentative steps forward. The cats closest to him look up; one meows, another grooms its paw. "Aye, they seem harmless." He moves a little closer and leans down to pet a black one, small, probably still a kitten. It starts to purr, turning its yearning green eyes up at him. "Aaaw, who's a good kitty?"

"Um, I've seen n-nature shows where the l-l-lions are purring during the k-kill. Just because they purr and l-l-let you pet them doesn't mean they won't jump you." Muffin takes wary steps back, ready to run if the cats do start jumping his crewmates.

The engineer turns contemptuous eyes on the boy. "Are you really a pirate? We attack people on the open seas and you're ready to run away from a gang of cats?"

"That is n-n-not a gang of cats. Th-th-that is a c-cat army."

The drunk rubs a grey mix behind the ears as he poses the question. "Do you suppose they're following the captain as well?"

"That's assuming that they're even following us." The driver stands up, blows cat hair off his hands.

"Come on. You think they're not following us?" The drunk's doubtful eyebrows hover high on his forehead.

"I'm just saying, let's not make any assumptions about these cats." He casts another wondering look at the cats. "I don't know what they're doing here. And it doesn't matter."

The cats march on with the pirates. Their tiny feet are preternaturally soundless.

Walking backwards for a minute, staring at the army behind them, the drunk pivots suddenly to face forward. "Let's hurry it up. I need that drink."

Muffin is way ahead of them, practically running in his eagerness to put some distance between them and the cats. "D-do you think there's anything stronger than b-beer?"

"Absolutely. I've hidden away some of the hard stuff under the beds." The drunk moves a little faster to catch up to Muffin.

Once the driver can no longer hear the speedwalkers, he turns to the smaller woman at his side. "So you thought about it?"

Miss Dynamite doesn't meet his half-open eyes. "I thought I was pretty clear already."

"Look, I know you want to get back into proper engineering instead of just building bombs and fixing boats. And I'm tired of this side of the world. I want to get to the West again; North America, Europe, it doesn't matter too much."

"I'm not about to just abandon the captain and everyone when they need us most."

"Why do they need us? They can find a new engineer and I'm a good sailor, but it's not like I'm irreplaceable. They'd get by without us. They'd find someone else to take our places." He lifts a hand slightly, moves it toward her as if to grab her hand? Touch her? He lets it drop back down.

"Yeah, they could just put an ad in the papers: 'Multilingual sailors for pirate crew wanted. Doctorate in engineering a plus'." Her sarcasm is tinged with anger. They've already been through this too many times, ever since the boat sank.

"Come on, you know that's not what I meant." This time, his hand knows what it's doing and finds its way to her shoulder. "After all, we can't do this forever."

She shrugs the knowledgeable hand off. "I'm not saying do this forever. I'm saying, this for now. And anyway, I like sailing. I like being out on the ocean. And I'm in no hurry to get back to the West. It's not like I'm in hell or something." She speeds up and disappears into the dimly lit street ahead of him.

He sighs. Looks down at the cats that have pulled up alongside him. Crouches down and pets two at the same time. A third comes up and licks the back of his hand.

The driver arrives at the apartment to find the drunk and Muffin already halfway through tall tumblers of something unrecognizable. Something murky and brownish. "What are you drinking?"

The drunk laughs. "Funny story. I had several bottles of whiskey and the like stashed around the house, but nothing to mix it with. Which is fine by me, you know, I'll drink anything. But boyo here, he just can't handle it. 'Oh,' he says, 'I can't just drink it straight.'" In the fussiest voice the drunk can manage.

"I do n-not sound like that," Muffin protests immediately. "A person can not want to drink whiskey straight."

The drunk ignores him. "So a bit of poking about the fridge turns up nothing but a box of soy milk."

The driver opens his eyes all the way. "You're drinking whiskey and soy milk?"

The two men with the tumblers nod.

"Yeah. It's actually p-pretty good." Eating natto, that fermented soybean treat so popular in this country, has permanently destroyed Muffin's taste buds. "W-wanna try?" He raises his glass so that it is under the other man's nose.

It smells curdled. He pushes it away and some of the liquid sloshes out onto Muffin's jeans. "No, thanks."

"J-just because you don't want any doesn't mean you have to d-dump it on me."

"Anyway, where's, uh—"

"Our little scientist?" The drunk grins, a bit maliciously. "She came storming through here few minutes back. Seemed pretty pissed off about something."

"Shut up, boat sinker." The driver goes into the kitchen, grabs a beer from the fridge, then settles down on the floor, away from the stench of soy and whiskey, and stares at the TV with the other two. The TV showing incomprehensible programs with subtitles in cartoonish fonts, capturing random words spoken by the supposed celebrities eating food. He speaks this language and yet the show makes no sense.

"So is the point that they're eating?"

"Y-you don't like it?" Injured puppy eyes. "B-but the ramen l-looks so good."

"What is the meaning of all those cats?" the captain demands, slamming the door and storming into the living room.

"They're s-s-still there?" Muffin leans back and fearfully pushes the curtain aside to be greeted by whiskers on the windowpane. "Yah!" He leaps forward and falls out of his chair.

"They follow me the entire way to the delivery and the entire way back and then, when I arrive here, they have surrounded the building. If they did not move aside to let me pass, I would still be on the sidewalk. They literally opened a path for me to enter." She glares at the cat at the window. "What are they doing here?"

"Good to have you back, Cap'n. Can I fetch you a drink?" The drunk holds up his murky tumbler. "A soy and whiskey perhaps?"

Possibly practicing for when he actually does grow two heads, the captain stares at him. "You're drinking soy milk and whiskey?"

He sighs. "So you'd rather have a beer then."

She nods. "Thanks." Back to the cats. "Does anyone know anything about these cats?"

Muffin shrugs. Back on his feet, he takes a few steps away from the window and the whiskers. "After w-we parked the car, they started f-following us. Everyone else was p-petting them, that's probably why they followed us home. Everyone knows if y-you pet stray cats, they'll f-follow you home."

"They were already following us before we pet them," the driver points out. "I don't know what they're doing here, but they seem harmless."

"Well, they let us pet them and they purred." The drunk hands the captain a cold one. "I don't know if that makes them harmless. The princess here says that lions purr when they kill."

"Stop c-calling me 'p-princess'." The protest is lukewarm; his eyes never stray from the threat of the cat at the window.

The can releases its gas as the captain pulls the tab back. She drinks deeply and frowns again. "Harmless or not, I want to know why they are here."

"We could open the door, see if they come inside," the driver suggests.

"How will that help us discover why they're here?"

His shoulders do a little samba. "It probly won't. But all these cats surrounding this building, that's going to look pretty strange to someone."

The frown lines on the captain's face just grow deeper. "We must do something."

The drunk looks up from the people eating on the TV. "Aye, but what? Go out there banging pots? I think that'll draw just as much attention as the cats. And if they're all round the building, it'll be hard for anyone to put us to the cats."

The captain crosses the room to the window, yanks it open, and glares at the cats sitting on the ledge. The cats stare back, flicking tails and licking paws, but none move toward the open window.

"I think we should just leave them. Go to bed and see what happens in the morning." The driver finishes off his beer.

The captain sighs. "I think we have no other choice. Although what do we do if they are still waiting in the morning?" She shuts the window and, after a moment of thought, closes the curtain. "Where is our doctor?"

"In her r-room, I think." Muffin jumps up. "I'll g-go get her." Out of the room and back in seconds, with the girl clutching a beer and looking distinctly uninterested. Dull eyes cast downward, she sets herself on the floor next to the armchair Muffin settles into.

"I want to say, excellent work tonight. Despite the appearance of the janitor, everything went according to plan."

"A-all right! High five!" Muffin lifts his hand, pins his eager eyes on the girl, who looks away. He turns to the drunk in the chair on the other side, who instructs him to perform an unpleasant and likely painful physical act. Muffin drops his hand.

"There's more. This man wants us to do another job."

The driver starts and looks up. "Another job? I thought we were just doing this one thing for the cash. High profile bombing isn't our style. Isn't it enough?"

"I told him exactly that. But he replied that he can pay." She stresses the word 'pay'.

Eyebrows are raised all around.

"Pay? How much?" The drunk polishes off what's left of his

curdled drink.

The captain grins. "Enough money to buy six boats, should we choose to do so."

"So what's the job?" The driver leans back, folding his arms across his chest.

"A shop in Nakano."

"And what would we be doing?" The drunk uses the remote to mute the TV now that there is some talk worth listening to, but keeps one eye on the subtitles despite the fact that he is functionally illiterate in this language.

"Basically the same thing as tonight. He is insisting we wear the black clothes. We only need a small explosion, some items from the shop and we leave. I will go, and you and you." She points to the engineer and the driver. "It should be quick; we go in, we come out." She looks away, scratches her head. "There is just one detail to mention."

"A-ha!" cries Muffin.

Heads swivel to look at him.

"I j-just figured there h-had to be a c-c-catch," he mutters, suddenly embarrassed, and focuses his attention on his soy and whiskey, which is almost gone.

Heads turn back to the captain.

"The timing is essential."

The engineer holds her bangs off her forehead, wrist at right angles to her head. "How so?"

The captain lets her eyes rest on each of them in turn. "Well, we must wait until a specific individual is passing. Myself, I don't understand. He wants this person to be killed, then he should hire an assassin. I told him, 'We're pirates, not assassins.' But his response was that he does not want to kill anyone. He only wants the building to explode as this person passes."

"So I'm supposed to set up the explosives so that they what? Knock this whoever flying?" Scowls and frowns from Miss Dynamite.

"Yes, if that's possible."

She tugs at her bottom lip with her teeth. "Of course, it's possible. In theory, I mean. But the simple beauty of mathematics doesn't always translate into reality so well."

"As long as the explosion doesn't kill us or anyone else."

The bomber nods decisively. "I can make it work."

"Good. Those are the words that I wanted to hear." She turns to the drunk and his soy-and-whiskey partner. "The two of you will stay here."

"What're w-we supposed to d-do here?" A teenage tantrum brews on Muffin's twenty-something face.

"If there is any soy milk left, I suppose you could prepare more of those drinks."

The drunk lights up. "That's not a bad idea." He elbows the boy with a wink. "We could spend the whole day drunk, watch terrible dramas. Sounds good, yeah?"

But Muffin is pouting at being left behind. "Y-you always take h-him."

"He goes, you stay." The captain's voice leaves no room for argument or whining.

"So when are we meant to do this thing?" The driver leans forward to hold his head in his hands, eyes the captain doubtfully. "I thought the plan was to be out of the city in the morning."

"We work in the afternoon. We will lea—"

The engineer jerks her head up from her mental calculations. "'The afternoon?'"

"That's pretty vague." Doubtful eyes are replaced by sceptical brow.

"He is to telephone us."

Miss Dynamite's ire pushes her up off the floor, knocking her empty beer bottle over. "Phone us? So I'm just supposed to be on call? I can't function like this." Her feet are elephant-heavy as they carry her out of the room.

The captain lifts her left hand to rub her temple.

"Well, how did you expect her to react?" the driver says. His voice is half-lidded, menacing somehow.

"I don't believe it's in our best interests to walk away."

"You should have at least put it to a vote." He is accusative in a way that he can't control.

"You're right. I should have put it to a vote. However, as with the job today, it was yes or no, at that moment. I didn't have the opportunity to come back and discuss it." She allows herself to glare at him. "What would you have done if you were the captain?"

He accepts the reproach. He does not want to put the captaincy up to a vote. Not now. "Same as you, I guess. We need the money. We need to get a boat and get back out to sea. I just don't like the way this guy works."

The drunk, having lost interest in the conversation once it was clear that he would not be obliged to do anything, is drinking straight from the bottle of whiskey he had hidden under his chair. "Look, are we finished here? Famous people are eating weird food on the telly and I'm not able to hear them."

The first thing Muffin does when he wakes up is nervously pull the curtain back and take a tentative peek out the window.

The cats are gone.

And it's sunny.

He can't stop a delighted "yosh!" from escaping his lips and waking the light sleeper next to him.

"What the hell is wrong with you?" Parched, the drunk's voice barely makes it out of his throat. Too absorbed in the tasty treats on TV, too much of that bottle being poured down his throat. That little 'yosh!' slammed into his head like a bullet train gone horribly astray.

"S-sorry, I tried to keep that in." Sheepish grins. "It's j-just that the c-cats are gone."

"Get out."

A hungover dipsomaniac usually does not bode well for Muffin, so he makes a quick exit to the kitchen where he finds the engineer bent over the table.

"Good m-m-morning, Miss Dynamite!" he chirps. "What're you w-working on?"

She doesn't bother to raise her head. "The calculations for the bombs. Took a look at the site this morning, saw where the doors were, how big the place is, now it's all about figuring out where the bombs go. I've got it, I'm just double checking," she is quick to add.

"Don't you have a c-computer for that?"

The briefest, most imperceptible of nods. "Yeah, but I like to do it by hand."

"G-good for you," he offers, opening the fridge, hoping for breakfast and finding only beer. Even the soy milk has been finished. "Isn't there any f-food?"

"No, Cap'n said you're supposed to go to the store." Her voice is muffled by the flatpack table in front of her face.

"I'm s-supposed to go to the store? W-w-why do I have to go the s-store? Why can't your b-boyfriend go to the s-store?" She lifts her head suddenly and glares at him and he has the thought that maybe it's not such a great idea to piss off the girl with the explosives.

"Look, don't talk to me about him." She is practically growling. She's been avoiding the driver since he started with her again last night.

Muffin throws up defensive hands. "S-sorry. I didn't m-mean anything. I j-just hate that I have to do all these s-stupid errands."

"That's your job." Her voice is directed at the table again. "You're the youngest and the least experienced. That's how it works. You knew that when you joined. Now go get some money from someone and get us some breakfast. I'm hungry." She begins erasing furiously, then blows the eraser crumbs off the page like she can't get them off fast enough, then back to scribbling with her worn-down pencil.

The drunk is usually who Muffin turns to when he is told to go get some money from someone. Despite his almost perpetual drunkenness, he is an excellent purser. Possibly because he doesn't actually go to buy anything himself, which would most likely lead to large quantities of alcohol and nothing else being purchased. Except maybe some fried potato products. But Muffin is reluctant to face that hangover a second time. He stands in front of the door to their shared room, muttering to himself.

"What the hell are you doing?" The driver emerges from the room across the hall, clad only in greying sweatpants, eyes almost completely closed. In fact, the left one is completely closed. His visual system is operating entirely based on the tiny crack between the upper and lower lids of his right eye.

"Gah!" Muffin's bare feet leave the floor.

"For the love of christ," comes a groan from the drunk on the other side of the door.

"G-great, j-just great." Muffin turns to glare at the heavy-lidded man behind him. "You've m-made his hangover worse."

Rubbing his eyes. "Look, I didn't make it worse. You're the one who screamed." A crack appears between the lids on the left eye as well. He's already doubled his visual productivity and it's not even breakfast yet.

"I d-did not scream. Y-you just startled me and w-well, I-I, um, I vocalized."

He shuffles down the hall to the toilet closet. "Okay, whatever, you're the one who 'vocalized'."

Muffin turns to the bedroom door again, takes a deep breath, and pushes the door open.

On his futon on the floor, the drunk has his head buried under a pillow and is moaning softly. Muffin squats down just beyond the drunk's reach. "H-h-hey, um, the c-captain said I should g-get some m-money and uh, g-get some food for everyone."

Noises that may be malformed curses trickle weakly from the drunk's hidden mouth.

"Y-yeah, um, o-okay. So c-can you g-give me some money?" Muffin reconfirms his distance from the drunk, shuffles back a little.

Abruptly, the drunk flings himself upright. Any gradual creeping up and he will just fall back down due to the pressure in his head mounting with every slight upward movement.

"Gah!" Squatting Muffin jerks backwards, loses his balances and falls with a thud on his tailbone. "Ow, my t-tailbone!"

Both hands clasped over his ears. "Would you just. Shut. Up," the drunk growls with as much strength as he can muster. "What the hell is wrong with you."

Leaning to the side on one hand while the other gently rubs his bruised tailbone. "You s-scared me. What d-do you expect, l-lurching up like some kind of zo-zombie movie?"

"Look away."

Dutifully, the boy turns his head to the side. "Honestly, y-you think I'm going to be s-stealing from you? Anyway, it's m-my money too."

"Yeah, but I'm in charge of it." He fumbles around for a second, digging a certain amount of cash from one of his many hiding places. Tosses it onto Muffin's lap with the smallest flick of the wrist possible. Eases his head back onto the pillow. "If no one knows where I keep it, no one gets blamed when it goes missing. Now go." Imperious as if the futon under him were a throne.

Muffin looks back, sees the bouquet of bank notes strewn across his legs and carefully picks them up one by one, arranging them so that all the heads are facing the same way, all right side up. He stands, takes his French fashion designer wallet from his pocket and carefully tucks the money inside. "D-do you want anything special?"

"You, out." His words are muffled again by the pillow that has found its way back over his head. "And the receipt." He is a diligent dipsomaniac.

"'A-and the receipt,'" the Muffin mumbles, sneering and pouting at the same time as he makes his uncareful way out of the room. He pulls the door shut behind him a little too forcefully and the corner of his mouth turns up at the moans that follow.

He walks through the kitchen where Miss Dynamite is still scribbling and erasing at the table. "I'm going now. D-do you want anything special?"

"Cookies." She almost barks the word.

"F-fine, cookies. You're w-welcome." He really emphasizes that last bit, but she doesn't look up or acknowledge him in any way.

He quickly pulls on sneakers whose laces never get untied and digs through the pile of jackets on the floor next to the entryway until he finds his own, a black leather jacket he bought years ago that makes his neck look too skinny. Muttering inaudibly as he steps out into the gray afternoon.

The captain steps into the kitchen, opens the fridge, glowers at the empty shelves. "Hasn't he returned yet?" She slams the door shut.

At last, the girl at the table takes her eyes off the papers in front of her. "No. He left a while ago, though, so he should be back soon." Eyes back down.

The captain sits across from the engineer, tilts the wooden folding chair back so it's only balancing on the back two legs. The scowl never leaves her face, just changes in shape a little. She runs a hand through loose hair. Reaches into the front pocket of her jeans and pulls out an elastic, yanks her hair back into a ponytail. Leans forward and the chair slams back down onto all four legs. The girl with the pencil noticeably jumps. "Is there no coffee at least?"

The engineer lays her pencil down with a shaky hand. "Would you like me to check?" Just a hint of ire creeps into the question.

Shaking her head, the captain stands up, pushes the chair in. "No, I'll look in the cupboards."

The girl at the table watches as her captain digs through the cupboards in the tiny kitchen. Drums her pencil hummingbird-style against her notes. "You're worried about this job today."

The captain looks up from her search, eyebrows still pulled together. "I don't understand it. This man seems to want much more from us. Why does he lay out such strange terms and conditions, why does he give us so much money for such simple jobs?" She hardly slept last night, that eerie man appearing in her mind over and over the way her tongue searches out the partial protrusion of her bottom right wisdom tooth.

The girl brings the tip of her pencil to her mouth, starts gnawing on it absently. Quickly realizes what she's doing and yanks it away. "Yeah, there's something off about this whole thing. The Honda building yesterday, that was weird. Why couldn't we have gone through the door? There was a door. He didn't tell us anything about a door."

The captain leans back against the laminate counter, crossing her arms over her chest. "The boy with the ridiculous hair last night. He said that a man wearing a suit sent him to tell us that the police were coming."

"I believe his exact words were the cops had 'some serious resources on the way'."

The captain misses the wryness in her statement. "Exactly. And he was correct, but that's not the point. The point is who was it that sent him to tell us that and why. There was no need to send a messenger with such information. Obviously, the police will come to the scene of an explosion."

Miss Dynamite sits up straighter. "I thought you knew. I thought that's why you kicked him in the nuts like that."

She's moving her head slowly from side to side. "No, I merely dislike being told what to do." She brings her index finger to her chin, starts tapping it slowly. "But later I began asking myself who sent him. The boy said that it was a salaryman, yes?"

The engineer pushes her lips out as she considers. "I guess."

Nodding as if it's all coming back to her. "And a pair of ugly shoes."

"So does the guy who hired us wear a suit and ugly shoes? Maybe he sent the kid."

"Although I am certain he has shoes, I cannot say if he wears ugly shoes or not. I have seen his feet never. Nor have I seen him stand up, so I cannot say if he wears suits. Last night, he appeared to be wearing a T-shirt, which is usually paired with jeans. So I do not think he is the man paying the boy."

"Well, if it wasn't that guy, then who was it? Who would want us to get away without being picked up? It's not like we were handing out Christmas presents to orphans, we did cause an explosion."

"That's the issue that's really perplexing me. Why would anyone want us to escape so smoothly? Other than the man who pays us," she adds. "Perhaps he hired someone to watch us. I really feel like we haven't been told everything. The man himself is unsettling and hardly allows me to even see his face. I have seen him in a fully lit room never. And now today we have this job."

"I—"

"Hey, g-guys!" Muffin is in considerably better spirits as he crashes through the door with several jammed-full plastic bags in each hand. "I got d-d-d-delicious food treats for everyone!"

The captain crosses the room and relieves him of two of the bags. "Close the door," she instructs without returning his smile.

He bites his lip, then his tongue. For a moment, he is frozen, a statue of himself, and then he does what he's told. Yanks his shoes off, brings the other two bags up into the kitchen.

The captain has already unloaded one of the bags and is started on the second. "Did you buy coffee?"

Muffin is taken aback. "Huh? N-no, why would I? There's

some right here." He opens the cupboard closest to the gas range, flourishes like a game show hostess with his free hand.

She looks up and sees the coffee canister in full view in a cupboard she looked in before. "Oh. Oh, that's where it is. Of course, it would be in the only cupboard I didn't look in." A doubtful glance from the engineer. "Will you make us some coffee then?"

"Your w-wish is my command, *mon capitaine.*" He bows deeply with a Victorian, rather than gameshow hostess, flourish.

"For the last time, don't call me that."

"Yes, ma'am." He prepares the coffee in silence.

After coffee and a breakfast of eggs and toast, the captain glances at the clock, then leans forward to rub her temples with the tips of her fingers, elbows still on the table.

"M-more coffee?" Muffin asks brightly, standing next to her with the millionth pot of coffee of the day.

She gives a brief nod, continues rubbing her temples.

Muffin pours. Waits for a word of thanks that is not forthcoming. Grumbles his way back to the coffee machine.

"We had better get ready. You..." The captain looks around. "Where is the drunk?"

"He's s-still abed. I just went to bring him some c-coffee. Want m-me to go get him?" The corner of his mouth slips up his cheek.

"No, it's not that important. Just tell him when he is not 'abed' that he needs to prepare for our departure. We're leaving according to our original plan, just a day late."

"Aye aye, c-captain." He salutes smartly and she glares.

"Didn't I tell you to stop that?"

"Well, actually, y-you told me not to call you 'mon c-capitaine.'" Furtive eyes avoid her gaze. She might have told him that once a long time ago.

She's ignoring him anyway. "Have you prepared the explosives?"

Miss Dynamite nods and grabs her pile of papers from under

her chair. "Yeah, it's all here." She sorts through them and finally yanks one out. It's covered in straight lines and pretty pictures. And some numbers. But mostly pretty pictures. She lays it out flat in the middle of the table so the driver and the captain can see, proceeds to outline how much explosive she'll use, where it'll go and where they don't want to be standing unless they also want to be caught in the blast. "It's not really enough to kill anyone, I don't think. I mean, not unless some freak accident sent a piece of glass flying into someone's eye socket and through to their brain or something."

Captain and driver both raise their heads, then their eyebrows, then stare at her.

"I'm just pointing out the possibility." Defensive against the macabre accusations in those raised eyebrows. "It could happen. Although it's not very likely." Hastily tagged on.

Muffin is clearly not going to be involved in this conversation, so he wanders off into the living room for the mid-morning 'wide shows'. Although they are meant to be somewhat newsworthy, they end up just being groups of random celebrities gossiping about random events. Some of them have other celebrities special guest star, but it's not clear how that works. If the random regular celebrities change from week to week, as they often do, how can anyone be a guest star? Muffin eases himself down into the sofa, clicks on the magic box and allows the talentless talent on the screen to sweep him away.

The engineer pops her head through the doorway. "We're off."

He tears his gaze away from the lady with the onion-shaped hair. "O-k-kay, good luck. Hope you s-steal everything and hurt everyone y-you're supposed to."

She frowns. "You don't have to say it like that."

"L-l-like what?"

"Whatever." She rolls her eyes, pulls her head out, then pops it back in. "Oh yeah, Captain said you're supposed to have dinner ready when we get back."

"She d-did not. She n-never asks me to cook."

The engineer shrugs. "Okay, fine. I say you're supposed to have dinner ready when we get back."

"You c-can't tell me what to do."

"I just did." And her head is gone, leaving him no opportunity to throw something at it. Although the only thing he has at hand is the remote and he needs that. There are many other wide shows to be watched, more talent to be scrutinized, like the mystery of the onion-haired lady.

"Drive past once," the captain instructs the driver as they approach their destination.

The destination being a shop full of Buddhist gear. They are about to blow up a religious goods shop.

"Are you sure we have to blow the place up?" The driver keeps his eyes on the road ahead of him.

"That's the job." The captain stares past him, through his window to the shops lining the other side of the narrow street.

"But that lady probably keeps her family shrine in there. With the pictures of her ancestors in it. She probably makes little offerings of rice and green tea to it every day."

The engineer studies his profile dubiously from the backseat. "I thought you were an atheist."

"Yeah, but I'm not so sure about destroying someone's ancestors. Or the place where they live. That's what the shrine is, right? Just their house?" The driver lifts his eyes from the road to question the engineer in the mirror.

"Slow down slightly." A pat on the arm accompanies this, surprising him. Usually, the captain just expects the power of her voice to compel people.

He obeys, takes advantage of a yellow light that he could have made, stops. "How's this?" A bit smugly.

"I like the view, but perhaps she does as well." She indicates the woman in a grey kimono in the shop window. "Next time, don't stop."

"But—" He starts, then cuts himself off and waits for the light to change.

The light turns green. Silence in the car as he pulls it into the parking spot they selected earlier. Shuts off the ignition. Waits. Finally, "I don't like this middle of the day thing."

"It's part of the job. It must be done now, in this way, or we don't get paid. In any case, it's getting late. The sun will set soon." The captain pulls a mobile phone from her pocket, looks down at it expectantly.

"Hey, can we watch TV on that?" The driver raises his eyelids a little at the prospect of watching tiny mobile phone TV.

The captain doesn't even look at him. "We could, if you mean, is the phone capable of such a thing. We're not going to, however. It is a device for communication, not entertainment."

"Is he going to phone now?" The engineer finally finds her voice. "I thought he already phoned. I thought you already had the info." And that voice is accusing.

"A telephone call doesn't change anything. It's only in order to—" The tiny machine starts singing a popular song by a nasally singer. She quickly pushes a button as much to end the song as to answer the phone. "Yes?"

Neither the engineer nor the driver can hear the voice on the other end, despite the tense straining of their ears. They look at each other, look away quickly, the conversation from the night before hanging between them.

"Everything is ready." The captain pushes another button, places the tiny machine in the cup holder in front of her. "We have half an hour, more or less, until our mysterious victim arrives."

"What's this person look like?" She'll be the one watching, she needs to know all the details.

"Corduroy jacket." The captain slings a bag diagonally across her chest and opens the car door.

Miss Dynamite is not far behind, hoisting her pack full of explosives and other fun treats onto her back. "'Corduroy jacket'? That's it? What does that mean? Is it a boy or a girl? At least tell me what colour the jacket is."

The captain turns to look at her, shrugs as the boy locks the doors, gets his own bag over his shoulder. "That's the only thing he said. 'Corduroy jacket'."

"What if there are a million people with corduroy jackets?"

"Then select one. I can't give you any other information because that's all I know." The captain is firm and the girl gives up, accepts her fate. If she blows up the wrong person, she hopes they still get paid.

They separate when they get to the alley; the driver heads out to the main street to go in the front of the store and the two women turn into the narrow alley to break in the back door.

The captain takes out her lock pick kit. One of two criminal skill she has, thanks to her criminal ex-husband. That and punching people, but that's a skill she cultivated on her own. She's a good puncher. Being able to pick locks is not generally useful when raiding ships on the ocean. Most of the locks they need to open are attached to safes and usually Miss Dynamite removes those. Her punching skills are often useful, however.

The engineer looks studiously casual as she takes in the area around them. It's one of those tiny, jumbled alleys that are everywhere in this country, with two-litre plastic bottles all over the place.

"Hey," she says quietly, so as to both not disturb her lock-picking comrade and to keep from drawing any attention that may be waiting to be drawn somewhere behind some garbage in this alley. "What's with all the bottles?"

"What do you mean?" In the same low tone, eyes closed, feeling for the pins.

"There's all these plastic bottles filled with water, I guess. What are they for?"

Biting her lower lip a little as she reaches for another pick. "Those are to stop the cats."

"Other people have trouble with cats like we do?" She shudders. A couple cats are nice, but hundreds all together so silent are creepy and kind of scary.

"Got it." The captain stands up, slides her tools back into their soft case. Glances over her shoulder to see all the bottles. "Yes, those are to keep cats away."

"Does it work?"

The captain shrugs. "My mother told me once that the way the light flickers as it comes through the water makes the cats nervous, but I've never seen a cat run away from a plastic bottle."

She turns back to the door, raises her eyebrows in an are-you-ready kind of way. The engineer nods and the captain turns the door handle slowly enough to be silent, but fast enough so that they're not standing in the alley forever turning a door handle. Pulls the door back wide enough for her mate to take a peek inside. The girl looks, nods and slips through the crack as it widens enough to allow her through. The captain is quick to follow, easing the door soundlessly shut behind her.

"I'm looking for something more, I don't know, more organic feeling," they hear the driver explaining to the elderly proprietor. "Less lacquer, more natural wood. Do you know what I mean?"

The captain nods at the engineer. They reach into their bags and pull out their black work clothes, slip them on. A lot of details that can't be overlooked for this job. Head to toe in black, the captain turns toward the giant metal desk that fills half of the room. While she silently opens drawers and pokes through their contents, the engineer gets her gear out. Checks wires and the small details that make everything happen. Waits for the driver's cue.

The driver who is currently examining an unfinished butsudan, scrutinizing the shape and size, running a hand over the edges. "This seems maybe too organic. Maybe if it was stained? A nice wood stain could really bring out the natural beauty of the wood."

The woman in the kimono, half his size, looks up at him, possibly trying to disguise her frustration. "I don't think we have anything like that. Perhaps you would like to stain this one yourself. Many people prefer to add a more personal touch to their family altar."

He turns towards the door leading to the back of the shop, where several inhumanly large altars are standing. The people who buy these must live in castles. He has seen apartments in this country smaller than these personal shrines. "Well, what about these ones by the door?" He raises his voice to stress the last word.

Kimono Lady follows him back, glares at him in the most polite, doubtful way. "Now, dear." She reaches up to lay a well-manicured hand on his forearm. "Do you think you can afford something like this?"

Over her tiny, patterned shoulder, he sees Miss Dynamite slip out the door to the front of the shop. He's careful to keep his eyes on the woman doubting his financial standing. "Cost is not an issue," he tells her solemnly, looking deep into her dark brown eyes. "This will be the home of my family's ancestors. I can't cut any corners here."

A polite smile slips onto Kimono Lady's face; a little more real than the fake enjoyment smile she was wearing when he came into the shop, but still fake. "That is a lovely thought, dear. Let's take a look at this one. I really believe it is the most beautiful altar we sell." Her hand on his forearm turns into a lever and she steers him firmly towards the biggest, most lacquered butsudan in the shop.

Behind her, Miss Dynamite has locked the front door, turned the 'Oh no! Close!' sign, rolling her eyes at the poor English.

The driver listens to Kimono Lady wax poetic about the virtues of the enormous and obscenely expensive altar. "The centre is subtly illuminated with fluorescent lighting and while it's not very traditional looking, it's very traditional-feeling when you open the doors. The double doors offer additional protection for the precious go-honzon inside and open wide to fully reveal the glory of that icon." As she speaks, she gestures gracefully to different areas with a flat hand, while the other hand holds her kimono sleeve out of the way.

He tries not to laugh. The words seem too unnatural and used-car-salesman style to be coming from a tiny woman in a kimono in reference to houses for ghosts. Turning his laughter into assenting murmurs and small impressed-sounding exclamations, one eye on his little lover, waiting for her to let him know she's ready.

Which she does by lightly stepping up behind the little woman now circling in on the matter of cost and covering her mouth with her hand, pulling her head up and back a little.

Kimono Lady makes a muffled sound, frantically eyes the man in front of her. He shrugs. "Sorry." He looks at the girl muffling the sounds. "You okay for a sec while I change?"

She nods. He goes into the back and quickly pulls on the pile of black thoughtfully left out for him. Slips the head gear on. Sullen-faced at the number of weird stipulations for this job, at this veil-like thing that covers his whole head, only the veil is hard to see through. A mask would be so much better. As it is, he had to cut holes in his veil thing for his eyes. These things are not meant for running or climbing down the sides of building. He doesn't even know what they are for and makes a note to ask Muffin later; he grew up in this country, he should know.

Back in the front of the shop, he takes Kimono Lady from Miss Dynamite, who gets back to work. Work that consists of standing near the window and watching for a corduroy jacket, now that her system is set up.

The captain comes out from the backroom, looks at the driver who nods in answer to her unasked question. "It's all good." He has a good grip on the woman's arm, maybe too good. She is so small that too tight of a grip could break her arm. He keeps his other hand over her mouth, sees in her eyes her gentle disappointment over his fall from big-spending customer to thug.

The captain's gaze shifts to the engineer by the window. "Not yet," Miss Dynamite tells her. "You?"

Abrupt shake of her head and she heads into the back room again. She can't find the books. They have to be back here and they're not. Corduroy Jacket is going to come and she still won't have the books. She curses furiously in her native language and goes through the desk drawers again. Then the book shelves. Then the inventory racks. Where, kneeling on the floor and reaching for a box of beads at the back of the second shelf up, her hand hits the bottom of the shelf above and it is not flat and metal as it should be. She feels around a bit, gives the chunky rectangular object a yank and rips it free. Taped to the underside of the shelf in a plastic bag. Of course. She opens the bag and checks that these are them. One flip-flops its way down to the floor when she holds it up. Weird accordion books with illegible writing. These are them.

The driver looks up when the captain returns, bag in hand. "You got it?"

A brief nod as she passes him and Kimono Lady to stand next to Miss Dynamite.

"Nothing yet, Captain." The engineer feels rather than sees the captain near her, keeps her eyes on the street in front of the window, keeps herself out of view of the street behind one of the more elaborate butsudan.

The captain leans against the butsudan, ponders the old lady. Her mother always said that the more you wear a kimono, the easier it is to put one on. She tried when she was younger, before she got married, but it always ended up being her mother tying her into the thing. She could never do it herself. Although she never had much incentive to practice. There aren't a lot of places to wear kimono outside of Japan.

"Hey," the engineer says suddenly. "Is that the one?"

The driver brings Kimono Lady closer to the window, craning his neck to see their intended victim. But the captain is there before him, blocking his view, looking out, nodding.

"The one in the corduroy jacket, right?" Miss Dynamite confirms.

Another nod from the captain and they are all hustle-hustle into the back. Ducking down behind the enormous desk. That is, driver, engineer and captain are ducking. Kimono Lady is being pushed down against her will and emitting more muffled cries.

Miss Dynamite fiddles about with something and then they are all deaf for a minute. Ears ringing, they step out into the front, which is not much of a front anymore. The butsudan the driver was going to buy is on fire. He casts rueful eyes at it. It is the kind of place he would have liked his family's spirits to dwell.

"She goes out the window," the captain instructs him tersely.

His eyebrows shoot up, yet his eyelids stay relatively low. He is the only one who knows this, though, thanks to the veil. "Just throw her out the window?" Manhandling of the elderly is really not his thing.

Another nod and he shrugs. He is a pirate, after all. He tosses the old lady as gently as he can out the window and onto the street, while Miss Dynamite shoulders her bag and then the three of them are stepping out the window.

They obstacle-course their way around the cat-scaring water bottles, a non-scared cat, varying piles of garbage and a rusting miniature shopping cart in the alley. Slip into the car, yank head gear off, get the car going and then they're gliding down the road, turn after turn, until they are far from the shop and back on a main road that takes them to the apartment where the drunk and Muffin are idle, awaiting their return.

Or not. When they bang through the front door, the apartment is creepily silent and their left-behind crewmates are not where they were left behind.

The captain throws her bag across the room furiously. "Where the hell are they? I thought I told them to stay here." Glowering.

Both the driver and Miss Dynamite are taken aback, share a quick wondering glance.

"Uh, I don't know, Captain." The engineer is less vigorous in introducing her bag to the floor.

The driver is untying the traditional black shirt and letting it slide off his shoulders. "Groceries?" Shimmies out of the loose diaper-style pants, muttering peevishly about the way they have to be tied onto his body, why did no one in this country think buttons were a good idea, everything has to be tied onto you.

The captain slams herself down onto a chair. "They should stay here when I tell them to." She glares at the floor, then at her remaining crewmates.

The driver holds up defensive palms. "I didn't do anything."

"Goddammit." The English curse is unfamiliar but satisfying somehow in her mouth.

"Look, you're the captain, but you don't own us. We chose you, remember?" He is really trying to sound like there are no threats hidden in his words, like we chose you so we can un-choose you kind of thing. But he signed on to be a pirate, which means democracy. For totalitarianism, he could have run off with the Navy or some other strict organization seething with homoeroticism.

They actually hear her teeth grind. A horrible, heavy squeaking.

"God, I have to pee!" Miss Dynamite exclaims suddenly and runs out of the room.

The drawn-out, low-pitched squeak/grind continues, then stops abruptly as the captain opens her mouth. "I'm sorry. I've been over-sensitive."

He waits for an explanation, but none passes her lips. "Why?"

Shoulders go up, shoulders come down. "It's this whole business. You were right yesterday. I should have walked away from this job.

It's too bizarre."

Furrows on top of lowered lids. "How do you mean? It was pretty simple, like you said. In and out."

She shakes her head, leans back, crossing her arms over her chest. "Why the black clothing? Why the explosives? Why the waiting? Why that person in the corduroy jacket? Why steal the same item from two different places?"

He jolts at this last bit. "Say that again?"

She sits up, drops one arm onto the table in front of her, lets the other hang down by her side. "Yes, we stole the same item two times." In the most world-weary tone, as if she's already explained this to him a million times.

"But how is that even possible?" His eyes actually open completely when he says this and he is quick to let his lids fall back to their natural position. So much light and he can feel the pain on his retinas.

"They aren't exactly the same thing, of course," she is quick to add once he starts protesting the logic. She's been calling them the same thing since their unsettling employer told her everything yesterday in that disturbingly flat voice. But of course, what they stole yesterday and what they stole today aren't exactly the same. "This is what we stole today." She grabs her bag from where it lays beaten and bereft, slumped on the floor where it meets the wall, and upends it onto the table. Little accordion-style books come tumbling out.

He picks one up. Lets it fall open. Tilts his head sideways to try to read the writing. Finds that tilting his head does not help. He is illiterate in this language. "So?"

"So," she continues. "At the Honda building, what was hidden in the cabinet I was told to look in, the one protected by the alarm that the boy set off was the same. A little book."

His frown slips even further down his face. "I thought we were stealing some corporate manual or something."

Head shaking, ponytail swings back and forth. "I also thought that, but only a little book like this was in there. Covered in the same illegible script. I thought perhaps the man made a mistake, maybe we were really supposed to get some thing in some other cabinet. But when I took it to him, it was exactly what he wanted. He's paying us to steal strange little books. With the Honda job, he said only that there was some 'documentation' in a particular cabinet that he wished to have. And this time, he mentioned it would be a 'similar object'. 'To help you find it,' he said."

"What does that mean?" He flips the book back and forth between his two hands, juggling a fountain of tumbling pages.

"I would never have found them if I didn't know what to look for. Even knowing, I barely found them; they were taped to the underside of a shelf." She stops as the front door opens and the drunk and Muffin come in. With a cat.

"Not again." The captain is on her feet and peering out a window.

"Don't bother," the drunk says too late. "They're out there. The same army." He steps up into the kitchen, stands next to the captain at the window. "They followed us back from the supermarket, yeah."

"Sh-shoo! Shoo!" Muffin is trying to get the one that slipped inside to slip back outside. The cat eyes him, turns its head, starts licking its back indifferently.

The driver stands up. "Hey, is that the calico from yesterday?" Crouches down next to it. "Hey there, kitty."

The cat leaves off its grooming, looks up at the heavy lidded boy, starts purring, rubs its head against his calves.

"It is you." Grinning, he drags a hand over her back.

Muffin is dancing an antsy-pants kind of dance in the corner of the entryway. "C-could you p-p-put it outside?"

A slow daggered look from the driver. "Just come inside."

Muffin hesitates, unwilling to cross the cat's path or move

too near it, and entering the apartment requires him to do both. Finally, he bounces up and down a few times in preparation and leaps over the head of his crewmate. Almost over. The bottom of his foot catches the driver in the forehead.

"Jesus christ!" Daggers in his voice now too.

"S-sorry, sorry," Muffin is quick to pull out his placating hands and voice. "I j-just don't want to be near the c-cat. It f-freaks me out."

"Aye, we thought we'd go out and pick up some things for dinner and after." The drunk and the captain stare out the window together.

"And they followed you home?" Holding the edge of the curtain up with two fingers, the captain seriously considers the possibility that they have all gone crazy, suffering mass hallucinations or something of the sort. Mass hallucination makes a lot more sense than a cat army.

"Aye, same as yesterday. We were walking along, talking and there were cats alongside and then bam! We look behind and there's thousands of them." He steps away from the window. "Still harmless though. Lots more purring today."

"H-hey! W-what's with all the kyohon?"

They all jerk their heads around to look at the boy standing at the table, holding one of the accordion books between his hands, staring intently at it.

"The what?" The drunk can't even get his tongue around whatever the boy just said. Admittedly, he has already had a few drinks. But that's never been an impediment to speech.

The driver tries to contain his surprise. "You know what those are?"

Muffin glances up. "Y-yeah, sure. They're kyohon."

The driver exhales through clenched teeth. "What I meant was, what are they?"

"Huh? Oh, r-right. They're just special books for s-sutras." He's more intent on the thick hand-made paper in front of him. His scholarly focus drops down into frowns. "Although there're no s-sutras in here. Just regular words. I g-guess it's just a notebook." He flips it shut, scrutinizes the cover. "It says sutras on the front, though."

"How do you know that?" The drunk sounds almost outraged as he half-stomps his way to the boy's side. "Don't tell me you can actually read that."

"Of c-course. I did study classical literature in university. Y-you knew that." Blank stares, empty eyes. "You d-didn't know that? D-do you p-people know anything about m-me? I thought we're s-supposed to be a t-t-team!"

"Why should we know that?" The driver picks up one of the accordion books, opens it to a random page, sees the same mystifying mess of black ink as before. Shuts it. "You don't know what we did before."

"Yes, I d-do. Miss D-dynamite was an eng-gineer."

Bark of laughter from the driver. "Come on, that's an easy one. What did I do?"

"After d-deciding that music school was not for you — was it cello you s-studied or bass? — you worked a variety of odd jobs, d-driving taxis, teaching English all over Asia, even spending some time as a welding apprentice in tropical B-brazil where you met our previous captain, who took you on. I believe you were even involved in some criminal happenings in Hong Kong. Pre-preparation for p-piracy, perhaps?" With the slightest hint of told-you-so.

The driver closes his mouth. How did Muffin know about the bass? "Just tell us what these stupid books are about."

"I'd be d-delighted." He unfolds the kyohon in his hands on the table in front of him. "See, it says—"

The cat screeches in the most horrific way, the kind of screech usually reserved for giving birth or being run over, then jumps up onto the counter and squeezes out the window that is only half-open. Her butt gets stuck for a second, but she pushes through. She is a trooper.

"Aah!" Muffin jumps about thirty metres into the air, his heart seems to go even higher than that. Drops the book in the process.

"What the—" The drunk can't stop himself from clamping a hand over his heart.

Pounding footfalls grow louder from the hallway to the right and the engineer bursts into the room. "What the hell was that?" she cries out, turning her head from side to side, expecting to see the drunk flaying kittens.

The driver stands up, goes to the window. "A cat." Peering out, he sees that all the cats are gone. The captain to his left is noticing the same thing.

"The cats are gone." A fact. She is more unnerved by their sudden disappearance than their gathering here in the first place. Unless it can be explained away by the hallucination ending abruptly. She would like it to be explained away like that.

Muffin slumps down into a chair. "M-my heart c-c-can't take this. F-first they're here, then they're s-screaming their way out the w-w-window. I wish those cats would just l-l-leave us alone."

The driver eyes the scene out the window, wearing his dread on his face. He turns back to Muffin abruptly. "What do those books say?"

Muffin holds up a deferring hand. "G-gimme a second, okay? That cat s-scared the life out of me." With a slight look of satisfaction, enjoying the moment. He's in demand.

"Just read it," the driver insists.

Arching his eyebrows, an askance glance. "F-fine. I'm reading." Muffin grabs the book from where it fell on the floor when he had his first heart attack. "Well, this b-bit here is about Kannon, often represented as the goddess of mercy in the Buddhist pantheon. We worship her at temples a lot, you've probably seen some images. That isn't written d-down," he tacks on hastily. "I j-just thought you might be interested."

The driver glares. "We're not." Daggers are not enough, polar bears and badgers in his voice.

Muffin returns the glare. "F-fine." Focuses on the book again. "It's f-funny, it's talking about K-kannon, but it's not a sutra or a prayer or anything. Just describing an image of her, maybe a statue."

"You can't tell if it's a statue?" The drunk is slightly amused by this. "Are you sure you studied this or are you just trying to have a laugh on us?"

Muffin shakes his head, shrugging a little at the same time. "N-no, the word is the same, whether it's a s-statue or a portrait or anything. It's just an image of a bodhisattva."

"A what?" The drunk does not attempt to pronounce whatever the boy just said.

"A b-buddha. You know, a g-guy who has conquered all his earthly d-desires and is free from this world?"

"I thought there was just one Buddha." Looking back over all the things he's heard about Buddha, he thinks it's not just the drink making him think that Buddha was some fat grinning Indian fellow.

Eyes rolling so far back, they may never return. "Th-that's what everyone thinks. S-so anyway. There are m-measurements written down, probably the size of some image somewhere."

The captain is suddenly much more interested. "'Some image somewhere'? Where?"

"H-hold on." Scanning intently. Mumbling to himself. "It says Hase, s-something about a temple in Hase." A moment of thought leading to illumination and he almost lifts a hand for a high five. "Oh! Hasedera! It's really f-famous!" Back to the book, there must be more.

The drunk is about to reveal more of his ignorance to ask what or where is Hase, or Hasedera or whatever, but Muffin cuts him off before he can start. "There's s-some stuff about a jacket in here too. Whoever wrote this, it d-doesn't make any sense. What do jackets and a temple have to do with each other?"

Both the driver and the captain almost pounce on the boy at the mention of jackets, but it is the driver who gets the words out first. "Jacket? What about a jacket?"

Taken aback, the boy rocks unsteadily on his chair, which he has carelessly tilted too far back. "Uh, I-I-I don't know."

"Well, look." The driver urges Muffin on with his eyes. "We don't have all the time in the world here."

A few more seconds of reading and brow furrowing. "C-corduroy. It says right here, a p-person in a corduroy jacket. Why would someone write modern loan words in this old calligraphy style? Usually this kind of writing is reserved for Buddhist texts and twelfth-century novels." A dreamy smile slips onto his face. "T-twelfth-century novels are t-too often o-overlooked in the l-literature world today."

"You don't think...?" the engineer starts but doesn't know how to finish.

The captain can't finish the thought either. Why would there be a reference to the person they just blew up in a book that they stole while doing it?

The drunk and Muffin exchange perplexed looks. "What?" the drunk says finally. "What has got your knickers in such knots?" Maybe he should keep his afternoon drinking to a minimum; he is missing too much today.

"Just keep reading." The driver leans closer to the boy with the book spread out in front of him.

His eyebrows crawl all the way up to his hairline, but Muffin does what he's told and stares intently at the accordion book. Still basking in the glow of being useful finally. "It's g-garbage. I m-mean, I can read the words, but half of them don't make any s-sense in this context. Whoever wrote this is a t-terrible writer."

A dramatic moment as the door bangs open. No storm raging outside though. All of them jump, some more than others — the boy may need to be peeled off the ceiling later. "How unkind of you to criticize a struggling amateur." A voice smooth like he's leaning against the wall and smoothing the lapels of his suit jacket, but when they turn to look at him, the man in the suit is shredded. His suit is shredded, at least, and his face and hands don't seem to have fared much better. His shoes, however, are polished and new.

"Who are you?" The captain is ready to jump him, if necessary, but she gets closer and the stench repels her. Steps back a little towards the table, waving a hand in front of her nose. "Jesus, you smell like cat urine." The appropriate curse in English slips effortlessly out of her mouth.

He doesn't look up, just runs his left hand over his scattered hair, returning it to its place on his head, while his right hand rests in his pocket. "Yes, I'm sure I do. A number of cats relieved themselves on me." The way he stresses and stretches 'relieved' is practically obscene.

Muffin can't collect his jaw from the table, so the drunk reaches over to help him out. "The cats? Are you telling us that all those cats attacked you?" The drunk is sceptical, yet the smell of cat urine is undeniable.

Finally, he raises his head. Looks each of them in the eyes.

When the man's eyes meet his, Muffin's heart stops again. He tells himself not to pee his pants. That would be very un-pirate-like. A very un-pirate-like, distinct possibility.

"Yes, the cats. But they're not quite strong enough. Not while all the pieces are in play." Here he smiles and shivers run down spines. "I would prefer it if they did not get any stronger." The engineer slumps to the floor as he passes his cool gaze over her.

The driver opens his mouth, cries out, reaches for her, goes to kneel next to her, but none of these things actually happen. His body is broken. He's still sitting in the chair across from Muffin, whose jaw is still being held shut by the drunk. He tries again. Still he sits in his chair.

The captain has a voice, but no motor control. She stands frozen with her scent-waving hand in front of her nose. Does mass hallucination explain sudden lack of motor control and unconsciousness? "What do you want?" Unable to move her eyes even, she continues to stare at him. Her tone would have more impact if her facial expression was appropriately angry, but she is still wearing the you-stink face.

He lets his eyes rest on the boy and Muffin goes limp, head hitting the table with a bonk. "That's what I want." He indicates the pile of accordion books. "And that's what I'll be taking. I do hope you don't mind." His smooth smile, his smooth voice, he practically glides across the kitchen to the table, collects the books with one ever-so-smooth pass of his hand. "Lovely."

Not able to see him anymore, but apparently she's the only one who can still talk, so it is her duty to speak up. Plus, she's the captain. It's her job to pretend to be brave even when she doesn't understand what is happening. "Those are ours." The pouting tone of a five-year-old on the playground.

"Aah, yes, yours." He is gliding back towards the door. "Yours because you stole them from a lovely old lady?" The upturn into a question is malicious.

"Who are you?" she demands again and strains fiercely to move any of her muscles, but produces only a tiny grunt for her efforts.

"That is the question, isn't it?" He smiles graciously. "I do apologize, but I'm afraid I can't stay. I have so many other people to see today." He wipes away a trickle of blood from his forehead that has crept into his eye. Even that movement is frictionless, fluid. "I also don't relish the thought of your protectors relieving themselves on me again and I feel that they'll be here soon."

And he's gone.

And she can move again. Her hand starts moving in front of her face again to prove it. She quickly stops it and turns around to face her crew.

The driver has already leapt forward off his chair to the floor where Miss Dynamite is groaning. "What happened?"

He helps her up, sets her down on a chair as she rubs her head. "I think we all want to know that."

She frowns. "Did he just look at me and knock me out?"

"Unless a bee stung you and you're mildly allergic to bee stings," the drunk offers, pauses. "Are you mildly allergic to bee stings?"

"No." She doesn't know why everyone says there's no such thing as a stupid question. "And besides, it's cold. Bees aren't just flying about in this weather."

He shrugs it off, reaches out and pulls Muffin's head up off the table. "Oy! Boy!" Shouting in his ear.

The boy jerks back in his seat, yanking his head out of the drunk's hand. "Ow! D-don't yell in my ear! You'll cause permanent d-damage!" He rubs his forehead where he slammed into the table. "Ow. What happened?" He jolts backward suddenly, tips his chair over the balancing point, clatters to the floor. "That-that-that guy! Is he g-g-gone?"

The drunk reaches down to help the boy and his chair back up. "Aye, he's gone."

The captain sinks down into the chair next to Muffin. "I think the more important question is what happened here."

"Crazy guy came in, we couldn't move, you ineffectively trashtalked him, he stole the books." The driver sums it up in point form while pushing the hair off the engineer's face, looking for signs of injury.

"I did not ineffectively 'trashtalk' him. I had an ineffective conversation with him." She lets it go. "That doesn't explain what happened. Why couldn't I move? I was paralyzed."

The driver takes his seat across from Muffin again. "At least you could talk. I was just frozen. None of me would listen to what I was saying."

"And the cats. The cats attacked him?" This the drunk finds unbelievable.

"He said they 'relieved' themselves on him." The girl shudders. Then light bulbs are popping in her head from the sudden surge. . "Hey, did you see his shoes?"

"Hey, did you hit your head too hard?" Mocking her tone. "What have his shoes got to do with anything? A crazy fellow busts in and you're after his shoes?"

Glares from her and her lover. "Shut up, you jackass." She turns to the captain. "Remember that kid from the Honda building?"

The captain waits for her to continue.

"You know, the one that you kicked in the nuts."

Small winces from the men assembled at the table, vigorous nods from the captain. "Oh right, that boy with all the hair in his eyes."

"Didn't he talk about the guy's shoes?"

The light from the engineer's eyes sparks up in the captain's. "He did. He said they were loafers, ugly, the man was extremely attached to his ugly shoes or something similar."

"I know maybe I'm reaching here, but the only thing that was still vaguely intact with that guy were the shoes. And they were all shiny and new looking. Even though his suit was shredded and he was bleeding all over the place. And the cats pissed on him, right? They'd have to have pissed on his shoes, right?"

"Are you saying the shoes are magic?" The drunk just can't stop with the sarcasm for this girl today.

"No, I'm not saying the shoes are magic. I'm just saying that he was wearing ugly, shiny shoes and maybe that's the guy who paid the kid and maybe he's more involved in this thing that we think." She stinks her tongue out at the drunk and he grabs for it. "Fuck you."

"Up yers," he sends back.

"Would you t-two quit it?" Muffin grasps the kyohon in his hand a little more tightly, turns his chair to face the other direction.

The driver frowns. "So what do we know?" Suddenly realizing how sleepy he is, glances at the clock. So late.

The captain stands, paces a little, then opens the fridge and digs around inside, finally emerging with cans of beer in each hand. "Beer?" She passes them to outstretched hands, takes her place at the table again. "We know nothing. We exploded an office at the Honda building, stole some little books—what did you say they were called?"

Muffin is facing them once more, the beer has won him over. "Kyohon. B-but only if there's s-sutras inside, I don't think these h-had any sutras inside. So I d-don't know what to c-c-call them."

"Well, we have to call them something," she returns. "We stole these kyohon from Honda and then we stole them from an old lady today. We also deliberately waited to set off the explosives for Corduroy Jacket."

Here, the drunk raises a whoa-stop hand. "'Corduroy jacket'?"

"Some person wearing a corduroy jacket walking by the shop. We had to wait for that before we could blow the place up." Twisting her mouth up contemplatively. The engineer saw Corduroy Jacket's face. Didn't look like the kind of person you'd want to blow up. But then, she probably doesn't look like a pirate.

The fuses in his head are coming together. "Is that why you all were doing little dances when the boy here was talking about jackets?"

"I get it." Muffin is nodding approvingly, glad that he was not alone in not knowing what that was about. "And then?"

"And then guy busts in and puts you to sleep." The drunk finishes his beer, scratches his unshaven chin. "Anyone like another?"

The captain and the driver indicate that they would.

"So what do guy and the books have to do with each other?" The engineer.

"The cats." The driver accepts a beer from the drunk. "Don't forget the cats."

"W-what do the cats have to d-do with it?" Muffin is slightly sneering, slightly scared.

The driver shrugs, drinks deep. "They're weird, that guy was weird, the books are weird."

The captain is nodding slowly. "You're right. Those cats are somehow part of this. He said they attacked him."

"D-does that mean they're on our side?" Muffin rubs a hand over the black stubble covering his head.

"What's our side?" Miss Dynamite offers in response.

The captain downs the rest of her beer, looks at the clock on the wall. "We're all tired, it's been a very odd day. Why don't we go to bed, and maybe we will find sense in this in the morning?"

The drunk laughs slightly derisively. "Aye, the army of cats that's been following us attacking a man who paralyzed us with a look is going to make more sense if we just get some sleep."

"Right." The captain lays her hands flat on the table and pushes herself up. "It's agreed. We talk in the morning, we sleep now." And she's down the hall, in her room, flopping down on her futon.

The driver pushes the covers aside and pulls a sweater lying on the floor over his T-shirt since it is freezing and they only have those kerosene heaters in this place. Heaters which need to be turned off at night or they'll set the house on fire or poison you with their fumes or both.

Buttoning the top button of his jeans as he cat-foots his way down the hall to the kitchen. The kitchen with the lights on. The kitchen with the boy sitting at the table. He groans. Yanks open the fridge. "Can't sleep?"

Muffin is nursing a cup of something steamy. "The c-cats are back." Glum. "I can feel them outside. They're k-keeping me awake."

"The cats are back?" Popping the beer tab, he walks to the

window, pushes the curtain aside, peers out. With just the one street lamp and that almost hidden behind the building next door, it's hard to see anything, but as his eyes adjust, he can make out the pointy silhouettes of ears. "So they are." He lets the curtain drop, crosses the room, sits down across from Muffin, brings the can to his lips.

The boy seems practically gothic. Not gothic novel, but gothic rock. Where's his black lipstick? "I can feel them out there, r-r-reaching out with their w-whiskers, taunting me."

"Taunting you?"

He sighs, puts his cup down on the table. "Not like they're t-talking to me, just they're out there, sitting there, w-waiting. And I have no idea why."

Shrugging, more beer going in his mouth. "None of us do."

"B-but I seem to be the only one freaked out by this army of c-cats."

"I think you're freaked out about everything. You need to relax."

"I can't relax with those c-cats out there." 'Cats' comes out sounding like 'cash' and the driver wonders if his young friend isn't hiding something stronger than cocoa in that steaming mug.

He pulls the mug towards him and takes a sip. Winces. Whatever Muffin is drinking, it tastes like gasoline. "What the hell is this?"

Muffin snatches his mug back. "That's my d-drink. You get your own."

He holds up his beer can, waggles it in the air a little.

"Sh-shut up." The boy is clearly in his cups. "I thought if I had a little d-drink, I could fall asleep. But all that's happening is I'm getting d-dr-drunk."

Despite himself, a smile spreads across his face. "That does tend to happen."

"Shhhhut up," the boy snarls again. "You're such a-a-a—mean guy!" Suddenly, he jerks himself up, so quickly that he almost tips

— 175 —

over his precious mug of turpentine, and liquid sloshes over the edges onto the table. "D-did you hear that?"

He's rolling his eyes. Great, Muffin is a paranoid hallucinatory drunk. Just great. "There's nothing. You're imagining things."

"Oh, am I?" Is the boy's chest actually puffing up? Before the driver can decide, Muffin has pushed himself up off his chair to his unsteady feet. "Well, I'll sho-show you." He starts off in the direction of the door, not exactly making straight for it, but getting to it in a general sort of way.

"Show me what?" Exasperated. With a fond glance and loving pat, he puts his beer down on the table and follows Muffin to the door, ready to throw his arms out and catch the boy if necessary. When necessary.

But Muffin makes it all the way to the door, turns abruptly and shoots him the evillest glare he can muster. Which, admittedly, is barely a glare. "T-take a look at this!" Flinging the door open.

To a thud and "Ow! Fuck!"

Muffin is surprised by the success of his accusation. There really is someone out there making noise. He thought it was just a cat. The action of flinging the door open has caused a reaction in his slightly drunk unsteady self and the teetering that began at that moment finally sends him to the floor with a thump.

For a second, the driver is unsure. Should he go outside and deal with whoever said that, whatever thumped into the door? Pick Muffin up off the floor? Get the captain?

Looking down at Muffin who is making no attempt to stand and actually seems to be paralyzed with fear, the driver takes a deep breath, squares his shoulders and several other clichés and steps out into the crisp night air.

"W-w-wait!" Muffin cries out, frantic, but it's too late. The driver is poking his head around to the other side of the door.

"Hey, ow." New Wave is sitting on the concrete walkway in front of the apartment, rubbing his head, sending his asymmetrical hair swinging from side to side.

"You?" He's not sure whether to be relieved or even more uptight. New Wave seems harmless enough, but then, the first and last time he saw him, he was taking a knee to the groin from the captain.

"Man, uh, li'l help?" One hand reaching out, the other still rubbing his head.

A pause long enough for an imaginary shrug and he offers New Wave his hand, pulls him up. "What are you doing here?"

A lit cigarette appears in one hand and the driver wonders where it came from. He's sure he didn't blink and anyway, a blink's not enough time to get out a cigarette and light it. "Why'd you uh slam the like door into my uh, you know, head?"

"My question is better." Backs up a little so he's standing directly in front of the doorway. The calico pushes out of the gloom and entangles herself in his legs. Purring.

Inhaling deeply from his cigarette. "Totally, that's uh cool." Exhales a miniature storm cloud. "Like, uh, wow. Lotta cats." He crouches down, makes clicking noises with his tongue. Holds the cigarette-free hand out in front of him. "Hey, kitties."

Another cat, looking like someone slammed a Persian and a Siamese into each other and they somehow combined to become one being, comes forward, stares intently before pulling its head back and trotting off into the night. A cat approaching from behind suddenly flinches at the smoke from his cigarette, jumps back into the dark. He laughs. "Like sorry, cat!"

Purring from the cat tangled in his legs reassures the driver. At least the cats aren't attacking the chain-smoker, although they aren't exactly cozying up to him either. But he still wants some kind of answer. A kid who was supposedly paid to warn them about the arrival of the police should not be standing on their doorstep. "I'm waiting."

Nods his head purposefully. "Right, uh, yeah. I uh, you know, saw all these cats, like what? I'm thinking."

The driver's eyelids are less droopy. "You what? Live here?"

Smiles, head shaking, the hair swings hypnotically. "Man, uh, no way, I uh just like you know."

"You know?" Was he this hard to talk to the last time? The only thing he can remember about that is the knee and winces again.

The shaking turns to energetic nodding. "Totally."

"Totally what? What are we talking about?"

He finishes the cigarette, starts to flick the butt away, then stares at the shapes of the many cats in the darkness, drops it to the ground in front of him and crushes it under his long and pointed shoes. "So uh, you know, then I uh remembered, oh yeah, message, right."

A noun. He pounces on it. "A message? You have a message for us?"

"Man, I heard you uh, like, have no boat, right. And you know, I know this guy who like uh knows this guy or whatever and yeah, he's uh like got this boat, you know?" Raising his eyebrows, like there's some subtext here that the driver should be hearing.

But he can't filter out all the verbal garbage to hear the main text much less any subtexts. "Wait. How do you know we have no boat? And why do you think it matters? Lots of people don't have boats."

The box that the previous cigarette must have come from is suddenly in his hand. "You're uh pirates, right? So uh like pirates you know, they have uh boats, so whatever." Pulling a cigarette out.

Making whoa-whoa hands. "Okay, but see, that's what I'm asking. How do you know that?"

"Oh, like man," Lighting, inhaling. "I uh you know like heard it or whatever." Smiles like sunshine and tosses the hair out of his eye. "If I were uh you know, you, right? I'd be more like into uh getting some kind of whatever, like boat or ship or you know. Pirates should like uh sail, right." He nods his agreement with himself. "Totally. Gotta sail, man."

One eyebrow is hitting the sky. "So you came to tell us about a boat?"

Some groovy head bob-nodding. "Totally, totally." Leaving the cig to hang from his lips, he rummages around in all his pockets. The pockets of the too-tight velour suit jacket spit forth a piece of crumpled paper. "All right, uh, found it." Mumbled around the cigarette. Thrusts it towards the driver, grabs his cigarette with his free hand. "So yeah, like here."

He reaches for it a little warily, although how could a crumpled piece of paper could be dangerous. It can't even give him a paper cut, all the edges are too worn down. He smoothes it out between his hands. An address in the city. Glancing up at New Wave. "This guy's got a boat?"

"Yeah, uh, I told him you would like maybe you know. So it's cool, right." Turning his head to look behind him. All the driver can see is the leftover streetlamp light, some cats, but either New Wave is crazy or he sees something more. Or both. In a hurry all of a sudden, dropping his cigarette briskly, crushing it with his heel. "Man, uh, I am so late, right." And he's taking the stairs to the ground two at a time before the driver can even decipher and respond.

Staring into the street, New Wave is gone too quickly. He should still be able to see something of that boy with the asymmetrical hair, but there's nothing but the cats. Shaking his head, shaking it off, he looks at the paper in his hands again.

Looks up. Is that a girl walking down the street suddenly? He squints to see her in the barely-there light from the lone street lamp. Wearing a tiny top hat and a voluminous short dress, she looks like one of the fashion types he usually sees in the more hip parts of town. He stares intently, looking for details in the dark, then rolls his eyes, shakes his head again. Too many crazy happenings are turning his brain around. People are allowed to walk down the street.

Turning to go back into the apartment, he trips on Muffin who is sprawled in the hallway where he fell. And fell asleep despite his apparent fear. Ignoring the temptation to kick him awake, he steps over the snoring grumbler, sits at the table, rediscovers his beer, lukewarm. Drinks it anyway with the crumpled paper spread out on the table in front of him. Finishing the beer, shoving the paper in his pocket. With a final glance at Muffin still out cold, down the hall and slipping into the bed kept so toasty warm by the engineer.

"The boy with the strange hair came here?" The captain paces, glaring at first him and then the boy with the hangover. "And neither one of you thought to wake me up?"

The driver lifts his shoulders, pulls his coffee mug closer. "I didn't think it was a big deal. And he," Jerks his thumb at Muffin. "was very drunk."

"C-can we please lower our v-voices?" Pleading whisper from the boy clutching his head.

"Gah!" The drunk pushes his chair back abruptly. "I can't stand his whinging! Please let him go!"

Dismissive waves. "Fine, go. Sleep, whatever. Don't drink so much next time."

Keeping his eyelids as low as possible while still being able to see, Muffin shuffles down the hall to the relative quiet of the empty bedroom.

"Anyway, there's nothing else to tell. He took off before I could get any good explanations for anything. I could barely understand him in any case. He mostly just says 'you know'."

"Know what?" The engineer frowns.

"That's just it."

"So he handed you this address and departed?" The captain waves the crumpled paper.

"Yeah, basically."

The engineer's frown deepens. "How did he know we're pirates?"

The re-seated drunk tilts his chair back. "What's more interesting is how did he know we're here."

"Which is exactly the reason we should not be here." The captain is firm. "We need to leave. Our employer has another job, but we refuse it. Just take what we have already and sail. I don't want to be a part of whatever is happening here."

Bobbing heads around the table.

"Where do we go then?" The drunk is the one to voice the question that's in all their heads. "With this new wave kid knowing so much about us, seems like what we planned is not so safe."

The captain sits down. "That's true."

The engineer breaks the silence finally. "I know you're going to shoot this down, but I'm interested in seeing this boat the kid was talking about."

"You're right. I'm 'shooting it down'." The captain digs out her flat, no-discussion voice.

The drunk stares at Miss Dynamite. What does she want with the boat? Is she drunk? If she's been in his stash, he may just kill her. Perhaps too much drink has made him paranoid or maybe paranoia is just what happens to all pirates sooner or later. His old crew were all conspiracy theorists. "Why?"

"We're going to have a hard time finding a boat right now. This was the problem before, remember? We all agreed that buying a new boat, rather than stealing one would lead to less trouble later, and you know, make it easier to work at sea without getting pegged by the Bureau, et cetera, et cetera. Which is why we're even doing these stupid explosion jobs in the first place. But I mean, come on, no one's going to sell us the kind of boat we need on such short notice. So we're back at stealing one."

"Sooooo...." The drunk is wishing she would wrap this up so he can make fun of her. Also, he wishes he had irished up this coffee.

The engineer deigns to lower her eyelids at him. "So, if this New Wave knows of a boat to be had on such short notice, maybe we should take a look."

Now he can make fun of her. "The whole point of taking off now is that New Wave knows way too much about us and this situation is getting out of control. Isn't buying a boat from him just more of the same?"

"Okay, first of all, we're not buying a boat from him. We're buying a boat from—" She turns to her lover to fill in the gap.

"A friend of like uh a friend, you know." A better imitation of New Wave would have squeezed another 'you know' in there somewhere.

Back to the drunk. "Plus, it's a boat, you jackass. Once we take it out to sea, New Wave doesn't know anymore about us than if we nick a boat from somewhere else."

"What if he attaches some kind of sensors?" Even he realizes he's grasping at straws.

"Sensors?" The driver raises his heavy lids. "You think he has Batman tools or something?"

This coffee needs liquor or the drunk cannot sit through this. "I'm just saying." A poor defence offered as he goes for one of his many secret stashes.

The captain sighs. "Whatever our dipsomaniac may think, the engineer has a very good point. Acquiring a boat legally now doesn't look promising. What do you think?" Turning to the driver.

Who is slowly nodding his agreement. "I think we should at least take a look. If we can get a hassle-free boat and be back at sea within the next day or two, it's worth it. Especially since I very much doubt the boat will have tracking devices planted on it." Raising his voice for the last sentence to make sure that the drunk reaching under the sofa for a bottle of rum hears him.

"Well, that makes three of us then, so that's a majority." The captain pours herself more coffee from the carafe in the centre of the table. "Would you two like to take care of it?"

Before the driver can speak, Miss Dynamite is piping up. "Don't you think we should all go?" If they are alone, he'll start with the leaving-the-pirate-life talk. At night, she pretends to be asleep before him just to avoid this conversation.

He shoots her a look from the corner of his eye that she ignores.

"No, I think hangover boy and the drunk should stay here, work out some details, prepare."

"And you?"

Drinking deeply from her coffee mug, putting it down in front of her, leaning over to stare into it. "I think I will have to go and have a talk with our 'boss.'" Even though it's some sort of poorly acted horror film every time; the officious servant leading the way to the dimly lit room, the man himself seated in a tall leather chair behind a large mahogany desk, shadows always falling in such a way that she can never quite make out his features. And when he speaks, his voice is so smooth and emotionless, it's almost inhuman.

The ride is uncomfortably silent. The girl avoids talking about leaving, but everything else that pops into her head — the cats, the crazy guy in the suit — are things she would rather pretend are not happening. The boy points out interesting combinations of vending machines that catch his eye on the side of the narrow road.

"Look." He jerks his head to the left. "Rice and batteries."

She looks.

Finally, "We're here," as he pulls into a parking spot, unlocks his seatbelt, turns the car off.

She looks around hesitantly, undoes her own seatbelt and guides it back to its source. "Are you sure? This doesn't look like the docks."

Out of the car, he shrugs. "I know. The ocean's not that far away, but still, this is where people live, not boats." He reaches in his pocket, yanks out the crumpled paper New Wave gave him, hands it to her. "But the address on this paper is just over there." He gestures to the north.

She frowns as she examines the hastily scribbled address. "Are you sure?" she asks finally. "Maybe you made a mistake. You can't find a place in this city just because you have the address. Everyone knows you need a map to find anything in this town."

"Except for the fact that I know this neighbourhood." He starts walking away from the car and she is quick to follow.

"You know this neighbourhood?" Eyebrows forming two sides of a triangle on her forehead, she slips her top teeth over her lower lip.

"Yeah, I lived here back in the days when I was 'seeing the world' as Muffin puts it." He grabs the address from her hand, glances down at it, glances up, down again. Nodding. "This is it."

"This? But this is just an apartment building. Where is this guy going to have a boat tucked away?" She stops moving forward, looks back at the car. They could give up on the idea of a boat, just become land pirates.

He's already holding the door open. "C'mon, it's on the fourth floor."

She enters reluctantly.

When they knock on the door, a guy in a hole-ridden T-shirt that probably used to be white and jeans of an unidentifiable colour opens the door, cigarette dangling from between his lips, randomly bleached hair sticking out at random angles. "Yeah?" from around the cigarette, not even bothering to fully open both eyes. His right eye, in fact, looks glued shut by sleep scum.

"Yeah, we were sent to talk to you about a boat." The driver stares at the chunks of bleached hair matted in places to the guy's head.

His eyebrows jump up, freeing the glued-down eyelid. "Oh, you're the pirates." It would be an exclamation if he took the cigarette out of his mouth. "Right, yeah, I was expecting you guys sometime." He steps back, taking the door with him, waves them inside. "Come in, come on in."

The engineer shoots her lover the briefest of nervous glances, but he's already nodding and chatting and walking through the door and she has no choice but to follow.

The inside of the apartment looks like its owner. Open pizza boxes with cheese still clinging to the insides are piled high in the kitchen/hall that leads them into the living room/bedroom/only room. Which is covered in manga, overflowing ashtrays and tissues. Used tissues. The engineer crosses her arms tightly across her chest, steps closer to the driver.

Matted hair falls in his eyes as he leans forward to sweep the tissues and empty chip bags off the bed/sofa. "Please, have a seat."

The engineer shoots imploring eyes at the driver, eyes that ask that they not sit, that they run away from this garbage can. But the driver does not speak eyeball, so she tries to avoid the stained areas as she gingerly places her bottom on the edge.

Dirty Pig clears a space for himself on the floor, sits cross-legged, the cigarette never leaving his lips, the cigarette that he may or may not be smoking. It's lit, but smoke never comes out of him. "So you're here for the boat?"

"Yeah, the kid with the new wave hair said we should talk to you." The driver shifts his gaze from the matted hair to the non-smoked cigarette, waits for the guy to inhale, exhale, make use somehow of the accessory between his lips.

Nodding as if he's trying to shake the information out of his head and into their ears. "Right, yeah, he said he was gonna tell you." Lifts a hand, runs it part of the way through his hair, but it gets stuck and he has to gently wriggle it free.

Everyone waits for everyone else to speak.

In the end, it's the driver who pushes ahead. "So what kind of boat is it? Can we see it?"

"Right, yeah. There's what? Five of you?"

The driver nods.

"So yeah, it's good for five people." The cigarette has burnt down so that it is dangerously close to burning his lips, but he seems unconcerned.

The driver waits for more information, which does not come. "So can we see it?"

Dirty Pig slaps his forehead, stands up. "Right, yeah. Of course you want to see it. Hold on." He takes a few steps, opens the closet on the other side of the room, starts rummaging around. Tosses out a heavy Swedish dictionary, which is followed by several T-shirts, all in the same condition as the one he is wearing, what could be an uninflated inflatable Hello Kitty chair and several cans of cat food that make a thunk as they hit the floor in front of the bed/sofa. At last, clutching something small in his left hand, he returns to his circle of cleared space on the floor with a new cigarette somehow attached to his lips. Hands the small thing to the driver. "There she is. What a beauty."

It's a framed photograph of a boat. The driver lifts his gaze over the edge of the frame to look at Dirty Pig. "Uh, this is just a photo." The driver should have expected this when New Wave pushed the crumpled paper into his hand. After all, what would a kid who can't form a sentence know about boats?

His nodding causes ash to drop from the end of the cigarette to his leg. "Yeah, I just took it. Nice-looking boat, right?"

The driver hands the photo to the engineer beside him. Her nose shoots up her face and her head shakes microscopically from side to side. He scowls and mouths the words 'take it' as he pushes it at her. She extends a hand slowly to take it by the corner with her index and middle fingers.

"Look." The driver turns back to Dirty Pig. "We kind of need to see the actual boat."

His crusty eyes open wide and he almost opens his mouth enough for the cigarette to fall to the ground. "The actual boat?"

"Yeah, you know, the thing that the picture is of. The big object that floats in the ocean?"

"Well, I don't have it here." Dirty Pig is giving the driver the street-weirdo look.

He sighs. "I realize that you don't have it here. Where do you have it? We need to see more than just this picture."

Dirty Pig stretches his hand out to the engineer and she drops the picture in it, pulling back quickly to avoid actual physical contact with him. He holds it up to them, then looks at it, caresses the frame. "But look, man, this is a great photo. Can't you just feel her power?" Raised eyebrows pass from driver to engineer. "She's the perfect vessel for pirates. She'll take you around the world, never stop."

"It is a great photo." The driver admits that he can feel the raw power that the boat carries in it just from looking at it. "But it's not quite the same as looking at the actual boat."

Shaking his head as if he refuses to believe that. "No way. Look again." He pushes the picture closer to them, smoke from his dangling cigarette like clouds passing in front.

The boy's heavy lids grow heavier and the rigid fear of touching something slips out of the body of the engineer to his left. The boat in the photo fills his vision and his head and is he inside it? Is he inside the photo? He looks to his left and the girl is standing next to him.

"Uh, we're dreaming, right?" She is the first to speak.

He grabs her hand. "Group hallucination. We must really want to see this boat." He tries to stay nonchalant, keep his heavy lids weighted down, tries to believe his own explanation. "We're here, so we might as well check it out."

They both have gone crazy. He sounds way too casual in this very not-casual situation. But then, she supposes, freaking out is not going to do any good. "Uh, yeah. Group hallucination. Let's check it out."

They poke their heads in all the places they're meant to poke their heads and those places are physically present; the boy with the heavy lids wanders around checking the space, the engineer takes a look at the engines. The twin diesel engines. She feels the grease on her hands, the cold metal, smells her old friend diesel everywhere, and she knows that if she had the key, she could start it up and hear the smooth duet. She looks for a maker name, but none to be found anywhere. Is she hallucinating the perfect engine? She should write down the specs.

"How is it?" Poking his head in.

Eyes like saucers as she raises her head to meet his look. "The most amazing engine I've ever seen on a boat this size. Enormous displacement, way bigger than I even thought was possible on such a small ship. She could easily get a top speed of 46, 47 knots. This thing could go the speed of light if I tweaked it a little."

"Yeah, the rest of the thing is the same. Living quarters are perfect, three separate cabins, one even has bunk beds. Mess area complete with top-of-the-line accessories. There's even a deep freezer in there. And a TV, DVD, et cetera, et cetera, everything like it was made for us. I don't get how it all fits on a boat this size. I mean, from the outside, it only looked like maaaaybe 12 metres long." Shaking his head. "We must be hallucinating the perfect boat."

She laughs, stands up, wipes her hands on her jeans. "Well, it is our hallucination. Why wouldn't we create the perfect boat?"

He can't hear his laughter and his lids are heavier than usual. They get lighter as he raises them and meets Dirty Pig's eager gaze.

Grinning to split his face in two. "So? You loved her, right? Yeah?"

The engineer takes the lead. "Uh, what I saw I loved."

"Right, yeah. That engine, it'll purr like a cat after lunch. You saw the way it's put together." He places the photo next to him, on top of what might be a plate of last week's dinner. "So you'll take her?"

Frowning, the driver does not know how to handle this. Should he buy a boat he hallucinated from looking at a framed photo? From a person who clearly cannot afford to own a boat? A person recommended to them by a kid who appears to be incapable of forming proper sentences? And then the girl is talking again.

"We'll take her." So firmly, as if she is not doubting her own sanity.

And maybe she's not. The boy sees the gleam of a religious zealot in her eyes and wonders if the hypnosis controls her now, if she'll live in the boat in the photo forever. He'll miss her if she does. Finding himself unable to protest, though. Finding himself unable to move or do anything, in fact.

Until he hears the low rumble of the engine of the car and in front of him, the steering wheel comes into view. Jerking his head back, the red light at an intersection greets him. "What—"

Cut short by the engineer throwing herself forward. "What the hell just happened?"

He shakes his head. "I don't know. What are we doing here?" Brutal honking from behind and he looks up to see that the light has changed. Eases the car forward. He looks around for something familiar, but this is nowhere he knows. "I'm pulling over."

With the car safely off the mystery street, they stare at each other as if the answers will be written on one of their faces. No answers, just lip gloss on the engineer.

"All I remember is sitting on that sofa and you saying 'We'll take it.'"

"I said that?"

"Don't you remember? After we hallucinated, you told him that we'd buy the boat and I thought you were nuts."

She is on the verge of tears, gulping in air. "I remember telling him I liked the boat and I was thinking of some way to get out of there. And then I was here." She clutches at his hand. "Do you think I fell on the floor?" The thought of touching that floor with all those used tissues is almost enough to cause her to break down entirely.

"I think whether you fell on the floor is beside the point. We don't know where we are or how we got here."

Nodding. She knows this, but panic squeezes her insides when she thinks about any part of her coming into contact with anything on that floor. Deep breathing. "You're right. We need to find out where we are." She releases his hand, rolls down the window and pokes her head out. "The sign at the intersection says 'North Elementary 5.'"

He rolls his eyes. "That tells us nothing. There's an intersection like that in front of every elementary school in this country."

She brings herself back into the car, turns to him. "I think we're going to have to get out and look for an address on one of the buildings."

"Good idea."

They have to walk half a block before they stumble upon a building with more than the building number written in white letters on the glass door.

They stop dead staring at it for a minute. "Does that say 'Kanagawa'?" he asks. "I suck at Chinese characters."

For a moment, she can't answer. "Yeah, that says Kanagawa." Kanagawa, that's not Tokyo. That's not where that kid's apartment was. "And after that, those two characters, they say 'Kamakura.'"

"Kamakura?" It takes him awhile to spit this word out. "Isn't that the place where the big Buddha statue is?"

She nods slowly. "And an hour or two away from Tokyo."

"How did we get all the way out here?"

"Seems like we drove." That clutchy panic is back. "How long have we been gone? The captain's probably back and everyone's probly wondering what happened to us. And we're in Kamakura. What is going on?"

He peers through the glass door of the building to the clock on the wall, performs a quick mental calculation. "It's been more than five hours since we left."

She tilts her head back so that the sky fills her view. "So it'll be dark soon?"

"I guess. What should we do?"

"Figure out why we're here? Call them? Go back? Find an explanation for why we were inside a photo boat and are now on the streets of an unfamiliar city?" Her mind may actually snap from the impossibility of the last few days. She is just an engineer, after all. She was trained to seek out physical stresses, not physical impossibilities.

He drapes his arm over her small shoulders. "Hey, don't freak out. We'll figure this out. Maybe there's something in the car or something."

More deep breathing. "Check your pockets," she instructs abruptly, checking her own at the same time.

He pulls up nothing but lint and the car keys, turns expectantly to the engineer, who is unfolding a piece of paper. He peers over her shoulder. "A receipt?"

She scowls.

He scans down faster than her. "For the boat? And there's a note at the bottom."

"'She'll take you round the world, so take care of her. Everything you need to get her going is on board.'" She reads it aloud. She is the audio learner type. "And then an address. So, what? Is this from that dirty weird guy?"

"Who else could have written it and slipped it in your pocket while you were zombified?" He takes her arm, steers her toward the car. "Let's go check out that address."

"Shouldn't we call the drunk and tell him where we are?" She wants the captain to know that they haven't run off together like the driver wants.

Unlocking the car, climbing in. "We'll call when we have some idea of what's going on. What could we say now? 'Hi, we looked at an imaginary boat and decided to buy it?'"

The address leads to the docks and when they show the receipt to an elderly man in a small office nearby, he leads them unsteadily down to a gated entrance, gets the key in the lock of the gate on the third attempt, ushers them down several wooden walkways before stopping in front of a boat at the end.

He reaches out with a hand whose liver-spotted skin is so loose, the girl stares and waits for it to actually fall off.

The loose-skinned hand caresses the hull of the boat tremblingly. "This is one of the finest boats I've ever seen."

"Well, that's what the guy who sold it to us said." A feeble laugh tacked on to the end. Is there even a guy who sold it to them? The thought jumps into his head that maybe they've always owned this boat, maybe there are no pirates, no new wave kid, no freak with a photo, just him and the engineer losing their minds. But no, he has the receipt.

The old man turns his watery eyes on the driver. "That boy is no liar. Always takes such good care, comes at least once a week to take 'er out. Nice boy, nice boy." Nodding to confirm his words. "So you plan to keep her here too?"

Such hope in the old man's eyes that the driver is reluctant to speak. "Actually, we're planning on travelling quite a bit so..." He lets his sentence trail off, as if not saying the words will not break this tiny man's heart.

He nods so slowly that it's almost imperceptible. "You kids always have to see the world."

The crack in his voice sounds like tears are on the way and the engineer is quick to act. "But uh, hey, we're not going to be leaving until tomorrow, so you know..." She doesn't know how to end her sentence. So say some final words? So have a last evening together? So get used to it?

But her words at least stop him from busting out crying on their heads. "Well, I'll have one more night with you, won't I, girl?" Patting the side with the loose-skinned hand. Fond glances exchanged with the mast.

The girl shudders.

The boy forces a smile. "Well, uh, I guess we'll just go aboard." He hopes he sounds cheerfully dismissive.

For a moment, the old man does not respond, continues to caress the hull. Finally, tears himself away. "Of course, must be so exciting. New boat an' all. An' such a lovely new boat at that." Reluctantly pulls his hand back, struggles a little to push it into his pocket. Did his skin catch on the edge of the pocket? The engineer watches in horror. "Well, I'll leave you to that then. If you need anything, I'll be in the office. Anytime." He smiles expectantly.

The driver holds his forced grin on his face. "Yeah, if we need anything, we'll definitely call you." He tries to sound firm, firm in a go-away-thanks kind of way.

The old man casts longing eyes at the boat one last time and then waveringly shuffles back the way they came. After he's gone a few steps, the driver and the engineer can hear him start to brokenly hum; hum, fade, hum, abrupt stop, hum.

When she feels he's out of earshot, the girl clutches her lover's arm tightly. "Are you as disturbed as I am?" she hisses between her teeth.

He can only nod, mesmerized by the old man's slow shuffle step and stop-start humming.

She tries not to follow the old man with her eyes, tugs at the boy's sleeve. "C'mon, let's see if we were hallucinating or not."

He starts to step forward but is held in place by her grip on his arm, her feet rooted to the dock. "What?"

Her grip gets tighter. "What if it is just like we saw?"

He shrugs. "Then we made a good investment." She glares. "I mean, what do you want me to say? I have no idea what is going on anymore and if I start thinking about it too much, I'll go crazy. So just say, 'Huh. That's weird,' and move on. Going crazy is not going to change anything. You think too much."

She peels her fingers free, shoves her hands in her pockets. "I know that going crazy is not going to help, but nothing makes any sense. I just want something to make sense. And I just know we're going to get inside and everything is going to be just like it was. And how is that even possible?"

"Hypnosis? Surprisingly accurate hallucination? In any case, huh. That's weird."

"Okay, okay. Let's just get it over with."

One complete tour later. "Huh. That's weird."

The driver grins at her. "See? It helps, doesn't it?"

"Surprisingly, it does." She is still sane after seeing the same engines as she saw in the photo/hallucination earlier.

"So I guess this is why we zombied our way to Kamakura." He takes a peek out the porthole. "It's getting pretty dark. We should figure out what we're going to do."

"We should probably call the others first and let them know where we are. But I don't want to use any of the equipment on board until we have a chance to check it all out." Frowning.

"Good idea. So we'll what? Use a payphone?"

"Did you see one nearby?"

"There's not going to be one on the dock outside." Sitting down in a chair that has just the right amount of support.

"So we go up to the street, walk around?"

"Yeah, seems like that's our only choice. And maybe there's somewhere we can get some food or something. You hungry?" He watches her nod, realizes he'll have to stand up again. Dismayed. The chair is so perfect. He looks forward to getting insomnia here and getting up to stare at the wall with a drink.

"I j-just asked you a simple question. Why c-can't you even answer m-me?" Muffin places clenched fists on his hips, narrows his eyes.

The drunk rolls his eyes so far back in his head, his irises may never be seen again. "I gave you an answer. I don't know where they are. When I came back from the shops, no one was here. What part of this do you not understand? Do I need to speak your native language, is that it? Has your English failed you?"

Will it come to blows? Muffin begins pushing his sleeves back in anticipation. Interrupted by the phone. It rings and rings as they stare each other down.

The drunk flops back into the easy chair below him and turns back to the TV. "Are you not going to answer that, boy?"

For a moment, nothing but the sound of his teeth clenching, air being sucked between them. "F-fine. Fine. I'll g-g-get the phone." Muffin stomps over to the machine, yanks the receiver from its cradle. "Takahashi residence." His mother trained him too well and he gives the fake name he gave to the estate agent. Becomes Takahashi.

"Hey, is the captain there?" The crackly voice of the engineer reaches his ears.

"She's n-not back yet. Where are you?"

A strained silence. He hears her breathing, sharp intake through her teeth. Finally, "Kamakura."

His eyebrows fly up his forehead. "Kamakura? What are you d-doing there?"

The drunk listening in feels his eyebrows jump as well. Even he knows that Kamakura is not Tokyo. Leans forward.

More hesitant air through the teeth. "Buying a boat."

"B-b-buying? You c-can't buy the boat! The c-captain said to loo—"

"You bought the boat?" Out of his chair and ripping the phone out of the boy's hand before he even realizes it. "What the hell is wrong with you? You can't just buy a boat! I agree to all purchases, I'm the fellow with the cash!"

She presses a hand against the phone booth wall, stares at the driver standing outside, waiting for her, watching traffic crawl by. "Look, we'll explain everything when we get back. We just wanted to call and say we're okay and we'll try to be back soon. Where's the captain? Why isn't she there?"

His indignant self falls to the floor. "Well, we don't quite know."

"What do you mean, you don't know?" A sudden lump in her stomach. "How can you not know?"

"She went out, we went out, we came back, she didn't. We don't know."

Muffin jumps as he spies a cat in the window. "The c-c-cats are back!" he calls out.

"Would you shut up?" The drunk puts his hand over the mouthpiece as he shouts at Muffin, but his voice is still loud in the engineer's ears.

"Y-y-you sh-shut up!" The boy marches over to the drunk, knocks the phone from his hand. Steps back, takes a deep breath.

"I'm on the phone, you git!"

"Hey!" The engineer is yelling into her end of the line, but no one is listening. Clearly, she has been forgotten and she's about to hang up when

BAM!

The drunk and the boy stop their shoving and turn to the door.

"Oh, don't stop on my account." The silky, fingernail-polishing voice brings shredded suits and shiny shoes to the front of her mind and she freezes. The phone is glued to her ear.

"You!" The drunk almost spits out the word.

"Yes, me." His suit this time is pristine. No cats pissing on him today.

"H-h-h-how d-did you get p-past the c-cats?" Muffin reaches to the drunk for support, but the drunk pushes his anxious hand away.

A carefully casual shrug. One hand holds up an unconscious

or dead cat and he grins. "It seems that I have gotten stronger." He tosses the limp animal to the floor with a sneer. "Distressing, I suppose. Maybe you should rest for a while." Looking up suddenly to meet Muffin's eyes and Muffin is down for the count.

The engineer hears the heavy thud of the boy landing next to the phone receiver on the floor. Casts a mute glance of terror at the driver outside the booth.

Who is nodding authoritatively to himself, having just decided that they'll have to buy a map to find their way back to the city, and is looking back at his lover to see if she's done yet and seeing fear instead of resolution on her face. He yanks open the door and she thrusts the receiver to his ear.

"Well, at least you've done me one favour. Don't know how much more of that kid I could have taken." The drunk is trying out real courage for once, but finding it less effective than the kind he gets from the bottle. "What do you want? Did you not already take all that's worth taking?"

The man in the suit drags his index finger along the edge of the counter as he moves leisurely toward the drunk. "Yes, yes, I did. In fact, I may have taken more than you're aware."

Edging backwards as the man in the suit inches forward. If he can send a person to sleep with a look, the drunk is very much not interested in a touch. "Did you? And what might that be?"

He stops his advance abruptly, slips a manicured hand into the inside pocket of his suit jacket. The drunk hears the slight rustle of the fabric as an envelope is pulled out and waved in front of his eyes. "This contains all the answers you need." Places it flat on the counter, slips his hand into his pants pocket, leans back a little. "You may want to have your errant crew members return as soon as possible. What needs to be done is not in Kamakura." The right side of his mouth reaches up, but doesn't make anything like a smile. "So let's—"

And he's stumbling backwards with a new screaming fur hat.

And another. And another. Until the drunk recovers enough to realize that the fur hats are cats. Screaming as if they're birthing babies and flying in from the door, the windows, even down the hall behind him and the drunk wonders who left the windows in the bedrooms open, feels his heart clench at the thought that maybe no one did and the cats just got it open on their own.

The man in the suit loses his footing under the barrage of cats and falls backwards to the floor. The cats quickly cover him, removing him from the drunk's sight entirely. The drunk who can't seem to get his mouth to close.

Muffin pushes himself up on his elbows, rubs his head with one hand, which falls back down as the squirming mass of fur comes into his view. "What—" And he shoots up off the floor as a hand suddenly breaks out of the fur and stretches fumblingly to reach the edge of the entryway. The fingers clamp down and the whole mass inches forward. The giant hairball spurts forth three or four fully formed and separate cats who run out the door at a trot, seeming less urgent than when they came in. More cats break free as the hand pulls the mass closer and closer to the door and the form of the man underneath comes back into view.

Eventually, the head is free of all cat-hats. The mouth moves and they hear a weakened version of the nail-filing voice. "Would you be so kind as to tell them I'm leaving? They seem to need more than just my word."

Finally, the drunk is able to close his mouth. "I don't have any control over what they do. The cats do as they please." He grins a little.

"Yes, I suppose they do." What sounds like a sigh. His other hand is free of cats and so it joins the struggle, two hands working together to drag his cat-covered person forward. When his torso is out the door, his head on the concrete of the hall in front of their apartment, enough of the cats have jumped off him that he is able to pull himself up into a crouched stand. Blood drips from his pant legs and the end of his sharp nose. "If you would read the information I left for you—"

A cat sitting in the entryway, recently removed from the man and his suit, hisses loudly and he nods. "Yes, yes, I heard you before. I'm going. If you had just asked in the first place—"

The cat hisses again, joined by the two cats sitting on the drunk's shoes.

The man in the blood-stained suit raises his eyes. "The cats cannot be with you every moment."

The drunk feels that this is one of those times where it's beneath him to reply, courage from the cats is better than the natural kind or the kind from the bottle, and so he merely stares and waits for suit guy to shuffle away, dragging his left foot as if he no longer controls it. He hears suit guy's shuffle-drop down the steps and onto the street and only then does his breath jump out of his lungs. He falls back against the fridge behind him.

"W-w-w-w-what—what j-just happened?" The boy on the floor is still propped up on his elbows.

"Hey! Hey!" The driver is screaming into the receiver as loudly as his vocal cords are allowing, scaring the hell out of an elderly couple wearing red reindeer sweaters walking by with their tiny dog wearing a tiny matching sweater. Whether it's the yelling or the English that scares them, he'll never know.

Wide-eyed, the engineer is mute, willing the drunk or the captain or even the boy to just pick up the phone and say something.

Muffin hears the tinny voice, wonders if that's it, if his mind has finally snapped. But the tinny yelling persists and looking around, he finally spots the receiver on the floor. "Y-y-yes, we hear y-you. Stop y-y-yelling."

"He—Jesus fucking hell," the driver on the other end abruptly cuts off his shout. "What happened? Are you guys okay? Was it that guy in the suit?"

Before Muffin can get a word out of his clenched throat, the drunk has yet again snatched the receiver from his hand.

"Did you hear all that?"

"Yeah, what the hell happened?"

"That guy in the suit came back, cats jumped him. Really fucking incredible to see, actually." The drunk spies the envelope still on the counter. "Left a message of some sort for us as well."

"What message?" while the engineer tugs on his sleeve with a pleading look. Are they okay? she mouths and he nods briefly.

Tearing it open, scanning it intently. An involuntary "Christ!" escapes his lips.

"What? What does it say?" Why aren't they there? An hour's drive at the least! They're no good here.

"That bastard's got the captain!" More intent on the letter now, trying to find the hidden details, the clues that will get them their captain back. "Says we've got to do this job if we want her back."

Muffin peers over his shoulder, reads the fine print. Grabs the phone back from the drunk. "Y-y-you guys have to get b-back here right away. It s-says that if we d-don't blow up some p-place tomorrow night, he'll kill the c-c-c-captain!"

"We're on our way." The driver slams the phone down and looks up to the questions on the engineer's face. "Yes, it's that suit guy. And he's got the captain. We've got to get back."

Her hand flies to her mouth to cover her gasp. "Captain!"

And then they are pounding the pavement back to the car, slipping behind the wheel and squealing onto the street, but not fast enough. But too fast when the driver realizes he has no idea where Tokyo is in relation to here.

"Read it again," the engineer insists, pushing her palms flat against the kitchen table.

The drunk sighs, rolls those rollable eyes. "We've read it thirty thousand times already. We know what it says."

"Read it again," she growls through clenched teeth and he lets his eyes roll back to the front of his head, gives in.

"Fine. It says,

'Pirates. I don't have no time for fancy talk or the like." The drunk enunciates each word carefully. "I reckon if I had met you all some other time, I might even have liked you. You're a crazy bunch of kids. But well, that ain't the way it worked out, now is it?' What the hell is he even on about?" the drunk snarls. "Why do we have to read this again?"

The engineer just glares.

"Christ. Fine." The drunk drops his eyes again. "'Turns out your captain has got herself involved in some of my ventures. I don't quite know how, but I ain't one to look a gift horse in the mouth. She's been handling those books and well, I guess handling you and that's enough for my own purposes. Seems like she is a lady with direction.'" The drunk pauses to take a sip of the beer in front of him. "'To keep things on track, I'll be needing you all to turn up tomorrow morning at exactly eleven o'clock. If you just do as you're told, we won't have no more trouble.' And then it's just an address." He flings the letter down on the table. "Is that enough or shall I make my throat bleed for you, pet?"

"Shut up before I rip your tongue out, you drunk fucker."

The three men jerk their heads back in surprise. The drunk even snorts a little beer up his nose and begins coughing violently. Muffin automatically reaches over and pounds his back, without taking his eyes off the tiny cursing engineer.

"We don't have time for your goddamned attitude. We need to find the captain and you're not helping." She snatches the letter from where it came to rest. "We need to find this address tonight. We need to scope it out and see what the hell we can do tomorrow when we're supposed to meet this fucker."

Muffin raises a timid hand acknowledged by the angry engineer. "B-b-but if we just do what he says, we'll get the c-captain back."

Now all eyes are boring through him.

"You really think that we'll get the captain back if we do the job?" the drunk snorts. "Not bloody likely. They're not going to give her back."

"B-but why not?"

The engineer pushes down on the table with her palms, leans forward as far as she can. "He or they or whoever are clearly insane, making us blow up the Honda building and then some old lady shop? I mean, if this is the guy we're doing jobs for, he's nuts. Have you seen the look on the captain's face when she talks about him? Crazy people never do what they say. We have to rescue her."

"You certainly do."

And for the second time that evening, Muffin wonders if he has finally lost it. But when he pulls his eyes off of the engineer and whips around in his seat, he finds that no, that voice really did come from someone who is not a pirate. A pink-haired someone with red claws.

Who is smirking. "You all can close your mouths now."

"Goddammit. Why can't just one thing make sense?" The drunk drinks deep and wonders if he ignores her, she'll just go away.

She laughs. "Look, I'm not going anywhere. And we got problems. Your captain getting snatched was not part of the plan. We have to get her back. Now."

Huh. That's weird, the driver tells himself before he opens his mouth. "What plan?"

She runs her claw-nails through her tangled pink hair, hoists herself up onto the counter. "That's not really the issue now. There are bigger problems on your plate. Like your captain being not here. Without your captain, you can't help me." Sends those big green eyes back in her head. "And damn, do I ever need your help. All my plans just get shot to shit every time I turn around. Swear I'm going to kill that kid if I get my hands on him. I totally know he started all this. He's always fucking with my shit." Snapping her gum furiously.

The driver crosses his arms loosely over his chest. "What do you know about the captain?"

"I know that the alcoholic there is right; you won't be getting her back by just doing the job."

"S-s-so we shouldn't g-go tomorrow?" Muffin is less intimidated by the pink-haired creature than the man in the suit, even if she does have those claws that could slit his throat before he was done blinking.

"No. No." Frowning, she hops off the counter and starts pacing. "If you don't go, she's gone for sure. You won't be able to find her."

"How do you know?" The engineer braces herself to defend her intellect.

A dismissive wave of the claws. "Trust me. If I can't find her, you can't." Reaching the fridge, she turns and heads back to the entryway. Brings a lacquered nail to her mouth, runs it along her red-lipsticked lips. "You'll have to go. And don't bother staking it out or anything like that. She's nowhere near there. None of them are that stupid." The cracking of her gum being pulled about in and out of her mouth fills the room. "You'll have to do the job so I can find her. There'll be too much going on; he'll have to let his guard down."

The driver gives his head a little shake. "What? His guard? How are you going to find her? You'll just know?"

Stops pacing suddenly, looks up, puzzled. "Well, yeah. What did you think?"

Her nonchalance silences him.

The drunk stares intently at the can in his hand, counts back on his fingers. No, before this one, he definitely only had one drink. "So we do the job and you find the captain? Is that what you're proposing?"

Beams of sunlight busting out of her mouth, slipping past crooked eye teeth. "Finally, someone gets it." The other three pirates turn their eyes to the drunk with scrunched-up faces, cocking their heads from side to side. Maybe he is used to rational conversation with hallucinations. "You have to follow what the letter says. Exactly. Don't even give a hint that you are thinking of anything other than getting your captain back by doing what he says. You have no idea what these guys can do to you. They shouldn't even be doing this now, damn them. Things have gotten out of control. I just know it's that kid. I'm totally going to kill him." Presses a hand to her forehead, furrowed eyebrows. "I'll let you know when I've found her. You'll have to get her out. I can't interfere."

The driver brings a hand to each temple and starts rubbing. "But aren't you interfering by talking to us?" Even though he has no idea what she could be interfering in. Or who this 'kid' is.

She giggles. Twists one of the heavy-looking hoops hanging from her ears. "No. I can't interfere physically. Talking's fine. I mean, who's gonna know, right?"

The drunk squints his eyes to get a better look at her. Is he drunk or is she being barbecued? It's like the kitchen floor turned into pavement on a hot summer day. "Can't like really can't? Physically impossible kind of can't?"

More gum snapping, hand in hair, smoothing, patting, arranging. And then the hand is in front of the drunk, offering. "Keep this with you." The barbecue heat lines get wavier.

They all drop their eyes to the tiny object in the palm of the drunk's hand. It looks like a pocket watch, eighteenth-century style. When they raise the inevitable questioning eyes, they raise them to thin air.

"What the hell?" The drunk jumps up from his seat, stomps over to the fridge, the counter. "Where the hell did she go?" Whirling to face his comrades. "She was here, yeah? One about this high, pink hair, long claws for nails, ugly green shirt?"

The driver nods slowly. "She was here. Or we're all hallucinating." Meets the engineer's eyes over the table.

"Huh, that's weird," she forces herself to say. Waits. "It's not working."

Muffin's eyes dart back and forth between them. "Huh? W-what are you talking about?" It's probably about sex. When lovers talk, it's almost always about sex. "Is it related to s-s-s-sex?"

"Shut up." The driver's tone stays even, laidback. "So what do we do?"

"I still say we go check out the address in the letter." The engineer is firm. "We need to know what we're up against."

The drunk slams his hands down on the table. "NO!" he roars and his crew members almost fall off their chairs. "That little pink-haired one said we cannot do anything that might make that fellow who's got our captain think that we are doing anything but what he says. If we go tonight, we'll only be making things worse!"

The driver uncrosses his arms, recrosses them in the other direction, leans back in his chair. "So you say we should totally go with that girl? We don't even know if she's real. We could just be having a group hallucination."

"What I know is that things have just gotten stranger and stranger since we accepted that Honda job and strange follows strange. Doing things regular'll not get us out of this." The drunk slumps down in his chair, as if exhausted by that leap of deduction. "This girl makes no sense. The cats make no sense, but they saved us tonight." He raises his eyes to Muffin for confirmation, who is nodding slowly. "So I say our best chance is doing what she says. Not likely we'll find the captain on our own."

Muffin's nods continue. "I-I-it's true. Tokyo's so big. You c-can't even find a restaurant without a map. I've lived here all my l-life and I didn't even know this neighbourhood existed until I rented the apartment here."

The engineer props her elbows on the fake maple table, clutches her head in her hands. "But none of this makes any sense."

The driver shrugs, his chair creaking as he tilts it back. "Things haven't been making sense for a while. I agree with the wino here. Let's do what she says, see what happens. We don't really have a lot of choices in any case."

"We could at least go and see this place, maybe set up some kind of ambush or something. Why are you all so willing to surrender the captain to a pink-haired hallucination?" The engineer curses their non-science minds. "Following the nonsensical because things are nonsensical is not a plan."

The driver gets up, walks around the table to rest his hands on her shoulders. "Do you really think we could ambush that guy in the suit?"

She holds her tongue, stares at the table with hands clenched into fists against the sides of her head.

"That's it!" The drunk hoists himself out of his chair, heads for the room with the television. "Who's willing to play celebrities-eating drinking games?"

Muffin follows the drunk out of the room. "Ooh, m-me! Me! Every time someone s-says 'delicious', you have to drink!"

Hello Kitty is screaming at them to wake up. "Good morning! Wake up! Hey! Wake up!" she shouts in Japanese from the bedside table until the driver hits the flower on her head, knocking her off the table, but shutting her up.

Sitting up and rubbing his eyes. "Tell me again, why do you like that alarm?"

The engineer next to him groans. "Might as well wake up cute. Better than the stupid radio." Rolls over, raises an eyelid. "Time is it?"

"Nine. We've got to get ourselves together if we're gonna make it by eleven."

She props herself up on her elbows. "And then what?"

He stands, pulls on a T-shirt. "Look, you were out-voted last night. Don't start. We go, we follow instructions, we see what happens and take whatever chance we get to save the captain." Without waiting for her reply, he heads down the hall to the kitchen.

Congregating in the room where food is occasionally prepared, the pirates grab their bags, complete with black explosion gear, not knowing what that guy in the suit will be asking from them, and jump in the car.

The address in the letter is not far and they arrive early. Too little traffic, too few problems.

"So now what?" the engineer grumbles. "This is you guys's plan."

"We wait." The tone of the driver's voice slams her grumbling to the floor.

Eyes avoiding eyes and then knocking at the window sets them all bouncing in their seats.

The driver is the first to recover. "What are you doing here?" as he rolls his window down.

"Like, uh, man. Totally uh crazy like you're here, I'm here. Man." The boy with the asymmetric hair leans down to meet the driver's eyes. Lets his gaze drift around the car. "Oh uh, like hey pirates."

Muffin flinches visibly.

The drunk punches him hard in the arm. "What the hell is the matter with you? He's not done anything. Just said hello." Turns to New Wave. "Hello. What can we do for you today?"

New Wave's dark brows pull together. "Huh? Like do for me? Uh no man, I'm here for you know."

All eyes in the car are rolling rolling rolling, but it's the driver who voices it. "Do what? Why are you here?"

A shake of the head that sends the hair shimmying. "Yeah, uh, right. Got some uh crazy note you know. Like man. Can't figure it out, right? And uh, you know, thought like shoe guy might be uh paying, right? 'Cause man, I am like uh broke. Check it out." And he passes an envelope through the open window to the driver. "Says like come here, man. And uh like something about uh, not being you know late or what. Man, that guy is nuts. Letters." He snorts his disdain. "You know. Like who doesn't have uh email or what?" Looks around the car for agreement.

"I d-don't." The boy who spent too much time learning ancient Chinese characters and not enough time interacting with other humans.

They all turn to stare at him.

"W-what? I really don't."

"Not even on your mobile?" The drunk has at least five different email addresses and there are several he's sure he's forgotten.

"No, I d-don't have a mobile."

New Wave nods understandingly. "See, yeah, like no mobile, no mail. Makes uh sense, right. But man, I uh seen this guy with a you know mobile phone and uh you know he's no Luddite." Shifty glances from side to side. "It is him, right? Like the note you know not signed or what, but uh, who else, right?"

The engineer leans forward to peer past the driver. "Do you even know what a Luddite is?"

Shoulders raised high. "Some uh crazy guy with no mobile, right." Smiles triumphant. "Hey, like did we have a you know discussion or something just uh now?" He seems about to pat himself on the back when the driver intervenes.

"So you just got this note in the mail?"

Slow, pensive nods. A cigarette appears from nowhere and he inhales deeply. "Like, yeah, man. Just show up at this address you know. Something'll happen, right? Right." Jerks his head up, hits it on the frame of the car window. Rubs it with the cigarette hand. "Ow. Man."

"So there was nothing else?" The engineer persists.

The boy reading the note in the backseat holds up a slow-down hand. "W-whoa, hey. This n-n-note is for us!"

All heads spin in his direction.

"For uh you? Like you pirates?"

Muffin is firm in his discovery. He's spent years of his life analyzing ambiguous texts, he knows how to read between the lines. And there aren't even many lines to read between here. "Yeah. I-it says for him—" Eyes in the general direction of the driver's window where the boy with the asymmetrical hair is leaning in. "—but there's a s-second address here. And a time."

New Wave's eyebrows skyrocket off his head. "No way!" Drags deeply off his cigarette. "Maaaaan." Nods as if to reassure himself, slowly slowly.

Muffin casts skeptical eyes at the smoker. "But it's n-not even hidden. It's right here under the part telling you to c-come here." Holding the note up and pointing.

New Wave leans in, squints at the paper, pulls his head out of the window, leans back, inhales off the cig, exhales. Rocks back and forth on his heels. Finally sticking his head back through the window. "No way, man. Like, I uh read it uh before, you know, and that address was like not uh you know."

The driver looks at the paper, sees the address and realizes that he does know what 'uh you know' means. Wonders if understanding New Wave means he'll slowly lose his mental capacity from now on, until he is reduced to talking in right's and you know's.

"So what? We're just supposed to show up at that address?" The engineer storms around the kitchen. "And then what?" When no answers are forthcoming, she throws herself into a chair that groans at the unexpected shock. "And then what? C'mon, I'm asking here!"

The driver shrugs. "We see what happens."

An inverted snort of disgust as she leaps to her feet again. "That's a plan? How did we ever manage out at sea? I don't recall ever 'showing up' at another boat and 'seeing what happens'. We have plans, we're pirates!" Back to pacing furiously.

The driver takes a deep breath. "This is not the same as seafaring theft. The captain is at stake, we're hallucinating boats and pink-haired girls, nothing is the way it should be."

"Goddammit!" Slamming her small fists down on the table abruptly.

Making Muffin jump sky-high. When he gets his heart beating at a normal rate again, "I-I-I say, we go with all our gear, d-dressed and ready for a job. I think there'll be s-something. It's in the evening and that's the b-best time for c-criminal behaviour."

The drunk narrows his eyes at the boy. "I thought I told you to quit with the movie talk."

"B-but what else am I supposed to call it? Stealing is c-criminal behaviour, isn't it?"

The drunk shakes his empty can in response. "Could use another."

Muffin bites his tongue, takes a moment to breathe in and breathe out several times. "Anyone else?"

The driver raises his sleepy eyes. "Yeah, I could have another. Thanks."

Muffin opens his eyes wide at the unexpected word of gratitude. When was the last time anyone thanked him? Humming slightly, he moves towards the refrigerator.

When he pulls his head and three beers out, he sees legs dangling from the counter next to his head. Raising his eyes without raising the skull that holds them, he is surprisingly unsurprised to find the girl with the pink hair smiling down at him.

She waggles her red-tipped fingers in greeting. "Hey."

Righting himself slowly, casting a glance over his shoulder to see if anyone else sees. At the table behind him, discussions are heated and the engineer is refusing to give in to the madness. But no one is noticing that the madness has arrived. Turning back and she's still there.

"Yeah. No, I'm not going anywhere." Snaps her gum, answers his questions. "And no, they don't see me."

"S-s-so I see you." Tentative hand raised to his nose to indicate himself. "But they d-d-don't?" Slow as if letting words out of his mouth with less speed will make anything less confusing.

"Wow, you catch on quick. Look, this is no time for debate." She frowns, red lips pulled down sharply at the corner. Lifts her right thigh off the counter, pulls pieces of potato chip out of her skin. "You people need to clean up after yourselves. Damn." Brushing the rest of the crumbs of the counter before setting her muscular leg back down on the aqua linoleum. "Dollface the Science Queen there is really cramping my style and there is stuff that's got to be said. So listen up, scaredy cat."

"H-h-hey!"

"Just shut up, okay? When you go tonight, look left."

"L-l-l-left?"

More eyeball rolling. "Just do it. Look left. It'll—"

"Boy!" The drunk's sharp voice cuts through him and he whirls around.

"W-w-what?"

"Where is my beer? What is so fascinating about that counter?"

He turns to look again at said counter and it's empty. Great. Now he'll have to figure it out. What does he have to do with left? Reluctantly, he returns to the table with drinks warmed from being under his arms too long.

"Didn't she give you that watch?" the driver says suddenly, turning to the drunk

"It's right here." He pulls it out of his pocket and pushes it forward on the table. "So? It doesn't even tell the right time. Piece of crap."

The driver takes it, peers intently at the face. Not only does it not have the right time, it's not even working. The hands rest motionless on— "Hey! Isn't this the time in the letter?"

All heads leaning in, staring.

"So what?" The engineer is the first to thump back down into her chair. "So it stopped at one of the 12 possible hours. What does that prove?"

Shrugging. "Seems like a weird coincidence. And since all we have to go on is weird coincidences..."

The drunk drains the last of his beer, slams the can onto the table. "I said it before. We have to follow strange to find the captain. The watch being stopped at the same time as the letter is another strange thing to follow."

"B-but how can we follow a s-stopped watch?"

"It means that the letter is not a load of crap." The drunk is firm. "So we do what it says."

"B-but it doesn't say to d-d-do anything."

"Would you quit your whinging?" the drunk snaps. "There's an address. What do you suppose that's about?"

"So it's settled." The driver pushes his chair back from the table, stands up. "We go. Let's get our shit together."

"Why is it settled? Did we vote? This is insane! You're all insane! Showing up somewhere is not a plan!"

"So we vote. All in favour?" Three hands in the air. The driver turns to his little lover. "We voted. We go."

A note of exasperation leaps from her throat and she follows it out of the room with heavy feet.

"Princess is getting a little carried away," the drunk notes idly.

The driver stares down the empty hallway. "She'll get over it. But if we're going to be there in time, we need to leave soon."

The engineer comes out of hiding with a pack on her back when they are tugging shoes onto their feet. "I don't want to see the captain get hurt through your incompetence," she tells their looks of surprise.

"He—" Muffin starts to protest but the driver cuts him off with an elbow to the ribs.

Walking out to the car, it's more than the pain in his side that makes the boy moan. "W-what are they d-d-doing there?"

One of the cats on top of the car yowls loudly, causing them to all take a step back.

"Maybe they want to come with?" The drunk offers, starting to count them all with his slight nods of his head and quickly giving up faced with the futility of counting a mass of moving felines.

Muffin sinks to his knees. "N-n-no, no, no. Th-they c-c-can't come. I c-c-can't be in a car with them."

The driver yanks him up roughly by the elbow. "Jesus christ, get a hold of yourself. They're just cats." And he moves forward deliberately.

As they approach, the cats jump off the car in twos and threes until there is just the one sitting on the hood. It's the calico that the driver has been friendly with. He smiles when he recognizes her and lets go of the boy's elbow to reach forward and scratch her behind the ears. "What are you doing here?" he coos.

She meows in response, then hops down and nonchalantly makes her way to the driver's side door. Sits down, waits.

The engineer refrains from rubbing her eyes. "What is going on here?"

The drunk is taking it all in stride. "Strange follows strange, I'm telling you." And he opens the back door, slides in. "Come on, we've not got all day."

When the driver opens his door, the calico leaps up gracefully onto his seat, steps past to the gearshift, sits, casts waiting eyes at the driver. He shakes his head a little, says, "Huh, that's weird" to himself a couple times and follows her in.

During the drive, Muffin shrinks back in the corner of his seat, maintaining maximal distance between him and the cat, who turns her head to eye him intently every so often. Eye him like he might be lunch. "Why d-d-d-does it have to b-be in the c-c-car?"

"Do you want me to tie it to the roof?" The driver glances up at the boy's image in the rearview mirror. "It's not like I could have stopped her anyway. She just got in. And you saw all of the cats

— 213 —

before. You think they would have been okay with us tying their leader to the roof?"

"Their leader?" The engineer is doubtful and possibly mocking.

"Well, she does seem to be in charge."

"What does that even mean?" She seems about to fly off in a rage again, so the driver turns placating.

"Look, I don't know. I'm just telling myself stories to make something make sense, okay?" The sun is falling below the horizon, so he turns on the headlights, glances at the clock on the dash. Almost time, almost there.

The cat rubs her head against his arm, purrs reassuringly.

"Hey!" The engineer cries out abruptly. "Isn't that Corduroy Jacket?"

The driver turns his head in the direction of her outstretched finger. "Crap! Is it?" He slows the car to get a better look at the couple walking down the street.

Muffin peers out the window. "S-so that's who you had to b-b-blow up yesterday?"

Two heads nodding in the front.

"D-do you think this is where they live?" he wonders aloud.

Miss Dynamite whirls to face the driver. "We're almost there, aren't we?"

As he nods, it dawns on him where she's going with this. "Are we here to finish the job?"

The drunk pulls himself forward, almost squashes the cat with a carelessly placed hand, peers around the headrest. "You think we're here to kill the one in the jacket?"

"No way! It's too much! Why would we be told not to kill yesterday only to kill today? It doesn't make any sense." The engineer tries to keep the couple in view, but the car takes them out of her sight too quickly.

The drunk leans back again, folds his arms across his chest. "None of this makes any sense. Or need I point to the cat sitting next to you there?"

She glances down at the calico, who returns the look, purrs. She turns away. Hitting the drunk won't make this stop.

The driver pulls up to the curb, turns the car off. "We're here."

"Wh-where is here?"

The drunk scowls. "Do you not pay attention to anything? Where do you think we are?"

The engineer glares at each of them in turn. "So now what? This is your plan."

"Yeah, n-n-now what?" Muffin seconds the explosives expert.

"Get out of the car?" the drunk suggests.

"Wait here until someone comes?" from the driver.

"Well, we can't do both." She folds her arms, stares out the window.

"Well, m-maybe t-two of us can wait here and two c-can get out?" Muffin tries to bring the group together.

The drunk's forehead is deepening into a scowl again when the calico starts meowing at the driver. "I think..." He pauses for effect, for breath. "I think she's talking to you."

The cat walks gently over the driver's lap to the door, raises a multi-coloured paw. Looks pleadingly at the driver. Opens her mouth to meow, but no sound comes out, just meow-shaped air.

"The door? Uh, yeah, here you go." And he pulls the handle, lets the door swing open.

She jumps down to the ground. Turns her head to look at him over her shoulder.

Forehead ridges lining up, he turns to the others. "It seems like she wants us to get out."

"We're following hallucinations and cats?" Another freakout seems imminent.

"Yeah, come on." As the drunk pushes his own door open.

"M-m-m-maybe someone should w-wait here j-just in case the c-cat's wrong?"

"Get out of the car." The drunk turns narrowed eyes on the boy.

The engineer reluctantly drags herself out of the car, cursing under her breath.

The cat leads them across the street to a cluster of trees in a small park and stops. Winds herself around the driver's legs, purring.

"S-s-s-so we're here?" Muffin doubts the cat's leadership abilities.

"Ah, good. I see you got my message." The silky voice slips out from behind a slender white birch tree, a tree hardly wide enough for a child to hide behind, and then the owner follows it.

"Where's the captain?" Snarling, the engineer would throw herself at him, but the driver holds her back.

"Now, now. Let's calm down, shall we?" He pushes his hands into his pockets, rocks back on his heels. "I see you've brought a friend." He nods his greeting to the cat.

Who fluffs up and hisses.

"You know, we can offer you much more than the girl can."

The calico leaps forward and attaches herself to his leg. Reaches up with one paw and drags it down the leg above her head. The pant leg shreds to reveal strips of a nearly hairless upper thigh that quickly starts to bleed.

He winces. "Fine, fine. I was merely making an innocent remark."

The cat hisses again and drops to the ground. Arches her back as she returns to the driver's feet. Who can only look down at her, stunned.

The engineer ignores the cat. "What do you want?"

His party-style fake laugh sends shivers down her spine. "Oh, no, no. It's not what I want. I am but a messenger."

"So what's the message?" The driver gets his voice back.

In his hands, two bulging shopping bags. Muffin tells himself that they were there before only he didn't notice them because he was too busy looking at the cat.

"This is for you." When no one steps forward, he heaves a sigh. "Just take the bags. Your friend there," Indicates the calico with his eyes. "will see that I behave myself."

The driver takes a hesitant step forward, reaches out to take the bags. Steps back. Peers in. "What's all this for?"

"Do you see the building across the street?" He points to the five-story apartment building behind their car. "On the third floor, the middle window?"

The engineer has to squint as she counts windows. Maybe she needs glasses.

"That." A finger indicating the bags and presumably their contents. "Needs to go in there."

Taking a look in one of the bags in the driver's hands, the engineer is unsurprised to find the tools of her trade. "Why can't you do this? You're going to kill the kid in the corduroy jacket, right? Why do you need us?"

He makes tut-tut noises with his tongue. "There'll be no killing. What a terrible thing to say! When it comes to changing directions, everything must be done in the proper way, you see. Killing the 'kid' now would be pointless."

Muffin starts to swoon, sees stars, pinches himself to push the stars away. "I-I-I'm sorry, d-d-d-did you just say 'ch-change directions'?"

A quick nod. "Yes, of course. What else would we be doing this for?"

"Uh..." The drunk wants to say something, but nothing comes out. Finally, "Is that even possible?"

He smirks. "Ask your feline friend here."

The cat narrows her eyes, growls.

The man in the suit puts up a defensive hand. "Please, no need to get violent." His eyes dart from side to side and he slips the hand back in his pocket. "I see that you'd prefer to wrap things up

— 217 —

quickly."

The pirates follow his darting eyes and see small shadows moving on the edges of the thicket. Two cats step forward out of the gloom.

The drunk shifts his gaze back to the man in the suit. "So we go in, blow it up, get the captain back?"

"All things in due time," he responds smoothly. "We only need you to place it. The explosion will be handled by someone else. While you are in there, you'll see a set of headphones belonging to a certain gentleman caller."

"That g-g-guy we saw with C-Corduroy Jacket?" Muffin steps closer to the drunk as more cats come forward to surround them.

"Such a perceptive young man, aren't you?" The man in the suit turns his smooth smile on the boy, who flinches into the drunk, who pushes him away. "Yes, the young man you saw walking down the street arm in arm with his lover. He has left his headphones in that apartment and it would please us greatly if you would bring them out."

"Why don't you just go and get them yourself?" The driver is still clutching the engineer, both to restrain her and to hold himself up. Somewhere in this conversation, his last straw was broken.

Smooth chuckles. "Wouldn't it be so much easier if I could? No, I'm afraid I can't interfere."

"Déjà vu," the drunk mutters.

"But aren't you interfering now?" The driver's jaw is clenched more tightly than his hands on the engineer's shoulders.

"Talking's not interfering," he informs them in clipped tones. "Now, you really must be on your way or you'll be late. I'll be waiting here for you." And he slips behind the trees again, as if he was never there.

The trees are not wide enough to hide a man in a suit, Muffin says to himself and forces himself to unsay it. Pink-haired girls are talking to him, cats are everywhere, the trees are wide enough for a man in a suit.

The driver looks at each of them. "So?"

The drunk grabs the bulging plastic bags off the ground. "Let's get the captain back."

Inside the building, the engineer is unsure. "So you think it matters how the explosives are laid?"

The drunk shrugs. "Nothing was said. Put 'em where you'd like." Quick glances to his left, then right. "Should we be coming in through the front door like this?"

The driver fumbles with the cheap doorknob. "Do you think we'd be less noticeable climbing up the building to go in through the window?" He gives the knob a hard pull to his right and it comes free, screws tumbling to the concrete floor.

"W-we'll just say we're friends," Muffin suggest brightly. "We c-could say that Corduroy Jacket's having a party and we're g-guests."

The driver pushes the door in. " Let's go."

As Muffin crosses the threshold, he remembers, 'Look left.' But when he turns his head, all he sees are coats hanging from the wall. Is he meant to get a new jacket?

"Help me, will you?" Miss Dynamite is looking straight at him.

"S-sure. What do you need me to do?"

"What do you suppose these headphones look like?" The drunk steps over a damp towel on the living room floor.

The driver shrugs, lets his eyelids sink a little lower. "Regular, I guess."

"But if we take the wrong ones? What if they both have headphones?"

"We take them both. Just find them already." The driver heads down the hall to the bedroom.

Following the engineer's orders and Muffin is careful to keep his head turned mostly to the left, except when he really has to turn it to the right because there's no other way. But he sees nothing that's worthy of being told to look at it. There is an old banana skin under the sofa and he wonders if he should leave a note or if maybe that's what he's meant to see. Dismisses both ideas. As he's standing up, ready to dust off his hands in a satisfied fashion after a job well done, he spots a box on the table to his left. To his left. And it's not filled with banana skins or tissues, but kyohon. This is a left-side item worth picking up, he tells himself. So he does, slips it in his backpack when the engineer leaves the room to find the drunk and the driver. Waits for her to come back. Suddenly connecting kyohon with their earlier adventures. Is he stealing back what was stolen from them?

His errant crew members return triumphant, headphones in the hand of the drunk.

"Got 'em!"

"Are you s-sure those belong to the 'gentleman caller'?" Muffin is quick to ask.

"There's not any other headphones in the whole flat. These must be his."

"You guys got everything set in here?" The driver looks down at the engineer.

She nods. "Let's get out of here."

Somehow, it takes away the thrill of the job to walk out through the front door.

"Now, what about the captain?" the drunk asks as he hands the headphones to the man in the suit.

Turning them over in his hands, focused. "I'm sorry?" He lifts his head suddenly. "What was that?"

"The captain, you bastard." The engineer is ready to leap for his throat again. "Where's the captain?"

The headphones are gone from his hands. "You'll see your captain when the job is done," he says crisply.

"But the job is done!" The engineer stamps a small foot for emphasis.

He casts his eyes at the apartment across the street. "It looks quite whole to me."

"B-b-b-but you said... y-you-" Muffin's face starts to crumple and he turns his face up to the sky.

"Yes, yes, I said." A dismissive hand in front of Muffin's nose. "But until it's finished, your captain stays with us. And now," He glances down at the gold brand-name watch adorning his wrist. "I do believe it's time for you to be on your way." Making shoo-shoo gestures with his hand and the driver has to restrain the engineer again.

"Huh, that's weird." He leans down to put the words in her ear, squeezes her shoulders and then relaxes his grip.

With inquisitive eyes, she turns her head to look up at him, nods slightly.

"So you'll find us?" He directs this to the salaryman.

Impatient nodding, more shoo-shooing. "Yes, go. And take your friends with you." The man in the suit looks uncomfortable as he lets his eyes rest on the cats.

"Okay, then, great." The driver steers the engineer away, raises his lids to command the drunk and the boy with his eyes.

The boy who doesn't quite get it. "S-s-so what? We're j-j-just going to leave?"

The drunk who does. "Aye, that's what we're doing. We're going to go home and wait like the good pirates we are." Grabs Muffin's elbow, pulls. "Come along now."

Walking to the car and Muffin is crying out. "H-hey! There they are!" They all follow his hand flung out towards the end of the street. "The 'g-gentleman caller' looks c-crazy."

Disdain overtakes the engineer. "Can you please not say that?"

"Whatever. Get in the car." The driver is already looking away and unlocking the doors. "We have to get out of here." The calico jumps in first, takes her place behind the gearshift.

Muffin stares at the couple, wonders why their apartment is getting blown up, why the gentleman caller is moving like a robot, and then the drunk is yanking him by the elbow again.

"Would you just get in the car?"

And when he does, she's already sitting next to him. "You got it, great."

All heads are turning.

"What?" The driver's eyelids can't go much higher.

She gestures frantically and all he can see is a red blur pushing back and forth in front of his face. "Just go! Just go, don't stare at me. Christ, what the hell is wrong with you people? He'll see me for sure that way."

Starting the car as fast as he can, the tires squeal a little as he pulls away from the curb, cutting off a small, white car, whose driver shouts profanities after them.

Turning the corner and they feel rather than hear the explosion.

"So what—" the drunk starts and finds the pink-haired girl's hand clamped firmly over his mouth.

"Shh!" Eyes closed, eyebrows pushed up against each other. Red lips forming fast shapes.

The driver glances at the engineer, raises his own eyebrows, opens his mouth to speak.

"Got her!" And the heavily made-up eyelids fly open. She retracts her obstructive hand. Smiles sweetly. "Sorry, just needed some quiet there."

"G-g-got who? Where? W-what?" Muffin leans forward to rest his heavy head in his hands.

"Your captain. Turn left here."

The driver obeys with a hesitant glance in the rearview mirror.

"Hallo, honey," she coos as she leans forward to run her hand over the calico back on her perch behind the gearshift. The cat meows and purrs in response and the girl giggles and nods, possibly in agreement.

"Will you please tell us what the hell is going on?" The engineer's voice is flat and hard.

"We're saving the world." Dryly and with a theatrical wave of the hand. "Is that what you want to hear?"

Before the engineer can let her clenched fist fly, the driver steps in. "He said something about changing directions."

She snaps the ever-present gum. "Yeah, things are a little out of whack right now, thanks to that little bastard. Trying to get it back in order."

"What d-does that have to d-do with those p-people who own the apartment?" Muffin wonders.

"The little one—left here," Interrupting herself to lean forward and lay a hand on the driver's shoulder. "You're going to miss it."

"No, I'm not." Jerking the wheel abruptly, engendering angry honks from behind.

"So yeah, the little one is pretty much the key to the whole thing, so, you know." Leaning back, blowing a small bubble that pops as she drops her head against the headrest. Snaps her gum.

"Are we talking to that new wave kid again? 'You know' what?" The drunk runs his eyes up the pink-haired girl's bare legs to where they meet her short skirt. Tilts his head to one side and cranes his neck a little.

"That's the one I'd like to get my hands on. I don't know why he always thinks his stupid shit is so hilarious." Snap snap snap. "Okay, it's here. Stop here." Tapping the driver on the shoulder with the lacquered nails.

He pulls up to the curb in front of just another apartment building. Glancing around and seeing just another neighbourhood. Cuts the engine. "So now what?"

"We f-f-figure it out ourselves?" Muffin suggests timidly.

Engineer and driver whirling around and meeting eyes with the drunk and the boy. "What happened? Where is she?" the driver shouts.

Four shoulders rising together.

"I haven't any idea. She did that barbecue thing and then poof!"

The engineer slams her head back against the headrest. "I knew this was a stupid plan! I mean, it's not even a plan! Now what are we supposed to do? We're somewhere in some stupid place and the captain is probably a million miles from here!"

A placating hand on her leg. "Look, why would she drag us all the way out here unless this is where the captain is?"

She knocks the hand away. "Why wouldn't she? How can you trust a hallucination?"

"Hey! She's not a hallucination!" The drunk's eyes are still full of long legs.

"We're stopped in front of this building, right? Why don't we just go in and check it out?" The driver tries to prevent a return to the debate on the reality of the pink-haired girl.

Muffin is already pulling on his bravery boots and opening his door. "L-l-l-let's check it out."

The engineer is muttering under her breath about how "just check it out is not a plan at all," but the others ignore her, walk up to the door. Exchange raised eyebrows.

"So we just go in, yeah?"

"I g-guess that's the p-p-plan." Muffin's bravery boots are not of the best quality.

The driver nods in a guess-so way. "So we'll just open it and go inside." Lids lowered, hands in pockets, trying to be nonchalant.

The engineer stares at each of them in turn, disgusted and incredulous. "You pussies!" she spits out finally and grabs the door handle, turns it, pushes the door in.

The three men wince almost invisibly but she sees it. "How is that any of you are pirates?"

"Okay, we're pussies. Let's just go inside." The driver edges past her and in through the doorway.

"What the—" The drunk gapes.

"How c-c-can this place b-be in this p-place?" Muffin turns around in the cavernous hall. Squinting in the dim light for a better look at the walls or where the walls even are.

The engineer cannot stop herself from rubbing her eyes. But when she's done, the hall is as big as before and she can't see the ceiling no matter how she peers into the darkness above her head.

"Clearly, this is the place." The driver starts moving forward, almost trips over the cat at his feet. "Hey, I thought you were in the car." Scoops her up in his arms. "Come on. I don't want to lose you in here." Her chest vibrates against his wrists.

The other three follow him forward, the drunk still gaping, Muffin turning round and round to stare with doubting eyes.

"Hey! What's that?" the engineer says suddenly, stretching a finger forward.

"A f-fire?" Muffin scrunches his face up but it looks like when the pink-haired girl leaves. All wavy lines and it's hard to make out a shape.

"No, I think it's candles. Come on!" The drunk breaks into a run. His feet make no sound as they fall. The footsteps of his comrades also do not reach his ears.

Closer and they can all see that it's not candles but the captain wrapped in string after string of outdoor Christmas lights. The engineer opens her mouth to cry out, but before she can make a sound, the drunk's hand is tight against her lips, his eyes intent on her. Eyebrows raised in a way that can only mean shut the hell up.

When he lets go, she sees the man obscured in the gloom behind the captain's unconscious head. Glancing at her crewmates quickly.

The man leans forward, brings the plug-in at the end of the string of lights in his hand to meet the end of on a string hanging off the captain, shuffles to the side, begins slowly wrapping the new string around the captain's arm.

The driver sees his lips move and realizes that the flat monotone rumbling that he thought was some kind of electrical appliance is this man muttering-mumbling-chanting. The cat in his arms squirming suddenly, too energetic for him and she breaks free, jumps soundlessly into the shadows around them.

Is that a desk she's lying on? Muffin's eyes becomes slits on his face as he squints into the dim in front of him. Jumps out of his skin at the touch on his forearm.

The driver raises his eyebrows a little, gestures to the left where the man isn't, where the shadows are. And where Muffin is pretty sure he doesn't want to go. The dark is not really his thing.

But the driver's gentle touch on the forearm turns into a sharp elbow in the ribs and he reluctantly moves forward. The drunk and the engineer are on all fours and moving in the other direction, towards the man and the bottom of the desk. Muffin reflects on what the plan could be and hopes he doesn't pee his pants when it is put into action.

After a few steps, the driver grabs his shoulder and pushes him to the floor. When he looks up questioningly, the driver motions for him to keep moving. Rubs his head and hopes all this crawling around is going to help the captain.

When the driver steps forward, he notes the sudden sound of his footsteps with a "Huh. That's weird."

The man with the shiny lights filling his arms whirls around, faces the driver. "What are you doing here?"

His jaw hits the floor and for a second, he is completely unable to pick it up. "Me?" he pushes out finally. "What are you doing here?"

The old man the driver last saw shuffle-humming his way up the dock recovers faster, reflexes like lightening and the lights clatter to the floor, replaced by a small knife. Held over the captain's neck, the loose skin on the back of his hand grazing her cheek. "This ain't how it's meant to be done, but if I have to..." Trailing off with an ominously soft smile.

The driver throws his hands up. "Hey! Whoa! I'm just here! I'm not going to do anything crazy." As much a warning to the others as a reassurance to the old man.

"So what are you going to do?" Almost petulant, but the knife does not waver. He narrows his eyes, glares suspiciously. "How did you even get here?" Light bulbs shattering over his head. "She sent you, didn't she?"

"Look," Slowly lowering his hands. "I don't know who 'she' is. I just want the captain back. What do I have to do to get her back?" Casting his eyes about in the gloom for his crew members.

The old man leans forward a little and his free hand comes forward to smooth the captain's hair back from her slack face. "Oh, you don't get her back. You took my boat, my beautiful baby. You don't get both. One or t'other, you see. I need the boat or the girl. One or t'other."

"You can have the boat back." Spitting it out, desperate, eyes always on the knife. "We don't care, we just want the captain back."

Slow shakes of the head. "You kids always want to have your cake and eat it, too. No, no, too late for that. You made your choice." Pushes the blade harder against the captain's neck.

"Stop!" he shouts, taking a short step forward. "Please, don't hurt her. We didn't know it was a choice. Let us have her back, just take the boat."

He lifts the knife to wave it in front of his leathery face. "Oh, no. Don't get me wrong, I don't want to kill her. Just you need the way to change the directions, boy." Nods to himself. "Yep, gotta have the way."

"The way?"

He waves the knife-hand contemptuously. "Now, don't tell me you don't know what's goin' on. I know you know; she been talkin' to you."

"Look, I think you've got things wrong. We don't know what's going on. We just wanted to get a boat." Visitations from a cryptic pink-haired hallucination does not count as knowing what's going on.

The decaying man drags an intent finger along the captain's motionless side, slowly moving towards the driver, who looks away hurriedly when the extra skin on his hand droops and pulls against the desk under her. "In any case, I have some work to do." He looks up suddenly, meets the driver's hostile eyes. "If you don't mind." Flicks his eyes to the left.

And the driver goes flying, slamming into a wall he can't see.

Which is about all the engineer can take. "Aaaaah!" She throws herself at the little man's back, clutching tightly as her momentum pushes him forward.

Into the drunk and his waiting knee. Who only wishes he had a beer bottle to smash against the desk and make this a proper bar fight. But the bottle of rum Muffin brings down on the old man's head breaks nicely enough, he notes.

Clutching the broken bottle's neck, staring at the heap of loose skin on the floor, Muffin hyperventilates and longs for a brown paper bag to breathe into. The drunk claps him soundly on the back.

"Well done, pet." He lets the clapping hand rest on the boy's rigid shoulders. "He'll not wake up for a while."

"Move it!" the engineer hisses as she unplugs Christmas lights as fast as her hands can find the joins. "You saw what he did to my poor sleepy-eyed boy. Who knows when he'll wake up? He's probably not even human. Can't you see how his skin is falling off?"

The drunk removes his arm from the boy and frees the captain's left arm from the white lights, while the boy is frozen in position, breathing erratically and staring at the shadow pile of skin and clothes on the floor. If it moves, his heart will stop. Is it moving? It might be moving.

A hand on his shoulder and the bottle neck in his hand falls to the floor, clinking as it rolls away, as he swoons to the floor after it. The driver stares down at Muffin's unconscious form. Looks up at the drunk who is busy freeing a leg. "Did he just pass out?"

"Check if he's gone in his pants," the drunk advises sagely.

The engineer tosses the last of the lights to the floor, gets to work on the ropes holding the captain to the desk. "Are you okay? He threw you or whatever pretty hard."

The driver nods as he crouches down to pick up the boy, realizes she probably can't see his head moving in the gloom, darker now that the lights have gone out one string at a time. "Yeah, I'm fine. My head hurts, though, and I think I'm going to have some really big bruises." Thankfully, Muffin weighs next to nothing and the driver easily hoists him off the floor, supports him with an arm around his chest. "You got the captain?"

"Just about. Hey! Give me a hand, you bastard!"

The drunk doesn't look up from his pillaging of the desk. "We came all this way, following the strangeness. Maybe something to explain it is here." Grins, stands straight, triumphant with bottle in hand. "And if not, seems like Mr. Skin there likes more than a little tipple in the afternoon. Is this where you got the—Oh, he's still out?"

"Yeah, and getting heavy. C'mon, let's just go. We have to get out of here before he comes to."

"Someone has to help me, I can't hold her up by myself." The engineer tries valiantly to do so, but is being crushed under the taller and heavier captain.

The drunk empties drawers into his bag hurriedly. "Sort through it later, yeah?" Picks the captain up off the engineer. Peers down at the man on the floor. "Is he moving?"

The engineer follows his gaze. "Crap, I think he is. Come on!"

Moving as fast as they can towards the door, but the unconscious members of the group are really slowing their progress and none of them are exactly sure where the door is.

"Are we even going the right way?" the drunk asks.

The engineer glances about nervously, looking for a landmark, a footprint, anything and coming up with only more darkness. "We should have left some bread crumbs."

"Yep, should have." The creaky voice from behind freezes them to the spot.

The engineer moves her eyes as far to the side as she can. And he's pulling himself off the floor in the corner of her eye. Flowing upwards.

"Now don't think I can't see you in the dark just 'cause you ain't movin'." His amusement makes her sweat freeze. "I don't need light for nothing but making the way. And I believe I was not quite done, so I'll be needing that lovely lady there."

And the weight of the unconscious captain rises from the gaping drunk's shoulders and he reaches up to grab a leg, but catches nothing but air. "Ouch! Jesus christ!" He looks down to see the calico digging her claws into his leg below his pocket. As soon as his eyes land on her, she releases and raises the paw to the pocket itself, scratches at it a little and something solid bumps his leg.

The watch! He reaches in and pulls it out, stares at it expectantly.

Other than catching what little light there is in the room and reflecting it back into his eyes, it does nothing.

"Goddammit," he curses under his breath, moving his hand so the piece of crap stops blinding him.

And starts blinding the old man. "Aagh!" The captain falls to the floor with a thud.

"Ha!" the drunk cries triumphantly, turning and twisting the watch to catch as much light as possible. "Take that, you bastard!"

The engineer and the driver stare. "That's what the watch was for?" the driver says finally.

"Just get the captain!" Pleased with the blinding trick, but the drunk doesn't know how long it'll hold out. "And maybe poke him in the eye or something."

Shuddering at the thought of approaching that poorly disguised pile of skin, the engineer chooses the first option, rushes to where the captain fell from the air. "I still can't carry her!"

"Then drag her!" the driver snaps. When the boy draped over his shoulders wakes up, he will punch him in the face.

She hooks her arms under the captain's armpits and shuffle-steps backwards. "Sorry, captain," she grunts.

"You don't think it's that simple, do you?" The old man is standing above her suddenly and she gulps her breath back.

"Damn it!" the drunk cries, clenches the watch in his hand. "You stupid piece of crap!" he shouts at it and hurls it away.

Into the old man's head.

Who goes down.

"Huh." For a moment, he can only stare at the watch on the floor next to the old man's loose hand. "Didn't see that coming."

"Get him off!" the engineer is shrieking. "He fell on the captain! He's so gross!"

He moves to drag Mr. Skin off of the captain's legs. Flinches backwards and gags at the touch the man's bare arms. The loose skin that looks like skin does not feel like skin. It does not feel like anything the drunk has ever touched, but somehow makes him relive gagging on a mouth full of clammy pink molding material at the dentist.

With the engineer, he hoists the captain off the floor and they run lopsidedly forward, carrying her between them. "We've got to get out of here already. I've used all my luck for the rest of my life.

If he wakes up again, it's the end for us."

"But we still don't know how to get out of here," Miss Dynamite pants under her half of the captain.

The driver jerks his head to the right, indicating the calico at his feet. "We'll just follow the cat."

"Follow the cat? That is—"

Before she can shift into highly outraged mode, the drunk cuts her short. "You still think any of this can be explained by anything rational?" She snaps her mouth shut. "We follow the cat."

Who struts off into the darkness as if on cue and they hurry after her.

The darkness gets thicker and thicker and the cat disappears from sight. The drunk and the engineer shuffle along a metre or so behind the driver, but all he can hear is the soft padding of the cat in front, relies on his directional hearing to guide him forward.

And then the door jumps out of the black in front of him and he pushes it open eagerly.

Silence as they stumble out into the night and move towards the car. Inside and the driver pushes down hard on the gas pedal, hoping tonight is not a speed trap night. Muffin's head bangs against the window in the backseat every time they go over a bump, but no one bothers to rearrange the unconscious boy.

"Is the captain okay?" the driver asks finally, raising his eyes to the rearview mirror to look at the engineer, gently supporting their still slumbering leader.

"I don't know," she confesses helplessly. "I mean, her heart's beating and she's breathing, but she's not waking up. Shouldn't she be waking up?"

The drunk turns around in the passenger seat to reassure her with a knowing eyebrow waggle. "She's been drugged, yeah? Seems like the most likely thing. And some drugs take a while to wake up from."

"I thought you only drank." The driver takes his eyes off the road briefly to glance at the drunk.

"Aye. But drugs can be right handy for a pirate who needs to have a customs officer take a little holiday."

"Wh-whu?" Muffin's head twitches and eyelids flutter. Lightening bursting his skull open and his eyes fly all the way open. "Aaah! H-h-h-help!"

The drunk leans forward to introduce an open palm to the side of the boy's head. "Quiet, you! You're lucky to be here!"

"I think I speak for everyone when I say, fainting on the job is not cool." The driver eases the car around a corner and into their parking spot. Shuts the ignition off, turns to glare at the boy, arm hanging over his headrest. "Your ridiculous faint just about kept us there with Mr. Skin."

"F-f-f-fainting?" Since the beer bottle is gone from his hand and they are in a parked car, he realizes that he is missing a good portion of time. Which is explained by him fainting. "I f-f-fainted?" So much for being a pirate.

"The only reason we didn't leave you there is because you saved our asses with that bottle over the head." The driver slams his door shut. Walking up to the apartment, "But that's it. The next time you pass out or do anything else that screws us up, we leave you. Agreed?" Looking to the drunk and the engineer, captain draped between them, for support.

"I think there should be some penalty punches," the drunk suggests eagerly and Muffin winces visibly.

"You keep bringing up penalty punches and we keep turning you down. Enough already!" the engineer snaps. "When someone screws up, we are not going to punch them in the face. Period."

"Fine." Sulking but hiding a smile. She didn't mention punching him for sinking the boat. That's progress.

In the room with the TV, they stand and stare at captain laid out on the sofa. Stare at each other.

Finally, the drunk slumps down in the armchair. "So now what?

You think we should slap her or what?"

Seething fireballs from the engineer. "No. I don't think we should slap her."

"Then what? We should try to wake her up."

"If it's d-d-drugs, maybe w-we should take her t-t-to the hospital," Muffin suggests timidly.

"And tell them what? Crazy little hillbilly with a lot of skin tried to make her the way and do some direction changing? Aye, you go ahead. Let me know how it turns out."

"What about that stuff you grabbed from that desk?" The driver sits down and leans forward, elbows on knees, hands hanging loosely between his legs.

The drunk reaches to the floor for his bag, dumps the contents out. Stares. "I think the vodka might be good for something." Takes the bottle in his hand. Frowns. "Too bad it's empty."

Muffin crouches down, brushes papers aside. Grabs one at random. Casts uneasy eyes up at the engineer. "I-I-it's a receipt for the c-c-c-hristmas lights."

The engineer is on her knees next to him. "What about everything else? There has to be something here." Snatching up papers and throwing them aside when they turn out to be nothing more than receipts. "Did he just keep a drawerful of receipts?"

"And empty vodka bottles." Dangling the bottle in the air in front of her before tossing it aside. "And I guess he had that rum before the boy smashed it over his head."

The familiar snap-snap of gum turns their heads She's standing behind the sofa, gently pushing strands of hair off the captain's forehead. Flicks her eyes up. "He already started, huh?" So quietly that they have to strain their ears to hear her. "Crap. It wasn't supposed to get like this."

"What wasn't supposed to get like this?" the driver demands. "He said he was making her 'the way'. What does that mean?"

Sighing, she balances her seated self on the back of the sofa. Runs a clawed hand through tangled pink hair and the drunk notices a small tattoo on this inside of her wrist. He squints to make it out, but figures now's not the time to play 'Show me your punk rock style and I'll show you mine.' "You should read those books, okay? I can't say anything. Rules."

The engineer lunges forward but the pink-haired pixie is faster. Inhumanly faster. First she's on the back of the sofa, then she's perched on the arm of the drunk's armchair. And the engineer tumbles forward onto the slumbering captain, picks herself up, turns around, furious. "Screw your rules! You started this! You can't just show up and then not tell us why!"

The pink-haired girl rests her weary head in her hand and heaves an Olympic sigh. "Okay, look. If I don't follow the rules, then I'm just like him and I'm no good to you at all, all right? Wrap your head around that, dollface, and deal with it." Snaps her gum for emphasis.

"L-l-like who?" Despite himself, the words jump from Muffin's mouth.

She glares up at the ceiling. "What did I just say, monkey?" Shakes her head a little and looks up at the driver. "You seem smart, sugar. I'm sure you'll figure all this out. But you better do it pretty damned fast. I was hoping he hadn't started, but since he has, your captain is his until it ends."

"She's barbecuing again!" The drunk cries out with annoyance, watching the girl turn into a distant vision on a hot highway.

And the armrest is empty once again.

"Goddammit!" the engineer explodes.

The driver is more pensive. "What did she mean by 'read those books'? What books?"

"I know!" Muffin leaps up and dashes into the kitchen where his bag is still resting against the wall, rushes back into the living room, grateful to have something to validate his continued existence as a pirate. Yanking the box out of his bag, slamming it down on the low coffee table. "This! She t-told me to look left when we went to b-blow up that apartment, only I didn't know what she was t-t-t-talking about and at first, I thought m-maybe she wanted me to take all the tissues I k-kept seeing or that old banana skin under the sofa, b-but then when Miss Dynamite was s-setting things up and I was helping, I saw this b-b-box on the t-table and it looked all w-weird and so I thought that this h-h-h-had to be—"

"Enough!" Another moment of nervous babble from the boy and the drunk will be forced to put his penalty punch policy into action, despite the opposition of his fellow crew members. "She told you to look left, you saw the box, you took it, yeah?" Muffin nods mutely. "So there are books inside then?"

"It's those k-k-kyohon from before." So quietly, he's almost whispering, trying to shrink further into himself and not really having much success. His height is an obstacle to his self-annihilation.

Furrows on the driver's face. "Those weird books we stole from the old lady? Why were they in that apartment?"

The engineer gasps, hand flies to her mouth. "You don't think Corduroy Jacket is working with Mr. Skin?"

"Do we have to give them such ridiculous names?" the drunk moans.

Hands on hips. "Do you have anything better?"

Shrugs. "Why not Yuki and Tomo? You know, give it a 'land of the rising sun' theme."

"Shut. Up." she hisses from between her clenched teeth. "Their names aren't the point. What are the books we stole doing in that apartment? That's the point, you asshole."

The driver finds his placating hands yet again. "Okay, look, let's just look at the stupid books."

Muffin is eagerly thrusting them forward. "H-h-here they are."

Each of them with flip-flop books in hand, furrows on brows.

"Why the hell did you give me one?" the drunk complains. "I

can't read your silly picture language."

"You read the s-subtitles on the TV," Muffin notes as he gives the kyohon in front of him a once-over.

"No, I don't. I just like the way they look on the screen. Cannot understand why everything everyone says has to be written down in colourful letters all over the screen."

"If you c-can't understand them, how d-do you know it's even what everyone is saying?"

Shrugs. "Seems like there'd not be anything else they'd write." Lets the book in his hand flop open to the floor. Turns it to the left, the right, flips it completely, looks up accusingly at Muffin. "Hey! This one's not even the right language! Are you trying to have a bit of fun at my expense? Give the fellow who can't read the book in a different language?"

Muffin reaches out, grabs the book from him. "W-what are you talking about? They're all the same l-l-language. I haven't even looked at any of them yet; how c-could I pick one for you?" Runs a hand over his short, black hair. "Huh. This one is d-different."

Folding his arms and leaning back, adding in some self-righteous nodding. "Aye. It's always make fun of the drunk, but he's not always wrong, is he? Well then, what's it say?"

With tangled eyebrows, Muffin pulls words off the page. "L-l-lo! In th-that ancient place with the rocks thrust up b-by the sea, from deep within c-c-came the powerful voice. 'G-go forth now. Seekest thou that which no man hath f-found. Into the light...b-bringst it and movest thou the very earth.' B-bid by this...thunderous voice not his own, the man fought the w-waves before him to...s-seek out the object b-bidden...'" He runs his eyes down the page, looks up. "It g-goes on like this for the whole thing."

Silence as they consider this, then the driver speaks. "But what does it mean?"

Shrugs all around.

"M-m-m-maybe it's some kind of epic prose p-poem or

something." Still unwilling to draw attention, but this is one area that he is familiar with and he never gets the chance to discuss it. "It reads l-like the Kojiki from the s-seventh century which was thought to have been s-started not long after Ch-chinese characters began to be—"

"Okay, you can stop there." The drunk holds up a protesting hand. "Epic poem means unreadable. That's all I need to hear."

"But that's not the c-case at all. In this country's tradition, poems are—"

"What did I say? No need to wax poetic about the poems. Let's keep looking through these things, maybe there's a Coles Notes version in here somewhere."

Muffin wants to rail against the drunk for being uncouth, uneducated, uncultured, but as a pirate, shouldn't he appreciate those very qualities? He wonders again how much of the outside world he must give up to live a life of seafaring crime. And if it's worth it when there's not so much seafaring being done. And the crime is mostly blowing stuff up.

"Christ, this one has our jobs in it." The driver wasn't sure at first — he does not have the formal education in this language that the engineer has — but several re-reads have convinced him that there is no other way to interpret the page in front of him.

"By 'our jobs', you wouldn't happen to mean the explosions and the like?" The drunk casts surreptitious eyes toward the bottle tucked away under his chair.

Nodding. Eyes firmly fixed on the page in front of him. "There's nothing else it could be. The explosion at the Honda building, the job at the Buddhist shop, it's all here. Even what we were there for."

Muffin raises his head. "Wh-what were we there for?"

The driver opens his mouth to answer smartly, realizes he has never been too clear on that himself actually. Lets his eyes drop back down to the page in his hands. Lets his jaw drop.

The engineer is out of her chair and poking her head over his shoulder in seconds. "What? What is jaw dropping here?" Runs her eyes down the page eagerly, looking for whatever her lover has found.

He spares her the effort. "We were there to change directions."

The drunk forgets the bottle and leans forward. "Say that again?"

"Yeah, change directions." Slides a finger across the page to underline his thought and the engineer follows.

"It does say that. I think. 'When up returns to up, the directions themselves will be changed and the world will begin anew.'"

"What does that even mean?" The drunk's sense of outrage extends to the fact that the bottle was out of his reach when he grabbed for it under the chair.

"You c-can't change d-direction."

"Someone obviously thinks you can and they are seriously fucking with our shit." The driver doesn't take his eyes off the page. "There's also some stuff about a ritual. At least, it seems like a ritual. Stuff about 'making the markings of the way' and a lot of stuff about lights."

"Lights?" The engineer follows his gaze down the page. "Oh there. What the—'make the marking of the way on the idol and adorn it in light'?" Tearing her eyes off the page. "The captain!"

Puzzled eyebrows from Muffin. "You think it's about the c-captain?"

"She was wrapped in Christmas lights when we got there," the driver concedes. "And that guy did keep saying he had to 'make the way' or something."

"Aye, but what about these 'markings of the way'? And this 'idol' bit, is that meant to be the captain then?"

Muffin stands up, stretches an arm out towards the captain, slapped away by the engineer.

"What do you think you're doing?"

"Ow! Ch-checking for the marks. I j-just thou—"

"I'll do that." She leans over the inert body of her captain. Squints and sees nothing.

"Maybe under her clothes?" the driver suggests timidly. He knows the engineer does not think he harbours any interest in the captain, but he saw the slap Muffin got.

He only gets a glare as she secretively lifts the captain's shirt slightly and peers in through the opening at the bottom. Sharp intake of breath. "There are marks! These are definitely 'markings of the way'." She lifts the captain's shirt a little higher and steps aside for the others to see the hundreds of tiny black arrows covering the captain's stomach.

Muffin leans forward but keeps his bottom firmly planted on his chair. No need to appear too eager to see the captain's flesh. "Are they all p-pointing up?"

"If by 'up', you mean towards her head, then yes. Except for this one." She points to a single arrow pointing to the captain's left, apart from the group on the stomach. "Does it say anything about a 'marking of the way' that points the wrong way?"

The driver's eyes are back on the page in his hands, skimming, scanning. "No, nothing about left. Just up and this crazy crap about up meeting up."

"P-pink Hair did tell me to look to the left for the books. Maybe there's s-something with that?"

"Maybe. But that doesn't help us at all. We still don't know why left." The driver lets the book in his hands fall to his feet.

"We don't even know why up." The drunk reaches for the book at the driver's feet. He can't read it, but he likes to look like he's contributing.

The engineer finally lets go of the captain's shirt hem and the worn black T-shirt settles over the arrows. "Does it really matter which direction or what it means? It's some crazy person thinking he can change directions. Which is obviously impossible. We just have to get the crazy old man to fix the captain. He did this to her, he can undo it."

The drunk lets out a cry of frustration. "D'ye really think that the direction does not matter? Or that we can just make everything better by asking sweetly? 'Oh, please, sir, Mr. Skin, please won't you wake the captain up? We're awfully sorry for all the trouble we caused.' What about the cats? The crazy man in the suit? The little pixie who barbecues in and out of the flat? Get yourself back to reading and find out why up and why left and then we'll find out how to 'fix' the captain. Are you clear on that, pet?"

Her mouth snaps open indignantly. And stays open. And slowly closes. She sinks down to the floor in front of the captain and takes a book from the pile.

Muffin exhales. Gets back to work with his own book, the epic poem.

The driver stifles a yawn, glances at the clock on the wall. Too late to be doing this.

"This is the one we read before." The engineer's voice pulls him back. "The one about the corduroy jacket and Hase."

"Does it tell us anything new?" The driver keeps his yawn in check.

"Uh, let's see. Not really. There's the bit about the jacket, the temple in Hase, um...Oh hey! This is new. It says Corduroy Jacket was already in Hase."

"What?" Muffin can't stop himself from ripping the book from her hands. "How c-could that be? I thought Corduroy Jacket was supposed to g-go to Hase." He scans the page. "You're right. 'The m-meeting in Hase was unexpected. Up was revealed and those who seek to d-destroy the directions will find you; they need you now. She put the game in motion, but you who wears c-c-corduroy, you are the key. The question of up lingers, and it is you who knows the answer. Anticipation b-builds; will you remember that answer when the t-t-time comes? Choices must be made. Who will hold you u-up?' Who wrote this? N-n-no native speaker would write like this. It's so c-clumsy."

"Okay, fine. It wasn't a native speaker that wrote it. So we're looking for someone not from around here?" The annoyance she feels at the theft of her book creeps into her voice.

"I think we're looking for this 'you who wears corduroy'," the driver offers suddenly. "I don't think whoever wrote these book things is going to be any help with the captain. But it seems like this corduroy kid is just as fucked as we are. Maybe we need to hook up and work this thing out."

"So we go to this Hase place?" The drunk glances at the captain as he speaks, but there's no change there. Will they have to cart her all the way to wherever this place is? "Can we not just go back to the apartment and see if we can meet there?"

"Uh, we did blow that place up." The engineer leaps on the opportunity to snap at the drunk. "Pretty sure no one lives there anymore."

"Does it say anything else?" The driver rests his hands on his knees.

Muffin lets his eyes crawl over the rest of the book, slowly shaking his head. The driver is leaning back when the boy's head pops up excitedly. "Yes! I think this is a t-t-time! I think there's a time for the next m-meeting! OK, well, I d-don't know if it's for a meeting, b-but there's a time!"

"You're having us on," the drunk cries as he stretches forward to peer at the book.

"No! No, l-l-look here." Muffin's finger trembles as he points to a place six page-folds down. They crowd around. "S-see, right here. It says a t-time."

Squinty shifty. Finally, the engineer, "That's a time?"

"I cannot read it," the drunk confesses without shame and sits back down. Waits for the exposition. Wonders why he bothered to get up in the first place.

"This isn't j-just some string of random characters. At least, I d-don't think it is. I think it's a date and a time, not any modern t-t-timekeeping though. I remember reading about the old l-lunar calendar and I'm pretty sure I've seen this w-word there."

"So it's a time, but you can't tell us when?" The drunk bets that if he stretched his arm far enough to pull a muscle he could finally grab the bottle tucked away in the underside of the dusty rose upholstered chair. All eyes are on Muffin and the book. No chance of a lecture from the engineer on his drunken ways.

Muffin doesn't even look up. He can't believe that anyone would use such an ancient timekeeping system and feels a scholar's delight at this language puzzle. "I c-can't tell you when yet." Grinning. "But I know where to f-find the answer."

"The Internet?" The driver has never bothered to look anywhere else for answers.

Muffin deflates. "Yes, the Internet."

The drunk takes the moment to pull the bottle out.

"Are you sure you d-don't want to come?" Muffin calls out as he pulls his shoes on. "The Internet café is just down the street. I-I-it's not so far and research is faster with more p-people." Trying to be upbeat, but that crazy guy in the suit out there somewhere, possibly with the crazy hillbilly, is making him grab for security blankets or pirates stronger than he is.

"No, we best stay and read the other books," the drunk informs him casually, as he flips through the channels on the TV and takes a swig from the bottle in his hand.

Muffin does not point out that the TV is not a book. Instead, he lifts his tired backpack onto his shoulder and pushes his way out the door. Prays that the guy in the suit is not on the other side of it.

TV celebrities squeal their delight at lovely hotels, delicious food, kind waiters while the engineer and the driver read and rub their eyes.

"Maybe we should just go to bed," the driver says at last, letting the yawn in his throat break free.

"And leave the captain like this?" The engineer is sleepily indignant.

"She seems fine." The drunk doesn't look up from the screen. "I mean, she's breathing quite well. Not a life or death thing we have here. We could do with some sleep."

Her mouth drops open and a chime comes out.

"Hey! You're the doorbell!" The drunk almost falls out of his chair.

The driver is up and headed to answer it before he is called on to mediate between the two of them yet again. At the door, he hesitates. Maybe opening the door is not such a great idea when they are apparently under attack by captain-sacrificing hill people. Shrugs, opens it anyway.

Tiny waggling fingers fill his vision. "Hel-lo!" Sing-song and high-pitched.

He jerks his head back from the fingers before they take one of his eyes out. "Uh, hi."

The hand drops and his gaze follows. The girl is short and smiling. He thinks she might be lost, judging from her Victorian apparel. Or maybe she lives in the neighbourhood. He's sure he saw a girl in a top hat that night when the new wave kid came by. In any case, she's a long way from Yoyogi Park where the fashion-obsessed parade around and collect the stares of tourists. Her smile is unwavering and her teeth are abnormally white. And still she says nothing.

A confused smile on his own face. "Uh, yeah. Can I help you with anything?"

She tilts her head to the side, peeps around him inside the flat. Her little pink top hat does not fall off. He assumes it is pinned to the long hair falling smoothly past her shoulders, so black that he almost can't see it in the night around her. "Do you have those little flip-flop books?" she asks, pertly, popping her head back up and twirling her parasol on her shoulder. The little pink bag dangling from her wrist sways.

"The kyohon?" He almost reaches a hand up to help his mouth close, but he manages to get the job done without the helping hand.

Short, sharp nods. "Yeah, I kind of need them. If you don't mind." Turning up to him black eyes that take up half her face, tears trembling in the corners. "It's kind of important, you know?"

Suddenly, more than anything, he does not want her to cry. He will do anything to keep her from crying. If those tears start falling, he will- he will- he will-

The engineer is startled to see the driver stumble back into the room so abruptly. "Hey, who was at the d—?" Her own question answered by the wide-eyed parasol-twirling doll person taking small, clipped steps behind the driver.

She turns to the engineer and smiles broadly, twin rows of straight, gleaming teeth. "Hi. I hope you don't mind. I just need to get those little books and then I'll get going." She extends a tiny finger in the direction of the pile of kyohon on the floor.

"Get the kyohon?" Both the drunk and the engineer are on their feet in seconds.

"It's really important," she tells them earnestly, a tear threatening to spill out of her right eye.

The drunk cannot look away from that tear. He wills it not to fall. He begs it in his mind to stay there, to stay in that eye, please don't come tumbling down that pink cheek.

The engineer pushes forward urgently, reaches into her pocket and pulls out a handkerchief to offer the girl, who takes it delicately, careful not to let her small bag slip too far forward on her wrist. "Please don't cry." The engineer's horror at the girl's tear is overwhelming her. She wants to pull towels out of the closets and lay them at the pink-booted feet of this wide-eyed stranger.

The girl beams as she uses the handkerchief to gently dab at the corner of her eye. "Why, thank you so much. That is so sweet of you." The engineer lets her breath out as the tear disappears, only to suck it in sharply as another one takes its place. If she cries.

"I'm sorry I'm such a pain, but could you maybe put those in a bag or something for me? I'll never be able to carry them like that." Her pearl teeth find her lower lip as her eyebrows find each other. "My bag is just too small."

The drunk is on the floor before the words have even reached his ears. Scrambling with the books, collecting them and dumping them in the bag the engineer is shoving at him. Jumping to his feet and thrusting the paper bag from the bakery at her.

She takes it with the index finger and thumb of the non-parasol holding hand and the pink quilted box bag threatens to slide off her arm and onto the floor. The driver is quick to lean forward and nudge it back. "God, you guys are just so nice!" Looks down at the bag of kyohon with upturned lips. "And the books smell like fresh bread!" Beaming at each of them in turn and each of them, in turn, breathes a little easier. Smiles mean no tears.

Tilts her head to the side and raises her shoulders neatly. "Well, I guess that's really all I came for. I should get going. But thanks. You guys are really super!" Turning on the heel of a platform lace-up boot, small steps toward the door, trailed by the three pirates.

"Are you sure you're okay?" the driver asks nervously. "Can we get you anything?"

"Would you like a drink?" The drunk grabs a bottle from the table.

Reaching the door, whirling about on that same heel, petticoats catching air. Grinning broadly. "No, thanks. I really have to be going. I have a ton of stuff to do today."

The engineer trips over her own feet to open the door.

Top hat jauntily askew, a twirl of her parasol and a turn of her boot and she is out the door into the night. On the road, she twists half around and waves her fingers at the pirates frozen in the doorway. "See you later!"

"What are you g-guys doing standing in the d-d-d-doorway?" Muffin fears for a moment that they were waiting for him, plotting to jump him and steal his research, his lunch money, his life. What is it that pirates steal from other pirates? They would take that from him.

Three heads shaking.

"What the hell?" the drunk sputters. "What the hell is going on here? What happened to that little princess bitch?"

Muffin presses his lips together, reaches his free hand up to scratch his shoulder. "'L-l-little princess bitch'?"

"Goddammit!" the engineer explodes. "How long have we been standing here?"

The driver groans and brings his hands to his head. Runs them through his hair. Leans back against the doorframe. "We did not let her take the books. Say we didn't let her take the books."

Muffin's eyebrows fly off his forehead. "What? The b-books? You mean the kyohon? Someone t-t-took the kyohon?"

The driver opens his mouth to tell all, but the drunk is grabbing collars and yanking them all inside. "Bad enough we've been standing out there for who knows how long. Inside, everyone."

At the kitchen table, Muffin shakes his head at the explanations that fill his ears. "So a little girl in a miniature p-pink top hat, a Lolita, came in and t-took the kyohon and not only did you not stop her, but you actually put the books in a b-bag from the bakery?"

"Look, it's bad enough that it happened. Let's not dwell on it." The driver's hands press a little harder on his temples. "What did you find out?"

Muffin mentally straightens his back. Yanks some sheets of paper out of his bag. Peers at them. "You know, the c-cats followed me to the Internet place."

The drunk waves his hand for the boy to wind it up. "Yeah, great. Cats. Internet. What did you find?"

He lays out his papers so the others can see. "It w-wasn't easy, let me tell you. See here, f-f-first I had to—"

"You have to admit that penalty punches are a good idea." The drunk looks to the engineer for agreement.

"You do make an interesting point." The engineer directs narrowed eyes at the boy, who swallows loudly and gathers his papers.

"The p-p-point is, it's tomorrow. Something's happening in Hase t-tomorrow."

"Tomorrow like today?" The driver looks out the window at the sun coming up.

Muffin shakes his head vigorously. "No, no. T-tomorrow in the regular world. Tomorrow like we go to sleep tonight and w-wake up again." Pauses, scratches his head to get the times straight in his head. "N-no, wait, you're right. Tomorrow like today. We go to s-sleep and wake up and that day." He's never been too good with time. He prefers the solidity of words written centuries ago. They never change.

"Tomorrow when? Tomorrow morning?" The driver was hoping to sleep in. "And what? What is going to happen tomorrow?"

Muffin looks down at the table, chewing the inside of his cheek. "I, uh, I couldn't find anything precise, no d-details. I mean, it says s-something, but I can't figure it out."

"So what? What did you figure out?" His surreptitious drinking is not helping him stay awake. Too much energy used up on that crazy skin man.

Muffin shrugs. "I think wh-whatever it is, it'll be sometime in the afternoon."

"Sometime in the afternoon?" The engineer would shriek but she lost the energy for that around the time the girl in the tiny top hat appeared. "How does that help us? Are we supposed to stake out this Hase place and hope that Corduroy Jacket or someone shows up? This is ridiculous."

"N-n-no, we don't have to stay there all day. I p-printed off a bunch of pages and I'm going to try and work it out in more detail. I just didn't want to stay away too long in case s-something happened." He lets these last words sink in. "Plus, we're tired and I'm not sure I'm reading things right and anyway, it s-seems like a good idea to sleep and look at it with fresh eyes."

The driver places his palms flat on the table, pushes himself out of his chair. "Good idea. The captain's not dying, we can't do anything until tomorrow at least. So we sleep and work out the rest later." He cuts the engineer off with a look before she can even get her words out. "Sleep now, details later."

It takes her a moment to realize that she is on the couch. In the apartment in Tokyo. At first, she is confused because she can't remember there being a couch on the boat. But the boat was sunk thanks to old grudges courted by the drunk and they're stranded on land. That's right. Rubbing her eyes and sitting up. Thinking hard, looking for an answer to the question of why she is on the couch.

She was in his office. And he was in his chair, in that dark room. And she was wishing that the lamp on his desk was a little brighter. It's hard to tender your resignation when you can't see who you're tendering it to. He stood up, moved towards her, but awkwardly, not smooth like she had somehow expected. Almost able to discern his face, she squinted to bring it into focus.

And then she was here on the couch. She can find no connection. She is certain now that this is the couch from the apartment, that her crew is somewhere nearby. She even assumes that the cats are outside. Runs a hand through her hair, dismayed to find that it is loose about her shoulders. She reaches in her pocket for an elastic, but finds none. Frowns. Looks out the window. Judging from the light, it's early afternoon. Afternoon on what day? Where is her crew? Why is it so quiet?

Slightly dizzy when she stands, she takes small steps into the kitchen. Notices the papers and the book on the table, leans over to look at them more closely. This is one of the books they stole before, the ones the man in the suit stole from them. She pulls out a chair, sits. What is it doing here? Flips it open, starts reading a random page.

"Robots?" The word on the page jumps out of her mouth. "The boy is a robot?" What boy? She can't remember anything about robots when they read it before, although she concedes that they did not finish reading it.

Muffin's eyes fly open. The blinds keep the room dark enough to sleep, but enough light creeps through for him to see the drunk on the futon next to his. "D-did you hear that?"

"Mfhkous." The drunk rolls over.

"Okay, it's-it's okay." The boy whispers quickly to himself. "There's n-nothing s-scary. The m-man in the suit is not in the k-kitchen. No one's in the k-kitchen. You're j-just hearing things. It's j-just stress. You're f-f-fine. Just g-g-g-go back to sleep. Just s-s-sleep, it's easy. Sleep."

"Goaroiuezfhj!" The noise coming from the drunk is angry.

Muffin forces his eyes shut. Wills sleep to come back to him. The sound of a chair pulling across linoleum flips his lids back up. That was a sound. There is someone in the kitchen. It's probably a cat. It's just a cat. Of course, Those cats are everywhere. One of them got hungry, came inside for a bite. Pulled back a chair to sit down at the table. Just a cat. He just has to go shoo it out and then he can sleep again. Easy. Nothing scary about a cat.

Except a cat that can pull chairs out from the table is scary. But he gulps his fear down, tentatively pushes back the blankets and crawls out of his futon. Out the door, not closing it behind him. He definitely wants the drunk to be awoken by his death cry. If he dies. But of course, he won't. It's just a cat. No danger. Nothing dangerous.

Tiptoeing into the kitchen and falling back loudly into the doorframe when he sees the captain at the table. "You're not a c-c-cat!"

The captain raises a puzzled face. "Of course not. Why would you say that?"

"What the hell is wrong with you?" The drunk rails as he jumps up from his futon and lurches towards the kitchen, ready to remove some of Muffin's internal organs. "We are trying to sleep and you're yell—" He stops short behind the boy. "Captain?" Pushes the boy aside, steps forward, sits down across from her. "Captain, you're awake."

"What is going on here?" The captain is both annoyed and afraid. Waking up on the couch, not knowing why and now her crew is acting like the dead are walking the earth.

"We w-weren't sure if you would wake up." Muffin sits down next to the drunk. "After we g-got you back, I mean."

"Got me back?" Her stomach's descent is quick.

"From that crazy bastard." The drunk is watching her carefully. "Do you not remember?"

A single sharp shake of her head and her unbound dark hair swings. "I told the man who has been employing us that we would no longer be able to work for him and then I woke up on the couch." The looks on their faces are not reassuring. "When was that? When did I talk with him?"

Muffin and the drunk exchange glances and the boy counts back on his fingers. "Huh, I g-guess it's only been two days."

"Two days?" Nausea suddenly overwhelms her. She holds it down. "Tell me everything."

The driver cannot get back to sleep and he curses the boy and the drunk under his breath. He looks down at the engineer, who is like dead. She can sleep through any horror. But if he can't sleep...

His sharp elbow sends her eyelids back into her head. "Whu? Huh?" Sitting up. "Time izzit?" Tilts her head to the side. "Izzat uh capn?"

"What?"

"Captain. Is that the captain?" Speaking slowly to get the words to come out of her sleep mouth properly. Without waiting for his answer, she is throwing on a sweater and running down the hall. "Captain!" Her first impulse is to throw her arms around their wide-eyed leader, but she restrains herself. "Captain, you're okay!"

Brisk nods. "Yes. These two told me what happened. Thank you for rescuing me." Gratitude that is real, but hard to express. The captain should be the rescuer, not the rescuee.

"You don't have to thank us." The driver shuffles into the kitchen to sit down at the table. "You can tell us what to do next, though."

Impatiently tucks her hair behind her ears. "Tell you what to do? I'm not even certain of the situation."

The driver shrugs. "Neither are we. But you're the captain, you must be better at deciding than we are."

"Give me some information to use to decide, then." She tilts her chair back slightly, arms crossed on her chest. "And some coffee." The last directed at Muffin who sighs and heads for the coffee maker.

"So this is the only book left?" The captain tries not to focus on the fact that her crew was overpowered by a little girl in a pink top hat. A miniature pink top hat.

The engineer nods. "It's the same one that we read before, only I guess we didn't get to read it all the way. It says there's something happening in Hase tomorrow."

"It also says the boy is a robot." The captain recalls her earlier glimpse of the book's contents.

"The who is a what?" Maybe the drunk is still dreaming. It's not like the captain to discuss robots over coffee.

Muffin is nodding vigorously as he places a plate of toast in the middle of the table. "Yeah. I-I read that, too, last night."

"You read that someone is a robot and you didn't mention it?" The driver is inwardly relieved. If the robot thing had come up last night, they still wouldn't have gotten any sleep.

"I f-forgot. I was tired."

The driver turns his attention back to the captain. "So who's a robot?"

The captain lifts her shoulders. "I have no idea. I merely saw the words on the page. I was about to read further, but then he came into the room."

All eyes turn to Muffin. "Yeah, the robot. I th-think it's that guy we saw with Corduroy Jacket. You remember when we went to do the j-job? And there was that g-guy? He's a robot."

The engineer's eyebrows are high and skeptical. "Are you sure? He didn't look like a robot. There's no humanoid robot that realistic."

"And there's no cat army, a little miss all in pink did not hypnotize us all, and we are not regularly visited by a pixie with pink hair." The drunk glares at her and reaches for a piece of toast.

"A pixie with pink hair?" The captain has not heard this story.

"So the boy is a robot?" The driver brings his 'Super Grandpa' mug to his lips and drains the last of his coffee.

"That's what it s-says. There's this bit about the boy being 'the interface between the directions.'" Muffin tries to make the quotation fingers, but judging from the look on the drunk's face, he made them wrong.

"So they're keeping the real boy to be the 'interface'?" The driver might need more caffeine to figure this one out. "What is the point of the robot?"

Shrugging. "M-maybe—"

The captain falls off her chair, cutting his response short.

"What the hell? Captain! Captain!" The drunk crouches down and shouts in her ear.

The engineer shoves him aside. "You're just making her deaf, you idiot!" She rolls the captain over onto her back.

Eyes shut, deep breaths. Slack jaw.

"Is-Is she asleep?" Muffin didn't know the captain was narcoleptic.

The driver places two fingers on her neck, counts the beats in his head. "She's not dead."

The engineer frowns. "I think she is sleeping. Like before."

"So...?" The drunk isn't sure what question to form.

"Halloo! Hey, anyone here?" The voice wafting in from the doorway is familiar to the driver for some reason.

He turns around, annoyed. "Of course we're here. You can see us from there."

Smoke rises from the lit cigarette in his mouth as he runs a hand sheepishly through his hair. Until it gets stuck and he has to carefully wriggle it free. "Right, yeah. I mostly just wanted to, uh, get your attention. You seem pretty busy, right."

The engineer takes a step backward. "What are you doing here?"

The drunk and Muffin exchange perplexed glances. "I think the better question is, who are you?" the drunk asks for both of them.

"So these are the other pirates, yeah?" Dirty Pig nods approvingly. "Yeah, the boat is perfect for you. The kid was right."

"What k-kid?" Muffin hopes that at least one question will get an answer eventually.

"About this tall." Raises a hand to his own shoulders. "Wears pouffy shirts, tight pants. Funny hair. Talks funny, right?"

The driver sighs. "The new wave kid?"

Satisfied nods from Dirty Pig. "Yeah, right. That's the one.

Funny kid. Likes to stir shit up, right?"

"Look, what are you doing here?" The engineer musters the sternest glare she possesses.

He raises an eyebrow, tilts his head towards the table. "Mind if I sit down? Long trek over here, right." Crossing the room and sitting before anyone has the chance to stop him. The engineer promises herself that she will burn the chair when he leaves. He looks down at the captain sleeping at his feet. "Oh hey, what happened to this one? Does she always sleep here? Weird." Leans back, hooks his hands together behind his head. "I couldn't sleep like that."

"She's not doing it on purpose," the engineer hisses.

"Let's get her back on the couch, yeah?" The drunk realizes no one is going to tell him who this dirty man with the bleached hair is, so he might as well do something nice for the captain. And get away from that smell.

Muffin grabs her feet, the drunk takes her shoulders and they shuffle-step to the couch in the next room. Lay her out. Stare down at her.

A cat jumps out from behind the sofa, climbs up to sit next to the captain's head, leans down, gives the captain's face a few sandpapery licks.

"Wh-what do you think is wrong with her?" If she dies, will the other pirates fire him? Muffin starts to think his career prospects are less than stellar.

"Dunno." If she dies, the other pirates are sure to get revenge on the drunk for sinking the boat. They've only been restrained by the captain.

"I mean, I'm no part of this, right?" Dirty Pig is saying when they return to the kitchen. Another cat appears, jumps onto his lap, looks up with a soundless meow. A smile from the man with the matted hair as he lifts a hand to run it over the cat's back. "The kid just asked me for a favour. Knew I had the boat and he needed a boat. And you know, me, I don't care too much. I can always get another boat, right? And the kid and I have been through some shit in the past, so I figure, hell, why not help him out? Right? Yeah. And when you pirates came by, you seemed all right and I figured you'd, you know, do my baby right. So yeah, that was it. That was all. The kid asked, I helped."

"So what are you doing here then?" Leaning against the wall on the other side of the room, Miss Dynamite grudgingly meet his eyes.

"Right, yeah." Lets the stub of a cigarette in his mouth drop to the floor, drops his head to watch it fall. Looking up with a fresh cigarette burning between his lips. The driver watches through heavy lids, lets it go. "So I'm nothing in this. I mean, whatever the kid wants to do with that crazy guy in the suit, his business, right? But then that old bastard starts messing around with my boat, coming by, chanting the chants and just, you know, fucking with my shit."

"W-W-Wait." The drunk holds up a hand, takes a seat across from Dirty Pig. "'Crazy guy in the suit'? And the 'old bastard'?"

"So you know them?" Nods of recognition. "Then you can see where I'm coming from, right? I mean, damn, that suit guy is one thing, but when that old bastard comes chanting his chants, that's when I get pissed, right."

Muffin cannot unfurrow his brow. "Is he t-talking about–?"

"Yes." The driver cuts him short. "So you're here because?"

"Because now I'm a part of this, dammit. Stupid kid." Dirty Pig's eyes narrow into a glare, which he directs at the floor. "When I get my hands on him, you know."

"So you're a part of this and that means...?" The driver waits for a useful answer.

He gets the street weirdo look when he should be giving it. "That means that I'm going to give you a little help. To fuck with his shit, right?" Satisfied, he leans back again. Lets smoke waft up to the ceiling.

The four pirates stare at the matted bleached head, then each other. The drunk shrugs, reaches for the coffee in the centre of the table. Sits. "You think I could bother you for one of those?" He indicates the lit cigarette with his head.

"Huh?" Dirty Pig sits up. "Oh, the cigarette. Yeah, right. Sure, here." Taking a hand off his head, a cigarette resting on his palm extended to the drunk.

The drunk takes it casually trying not to ask himself if it was stored in the fellow's hair, pops it between his lips, realizes he has no lighter, having quit smoking for the most part many years ago. But with men in suits and armies of cats all around, cancer is the lesser risk these days. "Got a light?"

Dirty Pig glances over his shoulder in his direction and the drunk realizes that the cigarette is lit. "Cheers, mate." Inhaling deeply. The smoke kills his sense of smell. A sense he doesn't need sitting next to a man who has not bathed recently.

The engineer pretends she did not see the cigarette find fire. "So how are you going to help?"

"What's that?" Dirty Pig's gaze meanders over to her.

"You said you were going to help us to spite him. So how are you going to help?"

Shoulders up high around his chin, sending the cigarette off at a new angle. "Uh, good question. Right, okay. Well, what kind of help do you need?"

"What kind of help can you give?" The engineer knows he came only to spread his filth.

Scratching his matted hair and a clump comes off in his fingers. He looks at it with raised eyebrows, tosses it to the floor. Visible flinching from the engineer. "Right, well, uh, got a lot of party tricks." Grinning, he places both hands flat on the table, glances at each of the pirates in turn. Raises his right hand slowly. A figure forms beneath his hand. Feet in blue sneakers, legs in brown pants, torso in yellow shirt, the closely shaved head revealed last.

"Hey!" Muffin delights in magic. He always wanted to have a

magician for his birthday, but his parents believed magicians were Western abominations. "I-It's the b-boy!"

"The boy?" The engineer leans forward slightly, catches Dirty Pig's scent, leans back. "You mean the one with Corduroy Jacket?"

Muffin nods excitedly. "Yeah, it's t-totally him. That's amazing, how'd you d-d-do that?"

Dirty Pig's grin spreads further. The cigarette in his mouth threatens to drop to the table, but stays glued to the thin bottom lip holding it. "Yeah, right. That's nothing. Check this out." The slow ascent of his left hand begins, while his right hand rests on the tiny head of the tiny boy. Again, feet but these ones are smaller and their sneakers are orange with blue stripes, legs in jeans, torso in corduroy and the engineer gasps. Before the head is even revealed, she is crying out.

"It's Corduroy Jacket!"

Dirty Pig nods in a slow groove. "Yeah, right. You know the players. So get this, yeah?" He takes his hand off the boy's tiny head and the miniature doppelgänger lurches forward across the table. Corduroy Jacket's double is released and for a moment, there is just the sound of tiny footsteps on vinyl-covered plasterboard as the two bump awkwardly around the tabletop.

"Okay, now yeah, this is where it gets good, right?" He places both hands together and then slowly pulls them apart. The cat on his lap jumps onto the table, hissing fiercely at the growing space between his hands. "Hey, kitten, simmer. It's just a little version. Your buddies could take him, right?" Placated, the cat returns to her position on the lap and the pirates can see the little man in the suit between his hands. He looks up, twinkle twinkle eyes at the engineer. "You ready? Check it out." And he removes his hands from Salaryman's tiny body.

The diorama on the table changes abruptly. The aimless lurching of the boy turns into a narrow focus on the tiny body in corduroy. The man in the suit follows. Is that a little evil grin on his face? The driver would rub his eyes, but he doesn't want to miss whatever comes next.

Corduroy Jacket looks up, sees the boy, cracks a smile, heads toward him. Muffin swears he can hear a tinny voice calling out.

The drunk watches the miniature smile slip off the miniature face and suspects he might be hallucinating again. At least this time he's not offering free drinks to girls in pink. A little shiny thing is in the boy's hand and he squints to make it out. A knife. The little boy has a little knife. His other small hand grips a teeny open kyohon. Even though it is nearly microscopic, the drunk is sure its pages are blank. And the little man in the suit is whispering something. The low hum of his smooth voice rises up from the table.

Corduroy Jacket turns away, starts to run across the table, but the boy is faster and before they have a chance to lean in closer, he's stabbing through that jacket with the little knife. The driver winces.

As he pulls his knife out, the body drops to the table, small pools of red liquid form on the table. The engineer has the sinking feeling that if she touched it, it would feel like blood. And smell like blood. And be blood somehow. She hates Dirty Pig even more now.

Salaryman leans over the wound, runs his hand over it, raises it to his lips, then the ceiling. Muffin closes his eyes, waits for the show to end. He feels slightly nauseous.

The sharp sound of hands coming together pushes them all back and the little people on the table disappear. The cigarette between his lips is almost burned to the filter. "That's the kind of help I can give."

The drunk squashes his smoked cigarette under his foot. After the dirty guy pulled out a chunk of hair and dropped it on the floor, no one will take issue with him dropping cigarette butts on the floor. "So you'll do scary puppet shows for us, will you?"

"The boy is going to kill Corduroy Jacket?" The driver tries not to let his eyes linger on the table and the missing pools of blood.

"And the man in the suit? He's behind it."

Dirty Pig laughs and his cigarette is long once again. "That little man only wishes he was behind it, right? He's just following orders, that guy. The boy too. You saw the book in his hand." Before the engineer can ask whose orders and what the book has to do with it, he's already moving on. "You pirates, you know those two, yeah? The one that gets stabbed, right, you don't want that to happen. Need to meet before that, right? Yeah, right."

"Well, that's the thing, isn't it?" The drunk stands and heads for the fridge. It's early, but he needs a drink and he's pretty sure he's not alone. "We know the where, but how about telling us the when? Or the what?"

Dirty Pig stares up at the ceiling, quiet for a minute or two. "Hase? You're going to Hase?"

The driver shrugs. "The books say there's something going on in Hase."

Slow, thoughtful nods. "Yeah. I know tonight is when a lot of stuff should go down. There's uh, times for things or something. I don't really know. But yeah, tonight. Pretty late, I think. Middle of the night-ish. Not sure of the time, I didn't check the schedule before I came. But you need to sort this out before then. Things are dire, right?" Affirms his statement with his own head. "You bought my boat, right. Yeah. So he'll be getting you in this either way. The old bastard doesn't like it when his toys get taken away. The girl takes them all the time and you should watch the shit fly, right?" Starts laughing to himself and matted hair bounces around his head.

"The g-girl?" Muffin wonders if anyone else knows what's going on.

"Yeah, right. You've seen her, for sure." He raises a hand above his head. "About yay big, crazy pink hair, claws." Shakes his head a little and ashes go flying. "She's a scary one. Cut your throat like that, right? I mean, she's all right if she likes you and hey, good thing she likes me." The engineer ignores the suggestive slant of his thick eyebrows. "But she doesn't like the old bastard, right? And you know, who does, right?"

"You bastard!" A shrill voice curses from the counter. "Fuckin' hell! I told you to stay out of this!"

Dirty Pig stands abruptly, shoves hands in his pockets, steps towards the angry girl next to the pink Hello Kitty toaster. "Hey, I said I would stay out of it, but then he is all, hey, help a brother out, right? And then guy with his chanting, what the hell do you want from me?"

Waving her red nails in front of her face, wrinkling her nose. "Jesus. What I want is for you to take a shower or something. Holy crap, you smell like the undead."

He rolls his eyes and turns away. "Yeah, right. Whatever. You're just on your high and mighty action. I bet you're all 'I can't tell you, that's against the rules.'" The last in the most simpering voice he is capable of accompanied by a disdainful hand in the air.

"That's exactly what she said!" The drunk assumes that the girl and the dirty boy are one of those crazy couples that fights in front of strangers and then goes home and has mad sex.

Knowing eyebrows raised in the drunk's direction. "See? That's how she is. She looks all punk rock with the claws, right? But she's all about the rules."

"Just. Get. Out!" She jumps off the counter and hits the ground with a stomp. "If you wreck this, we'll be stuck all fucked up for the next forever. And I know you get vertigo. You know he can't flip things like this. You trying to help them only helps him!"

Shoulders slumping, chin to his chest so the driver thinks he might set himself on fire with the cigarette ever present between his lips. "Right, yeah. It's just that the kid, you know, he was all—"

"I know how he was." Eyes narrowed and the drunk believes she really could cut his throat. Those nails are sharp and she is angry. "But you know that he is just fucking with our shit. He always fucks with our shit. And you always fall for it. Christ. How many years do you need to learn that lesson? You should have just kept the boat. Now we've got Precious in there taking a nap."

He shuffles toward the door. "He just gets to me, right. He just has this way and I always end up here." A member of the cat army threads herself through his legs, rumbling with sound. His shoulders lift a little, stooping to run a hand through its patchy brown and red hair. "Hey, thanks."

The girl with the pink hair steps toward him gingerly. "Look, I didn't mean to yell. Just that—"

Slowly bobbing his head, eyes still downcast. "No, I understand. Right, you're right. I should just stay out of it. He does this to me every time. I mean, yeah. I know he just likes to mess with shit, fuck things up and all."

Stepping up to her tiptoes, she plants her red lips on his dark cheek. Steps back. "So go. And take a shower. Seriously. You really smell like that time the dead walked the earth."

In that movie, Muffin adds in his head. In that zombie movie that they saw together. Because they have known each other for some time and do not need to explain things so much. Cradles his head in his hands. When did piracy become a battle between stinky men and eighties pop star refugees? He was so sure it would just be stealing from rich yachters.

Dirty Pig turns, raises a hand to them all. "Sorry to fuck with you, right. Just that kid makes me so mad, you know?"

The driver nods in what he hopes is an understanding way. "No, totally. He can be pretty annoying."

The cat climbs up the dirty pants of indiscernible colour to reach the shoulder of the unwashed shirt from the blue family and together they head out into the late afternoon. If only the sun was setting.

Expectant eyes come to rest on the girl who has made her way back to the counter.

"What?" she says. "Do I have something on my face?"

The engineer drums impatient fingers on muscular thighs. "What the hell is going on? Why did you send him away? We need to know what is going on and he was telling us."

She tilts her head to the side, bites her lower lip thoughtfully. "Well, he was telling you what was going to happen, I guess. But that's not what's going on. I think we're okay."

"No, see, that's what I'm talking about. We're not okay. What is going on? What is New Wave fucking up? Why is that filthy man so angry about someone chanting?" Slamming fists crash into the table. "This is not happening!" And then she's thumping out of the room and mouths are left hanging open behind her.

The girl with the claws pulls a hangnail from one finger with her slightly yellowed teeth. "Wohkay, your princess needs some time to cool down."

The driver's eyes linger on the empty doorway. "So tonight in Hase?"

Pink Hair jerks her head up from her hangnail maintenance. "Huh? Oh, yeah. Hase, big Kannon. Lots of action." Turns her glance back to her fingers, one of which is bleeding a little. Stares into space. "Okay, I gotta go." Scans the faces of bewildered pirates. "You guys okay without me? Yeah, of course you are." Heat waves in front of their eyes.

The drunk slumps down in the closest chair. "Do you think the dirty man and the pixie are...?" Raising the end of that suggestively.

Muffin lets his jaw hit the floor. "What? The l-l-little pink-haired girl and that horrible filthy man? How c-could you even think that?" Muffin has been harbouring his own secret crush.

The driver reaches in the fridge for a beer. "I think you're both missing the point." Pops the tab and pours the drink down his throat. "The captain is out cold and we're still nowhere. Is that boy going to stab Corduroy Jacket? Is he the one who is supposed to be

— 263 —

a robot or something? Dammit." Slams the beer can down on the counter behind him. Rubs his eyes with both hands. Tilts his head back and waits for everything to be regular again.

"The d-dirty man said that we had to get to C-Corduroy Jacket before tonight." Timid in the face of unfamiliar anger from the driver. The drunk's anger he is well acquainted with, but Muffin has never seen the driver make any sudden movement before. "I d-don't know what the ro-robot has to do with anything."

"Are you not going to see how our princess is doing?" The drunk gets up to reach around the driver and pull a drink from the fridge. Pauses. Grabs two and hands one to the boy without comment.

Muffin's eyes light up as he takes it.

The calico pushes her way between his legs as the driver rubs his temples wearily, stares down at her. "You got any advice?" Two days ago, he would not have considered asking a cat for advice. Today, he is awaiting her response.

A soundless meow as an answer. He leans down to pluck her off the floor, cradle her in his arms, rub her downy belly. "I guess we'll just go find Corduroy Jacket," he says finally. Captain by default.

The drunk raises a single eyebrow. "Aye, but we've no idea where Corduroy Jacket is."

He meets the drunk's eyes abruptly. "Well, we'll have to start where we last saw them." The driver tenses up, waits for the drunk to get obstinate, pick a fight.

But the drunk turns his eyes to the can of beer in his hands. He has no desire to be captain, be in charge. Captains take responsibility, go to jail with the crew, like his last captain. Lucky him to have this drinking problem and be passed out in some hole when the police came for them. "That would be the apartment, then. Do you remember how to get there?"

"I-I-I wrote down the address," Muffin volunteers eagerly.

The driver squats to lower the calico onto the floor. "I'll tell our explosives expert and we'll be on our way."

"She's n-n-n-not coming?" Muffin needs the support of the girl. She's less hostile to him than the drunk and less indifferent than the driver.

"Someone has to stay with the captain," the driver says over his shoulder as he makes his way to where the engineer has buried herself. Bracing himself for small fists pounding him in frustration over the incomprehensibility of the whole thing. Those fists may be small, but repeated pounding in the same area hurts. He resolves to let her beat him until she feels sated.

Muffin wishes he had stayed behind. The engineer would be so much more useful than him in the face of any possible danger. She can explode things. He tends to pass out. Sighing, he rests his chin in a hand propped up on the window ledge, staring at the city moving past his view.

The drunk turns his head away from the beer he brought along for the ride. "What is it, boy? Forget your teddy?"

The driver cuts the fight short. "Quit it. Just shut up. We're finding the kid in the jacket, that's it. No need to start something in the car, okay?" The driver turns left, pulls up to the curb. "This is it."

Muffin spots the patch of trees across the street where they met the scary man in the suit. Squints to see if the scary man is still there, remembers how the man just appeared in front of them, gives up.

They pile out of the car, make their way to the front of the building, stare up at the black space where the third floor apartment was.

"Now what?" The drunk says finally, crushing his empty beer can between his hands.

The driver shrugs, drops his eyes to rest on the calico lying on his feet who meets his gaze and offers a throaty meowl in response. "Go inside? See what's left?"

The drunk's already headed for the door.

"Wh-what if they're in there?" Muffin protests, following his senior crew members.

Careful to avoid the puddles as they make their way from the entry to the charred remains of the living room.

"Is this the s-sofa?" Muffin kicks a larger hunk of black gently and it crumbles to the soggy floor.

The drunk scans the room, asks himself what he expects to find. "So—"

"Man, this place, whoa, right?"

The cat at the driver's feet yowls at the boy with the asymmetric hair behind them.

The driver runs a hand through his hair. "What are you doing here?" Tired of asking this kid that question.

"Whoa, like uh, don't get all uh you know man." New Wave raises defensive hands; a lit cigarette dangles from his bottom lip. "I just uh came by to you know, find uh, that thing."

Even Muffin is rolling his eyes. "What th-thing?"

Groovy nodding. "Totally. Gotta uh, ask yourself, right, what thing, man. What thing. Like uh, this universe is like what it is or you know, totally the wrong way, right? Maaaaaaan." Impressed with his own depth, New Wave rewards himself with a couple lungsful of smoke.

The drunk prepares to launch a particularly virulent verbal attack, but is held back by the driver. "'The wrong way?' What makes you say that?"

The calico purrs against his calves.

More head shaking. "Whoa, like man, that's uh just it, you know? Man keeps giving uh me you know money to uh do crazy uh shit, right? Start to uh like wonder, which way is uh up, yeah?" He meets the driver's eyes abruptly and the driver starts to think that they don't even know the beginning of what's up with this kid.

The cat climbs up the driver's leg, up his torso, onto his shoulder, wraps herself around his neck, licks his ears.

"Which way is up?" Finding that he's asking the question sincerely, not as a joke the way he thought he would.

New Wave lets all the air in his lungs out as he shakes his head slowly from side to side. "Yeah, uh, like that's totally it, isn't it? You know, up. Man."

Muffin looks at the driver, looks at the kid, looks back at the driver, meets the perplexed gaze of the drunk. Missing something and he's not the only one. "What are y-y-you talking about?" Jabbing a finger straight up into the empty space in front of his face. "That way is up."

"For now." A pack of cigarettes is in his hands and he shakes a new one out. Lights it, inhale, exhale. "Right, like, what if uh, you know, that uh kid in the jacket, you know, like disappeared? Then what?" Regretful head shakes as New Wave pulls more smoke into his body. "Man, like, uh, that would you know change things, right." Smirking as he meets the driver's eyes.

"Aye, that it would." The drunk steps forward, moves toward the kid. Time for penalty punches and the girl isn't here to tell him different. "Why don't you tell us how?" Grabs the frilly collar of the eighties pop star's blouson, yanks him off the floor. "I'm thinking it's about time we get some answers from someone." And if he's honest with himself, this kid is the only one he feels safe threatening. That man with the shoes could shred him and he still has hopes for the pixie, even if she is shagging that dirty man.

Muffin claps his hands together eagerly, then drops both hands to his sides. Girlish clapping will not win him any pirate points.

"And you said you didn't need my help," the girl in the top hat says from the doorway. Clucks her tongue and takes a step forward.

New Wave laughs. "I think uh I can like handle a drunken, you know, pirate."

"Not drunk now." The drunk does not appreciate it when people automatically assume he is loaded. He has plenty of sober moments. But no one notices the sober moments. No, it's always look at the drunken sailor. What about the sober sailor? What about him?

The driver gapes and Muffin can see that this is the girl. Little girl in a funny pink top hat. And so many layers of lace and frill. He's seen the Lolitas on TV, but this is the first time in person. He's tempted to stare, but his mother raised him better than that. "Uh, l-l-l-look."

All heads are turned to look at him. Even the drunk holding New Wave up. Even the drunk is listening to him.

But he has nothing to say. "Uh, l-look." Stalling for time. With all this attention, he had better say something good. "We j-j-just want our captain back. We just want to know how to w-wake her up."

New Wave tilts his head back to talk to the small girl with the small purse. "See, like, uh, this one, you know. Someone's uh got some sense, right, like."

The girl narrows her eyes, pupils so black light is no longer escaping. "You want to know how to wake your captain up?" She takes a menacing step forward made less menacing by the squoosh of the wet floor under her black platform knee boots.

Muffin gulps comically and wishes he had never said anything and why isn't he at home with the captain anyway? Finds his voice. "Y-y-y-y-yeah."

Waist-length black hair sways from side to side as she tilts her head back and forth. "Um, okay." All hint of threatening is gone and Muffin feels like maybe things could work out after all. This girl seems reasonable, despite her ridiculous hat. Is that a rabbit poking its head out of her tiny bag? "The thing about that is that I don't actually care, right?" Smiling sweetly. "I don't even care about him." Jerking her eyes towards New Wave, still clutched by the drunk. "You're on your own, nerd boy." The boy with the asymmetrical hair who seems hurt.

"Hey, I thought you were like uh here to you know, give a brother a uh hand." Turning his head as far as he can with the lace of his shirt collar in the drunk's sweaty grip. The drunk whose arm is getting tired. He hasn't been taking advantage of the gym since the sinking of the boat. Being on land for him means going to galleries, seeing what new offerings the art world has for him. But secretly, because if the others found out, he would have depth and sensitivity. It would have been better if he had cut back on the art and spent a little more time with the weights. This kid is heavier than he looks.

One hand drops to a hip and frilly skirts move in waves around her thighs. "Okay, look. Number One, right? You're not my brother, okay? We had this conversation before. Remember? I told you not to call me that." The hand comes off the hip as she notices wrinkles in the white glove on the other hand, pulls the glove up to smooth it out. Satisfied smile. Looks up at New Wave again. "Number Two. I'm just supposed to get the books, okay? Got it? The books. And like, these guys still have one. And I need it. That's all. That's the only reason I'm here. Got it?"

Unsure whether he should interrupt or not, the driver interrupts anyway. "Um, yeah. So what do you need the books for anyway?"

A gloved hand flies up to her mouth, hiding a girlish giggle. "Oh, I totally can't tell you!" More giggling, shy eyes flicking about to every corner of the room. "But I mean, it's not like he can hear me or anything, right? And god, it's so awesome. I mean, I really want to tell someone."

New Wave is rolling his eyes. "Yeah, like, uh, right, okay, he can't uh hear you. Uh I think you like need to uh you know, figure out uh you know?"

Pretty pouting and Lolita twirls the parasol resting on her shoulder. "Okay, like, I am totally sick of that attitude, all right? That is totally why I am not here to help you." Raising her round eyes to the drunk with a trembling lip. "You can totally crush his neck, I mean, it's fine with me."

She's going to cry. Everything white in his head, all he can see is that trembling lip and the drunk is closing his hands around New Wave's windpipe.

"Like, uh, whoa! No fair, you know!" Choking and squeezing it out. "Can't uh give 'em the you know! Rules, uh, right!"

Raising her plucked eyebrows, rolling her eyes back, she raises the parasol and spins it above her head. "Yeah, right. Like I even care about the rules. You just think you totally know everything, but you totally don't." Pink tongue popping out from black lipsticked lips.

Muffin stares at the rabbit in her bag, while the driver lunges forward to pry the drunk's fingers off the boy's pale neck. The white, long-eared dwarf rabbit that is inching its way out of the black, patent leather box-style bag. Making its way out and leaping for his face.

"Aaah!" Both hands up beating at the mass of white fur attached to his face. "Mophllh!" Voice muffled by the angry mammal and he wonders if anyone even notices this thing scratching his face off. Unable to see, he can only hear the angry meowl of cats flooding into the small, charred apartment.

The calico leaps off the driver's shoulder and heads straight for the rabbit, tears it off the boy's face with a sudden swipe and the rabbit cries out. The high-pitched squeal that only rodents can make. Bares its long incisors.

Muffin drops to the floor, panting, enjoying the rabbit-free air.

"Oh geez!" Lolita cries with exasperation. "All I wanted was the stupid book. Stupid cats!" Stepping out of the doorway and gesturing scornfully with the hand not burdened by parasol and bag. "I am so over this scene. Your captain can sleep forever for all I care. Jerks." Her knee-high boots thunder as she stomps out of the wreck of the apartment. Hair swinging smoothly. "Come on, Mr. Fluffles."

The rabbit disentangles itself from the growling calico and crosses the room in three large bounds to follow the girl out, fluffy white tail wiggling.

And the drunk releases his grip on the boy's throat; New Wave falls to the floor, chokes a few coughs out. "Goddammit!" as realization dawns on him. "That little princess did it again, didn't she?"

Bracing himself as he nods slowly. Muffin has learned that the drunk has a tendency of taking it out on the messenger. "She s-s-started to cry and you started to ch-choke him." Eyes flick towards New Wave on the floor.

"Yeah, she uh like does that, right?" New Wave lights a cigarette and brushes the charred furniture off his velveteen pants as he stands. Taking a moment to smooth his black hair into the preferred lines. "Man, like, she uh totally has uh that crying thing, right? Makes me crazy, you know? Like what do uh I have?" Thrusts his cigarette in the air in front of his face. "These? Uh yeah, right. Like no one ever did uh my bidding for a cig, right? Plus, she thinks uh she's like so much uh better yeah? Even when uh you know it's like love or what, she's all uh gotta like find something, you know, better, you know?"

The driver finally manages to get his mouth closed. Then opens it again. "So is the rabbit her," Pausing, unwilling to even say it. This isn't a comic. "Henchman?"

A snorty laugh pops out of New Wave. Head shaking, hair flying and a few seconds of emergency grooming are once again necessary. "No, man, like didn't you uh see? It's a you know rabbit."

Great. The kid in the ruffled blouson is laughing at him. The rough tongue of the calico on his shoulder is small comfort.

New Wave tenses suddenly, eyes unfocused and the cigarette falls from between his fingers to the floor, where the firefighting water extinguishes it. Stares wide-eyed at the driver. "Crap. Like uh man. I gotta go. Lot going on, you know?"

The driver steps forward to grab his arm as he turns to head out the door. "Lot going on? Where? What? Tell us how to help the captain."

New Wave shakes him off, lights another cigarette to replace the one that was lost to the floor. "Man, no time, right? Got a train to uh meet, you know? But I'll uh stop by, right? We'll like totally you know, talk about your uh captain. See you at uh your place, right?" An urgency overriding his usual just-woke-up voice.

Muffin tells himself that when he blinked, New Wave sprinted for the door and made it down the hall before he opened his eyes again, but he's getting tired of lying to himself.

The drunk squats Asian-style on the soggy floor, hands dangling over his knees in front of him. "So what now, then?"

The driver pushes his hair out of his face, reaches up to run a hand along the calico's back. "Seems like we're not going to find Corduroy Jacket here. I'm open to suggestions."

The drunk rocks too far back on his heels and the watch falls out of his pocket, starts to sink into what was the carpet. He sees it over his shoulder, reaches a hand back to scoop it up. "What the—" Turns his face up to the driver. "It's working!"

Quick to crouch down, the wet soaks right into his socks. "Working? You mean—" The driver's not sure what it could mean.

Muffin peers down over the drunk's shoulder. "But it's t-telling the wrong time." Muffin frowns as he stares at the slow-moving minute hand, much too slow. "It's—"

"Of course, it's the wrong time. I've not set it and it was stopped for who knows how long." The drunk moves to set the watch, is stopped by the driver.

"Hold on. Just leave it. What time does it say?"

Squinting to see the tiny numbers. He knows he needs glasses, but glasses are not for a drunken pirate. "11:57," he declares finally. "More or less. I can't be counting the seconds."

The calico meows softly in his ear, but he doesn't need her advice.

"That's it, that's when it happens. We have to get to Corduroy Jacket before then."

Muffin's eyebrows are knitting a sweater. "Th-that's when that b-boy kills the one in the jacket?"

The driver stands up, shrugs. "I don't know if it's the boy or what, but whatever is happening, we need to stop it. We have to get that kid."

The drunk also rises, not taking his eyes off the gentle ticking of the old watch. "You think the kid can fix this?"

"All I know is that everyone is interested in this Corduroy Jacket. So if we get the kid in the jacket, we get the attention of someone who can make things right." Somewhere in his head is a voice saying this logic is spurious, but he quiets it with the knowledge that there is nothing else.

"So...what? We go back and hope that Mr. You Know Like Uh shows up?" Times like this the drunk wishes he hadn't got his old crew thrown in jail. He'd still be with them and there'd be no cats or watches. Just good old looting.

The driver shakes his head decisively. "No, fuck that kid. He's just fucking with us like all the others. We go back, get our stuff, get the hell out of that apartment." Meets the drunk's eyes, turns his glance to Muffin who quickly looks away. "We get the boat and we get to Hase. If we can't find Corduroy Jacket now, we will tonight."

"And then wh-what?" Muffin keeps his eyes on the floor.

The driver shrugs. "Hope that something else happens, I guess."

The drunk perks up as they pass the colander melted to the wall in the kitchen. "Maybe the little pixie will show up, tell us something useful, aye?"

"What if the d-dirty man comes?" Muffin's sense of smell is very delicate.

The engineer stares at the captain on the sofa, wills her to open her eyes, make a gruff command, speak in her lilting accent. Wake up. But apparently, the engineer's will does not have command over other bodies, despite her expectations. The captain's soft sleep breaths are unchanged.

She rests her elbows on her knees, cross-legged on the floor before the sofa. Sets her chin in her hands. Flicks her eyes at the clock on the wall. If they don't come back, what will she do? Maybe she could take the captain to her family. She doesn't even know if the captain has a family. There's no way she could show up at her own family's door. Maybe they could go somewhere new together. She's never been to Hong Kong. She could learn Chinese.

The door slamming against the wall in the kitchen shoots her to her feet, sends her into the other room.

"Grab your stuff." The driver bends, kisses the top of her head, moves into the living room, so quickly she thinks she imagined the kiss on the head.

Bewildered. "What? What's going on?"

"W-we're going to Hase." Confident, Muffin pushes past her towards the hall.

"Hase? Now?"

Nodding sagely. "Yeah, we had some trouble with New Wave and that l-l-little girl, the Lolita. So now we're going to take everything and go to Hase." Maybe he needs to call the realtor. They're really supposed to give one month's notice. And what about the futon? He heads down the hallway to collect the bedding.

The drunk moves around the kitchen, pulling bottles from random locations and stuffing them in a brown paper shopping bag. "Aye, so can we move it along, pet?"

"Don't tell me what to do, you lush." Stomps off down the hall after her lover.

"What about the c-captain?" Muffin asks the drunk, returning from their shared room with futon and blankets piled high in his arms, which hide his head from view.

The drunk places the last of the shopping bags full of liquor next to the door and looks up at the boy. "What's that? What are you bringing all the futon and what for?"

Trying to shrug but weighed down by the bedding. "I-I thought we would—"

"We've places to sleep on the boat. We'll not be needing those poor excuses for beds any longer. And we haven't any room for them in the car. Put them down and help me find where I've hidden the rum."

He sighs, tries to decide what to do. Bring it back to the room? Drop it all? The engineer will be mad about a pile of bedding on the floor. He'll blame it on the drunk, he tells himself as he lets go and futon and blanket hit the floor with a flump. He peers at the bags of alcohol lined up next to the door and is amazed that the drunk has not yet succumbed to alcohol poisoning.

The driver with a pack on his back followed by the engineer. "We ready? Let's get this stuff in the car. You take the captain." His eyes fall on the drunk.

A single raised eyebrow. "Then who will take the liquor?"

The engineer glares at him. "Just get the captain."

"How m-much further?" He wishes he hadn't had that grape soda at the rest stop. But it was a new kind and he finds the parade of new products marching through convenience stores irresistible. But his bladder is unhappy with his choice.

The drunk turns, scowls at the boy in the seat behind the driver. "If you don't stop asking that—"

"What? You'll stop and make him walk?" The engineer laughs. "When did you become our dad?" Shifts her shoulder so the captain's head falls back against the seat.

"I don't need your sass, missy." Feeling like someone's dad as he says it. Gives up, turns to stare at the road unfolding in front of them. "Oy, how much further?" Directed at the driver.

Adjusting the rearview mirror. "We're almost there." He meets the engineer's eyes in the mirror. "So we'll get the boat and you'll get the kid, right?"

"I d-d-don't know if this is such a g-good idea. We sh-should all go. What if one of the c-crazy people is there?"

The drunk snorts, lights a cigarette. "If there's only one, we'll be fine." Grumpy engineer noises get him rolling down the window.

"N-n-no, seriously."

The driver turns his rearview gaze to the boy behind him. "Look, someone has to stay with the captain. And we have to get the boat to this temple so we can get the hell out of here."

"How d-do you even know that we can get the b-b-boat to the temple?" Whining now, but he is feeling very sorry for himself and thinking that he might just like to retire and go back to the university and teach again. Teaching wasn't so bad.

"Because the temple is like ten minutes from the coast." The engineer wrestles her sleeping arm out from behind the captain. Winces as the stabbing of pins and needles starts. "There's no dock there, but we don't need a dock. And judging by the map, it's close enough that you guys should be able to get the kid and run like hell, be at the coast in a few minutes."

Muffin holds back a cartoon character gulp. "D-d-do you think running l-like hell will be fast enough?"

She shrugs. "It'll have to be." Unfolds the map on her lap. "See." Jabbing a finger at the paper. "Here's the temple. It's just shoop, shoop," Dragging her fingers quickly around corners. "And down. You'll have no trouble."

"Yeah, b-b-but what if the crazy—"

The drunk holds up a warning hand. "Boy, we're going. The crazy people will be there. We will handle them. Are we clear?"

The gulp escapes.

"Okay, I'm going to stop here. You guys ready?"

The drunk and Muffin all in black nod, Muffin somewhat glumly.

The engineer reaches across the inert captain to lay an uncharacteristically reassuring hand on his shoulder. She'll regret it in the morning. "You'll be fine. Just sit tight, wait for the kid to show up. I'll try to get there as soon as I can."

The driver looks at them in the rearview mirror, glances at the drunk to his left. "Just watch for Corduroy Jacket. And hope like hell that whatever happens doesn't happen before we get here."

Cold lumps in the boy's throat. He wishes the driver hadn't gone that far. Encouraging slaps on the back from the engineer and the driver and then he is out on the street with the drunk, creeping in the dark onto the temple grounds.

Crouching in some bushes next to the koi pond, the drunk stage-whispers, "So where do you think it'll be?"

"The m-m-m-main hall. Where they keep the image of K-kannon."

"And where's that then?"

He's glad the drunk can't see his eyes rolling in the dark. "It's the b-big building, the n-n-nicest one."

"And which one would that be?" A grand hand encompassing the coal night in front of their eyes.

The boy clicks on his flashlight. Flicks it around in front of him. Catches the corner of the stairs. "Up the s-stairs. C-c'mon, let's go."

"I had no idea the captain was so heavy," the engineer grunts as she pulls the sleeping body from the backseat of the car.

The driver grabs the sleeper by the armpits, leaves her feet to be held up by his girlfriend. "She's a tall woman. She should weigh something." Side-step crab walking down the dock with the weight between them. "Look, I know this isn't the best time—"

"Just don't."

"No, not about that." Goes to raise a dismissive hand, a hand that is back in place in seconds when the captain tilts precariously towards the water next to them. "I was just thinking." He takes a deep breath. Eyelids carefully at half-mast. It would help if he could see her face in the dark. But she wants this, he knows she wants this. "I was thinking, you're pretty much it for me."

The eyes that have been focused on the cracked wood beneath her feet as she tries not to veer off into the water are suddenly pried free, searching for her lover's face in the abyss near the captain's head.

He hopes she's listening. "And uh, well, I think that I don't want to be with anyone else and we have good times together and I'll give up the whole leaving thing, but I was thinking that maybe when the captain is awake again and this is all over, maybe you know, if you want to, we could get married?" All in one breath and totally not the way he rehearsed it in his head on the drive up.

Abrupt stop but the driver keeps walking so the captain's feet slam into her stomach. "I'm sorry?"

Relief at the questioning note at the end. "Do you want to marry me?"

"You want to marry me? I thought you didn't want to get married. I thought you don't believe in that."

She can't see your shrug in the dark, he tells himself as his shoulders rise. "I mean, I want to be with you."

"I think you should say yes."

The feet fall out of her hands. "Captain?"

The captain allows herself to be stood up by the driver. Pulls her shirt out of her armpits. "I was asleep again?"

The driver and the engineer nod, realize at the same time that she probably can't see them. "Yes."

She grins. "See, you should get married. You speak together." Looking around, trying to figure out the where and when, but only seeing darkness and hearing the ocean. "Where are we? How long have I been unconscious?"

The driver turns his mind from his lover. "Since this afternoon. Not so long."

The engineer takes the captain's hand. "We have to keep moving. We're at the dock to get the boat."

The captain lets the engineer lead her. "The dock? Then the others, they have already arrived at the temple?"

"We're bringing the boat around. They'll grab the kid and then we take off." The driver knows the plan sounds half-assed.

"Then we must hurry. Where is this boat you have purchased without authorization?"

"Do you really think this is the best place to hide?" The drunk's back is already sore from bending to fit under the souvenir sales desk.

"I-I-I've had it with your whining," Muffin hisses and his head hits the extra boxes of engraved candles yet again. "I'm n-not so comfortable here either, but did you see anywhere else to hide? Anywhere that wasn't in p-plain sight?"

The drunk raises his eyebrows. The boy has a bite, after all. He pulls out his flask, takes a swig of the rum inside. Silently offers it to the boy.

Muffin hesitates. Under his nose, the scent of rum mixing with temple incense. A scent which is kind of nauseating. But he takes the flask anyway. Drinks deep, feels the shot of fire all the way down to his toes. Hands it back. "D-do you think the captain—" The drunk's hand firmly over his mouth, the other hand gesturing to his ears. The hand is removed and Muffin does not attempt to finish his sentence. He listens carefully to the quiet footsteps as they make their way from the door to the alcove. Rustling sounds, rustling and a little clanking. The boy wonders what it could be, makes a game in his head of guessing. Hands rubbing together, followed by rings clanking? More than that. A hand in a box of marbles? Puppies with chew toys?

The light suddenly creeping over the counter above their heads blinds them. Only enough for a candle, the drunk tells himself while his eyes adjust. Got to be the kid. Somehow expecting that the man in the suit and his little pixie have no need of candles. He gets ready to step up, get this mission into action. Stops himself. Footfalls too close to his ears, too far from the candle.

"Just when I was beginning to wonder where you'd gone astray. The boy promised me that you'd be here tonight and yet, the hours kept passing without you. How delightful that you made it after all."

Muffin's blood is a cold gel pushing through his veins. He knows that voice.

The drunk grabs the boy's arm, gets his attention. The man with the shoes has frozen his blood as well, but he is used to having his blood frozen from time to time. What they need to do now is get in position and hope like hell that the driver gets here soon. Unless he sends the engineer. He better not send the girl. She's useless in a knife fight.

Flat feet slapping pavement.

"Hurry!" The captain calls as she pulls ahead of the engineer. "We're not going to make it!"

Cursing the captain's long legs. "Left!" she squeezes out with the last air in her lungs.

The captain veers abruptly to the left and is enveloped suddenly in the dark quiet of the temple grounds. She stops, debates the merits and demerits of using her flashlight. The merits — without it, they can't move forward — win.

"Up the stairs," the engineer whispers.

Curt nod from the captain and the light goes out. The engineer follows her up the stairs, moving as quickly as she can when she can't see more than the dark outline of the captain's swinging ponytail in front of her. Tries not to be distracted by thoughts of the driver. He wants to marry her. Rolling this marvel around in her head.

Muffin wills himself to have the power of invisibility as he creeps across the temple entryway. He ignores the flicker of the candles in the main room. Ignores the threatening silken voice of the man in the suit. Ignores Corduroy Jacket's senseless babbling. Trying to, anyway. But when someone starts talking about being upside down, his ears perk up.

The drunk, already safely hidden behind a small shrine to someone he has never heard of, resists the urge to run over and slap the slow-moving boy upside the head. If the man in the suit stops focusing on the kid, they're done. The boy moves like a snail. The man in the suit will have killed the kid before the boy gets to the other side of the room.

The man in the suit moves ever closer to the kid, whose heavy feet are headed for the giant glowing statue at the end of the room. The drunk marvels a little at the thing. He supposes it's that Kannon thing that the boy kept going on about. He didn't think it would glow.

"Do you really believe that there is something like a goddess of mercy? Someone to help people in distress?"

The drunk does not like the sound of that. Jerking his gaze from the boy who is finally hidden in the alcove opposite him. The man in the suit has his knife raised. The jewel in the hilt catches the light and sparkles blue and red for a second before he moves it towards Corduroy Jacket. Leaping from his hiding place, it crosses his mind that it's supposed to be that boy, the lover, that is stabbing the kid, not the man in the suit. He hopes Muffin hasn't passed out again.

Surprisingly, his footsteps make no sound. Like that time with the fellow with all the skin and the drunk expects a cat to appear to lead him out of the temple. He throws himself forward, planning to land on the much larger, smoother man, but only grabbing his jacket in his fist. Pulling hard and the man comes with him to the ground and stabs at his head.

Muffin wants to cry out, holds it in. He is not so oblivious as to have not noticed the lack of sound coming from the drunk's feet, from his own feet taking him to the drunk's side.

But it's not him that ends the silence. "You!" Footsteps suddenly audible behind him. He whirls around and the captain is thumping through the door, the engineer panting behind her.

The sleep must have done her good, Muffin tells himself as his own audible feet move him towards the drunk wrestling with the man in the suit.

The drunk registers the captain's appearance, doesn't take the time to look up. The knife in Salaryman's hand goes flying, landing with a dull thud on the other side of the room, inside the statue cage.

Surprised to see the drunk wrestling with the suit, the engineer notes that there is nothing requiring her presence. Under control. Only one crazy. Heads for the priest's area, starts shoving religious paraphernalia in her bag. Something here has got to be useful in making sense of what the hell is even going on. Take everything, sort later.

Corduroy Jacket turns timidly, wincing. "Me?"

The captain thumps over to the giant Kannon statue, impressed by the ridiculous size. She's never seen a religious image so large. And Kannon, the guardian of her mother's hometown. She takes it in with regret, no time to light a stick of incense and pray. "Of course, you. Do you think I'm speaking to him?" Jerks her head to indicate the drunk grappling with the man in the suit.

The drunk who finds his flask and uses it well. Alcohol is for more than just making him forget. A smug smirk at the crack the flask makes when it contacts the suit man's head. Shiny bastard with shiny shoes.

"You're the Kuroko," the kid in the corduroy jacket enunciates clearly.

You and the Pirates

You gape as the pony-tailed woman crumples to the floor before your eyes.

The engineer looks up from looting. "Captain!"

The captain. So Kimono Lady was right. Surprised at the confirmation that Kuroko have captains. Expecting that they're not really Kuroko since you can't imagine kabuki people running around temples attacking men in suits.

"What d-d-did you do to her?" Muffin tries to keep himself from jumping Corduroy Jacket.

"Uh..." Trying to keep yourself from running away. The Kuroko seem to be saving you now, but the one striding towards you and asking questions accusingly is reminding you that they have been trying to explode you. Maybe they just wanted to save you from Salaryman to blow you up themselves.

With the man in the suit safely unconscious, the drunk slides across the smooth temple floor to fetch the dagger from the other side of the metal cage surrounding the base of the statue. Examines it briefly as he walks toward the boy and the kid who appears to only be capable of gaping, shoves it in his bag. "Oy. We haven't time for this. Get the kid, I'll get the captain and let's get the hell out of here. Who knows when he'll decide to rejoin us?" Jerks his head to the unconscious man in the suit.

"The kid?" With a start, you realize that he means you. Before you can protest, the taller one, the one that sounds like maybe he's from this country, is grabbing your arm and yanking you forward.

The drunk gathers up the sleeping captain, apologizing to her in his head for the indignity as he tosses her over his shoulder. "Where's the boat, pet?"

The engineer closes her bag, hoists it up onto her back. "Don't call me 'pet', you asshole."

"Then tell me where the boat is."

She presses tight lips together. "Just come on."

"What boat? Where are you taking me?" And yet again, you reconsider your decision to leave Boy behind and come to an unfamiliar town in the middle of the night. This may not be the best plan you've ever had. "Let me go!"

"Don't start, kiddo." The drunk shifts the captain's weight; her ribs are so sharp. "We need your help, you need ours. Just shut up and come."

You want to laugh and then you do. "My help? Did you see before? Back there where Salaryman was trying to kill me? I don't even know why! I can't help anyone!" The note of hysteria creeping into your voice worries you. You should just accept the fact that you have a brain tumour, it has made you crazy and even as you speak, you are really just locked up in some institution somewhere, cackling madly to yourself while your friends and family watch helplessly. If you accept the cancer, perhaps you'll get better or getting better will stop mattering or something will start making sense.

"S-s-salaryman?" Muffin yanks the kid out the temple doors into the night which seems less black than before. "What a good name! Why d-didn't we think of that?" But the engineer and the drunk are not listening, walking faster in front, and he has to pick up his pace to keep up. If he loses sight of them, he'll never find the boat and then he won't even have to resign. They'll just leave without him. "S-so what do you call the girl with the p-p-pink hair?"

They know Pink Hair? You swallow another protest against being dragged about like this. "Uh, Pink Hair?"

Muffin beams. "M-me too!" Drops his voice to a just-between-us level. "Of course, the others d-do too, but they just never say it, I'm p-pretty sure." He knows that they are just trying to keep their cool, maintain their pirate images.

"So you see Pink Hair a lot?" Despite his accusing action with you before, this one seems a little friendlier than the others. That one that fought Salaryman, he seems surly. And the little girl seems very hostile. Of course, just because this one seems friendly doesn't mean they're not going to blow you up. Twisting your wrist, but the boy has a good grip and you're not going anywhere. And where would you go even if you could break free? Boy is not to be trusted and you don't have a house anymore. Good thing you're being kidnapped or you'd crouch down on the walkway and sob for a while.

"Um, n-n-not so much, I guess. I've s-seen her more than the others. But she k-kind of comes and goes."

"Don't I know it." If Pink Hair is talking to this crew, they can't be bad, right? Didn't you decide that you trust her, trust that she is not out to kill you like Salaryman? And they say you can help them. Maybe you can. And they did save your life in any case. You probably owe them something. Probably not since they have exploded you twice. "So where are we going?"

Muffin relaxes a little now that the kid has stopped with the wrist-twisting action. "Our b-boat."

"You have a boat?" Who are these people? You would stop and scratch your head if the pace being set by the two in front wasn't fast enough to make you stumble on your short legs. "Why?"

Muffin tugs the arm in his hand a little harder. He's losing sight of the drunk and the engineer, but he can hear the waves, secure that they can't leave without him. He can find a boat in the dark. "Uh, we're p-pirates. We roam the seven s-s-s-seas."

"Would you shut up?" the drunk roars from in front. "Have I not told you to stop with your movie talk?"

The engineer punches the shoulder without the captain's torso folded over it. "Dammit, keep your voice down. People live here, you know. The last thing we need is curious neighbours."

Approaching the road winding alongside the coast and the darkness is less, thanks to the streetlamps. You suppose this must be a major road to warrant streetlamps, and yet there is no traffic. You turn your head to see where the traffic is and stop so suddenly that the boy yanking you forward almost pulls your shoulder out of its socket. "What are you doing here?"

Boy steps further into the intersection and all movement stops. "What are you doing here?" Apparently noticing the Kuroko for the first time. "Who are these people? What is going on?"

The drunk meets the engineer's eyes with raised eyebrows. "That's him, isn't it?"

She nods. The little boy that was stabbing Corduroy Jacket on their kitchen table hours ago. Shudders. "Yeah, we have to get Corduroy out of here."

You start to step forward, but the boy holding your wrist holds tight. Frowning, meeting his eyes. "What? He's one of the good guys."

Muffin is paralyzed and praying that he doesn't pass out. He hopes Kannon can hear him. They're still close to the temple. Shaking his head quickly, nervously. "N-n-n-no, that's not a g-g-good g-guy."

"Come on, just come home with me. This is crazy." Boy is pleading with you, begging you with sad eyes to walk away from these Kuroko.

And it's not like you don't want to. Warned against trusting Boy, but is your only option trusting these people instead? You try and wriggle free, but the boy holding you has turned to stone. Remembering abruptly that you have another hand and it's still clutching the compass. Maybe the compass has some advice for you. Your fingers hurt as you force them open. Too much tension, too much clutching. The needle on the compass in the centre of your palm is spinning spinning spinning. Is this advice?

"Look, boyo. Just step aside. We've no interest in you," the drunk growls in the deepest, most ferocious pirate voice he can muster. But with so little rum in his system, it may not be piratical enough.

"Fuck you!" Boy snaps, surprising you. He is not usually given to cursing. At least not in English.

"We know your game, boyo. We might not know who your master is, but we know that you have one." Surprising himself with his cryptic tone. The drunk was intending to punch the boy in the face. Even with the captain slung over his shoulder, seems like he could swing hard enough to send the boy flying.

Boy's face switches abruptly from ever-concerned Big Daddy, the man who was humming creepily as you lay in the hospital bed, to empty eyes, blowing up your apartment style, and you take small steps backwards to hide behind the tall man still trembling and clutching your wrist.

The drunk steps forward, ready to punch as the boy moves toward them methodically. The boy who is much much stronger than he looks and is reaching in the drunk's pocket for the knife that he nabbed from the man in the suit. The boy who is shoving the drunk to the ground with that same lone hand.

The captain falls from his back, rolls once or twice into the road, comes to rest directly beneath the street lamp.

The engineer drops her bag and lunges for the boy with the knife and the empty eyes. Too much like the scene on their table and she curses Dirty Pig yet again. Dirty and bringing trouble. Dammit. "Daaaammmmm—!" she cries as she flies through the air, cut short by an arm thrown out and flinging her aside. Her head smashes into the unevenly paved road and she is back dreaming about tweaking the engine on the new boat.

Your teeth are clenched tight as you watch Boy, your Boy, the one who smokes too much and pants if he walks too quickly, that Boy, you watch him effortlessly knock these pirates aside and there is just the tall boy between you and him. The tall boy who is still trembling and clearly paralyzed. Great. Life and death and you get the nervous one. "Hey!" You shake the arm still firmly in his hand.

Muffin clenches, clenches, wills himself to hold onto consciousness. They said they would kick him out if he passed out again. But this boy is coming at him with a knife, the one with the jewel in the hilt that the salaryman tried to kill Corduroy with. He obviously wants to kill Corduroy too. And Muffin has no idea how to stop him. He wills himself to step back, step away, step aside, get out of the path of that knife.

Staring at Boy's back, you're not sure what to make of this. You were staring at empty-eyed Boy coming for your life and now you're staring at his butt. A fine butt that you have often admired, but one that is generally nowhere near his eyes. "Did you do that?" Not sure if you now have the power to move from side to side. That would be more useful than the up thing, though.

Muffin tightens his grip on Corduroy's wrist. The boy is in front now. The boy is in front? "I...don't know." Is he unconscious after all? But the steps of the boy in front of him falter, there's uncertainty there and Muffin realizes that he has somehow saved them. If Corduroy didn't do this, then he must have. Unless it was Pink Hair. But she is nowhere to be seen.

The drunk pushes himself up on his elbows, ignores the ache in his head, watches Muffin and the kid paralyzed in the face of the boy with the knife. And then they are behind the boy with the knife and he's not sure how that happened. And clearly, neither are they. "Run! Run! You stupid git!" The drunk starts pushing himself to his feet.

Run. Yes, run. Muffin turns abruptly and makes his feet hit that pavement. The boat is just across the street, the boat is right there, he can see it, he can see the driver, climbing to shore, heading towards them. Just run. Get on the boat, get Corduroy on the boat.

Climbing down the ladder, skipping the last few rungs to jump toward the rocks on the coast, the driver lands up to his knees in water. Sloshing through the water, but it's not fast enough, he can see the girl's pink skirts swing as she makes her way towards Muffin dragging the kid this way. Why didn't he just run the boat ashore? This boat of all boats should be able to handle it. The driver curses himself, curses the water still laying between him and the shore.

"Okay, so you have the book, right? Because he was sooooo mad that I couldn't get it from you before. So like, hand it over, okay?"
You wish you would stop feeling dumbfounded sometime soon. If this is your new permanent state of being, you may have to kill yourself. But someone else will probably do it for you, so no problem. The white rabbit poking its head out of the small pink box bag dangling from the wrist of the big-eyed girl hypnotizes you a little. Your eyes follow its pink nose twitching from side to side.
Muffin feels the kid slump down next down him, fall backwards into him and then slide to the ground. He gapes at Lolita, the rabbit, but still clutches Corduroy's wrist. He cannot let go. If he loses the kid, the drunk will definitely start the penalty punches. He opens his mouth, but nothing comes out. Clears his throat, Adam's apple up and down, tries again. "Wh-wh-wh-what?" One word clears his tight throat. Only four more to go.
But Lolita doesn't wait to hear the rest. "I said, hand the book over, dumbass. Geez. Are you deaf? Is that your problem? Want me to sign it for you?" And she does, deftly. The bag on her wrist swings so violently, threatening to go over, that the rabbit jumps

out. Squats on the concrete, perks its ears up. She smiles at it indulgently. "Look at you, Mr. Fluffles. All the way down there. What a good bunny! Yes, you are!" Crouching down next to him to coo in his face. "Yes, you're a good bunny!"

Muffin knows that he should seize this moment of distraction, gather up the kid and run as fast as he can for the boat. He can see it outlined in the dark, bobbing tantalizingly near on the surface of the shallow water. But the body connected to the arm he has in his grip continues to lay sleeping at his feet.

Finally, reaching the shore, water pouring out of his shoes and the driver is climbing the rocks to get to the street. No longer able to see what is going on, grumbling that Muffin needs to take the kid and run, but he'll be lucky if the boy is still conscious. A familiar voice turns his head. The calico on the rocks ahead of him.

"Hey, you're here!" Pulls himself a little closer to the cat. "The girl is just up there!" Jerks his head upwards. "The kid is up there too. I don't even know if you understand me, but—"

Hissing, the calico does not wait for him to finish. Bounding up the rocks, yowling.

Yowls that reach the girl's ears and she whirls, shining black hair swinging evenly across her face. "Why do those stupid cats have to come all the time?" Lower lip thrust out. Turns back to the rabbit twitching on the pavement at her feet. "You better get back in the bag, Mr. Fluffles. Those cats are so mean!"

Muffin promises that he will never say anything bad about the cats again, so glad that they are finally here, that there is something more than him standing between Corduroy Jacket and all the crazy people. Feels stable enough to focus on Corduroy, pull up, hook an arm through armpits and have a puppet person standing next to him. Eyes eager to see hordes of cats see a tiny pink top hat when they look up again. He stops breathing.

She tilts her head back but the hat does not fall off. Grinning mischievously and he remembers the girls in high school, the ones that were into 'compensated dating', they smiled like that. "Sooooo can I have the book?" A single gloved hand thrust out in front of her small torso, palm facing up.

"But-but I d-d-d-don't have the b-b-book." Why is he not somewhere else? What made him think he could be a pirate?

The coy smile drops into a pouting frown. "But I need it. If I don't get all the books, he can't do this stupid direction thing he wants and then I don't get what I want."

"Wha-what d-do you wa-wa-want?" If he keeps talking, will the rabbit stay in the bag? Those whiskers are twitching rapidly over the edge of the bag and he fears a repeat of the last time they met.

"Oh my god!" Thrilled, grinning, purse swinging. "No one ever asks me that!" Petticoats and underskirts keep swinging long after the slim body stops moving. "First of all, duh, of course I want like a ton of new clothes. But mostly," Slyly, darting black eyes from side to side. "I want to be up next."

Manners drilled into him from before memory kick in. "B-b-b-beg your p-pardon?"

She nods enthusiastically. "Yeah, he won't go for it probly. But if I totally get all the books and kind of you know, be in the right place at the right time? Then I can totally get to be the next up." She turns scornful eyes on the kid hanging from Muffin's arm. "This one did a terrible job. I mean, you're up, you could do anything! And what does this one do?" Eyes that demand an answer.

"I d-d-don't know. W-w-what?" He can hear more and more cat yowls but none of them are approaching. But the yowls are fierce and the hissing reminds him of that time with the Salaryman. Resists the comic gulp.

"Nothing!" The word pops out of her blackened lips. "Absolutely nothing! I mean, how totally lame is that?"

He has to concede that that is pretty lame. "Th-that is t-t-totally lame." So Corduroy Jacket is up? He's not sure all the dots are connecting for him here. "B-b-but wait, aren't y-you trying to k-k-kill...?" Lifts his arm to get Corduroy in her face.

"Gross!" Squealing and again the compensated daters are in his head. "No! I totally don't kill people. I'm just supposed to get the books."

"Jesus christ!" The driver scrambles over the rail separating him from the road. "Just run, you idiot! Get the kid to the boat!"

The small sharp head of the Lolita turns to glare at him, pointed chin leading the way. "Do you mind? We are having a conversation here."

Muffin stops breathing when the rabbit jumps out of the bag, leaps toward the driver. Face turning blue before he realizes that the rabbit is not coming for him. And the cats are not coming for the rabbit. He whirls around, the legs of the puppet person on his arm drag on the road.

A captain tug-of-war and he's holding his breath again.

"Let go of her, you bastard!" The engineer holds tight to one leg, but she is no match for the robot boy.

"Where are those bloody cats?" the drunk moans, the captain's pant leg slowly slipping out of his hand.

One of the bloody cats is hissing at the man in the suit.

Who laughs. "We're too strong now." Hands resting loosely in his pant pockets. "You have no power over us and you know it. We've got the interface, the way has been marked. Up will soon be ours. And what do you have?" A single raised eyebrow.

The calico growls and meowls deep in her throat.

The raised eyebrow drops to join the other in a scowl. "The girl will have the book soon." Snapping, testy.

You wonder if you're dreaming this, if you're having a dream where Salaryman chats it up with a gang of cats. Not even a gang; an army, a battalion. There must be thousands of cats. They're sitting on the stone walls lining the road, the paint-chipped, rusting railing that keeps careless drivers from plunging into the sea. A Persian unit blocking a side road, more Siamese than you thought existed covering several vehicles parked on the side of the road, a large contingent of Japanese bobtails advancing on Boy, who seems to be yanking on that woman's arms, the captain. She's the captain.

But if you were dreaming, would you dream that you had a man's arm jammed in your armpits? Would you dream that a rabbit was scratching the face off a man in black? Unless it's the cancer. But you decide to go forth as if it wasn't, as if you believed yourself to be cancer-free.

Muffin tears his eyes from the captain tug-of-war, feeling the body strung over his arm move of its own accord. "A-are y-you okay?"

You shake off the sleep. "We have to be over there. Where the cats are. I know you can't see them, but that's where Salaryman is." It seems like he is right in front of you, scowling at the cat, but the image is only so clear in your mind. With your eyes, you see nothing but darkness. The cancer has apparently given you some kind of psychic powers.

Muffin peers into the gloom. Corduroy is right, he can't see anything.

"You can do it, right?" You note the pleading note in your voice and let it pass. You've had a rough day, you can plead.

"D-d-do it?" Slow realization that 'it' is the moving that he did before only he doesn't know how he did it.

Your voice draws the attention of the girl cheering the bunny on in the fight against the man in black. "You are not going anywhere, okay? I need the book, your friend here has got it and you know, you should probly give it to me."

You raise perplexed eyes to the boy who still has his arm in your armpits. "What book?"

She cuts him off before a sound even leaves his mouth. "God, you are the worst! You should know this! The book, you know, the one that controls it all? The one you are supposed to protect? Because you know, it has all the rules and stuff?" Snorting with disgust at the blank look on your face. "God, I am totally a waaaaay better up than you!" She pauses, tilts her head back, thoughtful index finger tapping her chin. "When I'm up, I think I'll be that way." The finger flicks to the left. "Or maaaay-be, that way." Southeast.

"Or that way." Your eyes head over to the cats and Salaryman in the darkness. If up can be any way, if that's the game your cancer is playing with you, then up is that way now. Is this what Pink Hair meant when she told you to remember which way is up?

The rabbit's claws stop reaching his face, although the rabbit is still scrabbling away furiously. The driver notes the miracle with concern. Glad to be free of the rabbit, but not so glad to see a rabbit drifting off to his left. He pushes himself off the ground, watches other things float off to the left. The boy still holding the captain's arms, the drunk and the engineer on her legs, rocks on the ground, empty pop can. Stands. Finds that he is not drifting off to the left. Huh, that's weird. He breaks into a run for Corduroy Jacket and Muffin still clutching that wrist. Stops abruptly when they're not there anymore.

The Lolita drifts past and he grabs at her. "Where did they go?"

Frowning and shrugging. "Stupid up. Figured out how to be up. Now, how am I going to get to be up?" Crossing her arms firmly across her chest. "I can't do anything now."

The driver lets go, wincing at the petticoats, too much black lipstick and too many utterances of 'up'. Runs for the captain strung between the two sides.

Muffin looks down at his charge. "D-d-did you d-do that?" They are not where they were. He can't decide if he should be worried.

Nodding slowly, piecing the scene together. "Yeah, I think I did."

"Well done," the dry voice behind you offers up its dry praise.

You know it's Salaryman so why do you bother to look even? But looking and still not seeing that face, too far from the main road to have street lamps and all that you can make out are those perfectly tailored pant legs, the perfect hem, the perfect length. "What do you want from me?" In your mind, ripping out your hair and throwing it at him.

Smooth chuckles that you're too familiar with. "I want nothing from you. I want nothing at all. I have no desires." He looks up at you abruptly. "The little regime of your pink-haired friend is at an end."

His flat feet hit the pavement, crossing the distance between you in seconds, and he is ripping you from the boy's grip. A knife to your throat. Different from the one before, you notice with the lunacy of cancer.

Fingers tingling with emptiness. Finally not clutching so tightly, they lose all power. Muffin curses himself and wonders if he should just run away and pretend that he never knew any pirates.

Cats leap from various quarters, the roofs of cars, the tops of fences, from under bushes lining the road. The calico stays at Muffin's feet, purring softly at the approach of the driver.

He crouches down to briefly scratch her ears and then the driver is shoulder-to-shoulder with Muffin. "You lost Corduroy?"

"No, n-n-no. I c-c-can't, I-I-I couldn't—" Unable to finish his sentence. Couldn't what? Couldn't stop the crazy man in the suit? A good pirate would have died trying and yet he just stands here. "No, no, no w-wait. I can—" That thing he did before, he could do that again. He could do that again and the driver could do something. He grabs the driver's hand, gets a raised eyelid in return.

So what did he do? How did he do that? What was he doing? He was just wishing he was somewhere else, he was wishing he was not here, he was hoping that they would just move somehow.

And then they did. The driver is not sure how he ended up behind the man with the knife, but react now, understand later.

Punching hard, aiming for the kidneys. Previous experience has taught him that that is deeply unpleasant.

You fall forward as Salaryman lurches backward, momentum dragging the knife across your shoulder, and you wince. Look down at where Boy's too-big sweater has separated from its sleeve and your arm hangs out, blood trickling slowly down to your elbow and then off onto the ground. It's just a small cut, you can't understand why you're feeling so dizzy. You sink to the ground; you'll just lie down for a second.

The drunk takes a moment to marvel at the abrupt stop of the leftward drift and hopes the robot on the other side of the captain is less adaptable to sudden change. "Pull now!" he yells to the engineer gripping the other leg tightly.

"But her pants—" She can see a yellow side elastic peeking out on one hip.

"Just pull!"

Falling to the road behind them with the captain and her pants still together. The robot boy reels and the engineer is glad to see that at least one law of physics is not being broken here.

The drunk is already collecting their still sleeping leader in his arms. "Back to the boat, pet!"

The engineer hurries after him. "What about the others?" Peering into the shadows cast by cars and streetlamps, but no sign of her boyfriend. Her fiancé?

"They'll have to manage on their own. We've got to get her away from him."

The robot boy recovering his balance, taking tentative steps towards them, picking up the pace and the knife is above his head yet again.

Cursing under her breath, she darts ahead of the drunk. "This way!"

The driver sighs with relief at the league of Japanese bobtails pouncing on the man trying to stab him. That punch in the kidneys was not as debilitating as expected.

"I told you." Voice filled with scorn as he knocks a bobtail out of the air. "You." Another cat meets his square hand. "Are." The next cat yowls as it is struck to the ground. "Not." A kitten hits the pavement hard. "Strong enough."

Chuckling cut short by a hissing and obese Siamese jumping on his head from the roof of a delivery van, followed by its thinner cousins.

The man in the suit stabs at the fur on his head, but blindly and the cats dodge the attempted murders easily. The driver scrabbles to his feet and scans the road for Muffin and the kid.

Forcing his feet forward. Left, right, left. Don't stop, that's it. Corduroy is heavier than he thought but he holds on. Feels good to have this burden back, body slung across his elbows in front of his chest. Don't think of the salaryman. Don't think of that crazy girl. Just the boat. Just the boat. Chanting to himself to keep the fear from paralyzing him yet again.

A hand on his shoulder and he squeals. Cats stop and stare.

"Hey, whoa. Take it easy. It's just me." The driver supposes he should be glad that Muffin didn't pass out this time. "What happened to the kid?"

Muffin forces himself to breathe, kickstart that heart. Turns to show the driver the sleeveless arm. "I-I-I-I don't know. I-I d-d-didn't see. I j-just saw when, when—I-I mean, there w-w-was falling and, and—" Wills himself not to cry. He doesn't want Corduroy to die. He doesn't want himself to die.

"Hey, okay. It's okay. Probably that crazy guy in the suit managed to get a stab in." Nervous glance over his shoulder. "I'm not sure how long the cats can hold out. We have to go." The driver gets his feet moving faster. "The boat is this way, come on."

"Wh-what about the o-others?" Muffin is pretty sure that being a good pirate means not abandoning your crew.

"They'll meet us at the boat. Come on."

"Hurry! Hurry!" The engineer knows that the drunk can't run any faster with the captain over his shoulder, but still she shouts it out.

Panting, snarling obscenities under his breath. The drunk clutches the captain's thighs; she best not take it the wrong way if she wakes up suddenly. He can hear the robot boy's feet behind him, heaps verbal abuse on his own non-robot self. He can't outrun a machine.

Why didn't she bring a weapon? What the hell was she thinking? Frantic for something to slow that boy down, but only rocks at her feet, leading to the ocean, to the boat. Safety so close! She grabs the biggest rock she can find and flings it as hard as she can.

The drunk dodges the boulder, runs past her. "Throw them at him! At him!"

"Sorry!" She reaches for another rock as the drunk clambers down the bumpy path to the shore, to the dinghy she and the captain left tied up. Looks up to throw but the boy is already on top of her. Knife headed straight for her heart. "Gah!" The engineer throws herself to the side. She's out of practice. Can't even remember the last time she was in a knife fight. She tackles the boy's knees, rolling with him across the pavement, away from the coast and the drunk laying the captain in the dinghy.

The thing falling out of the sky onto Muffin's head effectively destroys the rhythm he had achieved with his left-right mantra. "Aah!"

The driver stops, turns and opens his mouth only to have it filled with fur. Spitting as the furry object falls to the ground. "Cat?" One of the Siamese unconscious at his feet.

"C-c-cats!" Muffin shrieks. A cat with reddish fur lies inert on Corduroy's chest while a skinny, hairless cat falls from the sky and slides down the rolled-up pants to the ground.

"Run! Just run!" The driver cannot explain the cats shooting through the sky, flying towards them, but is pretty sure it is related to the man in the suit. Or else the guy with too much skin and either way, running is the option of choice.

Shaking Corduroy Jacket to knock the red cat off, running as fast as he can, but the best he can muster is a kind of shuffling half-walk, half-run. The body draped across his arms is doing nothing for his balance.

The little girl in the top hat is in front of him, trying to hold her giggles in but not doing a very good job of it. "You think you can outrun him like that?" She stops even trying to contain her delight. "As if. Look, if you just give me the book, I can maybe, you know, get him to go easy on you. He just wants the kid, so you know."

The little voice reaches his ears and the driver turns, makes a run at her. She's just a girl in layers and layers of silk and cotton. If he can't take out the man in the suit, he can get this girl out of the way at least.

She turns to him with lips quivering. "Oh my gaaaaaaaaaawd." Dragging it out, hurt like he was squashing bunnies. "Oh my god. Are you going to hit me?" Tears piling up against her lower lids.

Muffin knows he's in trouble when the driver stops his frenzied attack run and starts walking towards him. Crap. How come she does that to everyone but him? With Corduroy Jacket draped over his arms, there's nothing he can do to fend off the driver.

"Christ." She is sitting on the roof of a car on the side of the road.

"Wh-wh-where have y-you b-b-b-been?" Muffin inches backwards away from his formerly laidback crewmate. If he breaks into a run, will it be like it is with dogs and bears? Will the driver sense his panic and view him as prey?

"Look, I told you a million times, I can't get inv—"

"Then wh-what are y-you d-d-doing here?" Although he wants to sound cool and in his element, he nearly shrieks the words at the girl with pink hair. The driver's lips are curling into a grin that Muffin has never seen before.

She shrugs. "The cats. They keep howling for me. Heeeey." She lets the word slide slowly from her mouth, grinning suddenly. "You're different." Tilting her head to eye him carefully. "Yeah, yeah. Looks like you're the one your friend there decided on." A quick nod towards Corduroy and then the grin on her face drops away. "Oh shit." Lower lip tugged in between her teeth as she watches the driver. "Where the hell is she?"

"He-llo!" Lolita steps out from behind the driver. "You miss me?"

Pink Hair jumps off the car, storms over to the girl in the top hat. "You are so not supposed to be here!" Reaches for Lolita's lace-covered arm, but the smaller girl jerks away. "Are you the one who started all this? You are in so much trouble."

The driver stumbles to a halt and Muffin lets himself breathe, but doesn't stop inching backwards. The body in his arms keeps breathing, just barely. Blood drip dripping to his feet. He tries to do that thing again where he just wishes he was somewhere else, but he keeps being where he is. It's not possible that his desperation is not just as sincere as before. Maybe even more desperate now since the driver's skills are well-known to him and he has no trouble visualizing his gruesome end.

"And what if I did? I was tired of waiting." The violent shakes of her head send long black hair flying. "You don't get to tell me anymore, okay. Your game sucks."

The girl with the spiky pink hair sucks her teeth dry. "It's not my game, you twit. It's the way it is."

"Well, he says that it doesn't have to be that way. And changing the directions is all it takes. And I'm going to be up." Defiantly, waiting for the challenge, but hoping it doesn't come.

"Yeah, right." Snorting laughter. "Did he tell you that? Did he tell you exactly how much work you have to do to force a change?" Snapping her gum furiously

Far enough away from the driver and the girls and their fight to turn around and make his feet move faster. Except he doesn't know where the boat is. He breathes deeply. Calm, calm. It has to be at the shore. That's where the ocean meets the ground. That's where boats go. Left, right. A cat shoots past him, yowling. He tries to move faster.

No weapons, but she does still have this rock. Robots smash like anything else, but she's still afraid that this boy is not really a robot. The engineer is not comfortable killing people. Not that kind of pirate. She brings the heavy rock down on the knife-wielding hand. The knife goes flying and the boy shouts out. Only blood pours from the hand. The engineer starts, mildly surprised. After all the buildup, she was expecting wires and oil. She smashes the hand with the rock once more. Partly to keep the thing/boy incapacitated, partly to find out whether it is a thing or a boy.

"Bloody hell!" No matter how he ties this rope, the drunk can't get anything to hold the captain while he tugs her up. Where the hell is everyone? Someone should be on board. He gets to work tying her over his shoulders. He'll have to climb the ladder with her.

Left, right, left. Just one foot and then the next. It's not so hard when the driver isn't chasing him. Wondering what the driver is doing instead of chasing him, losing his focus on his feet. Muffin looks up and there is the engineer. Startled by her warlike stance over the boy. The gentleman caller.

Footsteps hard behind him and he freezes. Muffin berates

himself that this is the stupidest thing he could possibly do, but his feet are just not listening. The slap on the back sends a yelp from his throat.

"Move it!" the driver tells him, pushing him forward.

"B-b-b-but you—The L-l-lolita—" Limbs trembling and he hopes he doesn't drop Corduroy.

"They're fighting. I don't know. Suddenly, I could move and I heard her." Nods toward the engineer. Eyes opening wide at the hand of his lover crushing the robot's hand with a rock. Wider at the sight of blood. "What the—Is he bleeding?" He breaks into a run.

She stares at the hand which has a wire or two popping out of it thanks to that second smash. Brings her weapon up against the side of his head. Now that she has confirmation of his robotness, nothing wrong with smashing his head in. Ha, smashed you good, she tells the boy silently as she looks up, meeting the driver's eyes. Jumping off the robot boy to throw her short arms around her boy. "You're okay!"

He briefly allows himself to embrace and be embraced, but the hand dripping blood and possibly motor oil is not slowing the robot boy down. His head is dented and that doesn't seem to matter much either. The driver shoves his girl behind him. "Go! Get to the boat!"

Supernova eyes popping out of her head as she stumbles backwards, then turns and runs for the shore.

The robot boy lurches forward. "I just want us to be together," he intones.

The driver keeps pace in the opposite direction. "Where's the boy?" Searching his flimsy excuse for a memory. "Where is the, uh, interface?" Ready to run at any extra sudden lurches.

No lurches, only stopping. "I have to get the interface." The robot boy turns on one heel, lurches back up the street to the temple, leaving a trail of dark spots on the concrete. Is it the blood or the oil that is leaving the darker stain?

"Come on!" the engineer shrieks, watching her boy trot after the robot boy. What is he doing? Looking around for a wall to punch. Run after him, go to the boat. Run after him, go to the boat. Muttering curses against him and the genome that made him like this, she runs after him.

The engineer's shriek startles him out of his chanting. Almost to the shore, Muffin knows her voice is close but he can't see her. Or the driver. Or anyone. Shifting the unconscious weight in his arms, trying not to pass out. He just has to get to the boat. Everyone is on the boat. They're all waiting for him there. They'll have a party when he gets there and the drunk will get him drinks. The cats won't come on board, but will hang around in case of trouble. Left, right.

Hissing whizzing by his ear. He follows the Persian's trajectory into the ocean with his eyes. Cats hate the water. Left, right. He bets she is angry. Left—

"She is, in fact, very angry."

Stop.

The man in the suit takes a few steps towards him. "Do you know why she is angry?" He lays a hand on Muffin's shoulder. "Because she knows she is not strong enough to fight me. And if she is not strong enough to fight me, do you think you could possibly be strong enough?"

His cologne smells expensive, unlike the slap in the face he used to get commuting on trains so jammed with people that men in white gloves had to hold them in to get the doors closed. Remembers that that is one of the reasons he gave up academia for piracy. "I-I-I-I d-d-d—." Breathes deep, inhale, exhale. "I-I-I don't w-w-want to fight you. I d-d-d-don't e-even know what's go-go-go-going on."

"Then you won't mind if I unburden you?" Manicured nails

at the end of slim fingers reach for the sleeper making his arms shake.

"That stupid twit!" The drunk rows faster. "Why does he always stop when he's attacked? He'll get himself killed in no time like that." Only able to make out the shadow of the man in the suit menacing the boy on the coast, but he's got a good imagination. He can fill in the rest of the details. He hopes he doesn't end up the only pirate left in the captain's crew. Sleeping now, but waking up to one pirate and having it be the drunk at that, she'll just be wanting to go back to sleep.

"I-I-I'm not s-s-s-supposed to le-let go." He keeps wishing he was somewhere else. Why can't he do that thing again?

The salaryman laughs, runs his fingers along the contours of Corduroy's inert body. "I'm afraid you won't be able to do that as long as this is bleeding so wonderfully."

Is he actually smiling? Muffin squints, but the features of the man's face never clear up. Like there's a barbecue under his face. "B-b-but I d-did it be-before." Feebly, a five-year-old getting ready to burst into tears.

"Yes, before. When your friend here was still conscious and not getting ready to meet the interface. You," How can a voice sneer like that? "My boy, you have nothing of your own. For some reason, your friend here has chosen you." Barks a laugh. "Leave it to this up to choose the weakest of all allies."

He opens his mouth to protest, snaps it shut. Anyone would be better than him. Unless there was a need for reading ancient literature. Hands down, he's got that one sewn up.

The drunk tugs the dinghy ashore far enough to make sure that it won't float away without him. He doesn't fancy swimming back to the boat. Pulling himself up over rocks, avoiding the cats that seem to be draped over every single one. Why are all the cats dead? Are they dead? Reaches down to check one for a pulse; do cats have pulses in their necks like people? Nothing in the neck. A steady but faint rhythm beats against the base of his hand resting on the cat's chest. Not dead then. Keeps making his way to the shore. Cats are okay, that stupid git is probably not.

The engineer knew she should have built those robot legs. The driver kept telling her not to bother, they're pirates, when would they need to out run someone? Spend the time tweaking the engine, he advised, oh-so-sagely. That's what we'll need to be faster. And yet here she is, muscles creating lactic acid due to a severe lack of oxygen. All the panting her lungs can do is not going to get oxygen to those muscles any faster. And she still can't catch the driver.

The robot boy is throwing fists, but slow and the driver dodges easily. Did the engineer smashing really do that much damage? She must know her mechanics so maybe he shouldn't be surprised by that. "Where is the interface?" Shouting it for the fifth time, but the robot still does not respond.

"Um, n-n-n-no, no, s-see, I k-k-kind of pro-pro-promised the, the others." Trembling arms move Corduroy Jacket away from Salaryman fingers.

"The others." The hand jerks away, angrily finds its way into a well-tailored pocket. "Where are the others now?" The non-pocketed hand reaches up to the shadowed head possibly to smooth down errant hairs. "My boy, it is just you and I here at this moment. There are no others. And all I want is this creature that burdens you so." He tilts his head to the side, somewhat jauntily, sympathetic eyebrows high on his forehead. "And you are burdened, aren't you?"

Nodding and shrugging to himself. It's true Corduroy is a lot heavier than he first thought. And this pirate thing is just not working out. And maybe he should just give it all up, go back to teaching.

She should just face it. These short legs will never get her there. She can hear her lover, but can't catch him. She follows the sounds up the hill, the stairs. The driver is climbing up to the temple? Curses the stairs. Gets to climbing.

Muffin's thinking about teaching and then he's being kicked. Or punched. Is he being punched really hard? He can't tell. He has never been punched in the back before. The blow from behind is sharp followed by a bloom of warmth and his knees buckle.

"Damn fools."

Pulling the sleeper tight against his body. Is he hallucinating? The pain is making his vision spotty so maybe. But that's the guy, the one with all the skin, the one that put the captain to sleep. Sinking lower and lower to the ground, willing himself to stay awake. Penalty punches from the drunk, don't think that he won't do it.

"All y'had to do was get up. 'No problem,' you said. 'Consider up taken,' you tol' me. So you won't mind tellin' me, if up is taken, what is this fella here doing with up in his arms?"

Muffin watches the dirty loafers circle the shiny new shoes of the salaryman. Telling himself to raise his head, but his eyes stay on the ground.

"We just have this time, y'know. Not like we can try agin some other time. Got to get it done when the markings is fresh. Dammit, you know that. We'll have to start over again and I'll be damned if I'm about to grapple with that damned kid again. Cain't hardly unnerstan' a word he says. And dammit, I'm tired of his tricks and games."

The smooth voice of the man in the suit, stilted somehow. "Of course, of course. Up is practically ours. He just has to let go."

"Well, he ain't gonna let go while he's standing upright, now, is he?"

Is that an uncomfortable silence? Muffin focuses on clenching and unclenching his toes. Passing out now is definite penalty punches and he knows they will throw him out and he can't go back to teaching now, not after getting the taste of adventure in his mouth.

"Yes, of course. But you know that he is protected, that is to say, well, we are incapable of forcing him to do anything. Even for us, there are rules."

"Rules don't say nothing about touching him. Just cain't take anything. Or kill them. I thought you knew that. Honestly, I'm starting to wonder what good you are."

"Of course, yes, the rule is no taking. I merely worried that by injuring the boy in an attempt to take up would lead to the same consequences."

Those sound like excuses to me! Singing it in his head. Realizing he may not be in the best mental state. He pulls Corduroy more tightly to him.

If the drunk was driving a car, there would be squealing tires against pavement at the speed of his stopping, dropping to the ground. Mr. Skin! The skin on the hillbilly's arm swings as he brings something shiny out to meet the boy's back. Blu-dee hell. He watches the boy wobble and drop to his knees. Rustling in the darkness to his left and he sends his eyes shooting off to his side.

Cats. Tiptoeing cats. On the tips of their toes. Are those things called toes? They might be called something else on creatures with four feet. Even as he gets stuck on whether or not cats have toes, more cats are creeping forward on the appendages that may or may not be toes. The drunk gives up considering the nature of the appendages, gets back to marveling at the fact that the little animals are walking on the tips of them. All of them. He wishes he was in on their plan; it appears to be something sneaky.

Only a few steps behind the robot boy punching through a pane of the sliding door to the main hall and shoving it aside. Robot Boy, or RB as the driver has taken to calling him, stumbles on the raised frame of the sliding door, recovers, steps out of the driver's sight. Who follows in a much less spectacular fashion.

He tries to ignore the wobbly shadows cast by the candles and crosses his fingers that there's no one in here praying or on any legitimate temple business. Focuses on RB who is putting his hand through another door to open it. Is it the blows from the engineer or just faulty programming from the start? Who would make a robot that didn't know any other way of opening a door than sending a fist through it? The driver slides his feet across the polished floor of the main hall, tries not to stare at the enormous golden statue looming at his side. This must be the Kannon thing that Muffin was so excited about. Is it glowing? Must be the candles.

At the top of the stairs, it's clear that she's lost him. But light from the candles guides her to the main hall, to the smashed door. Eyeing it with a raised eyebrow as she passes. Thumping footsteps hitting her ears and she knows that that can't be her boy. So...Robot? Suit guy? Her money is on the robot. Suit guy is after Corduroy who is with Muffin. Unless Muffin screwed up.

In the hallway off the main hall, RB stops sharply. Distracted by the glow, the driver almost walks into him, catches himself on his tiptoes. RB kneels, yanks a piece of the polished hardwood floor up, tosses it through the sliding door lining the right side of the hall.

She clamps her hand over her mouth to keep from shouting out when the huge chunk of wood comes flying through the wall at her. Jumps aside, watches the chunk and realizes that it is floor. The temple floor. And the wall is a series of sliding doors. Of course. Solid walls on a building would be too easy. Through the hole in the sliding door wall, she watches the robot version of the boy reach into the floor and pull himself slowly upright. Whatever he's got in his hands looks heavy. She tiptoes closer, trusts that her lover is nearby for some punching.

The driver holds his breath and tries to peek over RB's shoulder. Seeing RB's face and almost letting his breath out with some vocal action. RB raises one knee, uses the other leg to push himself up, the unconscious body of himself in his arms. The driver realizes this must be the real, non-robot version of Corduroy Jacket's lover. The interface. He is deeply disturbed by the identicalness of the two of them. Glad that the engineer worked her rock banging magic and marked the robot.

On the count of three, she tells herself. Three and jump, okay? If he's the man you're going to marry, he'll be there, ready to save you from robot wrath. One. Two.

The robot goes flying forward, the boy in his arms hits the wall/door at the end of the hallway. From his tackling position, the driver sees the engineer out the broken door, mouth hanging open. "Get the boy!" Using both fists to keep a continuous series of punches headed for RB's face. If he just keeps it up, maybe the robot won't be able to respond. Some kind of circuit overload. He knows nothing about engineering. Is circuit overload even a real thing?

Why does he always make her carry heavy people? She pushes a door panel aside at the end of the hall, grabs the unconscious boy's hands and pulls. He's much too big for her to carry. "Help me!"

The driver was there, ready to save her from robot wrath. Does this mean she should say yes? Is she looking for signs? Chastising herself for lack of scientific perspective. She gave up superstition with her family. She should make a list when she has the chance, pros and cons of marrying the driver.

The cats slink by him on the tips of their toes. He stays pressed to the ground, as close as he can get. No need to get the man with the extra skin coming over this way. The skin that is swinging wildly as he gestures angrily at the man in the suit. The drunk starts inching forward with the cats.

And then cats are jumping on top of cats and tottering forward like toddlers after too much sugar, kitty totems, while others are racing forward and the drunk's jaw hangs open slightly at the sight of cat after cat at top speed racing through and around the legs of the two men standing in front of the boy, leaving a path clear for the kitty totems who split, two toward the faces, two for the backsides. The men try to keep their balance as their feet are pushed back and forth by high-speed cats, while the wobbling cat totems close in on their targets, two towers for each man. A single paw from each cat in each tower reach forward to slash at the fronts and backs on the man with too much skin and the man in the suit, knocking them back and forth between the totems positioned in front and behind.

The drunk tears his eyes off the site of organized cat action and inches forward as fast as he can. As long as he stays low, the cats are keeping him hidden.

"Have you all gone deaf?" The man in the suit is unruffled by the tower of tortoiseshells tearing at his suit and his face, the hundreds of cats shooting through his legs. "You do not have any power. We have all the pieces. Well, nearly." Self-satisfied as he grandly opens his arm towards Muffin on his knees. "He's going to drop the last piece sooner rather than later. I think we all can see that."

His head sinking lower, Muffin feels the air move with the salaryman's arm. He bites the inside of his cheek hard, head jerks to the side, but he can't get his eyes to open again and he can't feel his legs. Has he been paralyzed? Maybe that's his spine that was stabbed. He lets the angst and regret come. He never even got to see the boat. He's dying a pirate virgin.

Before he can fully resign himself to death or at the very least, paraplegia, small stabbing pains shoot up from his right ankle, then his left calf, then his thighs until his entire lower body is covered with prickling, sharp pain, forcing his grip on conscious to get a little stronger and his eyelids to crawl up half a centimetre. It's a red cat. There's a red cat under his nose. Lets his eyes drift to one side, meets the round emerald eyes of a very fat Siamese cat, rumbling with loud purrs. Drift to the other side and he finds several kittens, meowing soundlessly. Then it must be the cats that are stabbing him in the legs. He frowns. Eyelids climb a little higher. Cats don't have knives.

The drunk watches as a large contingent of cats move forward from the gutter behind the boy, climb onto his legs, cluster around him, reach up with small paws. If they are trying to bury him in cat flesh, the drunk will have to mount a rescue.

He's close enough now to hear the man in the suit, mocking the cats' feebleness, Mr. Skin curses as he pushes forward, scattering the cat totem in front of him, and shakes one leg then the other to send cats flying into the ocean. The drunk holds his breath for a longish bit as he moves ever closer to the boy. If he can hear them, they can hear him, right? But the whirlwind of leg cats is quite loud. Lots of yowling. And there are still the three towers of cats, all hissing and scratching. The two in the eye of that storm likely aren't able to hear too much. He could use another drink of courage, but he thinks he might have lost his flask dragging the captain to the boat.

"Oh, fer Chrisssakes!" The sleeves of his plaid golf shirt cut into the excess skin swinging from his arms as Mr. Skin lifts them above his head and swiftly spreads them out to the sides of his head. The end of the kitty totems, of the racing whirlwind as cats shoot past the drunk's head. "Stupid cats. Goddammit. This ain't got nothing to do with you." The frown on his face lifts as he spots the drunk. "Now, you on t'other hand. Boy, you got something to do with this, now, don't you?"

The drunk suddenly understands why the boy is always freezing in the face of danger. Perhaps Mr. Skin is in fact talking to the boy, rather than himself. The ear to the ground hears the heavy footsteps of Mr. Skin's loafers. The loafers in front of his eyes. "Crap."

"You might as well stand up, boy. Or I'll make you stand up. Don't matter none to me."

He pulls himself up slowly, noting the cats fluffing Muffin's lower half like a sofa cushion. "What can I do for you then?" Raises his eyes to the face of his captor, regrets it. The hairless head almost looks like it's melting. The drunk tries to look away but finds that he is mesmerized by the interplay of light and shadow in the folds of the man's many wrinkles.

"Well, I sure am glad you asked, boy." The drunk shudders as Mr. Skin reaches up to rest a hand on his shoulder. He crosses his fingers that the hand does not move to any areas with exposed skin. "I jes' need you to help your friend here out. Look how much trouble he's havin', holding up that heavy thing. If he just lays it down, the two of you can jes' walk away. Won't be no problem."

The drunk glances at Muffin clutching Corduroy Jacket close to his chest and frowns. "That's not a thing, that's a person."

The hand on his shoulder gets a little tighter. "See, that's what gets you into trouble in the first place. If you all had just minded yer business and done what you're tol', there wouldn't be no problem right now." Tighter still and the drunk gasps. "Do what you're tol', boy."

Reluctant steps forward and the cats covering and surrounding

Muffin turn in unison to face him. Backs start arching and soon,
the whole lot are staring him down and hissing ferociously. "Here's
the thing, cats. I've no choice in the matter. That one," Jerks his
head towards the elderly man in gabardine. "Seems to think that
the boy here has to let go of our mutual friend."

The hissing increases in volume. A cat with no ears steps out of
the battalion in front of him. Squinting, he sees that it has ears,
they're just folded down against its head. It leaps for his face and he
puts the question of folded ears out of his head. He ducks and the
cat soars over him to attach itself to the face of the man with too
much skin behind him. The drunk wants to turn and see how the
cat manages to stay attached without sliding down pools of skin,
but is occupied with dodging other cats aiming for his eyes. He
needs those eyes.

Abruptly, the hissing stops and the drunk learns that silence can,
in fact, be deafening. Nothing is leaping for his eyes. He looks up
at the cats and they are all staring off into the distance, unfocused.
Listening. The listening ears abruptly drop flat against wide heads
and the hissing starts again. Wincing and bracing himself for more
flying cats when he notices that the narrowed eyes are focused
on the man behind him. And then cats are jumping, running,
pouncing past him to attach themselves to Mr. Skin.

"Dammit!" Mr. Skin waves arms, kicks legs, but cats do not soar
into the ocean.

Salaryman is running up the street towards the temple, a
battalion of Abyssians in hot pursuit.

The drunk scoots forward to the boy's side, trying to be not
noticeable. Let the cats deal with Mr. Skin. "Oy!" Grabbing the
boy's shoulders and shaking hard. "Hey! Are you still in there?"

Head flops back on his neck, too heavy. The drunk's face looms
over him. "H-hey." Surprised to find that his voice still works.

"Can you stand?" The departure of the cats has revealed a large
red pool surrounding the boy. Not waiting for an answer, he slips

behind the boy and snakes an arm under each armpit. Pulls up. When the boy is far enough off the ground, he quickly ducks under one of the armpits, lets the long body hang off his shoulder. And still Muffin does not let go of the kid. The drunk may have to rethink the penalty punches.

"Just leave him!" Why does he have to beat the thing into submission? She needs help here.

The driver keeps punching. RB is hardly bleeding and if he stops punching, maybe the robot won't be damaged at all and will just pull itself up and come after the engineer dragging its mirror image. Previous fisticuffs with the robot have taught him that it is much much stronger than him and if he gives it the chance, it will be on top of this game.

Behind her, an army of footsteps on the stairs. Fingers crossed that it's the cats.

"Drop it." The smooth voice of a man who spends too much on suits and the engineer feels nauseous suddenly.

The voice of velvet carries. The driver punches and jumps off the robot in the same move, stumbles, feels a sharp pain in his ankle, runs anyway. Ankles heal, that suit guy is crazy and going to kill his fiancée. Not his fiancée yet. She didn't say yes. Forces himself to ignore the doubt overwhelming him, but why didn't she say yes?

"Yes, the boy. Would you be so kind as to remove your hands from his person?"

The man in the suit's behind her at the top of the stairs, so she lets the boy's arms drop to the ground and turns around to face him. Knocked aside and hitting the ground hard before she can get a look. The temple gravel cuts her face.

"Wonderful. Thank you so much." The swooshing of wool-polyester blend pant legs in her ears as he steps briskly past her toward the boy. A swooshing that is quickly replaced by low rumbling growls. The engineer lifts her head and sees the outlines of cats pacing along the edge of the stairs.

"Too late, my friends." Crouched down next to the boy, pant legs carefully raised to avoid the damp of the night ground. One hand firmly clasping the inert boy's wrist.

The low rumble of the growl rises in intensity until an army of fire engines are lined up behind her, but none of the cats step forward. She pushes herself back to her feet, ignoring the scrapes on her face and hands. Stares at the man in the suit, tenderly lifting the boy in his arms. "What the hell is going on?" she shrieks, surprising herself. She was planning to jump him. "What do you even want?"

"Now then. No need for such emotion. I'll just take the boy here and be on my way. You can all go back to whatever it is you pirates do." Slow grin spreading. "Well, other than your dear captain. I'm afraid that, as the way, her life will regretfully have to be given up to our objective. It really is a shame that you bought the boat. The path was much more accessible with such a vessel. And of course, your captain would not be in the predicament she finds herself in."

Calm. Calm. She brings it down a notch. "And what predicament is that?"

"Now, really. I know very well that you are an intelligent young lady. This sleeping problem your captain has. It will only get worse, you know. One day, she will stop waking up." He moves towards her with the boy in his arms. "That day will in fact be today, now that I have re-acquired the interface."

She jumps aside as he steps smoothly toward, then past her to the stairs. The fire alarm growls start up again, but the man in the suit is unswayed. "In case you hadn't noticed, I do have the—"

The unconscious boy shoots forward out and down the stairs. A moment of indecision later, the engineer is chasing after him, hoping that he doesn't sustain any serious blows to the head.

Funny. He didn't think that would work. The driver lies on top of the man in the suit for a moment, basking in unexpected success. Delights in the sound of growls and hissing advancing. Does not see the fist headed for his face.

Brushing gravel and assorted accoutrement of nature off his suit. "Really. I expected more from you, to be honest. A tackle is so...so base."

Pulling himself up and wiping the blood from his nose, the driver sees a cat flying towards the man's head, forsakes the witty banter and runs past him to follow the engineer down the stairs.

The ocean is starting to get restless, he notes, as he tries to steady the dinghy enough to lower Muffin and the kid into it. Time to be on our way.

"Uh?" Why can't he get his eyelids to go up more than a centimetre? He just wants to know where he is. He thought the drunk was with him, but maybe that salaryman is in his head like in the movies.

"Bloody hell, boy! If you're awake, then can you not get in the boat on your own?"

Boat? Boat. Pulling together all his strength to lift one knee as high as it will go, hoping that's enough to clear the side. He's not going to die a pirate virgin.

Noise on the rocks behind them and the drunk holds in a groan. Is it going to be that man with the skin again? Because he has had about enough of that nastiness.

"Holy shit! What happened to Muffin?" The engineer sends sand and rocks flying as she pulls up next to the drunk.

Sighing with relief. "Explanations later. Help me get him in."

The driver tosses the boy into the dinghy behind the drunk and the engineer. The boy who is going to have a terrible headache if he ever wakes up, between falling down the stairs, getting tossed into the boat and the hit to the head he took from a lamppost when the driver swerved while running for the coast with the boy over his shoulder.

Not again, groaning in her head as she pulls herself up from the sofa under her. She frowns. This sofa is different than the last sofa. And darker. It's darker here. And moving. When she tries to stand, the bobbing of the floor sends her back down to the sofa. Of course. The boat. She's on the boat. The captain wonders why she is waking up alone again. Wasn't she in the temple?

Placing a hand on the wall behind her for support as she stands up, ignoring the pain in her head. She takes slow steps out of the room, wonders where the stairs to the deck are and how is it that this room is so big?

"Yeah, right, totally. I mean, how is uh this room so like big, you know?" She spots the glow of his cigarette before his asymmetrical hair. "I mean, like, man, it's a uh you know boat, right?"

"Yes. It is strange." Wary. He should not be here. She thinks.

"Maaaaaan." Drags it out as he approaches her. "Your crew is like so hot, right? They're uh like fighting right now, you know. With uh like that guy."

She sees the man in the suit in her mind. "What about the other one?" Trusting that she does not need to specify their former boss.

Nodding groovily. "Right, uh right. That guy. He's uh you know." It's not so dark that she can't see the half-grin spreading across his face as he takes another step towards her.

"No, I do not know. That's why I'm asking you." Without thinking, she takes a step backward.

"You like don't uh know?" Grin growing wider and wider. "That guy uh, he's like, a robot." Takes another step forward.

And she takes another step back. Should she be shocked that their boss is a robot? It explains the empty voice and the distinctly awkward feeling she had in his presence. But how many robots are there? "I find it hard to believe that there are two such highly functional robots walking around at liberty."

Back to rueful head-shaking. "No, no. You like uh don't you know." He takes a moment to make the ember at the end of his cigarette glow brighter. Exhales. "Just one robot, right? Like uh, the boy robot, you know, it took some working out. Man. Good robots are like uh hard to make, you know."

Grateful for the darkness that hides her dark eyebrows reaching for the sky. "Am I to take it that you built the robot?"

Producing an actual laugh to accompany the swinging hair. "Like, uh, no way, you know. I don't uh do things, right. Like, people uh do things for me, you know." Drops his near-finished cigarette, lights another.

"So you had someone build you a robot of that boy?"

"Yeah, you uh got it. Thought I'd uh like test it out with you like pirates."

For a moment, she can only stare. Tying strings together in her head. Letting the knots come together slowly. "So you're the one doing this?"

The glowing tip of his cigarette flies back and forth, light trails in front of her, as he waves his hands in protest. "What? Like uh no way! I told you, you know, I don't do things."

"You have others do things for you." She tries to keep her tone even.

"Yeah, right, but like getting people to uh do things can be, you know, really uh hard."

"So you use a robot?" Slightly unnerved that she is not only following his train of thought but adding to it.

"Exactly!" The hand holding the cigarette shoots out, points at her enthusiastically. "Thought like you pirates won't take me, you know, seriously. Seemed like a robot, like, that's get some respect, right?"

Her train diverges from his. "But why do you need our respect? What are we doing here?"

Grooves on his bobbing head. "What are we uh doing here?

Totally. Universe, man."

"No, this is not philosophy." Less inclined to back away. "Why did you need my crew to take you seriously?"

"Fine, like no philosophy." Tosses himself down on the bunk behind him, leans against the wall, peers at her with the one eye not hidden behind a curtain of dark hair. "I thought it would be you know fun to mess with him."

"'Mess' with who?" Restrains her fingers that want to make quotation marks in the air. She's just not that comfortable with English slang.

The orange tip of the cigarette twirls languidly in the dark above his head. "Oh you know, that guy."

A man with a head like a melted candle. "Who is he? Why do you need to 'mess' with him?"

"Well, he's all uh whoa!" Jumps off the bunk and throws his hands up in the air suddenly and the captain has to concentrate to keep herself from jumping away from those flying arms. "Turn the world upside down!" One hand takes the cigarette out of his mouth, the other falls back to his side. "Me uh you know, I could like uh care less. I mean, up, whatever. But like this guy, he's all uh gotta do it, right."

"Turn the world upside down? This is related to the person in the corduroy jacket, yes?" Wills herself to stand still, don't move backwards.

New Wave pushes air out between his lips. "Man, it's not just uh like related, right. It is the kid in the jacket." Brings the cigarette to his lips.

"Beg your pardon?"

"Yeah, okay, like uh, it's not my you know business to like tell you or whatever. The girl should you know." Grumped out like she's asked him to work overtime on a Friday.

"The girl should what?" What girl?

Long sigh, followed by a sharp drag off the cig. "Okay, look, uh. The uh innocent thing like isn't taking you know anyone uh anywhere. Miss Meddler herself. Like you're her choice, you know. She should be like giving you the you know deets."

At long last, she understands the complete meaning of the word 'baffled'. All her years of studying English come down to this. "I'm sorry. Are you speaking of the little girl in the top hat or the little girl with pink hair? I have not had the pleasure of meeting either."

"Pfff." Scornful. "Like uh, as if Lolita could even you know like compare. Loli, she's uh just you know trying too hard, right. She's the one who uh like started this, you know. Off schedule, right. She's got like uh some idea that you know, if she uh helps him or whatever, he'll you know." Yanks a pack of cigarettes out of his pocket, impatiently shakes a stick free. "But like, whatever, you know. As if. He's totally going to just you know stop the uh whole thing, right." Brings the stick to his lips, sets fire to it. Takes a drag. "But you know, try telling uh her that, right. She used to be uh such a great girl. We had uh like some you know awesome times. Except for that crazy rabbit." Shakes his head smilingly. "That thing will uh like chew your face off." She holds her breath. He's not talking to her anymore. "What's like uh stupid is you know, she could have moved up, right. Like she has you know talent. But she's all, need it uh now." Flicks ash onto the floor. "Okay, I like totally changed my mind, right."

Raising her eyebrows, but keeping her mouth shut.

"Your pink-haired friend won't uh tell you this, right. Too afraid of like 'breaking the rules'." His voice jumps an octave and he minces with his cigarette. "But like, man, whatever. You, captain lady, right, you need to like head to where the little you know girls go. Like, the girl in the top hat, my little Lolita, you know? She is totally uh where you want to you know be. Keep you awake, right?"

It's dark but she swears he is winking at her and then the ground is hitting her in the face.

"Do you think this is far enough out?" The wind blows the driver's hair off his face as he maneuvers the ship and he lets his eyes slip all the way shut, just for a moment, just to feel that breeze.

The engineer leaning against the rail, letting the sea kiss her, turns, rests her back against the same rail. Slides from side to side, elbows firm against the metal, providing a base to slide from. "Yeah, I guess. I mean, if they can sail, they can probably sail better than we can so we're screwed in any case, right?"

He reaches out with one hand to pull her towards him, gives her a smacking kiss on the lips. "Always the optimist."

She grins, pushes him away, herself back to the rail. "Hey, I'm just being realistic." Happier than she thought she'd be to have unstable ground under her feet again. Even with the captain passed out on the sofa, Muffin stabbed and two strangers filling two beds.

The driver slips the creature into neutral and lets it drift on its own for a while. The seas are not so rough and he has a feeling that this is the sort of ship that won't go where they don't want it to. Just like it has the engine they want and perfect living quarters. "Let's go figure out where we're going."

He loves the sound of her easy laugh as she grabs his hand and leads the way below deck. "Do you expect the drunk to have the answer or something?"

The drunk glances up from his needlework as the happy couple walks through the door. Acknowledging them with a slight nod, frowning as he plans his next stitch. No need to scar the boy for life. Although he may want that. The boy is always so eager to sound like a movie. Movie pirates have scars. Nodding to himself. Right, a little bit of a ragged edge to the thing. Stabs his needle through the edge of the wound, pulls it through to the other side, gives a tug to bring the two edges of the hole together.

The driver squats and watches over his shoulder. "Giving him a scar, huh? He'll like that."

The engineer crouches down next to the captain, strokes her hair, whispers soft things. "Do you think she was out the whole time?"

The driver jerks his head up from the drunk's quick needle. "Huh? I don't know."

"Did you hear him?"

"Hear who?"

"The man in the suit."

"Salaryman," the drunk says authoritatively, eyeing his work.

"Whatever. Did you hear him before at the temple?" Eyes turned to her boy.

Shaking his head. "No, what did he say?"

"That the captain would just keep sleeping. That today was the day that she stopped waking up."

"But we saved her, yeah?" The drunk's words are distorted by the needle clutched between his teeth.

"If we saved her, how come she's still asleep?"

The driver raises his eyes to the kid in the jacket and the 'gentleman caller'. "If it's finished, how come they're out?"

"Duh."

The drunk's heart leaps up in his chest and he stabs the boy. She's back! Trying to be casual as he turns. She's perched on the edge of the bed holding Corduroy. Pink hair as shocking as ever. "'Duh'?"

"Yeah, duh. Of course, they're still out. Duh." Snapping her gum loudly. "It's not finished obviously."

"Well, how do we finish it?" The driver grips the engineer's arm tightly. She's not leaping yet, but it's only a matter of time.

Whoa whoa hands up in the air. The light in the cabin reflecting off the red lacquer on her nails. "How many times do I have to tell you? Rul—"

"Yeah, yeah, rules." The engineer steps forward despite herself, despite knowing the driver is holding her fast. "How. Do. We. End. This?"

The girl with the pink spikes lets her red claws run gently down the edge of the unconscious face next to her. "I gave you all the tools I can. This one has the compass, he's got the watch." Eyes jump off of Corduroy's face to search the drunk's. "You do still have it, right?" Narrowed eyes and he fears how sharp those claws must be.

Shoves anxious hands into pockets, but behind his eyelids the watch is arcing through the air and hitting Mr. Skin on the head, clattering to a stop on the floor as he reaches down for the captain. But no, he picked it up then. At the temple? In the water? Maybe it went to the same heaven as his flask. "I'm sure the boy here snatched it up, he's good at picking up odds and ends. But as you can see, he's not really with us at the moment, so…"

Jumping to her feet, angry eyes getting to him before the rest of her. "You lost it?" She stares for a moment, then snaps her head, her body away, stomps over to the other side of the small cabin, drags her long nails down the wall in front of her. The engineer is surprised at how deep the gouges are. "You lost the watch." Shakes her head quickly from side to side, starts talking quickly to the wall in a low voice.

The driver's not sure that's even English that she's muttering at top speed. "Uh, I'm sure it's like he said. Muffin probably picked it up or something. We'll just ask him when he wakes up."

Whirling, red eyes shooting flames and the driver stumbles backward. "It's not like he says. Goddammit! Of all the people I could have picked! If he doesn't have it, then none of you have it. It's for him. You can't pass it around like a hot potato. Fuck!" This at the top of her lungs.

The engineer winces, betrayed again by a too-religious upbringing. "We'll find it." And then wishes she hadn't spoken as the fiery eyes settle on her.

"You'll find it?" Scoffing half-laugh as she pulls a quick hand through her tangled hair. "If you left it where he thinks you left it," Quick nod to the drunk staring at his feet. "Then you won't find it. It's gone. He has it." Rolling her eyes to the sky. "He'll find it. And your stupid rum."

Not sure who exactly 'he' is, but understanding from her emphasis that it is not a happy outcome for him to have it. The drunk wonders if 'he' will at least give him his flask back. A gift from his lover in Singapore. Not that they're involved anymore, but the flask brings back fond Singlish memories. "Well, what is it for? Maybe we can find something else." Trying to make this up to her, take it away so maybe he can get back to pixie fantasies.

Waving both hands in frustration. "No, no, you can't. Just—Crap. I have to think about this."

He barely sees the barbecue this time.

"So, uh…" The driver opens his mouth for witty remarks to exit, but he just gets an "uh".

The engineer slides to the floor in front of the captain-bearing sofa. "What does it even do? I thought it did what it was supposed to when he threw it at that horrible man." Shuddering at the memory of the melting skin.

The driver shrugs and joins her on the floor. "Guess not."

"Hayshueh."

Six eyes fly across the room to the boy with the newly forming scar.

He tries again. "Hey, what's ha…happening?" His tongue feels thick and heavy. Did the Salaryman drug him? Is this a drug dream? But the engineer is here. She wouldn't feature so prominently. Would she?

"We gave you something for the pain." The driver takes the steps to his side.

The drunk laughs. "Plus, you wouldn't let go of Corduroy. We had to loosen those arms."

Heart pounding, pupils pulling shut at the sudden light. "C-c-corduroy!" Tries to fling himself up, gasps at the hot pain when he rolls over, sits up.

The drunk frowns at the destruction of his handiwork. "Dammit, boy. I just finished that. And now you've gone and opened the bottom bit." Crouching down, grabbing his needle. "Hold still." Using the boy's shirt to wipe the blood leaking from the partially reopened wound.

Muffin's frantic heart slows when he sees Corduroy laid out in the bed across from him. Still unconscious, but still with him, so he'll take that as a plus. He flinches away from the drunk's needle.

"Dammit! I said, hold still!"

"TThhhorry." Tongue still heavy, but he's managing it. Eyes traveling around the room. The boat. He's on the boat. He's a real pirate, a seafaring thief. He's a criminal of the high seas. He was even stabbed. Maybe he'll get a scar. The captain on the sofa gets his thoughts off scars and the ocean's criminal element. "The c-c-captain'sh sleeping again?"

"Yeah, she was just passed out on the floor when we got here." The engineer keeps her voice neutral.

"D-do you think she'll w-wake up?" Feeling woozy. Maybe he should lie back down.

The drunk studies his work, decides it's good enough. Boy made it open again, boy can deal with the larger scar. "Aye, she'll wake up. Just a matter of when." Feeling his exhaustion in his bones. "But the real question is will I get to sleep?" Grabs Muffin's arm, tosses it over his shoulder, stands and brings both of them to their feet. "Would you be so kind as to show us to our beds?"

The driver pushes open the small door, "This way."

Scrambling to her feet. "But what about—"

"It'll have to wait, then, won't it?" The drunk maneuvers the two of them out the door, Muffin's head falling forward and jerking up as he tries to stay awake.

The sofa again. She drops her legs to the floor, brings her torso up to lean against the seat back. Sunlight pushing through the dirty glass of the small window gives her retinas something to process. The engineer snoring across from her, head and hand hanging off the bed, fingers grazing the floor. Her lover on his side, back turned to her, pillow over his head. At least, she fervently hopes it's the engineer's lover under that pillow. No time for big break-up scenes.

A sudden snort, followed by coughing that sounds like choking and the engineer's eyes fly open.

The captain is seated on the ceiling, staring at her. Her sleep brain rights her, makes the connections and the engineer is flipping herself right side up. "Captain!"

Muffled sounds from under the pillow next to her.

"How long?" Bracing herself for weeks, even months.

The engineer sits up, steals the blanket from the driver and wraps it around herself. "A few hours. Not so long." Rubbing her eyes. "You want some coffee?"

At the sound of his captain's voice, Muffin's eyes fly open. He's a real pirate and that is his real captain. Feeling compelled to see her, show off his wound somehow, prove to her that he is worthy of this thing she lets him do. He tries to sit up and cries out, hopes he didn't tear his stitches again. The drunk lectured him for a long time before he fell asleep. Muffin stares down at his naked thighs, wondering why they are naked, why he has the measles. Does he have the measles? Don't adults die from the measles? "H-h-hey! Wake up! Hey! Are y-you awake? Hey! Can you hear m-me?" He's going to need to go to the hospital straight away. This measles thing could be the death of him.

The drunk lets his head drop over the side of the upper bunk. "What?"

"I have the measles."

Pressing his eyelids tightly shut, get rid of the headache, the boy. But the boy remains. And the headache is only slightly improved. "You do not have the measles. The cats did that." Raised eyebrows and perked ears. "Is that the captain?"

He nods. "I think so. Where's Corduroy?" Remembering the cats, their little knives and more concerned about the fact that his arms are not clutching Up.

The drunk lands in front of Muffin awkwardly, nearly twisting an ankle. "Captain's bunk with the boy." He pulls on some pants and watches Muffin wince as he tries to stand. Giving in to the kinder self he didn't know he had, "Here, let us help."

"I'm not—What happened to you?" The captain interrupts herself and is on her feet before Muffin is even through hitting his head on the low doorframe.

The drunk sets him down in the chair next to the engineer. "The fellow with all the skin slipped a knife in him. He'll be fine."

The captain lifts his shirt to take a look at the wound. "Did you do this?" When the drunk indicates that he did, she frowns. "Your work is usually better. He'll have a scar."

"Aye, I thought he might want one."

Smiling, she lets the shirt drop. Takes her seat. "I was just saying that the boy with the asymmetrical hair was here."

"N-new Wave?" Muffin grins when the engineer pours him some coffee. Being stabbed changes everything.

"Yes. He said to me that we should 'go where the girls go'." The captain takes a sip of her coffee. "Frankly, I have no idea what that means. He seemed very distraught, as if the actions of one girl in particular were bothering him."

"Which girl?" The drunk mixes cream into his coffee before taking a sip.

"That was my exact question. He did not give me any real answer.

He simply became quite absorbed in the topic of 'Lolita'. I have no idea who Lolita is."

"The L-lolita." Muffin puts the emphasis on the 'the'. "It's the girl in the p-pink top hat. The one that m-m-makes you all c-crazy."

"Hey!" The engineer is quick to the defensive. "You weren't there. She'd do that to you too."

Before Muffin can open his mouth, the driver is opening his. "No, she wouldn't. She didn't. Last night, she came for the book, the one she didn't get that time. And she was asking, getting angry, whatever, but she didn't make him give it to her."

She shrugs. "Maybe she can't do that anymore. Maybe it was a one-time thing." She expects that she'll develop amnesia after all this is over, her scientific self rejecting the unreasonable memories.

Shaking his head. "No, that's the thing. She totally got me. I mean, I don't know what happened really. But I was going after him, trying to take the book. And then the pink-haired girl came and they fought. Something about some guy or something. I mean, I wasn't really there. I don't know."

"Od-d-daiba!" Muffin cries out and chairs rock back.

"What?" He whirls in his seat to stare the kid down. The drunk has never known a stab wound to affect the brain.

"Od-daiba!" Excitedly wiggling in his seat. Stops when he realizes that causes pain. "We have to g-go to Odaiba!"

Adding it to his medical street knowledge: Knife wounds in the lumbar region cause brain damage. "You want to go shopping?" The drunk is not native to this country, but he's been to the area in question and as far as he can tell, it is nothing more than a glorified waterfront shopping centre. Although he did enjoy the beer sold along the fake boardwalk. Nice touch for a shopping centre.

"N-n-no, no!" Shaking his head so that he gets dizzy and he has to force himself to stop. "No, it's wh-where the Gosulo go."

"The who?" The captain knew the boy might have trouble

dealing with actual fight situations.

"The L-l-lolitas. Gothic and L-lolita, actually."

"You mean, the girl in the top hat?"

"N-n-no." His scorn reaches out and gives each of them a slap. "No, the g-girls, the group of girls who w-wear the Victorian style clothes with all the—" Staring into space, frowning. "What is that c-called? The b-big skirts worn under other s-skirts?"

"Petticoat?" The driver volunteers tentatively, hoping no one asks him why he knows that.

"Yeah, the girls who, who wear the p-petticoats and so much pink and, and the very t-tall shoes? Hair in c-curls? M-maybe they have little hats? They're called Lolitas. And the G-gothic ones, they wear all that stuff b-b-but in black with v-vampire accessories. There's one sh-shop in Odaiba that is the b-best Gosulo shop in the country. B-b-b-but very exclusive. You have to know p-people to even know about it. And not j-just anyone can shop there."

Narrowed eyes, the engineer leans forward. "How do you know that?"

"M-my best friend from school, his s-sister, she's a Gothic Lolita. V-v-very dedicated. She knows all the p-people, the entire scene. A-anyway, it has to b-be that place. That has, has to be the p-place he was talking about."

The captain slaps her hands on the counter in front of her. "Then we go. Odaiba is not so far, it's on the water and so accessible to us, and if it's not the correct place, at least we are back in Tokyo. We may be able to get some answers somewhere else."

Muffin pulls himself up from his chair, wincing and against the murmured protests of his crew, feeling noble and conquering. Except for the hot pain in his back, being stabbed is pretty much the best. "I have to see Corduroy." And the compulsion he feels is stronger than he can say. He shuffles out of the mess (in movies, it's called a mess) and walks down the hall. If anything happens to Corduroy, it happens to him. Is it because of what the Salaryman said, that Corduroy chose him? He's sure that can't be true. He's the worst pirate. Without this slice of his back sewn shut, he'd be the one pouring coffee this morning. Suddenly realizing that he doesn't know where he is. "H-hey! Where is Corduroy? S-someone can help me?"

Crew dispatched, the captain is the last one within earshot. She stands up. It's about time she spoke to this person in the corduroy jacket anyway.

But the person in the corduroy jacket is wearing a sweater missing one sleeve, and still unconscious. The captain runs a light finger over the gash on the shoulder. "Just from this?"

Muffin leans back in the captain's easy chair. "The S-s-salaryman reached out with the knife and C-corduroy's shirt s-sleeve came off and there was that little c-cut, but I-I-I didn't think it was such a big deal, b-but then, asleep!" Most of the time, he feels like he is fluent in this language but then every so often, a word is not there, an idea he can't express and he realizes that fluency is still far away.

"And what about him?" Casting her eyes towards the boy on the second bunk.

"They're lovers." Voice lowered, confidentially speaking.

A single eyebrow crawls up her forehead, but only slightly. "He's here because they have sex?"

He frowns. "A-actually, I don't know why he's here. Someone s-said something about him being the 'interface', but I d-d-don't know why he's here now. I guess Miss Dynamite f-found him?"

"You should stop calling her that. She doesn't like it." Absentmindedly. "So someone found him and now he's here. And he's the 'interface'. What does that mean?"

Shoulders up high. "It, it was in one of the books. Don't y-you remember? You were there. He's a r-r-r-robot."

Jerking away from the boy. "This is the robot?"

"No, no. The r-robot is the one that replaced him. I'm p-pretty sure that's n-not the robot." He can't be sure, anxiety gnaws. "I th-think."

The drunk sits down in the open doorway, takes a drink from the unlabeled bottle in his hand. "No, that's not the robot. Our girl smashed the robot up pretty good. Or so I hear."

"I thought you were on duty." The captain doesn't like to nag people to their duties.

He shakes his head, shaking the bottle at the same time. "It seems that I'm not. This boat's not needing so much care. One man to take care of the whole thing." Arms open to encompass the entire boat. "Don't know how that can work, but I'm not opposed to free time."

"So who is that man?" Smiling at the decided possibility that it's the engineer.

The drunk scratches his head with his free hand. "Our little love bunnies have apparently become one."

Low moans rising from the bed behind Muffin. Who peers in at the shadowed face. "A-a-are you awake?" Rapid cursing in the native tongue of this country and Muffin recoils. Expresses stammered outrage in the same language and the boy's eyelids open all the way.

"Oh, I'm sorry. I didn't uh, I—" One hand on his head, one hand on the bed pushing the rest of him up. Eyebrows pulled tightly together. "What the—Where am I? What is going on?" The eyes under the eyebrows suddenly frantic and he is using both hands to vault off the bed, lands running, but sneakers screeching to a halt as he spots his lover. Crouches down next to the bed. "Did you kidnap us? Are you working with that crazy man? What do you want?" He draws closer to his lover, tries to be a shield against whatever happens next.

"No, we are not working with 'that crazy man'. We did not kidnap you."

Muffin raises a tentative hand. "C-c-captain? We k-kind of did."

Pursing her lips tightly. "Yes, we kidnapped you. But only because you were unconscious and the man in the suit was about to use his jeweled dagger on you both. I think you'll forgive us for 'kidnapping' you."

"So...what? Why did you save us? What do you want? Who are you?" He drags a tense hand over his shaved skull. "What is happening?"

"We were hoping you could tell us." The captain watches him intensely.

Legs crumbling from a squat to his ass on the floor. Hands on his head as it shakes a little from side to side. "I don't know. I don't know. We were having dinner and then we left. And the cat went crazy, I don't know. It just screamed and ran out the window."

"The cat?" The drunk comes all the way in the room, drops down on the edge of the now-vacated bunk.

The boy nods. "Yeah, some cat. I mean, I don't know whose cat. It was a big, fluffy Persian. It made this horrible noise and ran out when I was paying the bill. And then we left, we went outside, walking home. And the waitress came out, called us back and said we forgot this box. And the next thing I remember is waking up in some container or something."

"You woke up in a container?" The captain leans forward.

"Yeah, yeah, in a box. I mean, it looked like a box from inside. And there was light coming in the cracks and...I don't know. Maybe I was drugged. It's all so weird in my head."

"What's weird? What's happened?"

Scratching his head, then his arm, then the head again. Eyes casting about, coming to rest on the drunk. "You don't have any cigarettes, do you?" Sounding very apologetic.

The boy's eyes land on the drunk. Does he look like a smoker? He wishes that he hadn't bought those cigarettes yesterday. First pack he buys in years and he's caught out. "Uh, yeah." He tosses the box to the boy who quickly pulls one out, lights it while the captain turns her curious gaze on the drunk.

The boy inhales and exhales from the cigarette several times. "I'm kind of quitting." Stares at his feet. "But I think I might have to try again some other time."

"So the box?" The captain's eyes are back on the boy.

"The box. Yeah. I mean, maybe I wasn't seeing straight. I don't know." The cigarette hand pushes close against his naked scalp. "When I looked out through the cracks in the box, I saw this guy, um, this guy with like a lot of skin. So I don't know, maybe I was seeing things."

"Why do you keep saying that?" The stream of I-don't-know's is wearing on the drunk.

He lets smoke out in one heavy breath. "Because he stepped out of it."

"I'm sorry, what?" Perhaps her grasp on this slippery language is not as strong as she thought.

Shoulders raised, cigarette to his lips. "He stepped out of it. That's what I saw. This man was so wrinkled and his skin really sagged off his body. It was like his clothes held his skin on. And then he took his clothes off and then he took his skin off."

"Maybe you were drugged." Although the drunk has been the advocate of weird following weird, Mr. Skin stepping out of that skin is too much for him.

"What happened next?" The captain withholds judgement.

"He started shuffling around the box, saying something in this really low voice, just the same thing over and over."

"Ch-chanting?"

The boy nods excitedly. "Yeah, chanting. I always forget that word." Crushes the short cigarette in the ashtray on the small table at the foot of the bed. "He was chanting and, I don't know, doing something with his hands. I mean, I couldn't see his face or anything. Just up to his elbows or so."

The drunk can't keep the question in any longer. "So he was

naked then? After stepping out of his skin?"

Startled, the boy meets his eyes. "No, that's the weirdest part. He was wearing these tight pants and this kind of frilly shirt."

Gasps all around.

"You don't think?" The drunk can't quite bring himself to say it.

Gritting her teeth. "I do in fact think."

Bewildered eyes from both Muffin and the boy. "Wh-what? Who? What are y-y-you guys talking about?" Feeling like somehow he should know. He has missed some vital clue.

"New Wave," the drunk snaps. "That's the new wave kid he's just described."

"B-but, but—" He thought that New Wave was hired by the Salaryman. "But j-just the clothes, he d-didn't see his face or anything."

The drunk's disdainful eyeballs are rolling. "Who else do you think it could be, hmm?"

The captain nods crisply. "That boy with the asymmetrical hair has been everywhere we have been. He has been somehow involved in this from the beginning." Turning her focus back to the boy. "He chanted. What did he do next?"

More head shaking, shoulders rising. "I don't know. I think that salaryman, our stalker, that guy came in. I mean, I never saw him before, but the shiny shoes and the pants were the same as what I was told, so."

"The Salaryman?" Muffin can't contain a gasp.

"Not 'the Salaryman'," the drunk is quick to correct. "Just Salaryman. Like a name."

"And uh, Salaryman said that he had the way and, 'If you're done with the interface, I prepared the way.' And then, the guy with the skin, he says, 'Take the interface to the temple. Keep him away from up until I arrive. If the way is not marked when they meet again, we won't be able to do this.' It was just so weird, I remember every word." Shaking his head, bringing his hand to his lips, realizing too late that he has finished that cigarette. "I mean, I don't even know what that means. I must have been drugged."

"And then what?" The captain urges the boy on, ignoring the wide eyes of her crew members on her, but feeling their weight. Is it because she is the way? The arrows on her torso? The engineer told her, but she is uneasy with it. What does it mean to be 'the way'?

"See, I must be making this up or something. It just doesn't make sense. I mean, I saw him step back into that skin. And then, uh, I don't know. There was like some times when I thought maybe I was dreaming something, but I can't remember. It's all shadows and blurry images. And then I woke up here."

"That's it?" The drunk keeps his hands at his sides.

Heavy feet racing towards them and all faces turn to the doorway expectantly. Rewarded by the engineer slightly out of breath. "Odaiba. We dock in five minutes."

The captain pulls herself to her feet. "You stay here," she tells Muffin, who sets himself back down gladly. Moving away from Corduroy seems like an impossibility. "You and you, come." Out the door, up the stairs after the engineer.

The boy on the floor looks bewildered. "Me?"

Taking pity, the drunk offers him a hand. "Aye, you. It won't do to have the two of you together." Eyebrows pointed at Corduroy unconscious on the bed.

"But, but what about him?" On his feet reluctantly.

"Those two have to stay together. Trust us." Confidence that he doesn't feel. The boy is the interface, the captain is the way and the kid on the bed? If they don't understand this, how can they make it end?

"Obviously, we have to take the boy." The captain is not going to be moved on this. "They are pieces. We are pieces. We cannot have those pieces together."

"So you want me to take the boy?" The driver is not sure he approves of this plan. He'd prefer to have at least one pirate by his side if he has to watch over the boy.

A single sharp nod. "He can't stay here. Apparently, his lover and he have some kind of connection that the man in the suit hopes to use. And I appear to be part of that, so he certainly should not be with me. In addition, I seem to be unable to control my wakings. If I should sleep while out...we should be a group of three in case of that happening."

"That's why you should stay here, captain." The engineer makes one last plea. "We're just going to find the shop."

"I can't believe that git knows that this place is in Odaiba, but has no idea where."

The engineer comes to Muffin's defense. "We're lucky he even knew it was here."

"If this is even the right place," the drunk notes with the bottle in his hand.

"OK, if it's not the right place, you can punch him. Are you happy now?" The engineer just wants to get this over with, find the girl and get some answers.

She smirks when they are forced into some artificial shrubbery by precisely ordered columns of advancing lolitas. "Hmm, I wonder if this is the right place."

"Just shut up." The drunk tries to avoid bare skin touching the fake plants. He gets a rash.

The captain peers out from their hiding place as the lolitas shuffle forward on the deserted boardwalk of the oceanfront shopping centre. "What are they doing?"

"Going to meet their leader?"

The engineer turns to the drunk. "Are you saying that our Lolita is their leader?"

"I think she's proven that she can get people to do what she wants." With a shrug that brings his hand up against a plastic purple flower. "Dammit." Tries wiping the hand on his pants, knowing that it will have no effect and there will be welts popping up in no time. "We'll follow them, then?"

The captain nods with a frown on her face as she stares at passing feet. "Why do they walk with their feet turned in like that? And many of them move like horses."

"I always wonder that. I thought maybe it was a disease." Eyeing the wide variety of shoes and the engineer knows that her second guess — it's the shoes — is also off the mark. "But why would so many girls with the same disease belong to the same subgroup?"

The drunk's eyes are far back in his head. "Oh for—it's fashion." Exasperated. "Young girls do enjoy fashion and in this country, fashion means prancing like a show pony."

The last of the lolitas shuffle and prance by their hiding place. "Whatever the reason, they move quite slowly." The captain watches and waits for them to be far enough away so that she and her crew can emerge from the shrubbery and creep frustratingly slowly after them.

"It's probably under construction or something." The driver searches for an explanation as to the lack of customers in this shopping-mad city. "I mean, it would have to be, right? Otherwise, where did everyone go?"

The boy nods. "I've never seen a place in Tokyo so deserted. It must be closed."

Careful, quiet footsteps past darkened shop windows. "Well, the shops are all closed, so yeah. But in the middle of the day? It's got to be construction."

"Hey!" The boy shouts, then clamps his hand over his mouth. "Sorry," in a much quieter voice. He is not used to the spy game thing. "Um, but there's a shop there, 'Poupée de la Nuit'. That's probably it."

Following the boy's extended hand, squinting to read the Gothic style letters. "Yeah. That sounds very Gothic Lolita." He glances around, nothing but artificial palm trees. "Let's go check it out."

The boy swallows nervously several times. "Um, don't you think we should go back and get the others?"

"Why? You heard the captain; you guys shouldn't be around each other. And we're just taking a look." Keeping close to the walls. He can't see anyone, but he stopped trusting his senses about three days ago.

"I g-guess I just thought being a pirate was going to be more exciting, y-you know?" Muffin leans back, winces at the pressure on his wound, shifts his weight forward again. "But until they s-started asking us to blow stuff up, all I did was run errands and make coffee. I-I-I have degrees in c-classical literature and history. I-I was an associate professor. I was a rising s-star. I shouldn't be m-making coffee. Don't you think?" Eyes slipping around the room down to the inert body on the bed across from him. A heavy breath is the response he gets and he frowns. "D-do you think you're going to wake up soon? It's n-not so much fun by myself and I'm getting pretty bored, to be honest. Al-although you are a very g-good listener." Quick addition in case somewhere in there Corduroy is listening to him. No need to lower self-esteems. Sighs. Twists his head to take a look at his stitches again. He's pretty sure he'll have a scar.

The cat's voice sends him up off the bed towards the ceiling. On his descent, he sees the calico in the doorway. With the fat Siamese who sat in front of him when all the other cats stabbed him. It looks like that cat, anyway. He wonders how many fat, emerald-eyed Siamese there are in the cat army.

"C-c-c-cats." The cats are his friends. He has to learn to love them and not fear their stabbing little feet.

The Siamese waddles over to him and sits on the floor at his feet. Opens her mouth to speak, but nothing comes out. She tries again and manages to push some air through her vocal cords to produce an airy squeak, looks up at him pleadingly.

Seeing the plea in her eyes, but not knowing what it's for. "W-w-what? Y-you want...a, a cookie?"

She lifts a single chocolate paw and places it on the edge of the bed. Opens her disproportionately small mouth again.

"U-up? You want up?"

Heavy purrs push forward from her chest. The calico leaps on the bed opposite with a grunt.

This fat soft animal couldn't possibly hurt him, he tells himself as he reaches down and hooks an arm around her ample belly. Her weight startles him and he needs to put a little more effort into pulling her off the ground with one hand. He sets her next to him on the bed. "What d-do you eat? You m-might want to, you know, eat l-less of it." Defensive hands in the air at the accusing eyes she turns on him. "It's j-j-just an idea."

The calico scrabbles around on Corduroy and Muffin wonders if that's such a good idea, but lacks the nerve to remove the cat so lets her proceed. "Uh, are, are you l-looking for something?"

The calico meets his eyes, turns her head back to Corduroy. Meows. He realizes that the calico is not randomly attacking Corduroy, but is focusing on the pocket on the left side of the baggy pants. She turns yellow eyes on him again, more urgently. Louder meowing.

"O-okay. I hear you." Taking a step to set himself down on the bed next to Corduroy and the burrowing calico. The Siamese alone on the other bed opens her mouth to another silent pleading meow and starts looking around for a way down. Peering over the edge of the bed, pulling her head back. Gets enough air in her throat to squeak.

"I c-can't be there and here. J-just wait a minute, okay?" Back to the calico and her expectant eyes. "S-so in the pocket?" Assenting rumbles from her chest. As he sticks a hand in the oversize pocket, he feels something cold against his fingertips, decides that this must be what the calico is obsessed with, pulls it out. "A compass?" Frowning down at one feline, then the other. "I don't understand."

A soft paw on his wrist. A gentle mew.

So he turns his head back to the compass in his hand and sees that instead of the regular directions, it just says 'up' where 'north' usually goes. He stares at the two letters, frowning and hoping that something starts making sense. When hope runs out, he looks up. "I d-don't under—" He's not looking at the mottled coat of the calico, but the kid in the corduroy jacket. Really wearing a corduroy jacket now and hurrying away from him. "Hey! Y-you're awake!" He reaches out, but

You are taking the steps to the temple two at a time. You're late.

Steps to the temple? Is his wound infected? Has the infection reached the brain? He should have known better than to trust the drunk. He's still got the compass with its needle wobbling around 'up'. He stares at the retreating brown jacket and, shrugging mental shoulders, chases the jacket and its owner up the stairs.

At the top of the stairs, you wonder which way to go next. She just said the temple at Hase, but not which building at the temple at Hase. And there's eight or nine of them. Cursing under your breath. Is she some kind of crazy *miko*? No one but a shrine maiden would she make you come to this temple in the middle of nowhere just to talk to you. Not even understanding why you couldn't just talk on the phone, why it has to be all talk in person. But if Boy is getting something on the side, you need to know about it. He's been getting too clutch baby lately and if it's guilt based, you're done with him. Maybe you're done with him anyway. The clutch baby thing is getting a little old.

Corduroy is just standing there, staring aimlessly around the temple grounds as Muffin pants his way to the top of the steps. At least his back doesn't hurt now. Bends over, hands on knees, to catch his breath.

"Yoo-hoo!"

Jerks his head up at the sugary call. Why can't he hallucinate some supermodels if he is going to die of a terrible brain infection? Why does he have to imagine that girl?

You twist in the direction of the high-pitched shout out. "Me?"

Her petticoats bounce and swish as she nods and waves from the doorway of the largest building on the grounds. Black hair slipping over her shoulders, grazing the straps of the white bag covered in sparkly red hearts that is hooked over her elbow. "Of course, silly! I don't see anyone else here! C'mon!" White gloves beckon you forward.

Surprised to hear that he is not here. Muffin wonders where he is as he hurries after Corduroy, even while contemplating why he bothers.

Inside the big hall again, shuddering. Seeing the—Seeing Salaryman standing in front of him with that knife again. Starts praying silently to the enormous image of Kannon behind the Lolita.

Who cocks her head to the side, lower lip popping out. "Do you hear that?"

You shrug. "Uh, hear what?"

"Huh. Sounds like a little buzzing or something." Tiny shoulders slipping up. "I guess it's just me."

Not a *miko*, but definitely crazy. Unless *miko* recently went Lolita. And Buddhist. But you feel certain that the multitude of rock-dwelling spirits or any other member of the Shinto pantheon would not approve such a change in the structure of worship. "So look. I don't know why I had to come all the way out here, but I'm here. So what is it?"

"Oh yeah, totally. I can totally get that you're, like, annoyed." Bobbing her small head with black lips pushing forward. "I mean, it's pretty far." Lips spreading out into a grin. "But totally worth it, okay? Check it out."

Are you supposed to follow her behind the big statue? Is she even allowed to go back there? You thought that was some kind of priest-only area. Sighing. This whole trip was probably a waste of time. There's no point in even waiting for her to come back out. You should just leave.

If he's not here, then he's not really going into the altar area and following the Lolita behind the Kannon? Right? No Buddhist hell for him, this isn't real. Still, his heart pounds madly and he has to remember to breathe. The Lolita opens a little door at the base of the statue. Kannon has a door?

She stands upright again and sticks her tongue out at the ceiling. "Stupid jerk. You just can't handle a woman with ambition."

The breathing he's tried so hard to keep constant stops. She can't be talking to him though. He's not here. Plus, he has no problems with women with ambition. He supports gender equality.

Sunshine and smiles as she emerges from behind the statue. "So?"

You run a hand over your head, through your hair. A waste of time. And it's not like you have so much of it to waste. "So what?"

The sunshine slides off her face and those deep dark eyes are rolling past up and into her brain. "Oh god! You really suck!"

"Wh—Where did that come from?" Did she just make you come all this way to insult you?

The bag slides down her arm as she puts her hands on her hips and for the first time, you notice the floppy ears of a rabbit hanging over the edge. "Look, I know you think I'm fucking your boyfriend or whatever. So just think that if that's what you need. But this is all about you."

Did she just say that she's fucking Boy? "What? What is all about me?"

"See, it's obvious that you're not qualified for the job. So just forget it. Soon, you won't have to do it anymore."

You know all the words she's saying, but strung together in that order, you can't pull any meaning from them. Staring blankly. Are all Lolitas crazy? "The job?"

Without responding, she sets her bag down on the floor. "Mr. Fluffles, can you give me a little help? I don't think I can do this alone." Nose twitching at hyperspeed, the white rabbit jumps over the edge of the bag and sits quietly on the wooden floor.

"Do what alone?" Why do you keep standing here? It's obvious you're not going to get any answers. Was she kidding when she said she was fucking Boy?

Coal black eyes shooting daggers at you. "I said, just forget it." The rabbit's nose twitches even faster.

Muffin watches Corduroy fall to the ground for the third time since their paths crossed. Can't that kid stay on the old feet? Dutifully crossing the room to squat down, check for life. Reaching out to take a pulse, the compass drops out of his pocket and he reaches down for it. Notices the needle pointing unwaveringly at 'up'. Looks up at the Kannon above him, down at the kid at his feet, back to the compass. Which one is 'up'? Staring at the two letters as he tries to unpuzzle this. Maybe neither of them are up. After all, up is that way. Follows his thought with his eyes and the ceiling is much closer than he expected. And white. Isn't the temple ceiling made of unpainted wood?

Sharp pain in his hand and he yanks it away, letting the compass clatter to the floor. "Ow!" Eyes seeking out the offender and finding the calico. Ears catching the faint squeak of the Siamese still trapped on the other bed. He ignores the plaintive sound to focus on the calico. "Am I d-d-dying?"

The calico jumps down from the bed, heads for the door. Did she just flick her tail disdainfully?

He picks up the compass on the floor, sets himself down next to the Siamese who thunders her appreciation. Petting her absent-

mindedly as he stares at Corduroy. So the awake thing was a dream?
Hallucination? Brain infection?

"Do you hear that?" The boy raises anxious eyes as the driver
fiddles with the lock on the back door.

Almost laughing at how easy it is. Always overkill on the front,
with the bars and the shutters and then a flimsy tumbler lock on
the back door. "Huh? What? No."

"It sounds like a lot of feet."

Sighs and lets himself listen to something other than the lock.
Hears lots of feet. "A parade?"

He has the thought before the boy says it. "In a deserted shopping
centre?"

Back to the lock. He's not as skilled as the captain but this is not
the most difficult lock. A few more seconds of maneuvering and
he's got it. He pulls the door open noiselessly. "In." Quick hand
towards the open doorway. "I don't know what that is, but I think
we don't need to find out."

He looks up at the sun advancing across the sky. "Well, at this
rate, we'll be eating our breakfast here tomorrow morning." The
drunk was really hoping that they would get the night off of crazy.
Was it only a few days ago that he was drinking heavily and watching
subtitled telly?

The engineer leans back against an artificial banana tree,
complete with half-ripened bananas. "I'm getting kind of hungry,
actually."

Squatting, watching the Lolitas shuffle forward. "They seem to
be advancing on that shop." The captain lifts a long finger.

She turns, squints to block the sun. "What does that say? Poo—
Poh—Pow?" Panicking at the thought of a word she doesn't know.
She's not as smart as she thought?

"'Poupée de la nuit.' That's French that you're killing. Means 'night doll' or some such thing." The drunk pats himself on the back for showing up the smart girl. "Maybe we'll be meeting them there rather than waiting here for them?"

"Careful of the lace." The driver's warning comes too late and the boy walks right into layers of starched lace.

"Ow!" Surprised at the stiff, scratchiness. He thought lace was supposed to be soft. But he has not had a lot of experience with lace.

Grabbing the boy's arm and yanking him to the floor. "Shh!" He hopes his ears are lying to him, but feels confident that they are still truthful.

"Well, they're on their way back here now, so too bad, okay?" The Lolita's voice grows louder as she approaches the pile of lace petticoats they've buried themselves in.

"Look, uh, just send them you know, away. This thing you're uh like doing, it's you know crazy, right."

The driver holds in a cheap soap opera gasp, but the boy at his side can't quite keep his in.

"Hear that?" Defiantly stomping to the front of the shop. "They're already here."

"Like that was you know, breathing, okay. Unless your like army can you know float." His footsteps follow hers less aggressively.

"I told you, they're not an army, okay? God. They're a fashion patrol. I'm not telling you again. Geez." Thumping into the room.

And then silence and the driver feels that familiar lump of dread in his gut.

Multi-coloured lace ripped away from his head with a triumphant "Ha-ha!"

Taking a deep breath, meeting the eyes of New Wave. "Hey." Weakly. "What are you doing here?"

Lolita peeps through the crook in New Wave's elbow. "You?" She turns her outrage on the much taller man in the ruffled shirt.

"Did you know he was here? Oh my god. I can't believe I thought we could work it out. You were totally going to let those stupid jerks stop me. You're totally working with her!"

New Wave glares at the driver who crosses his fingers that the boy still buried in lace at his side knows enough to keep his fat mouth shut. Turns to the girl in pink at his side. "No, like, I had you know no idea, man. Like I'm sincere, you know? I wasn't like uh planning whatever."

Fists slamming down at her sides. "This is so like you! God. Totally. You always do this! You always think you can just control everything or whatever!" Heavy pink platform boots echo as she thuds over to the window, peers out. "And where is my fashion patrol?" she squeals in frustration.

"Are we there yet?" Eyes closed. How long can he walk in a straight line before opening them? Will he hit a fake banana tree?

The captain sighs. "No. We're not there yet." Her gaze starts to unfocus on the swaying skirts of the many lolitas shuffling towards the shop.

"I say we jump on their backs, get a ride." Eyes still closed.

"We can't do that!" The engineer manages to muster up some outrage despite the calming effect of so much pink and white lace moving gently from side to side, an occasional splash of black to keep things interesting.

"And why can't we? These lasses are not in this world. We've been in plain sight for ages and they've not taken any notice of us. I say we take advantage, get off our feet for a wee bit."

The captain cuts in before they really get started. "The shop is just ahead. We'll just keep following. It won't be long now."

"Aye, that's what you said ten minutes ago."

The shuffling and prancing in front of them turns into running and trotting abruptly. The drunk's eyelids fly open at the new sounds. "What the—?"

"Come on!" The captain is already racing after the doll girls.

The engineer picks up the pace. Is her fiancé the reason for the running? Is he her fiancé? Did she say yes? Maybe when they were on the boat? Cursing her own absent-mindedness.

"No! You shut up! You always do this! You think I can't handle it! You think I'm just a little girl! That is totally not true!"

The driver winces at Lolita's piercing voice.

"No, no, c'mon. Like uh, just you know, you're all 'I wanna be up' and like you don't even know, right." Placating hands out and expansive, ignored by the girl.

Stomping back and forth. "You just—God! It's not about me being up. You just totally don't get it."

Hands crammed deep into pockets. "Okay, I like uh don't you know get it. So tell me. Tell me what I like don't uh get."

Pulling his hands from his pockets, clutching them in her own, she gazes anxiously up at him. "I don't want to fight, okay? I just—I just need you to understand? I need to have my own thing."

He lets her hold his hands, but warily. "Your own uh thing is the like directions?"

She pushes him away, turns her head. "No! Just—God!"

Hoping that the debate is as heated as it sounds, the driver pulls himself up from the lace cushioning, digs around for the boy.

Slam as the door hits the wall and girls in full skirts pour in. Lolita smirks at New Wave. "See? Here they are."

He jumps back to avoid being trampled as the girls organize themselves on the sales floor. Lights a cigarette and brings it to his lips. "Yeah, like so what are you know they uh going to do?"

Soft feet on the floor as the boy and the driver head back the way they came.

Noises of deep exasperation pushed from her throat. "As if you don't even already know! You know everything, don't you? Why don't you just tell me what they're going to do?"

Shoulders up around his ears. "Like, uh, I don't you know, know. Go to your uh secret like meeting with the man in uh charge and you know kill him so that you can like take over?"

Painted lower lip on the floor. "How, I mean, what—" Arms fall to her sides and the small box bag drops to the floor. With an indignant squeak, Mr. Fluffles hops out and crosses the room to hide in the legs of the lolitas standing silently with toes pointed inwards.

Gentle, gentle. The driver pulls the door towards him as softly as possible. No need to attract attention. Pushes the boy out onto the boardwalk. Feels the eyes of hundred of girls in big skirts and high necked shirts on him. Freezes.

"What are you still doing here?" Lolita storms over to the driver, grabs his arm, drags him into the centre of the room and throws him down on the floor in front of New Wave. "Can't you see this is private?" The anger in her voice slowly disappearing until 'private' is choked out from a tear-lump-filled throat. "Can't you see that he," Disdainful sad eyes on New Wave. "doesn't love me, that he totally never loved me?"

"Hey! That is like uh so not you know true!" He puts a firm sneaker-clad foot forward, but the empty-eyed driver prevents any further progress.

The engineer freezes in the doorway, unable to tear her eyes away from her lover threatening the new wave kid.

The drunk grabs her sleeve, tears it pulling her to the floor. "Get down!" Hissing and inching forward for cover in the forest of white and pink tights standing between them and the top Lolita.

The captain holds her position outside against the wall. From the engineer's face, she knows it is the driver in there, but what about the boy?

"Hey, like uh, no fair." New Wave takes a step away from the driver. "You can't you know uh do that. Rules, right?"

"God, you totally are on her side!" She tugs a monogrammed handkerchief from a hidden shirt pocket. Watery eyes on the driver. "He's just so mean. I mean, having an affair with my sister?"

The horror of her wet eyes and the terrible unfaithfulness of the man with the asymmetrical hair overwhelms him. He reaches forward to take the pale neck in both hands and squeezes, holding his own breath. Anything to make her stop feeling so sad.

"No!" She hasn't said yes yet.

The drunk fumbles frantically for some piece of the engineer as she pulls herself off the floor and scrabbles forward. He gets a piece of her coat, but no engineer. Digs out the curses he learned in Singapore, yells them all at her in his head.

The captain whirls around at the light touch on her shoulder and relaxes when she sees the boy, but only slightly. She didn't hear his approach. Perhaps this is a sign that she should retire. It may be that she is no longer aware enough to be captain of a small band of pirates, especially with her sleeping issues taken into consideration. Is piracy still a viable career choice for her?

The boy raises his eyebrows questioningly, cocks his head toward the shop interior.

She shakes her head, fingers to her lips, and goes over outcomes in her head. The boy being with her is a very bad idea, but the others are inside. Would he make it if she sent him to the boat alone?

"Unlikely." Followed by chortles to her left and she raises her eyes reluctantly.

"I am delighted to find the two of you here together. You've made my job so much easier." Manicured hand sliding out of a pocket. "So let's be on our way, shall we? No need to disturb them." Slight nod of the head towards the shop.

Shoving the boy away, shouting for him to run, leaping for the man in the suit. Except the boy is still standing next to her, her voice does not reach her ears and her feet remain firmly on the ground.

"You remember this, don't you?" The man in the suit takes smooth steps towards them. "Here's another old favourite." Perfectly hairless hand reaching out, touching the boy's cheek familiarly, fatherly, and the boy slumps against the captain.

Crying out, raising a knee as he comes towards her. Not surprised by her knee staying where it is, her mouth still closed as his hand caresses her own face.

They both go down in the tackle. The engineer wills herself to be as heavy as possible, hold him down somehow. She crosses her fingers that if she just doesn't look at Lolita, she won't get all twisted up and attack New Wave.

Abrupt puff of air through his nostrils. "Is your like uh army here as tough as you know the guy who just uh got tackled by like his girlfriend?"

"Shut up!" Windows break and the drunk suspects he just lost the hearing in his left ear. "I told you they're the fashion patrol!" Right feet pop up around him and he rolls to dodge the inevitable return of those feet to earth. The shop that is not a shop is filled with the thunder of platformed feet advancing on New Wave. "You totally can't stop me! I'm totally going to kill him and then I'll be in charge! I'll be better than up! I'll be the one deciding all the directions!"

The drunk mutters angry threats at himself as he stands and pushes through the thumping lolitas. "But, lass, do you not know that he's the one doing the deciding?" If the boy was lying about the new wave kid stepping out of Mr. Skin, the drunk knows he won't get the chance to mete out the penalty punches.

Every lolita turns on her heel to face him, one knee still up, ready to continue the grudge march. Mr. Fluffles appears from their midst, hops tentatively towards the girl behind them all.

"What did you say?" Almost inaudible, but the daggers in her voice carry.

"I said, that's the one you're set on overthrowing." Index finger unwavering on New Wave. "He's been seen wearing some other skin." Frowning at the way that comes out.

Lolita and crew turn to the man in the frilly shirt. "What is he talking about?"

Eyebrows high, defensive hands raised. "Like uh, what, you know, how could—"

Black lips pulling back into a perfectly formed circle with a sharp intake of breath. A single gloved hand quick to cover it. "It's true, isn't it? It's totally true. You're him. That's how you knew. You totally knew everything. You totally planned this." A heavy pink-shoed step back. "Why would you do this? Why would you lie to me?"

Dark eyes aimed at the drunk, speaking to the girl. "Look, uh, you're all like totally crazy, right? I'm totally not even. Like uh, it's just uh a misunderstanding. I uh you know I don't like even know what uh you're you know." Head turning back and forth. Front door, back door, front door, back door. Back door. "I totally like uh have you know stuff to like do, okay? We'll like talk later, right." The tension in his legs belies his desire to run.

Knees buckling the second the door swings shut behind him and Lolita buries her face in her pastel pink gloves. "Oh my god. How could he do this to me?"

The engineer relaxes her weight-increasing efforts. The driver under her has stopped struggling and she lets herself believe that Lolita is not working him with her tears anymore. Meeting his clear eyes, she almost lets out an audible sigh of relief. But she lets the drunk hold Lolita's attention. Holds her breath, keeps that sigh in.

Run like hell? Keep her occupied? The drunk weighs the options in his head. Begrudgingly goes with keep her occupied. "So did you not know?"

Woeful head shaking. "No. I mean, totally like, how could I know?" Round, pits of tears turned on him suddenly. "I mean, I was gonna kill him." Lower lips trembles ferociously. "I was totally gonna kill him. I thought, I thought—"

He crouches down next to her and slips an arm over her shoulders. Glances up at the engineer helping the driver off the floor, together inching towards the back door. "Aye, but there was no way for you to have known, now was there?" He rubs her arm in a way that he thinks might be consoling.

"Yeah, but—" Hiccups. "I mean, why?" Muscles in her neck give out, head hangs forlornly and the drunk almost feels sorry for her. "I thought he loved me, you know? I thought—" Several sobs pull free from her throat.

He pats her arm as he looks around the room. Could he get to the door before she realized he was gone? "Now, then. Do you not think he might be doing this exactly because he does love you?" Hours of daytime telly finally working for him.

The hiccupping sobs stop suddenly. Black eyes focus on his face. "What do you mean?"

"Well, darling, a man will do many things for his lady. Did you not say that he was not able to handle your ambition? May be that he was trying to keep you near him." If she makes him talk more, he's doomed. That's all the terrible advice he can remember.

The engineer pulls her lover forward. "Come on!"

"But the captain? The drunk?"

"The captain obviously went back to the ship!" Why won't he just come? "And the drunk knows where we are. Come on."

"What if he gets in trouble with her?"

"He's not going to get in trouble with her. He's comforting her. She just lost her lover. She's not going to do anything now. Come on."

Sadness slides into vengeance before the drunk's eyes. "If he can't handle a woman who knows what she wants, then he is totally not even the guy." She flings her consoler aside, collects Mr. Fluffles from the floor at her feet and eases him into her handbag. "He is going to be so totally sorry."

Lolita feet hit the ground simultaneously and the drunk is surprised they were able to hold those knees in the air for so long. Rubs his head. That girl is a lot stronger than she looks. "So you'll be on your way to...?" Crossing his fingers that he doesn't get included in the plan for vengeance just for asking.

Derisive snort as she strides towards the door. "As if I don't even know where he is. He thinks he's so smart, thinks I can't figure anything out unless he tells me. He is such a jerk!" Bystanding lolitas throw the doors open as she approaches. "I know where this ends and I know he has the interface and the way. I just have to make sure I'm the one finishing this up." She smirks, running her hand down Mr. Fluffles' back. "I am so totally gonna be the one to close that stupid little door." Petticoats fly as the fashion patrol chases after her.

He lifts his tired carcass off the floor. Why couldn't she just tell him if she knows where this ends? Everything's a riddle with these people.

"Where's the captain?" The engineer elephants her way down the stairs and Muffin swallows his heart.

Pounds his chest to get things in there sorted again. "W-w-what? The captain's with y-you." He jumps up from the bed. "The c-captain's not with you?" He follows the sound of elephants to the engineer moving from room to room, frantic.

"She's not here?" Head in the mess.

"N-no, no one's here. Just m-me and Corduroy. What

— 357 —

happened?"

The driver comes up behind Miss Wild Eyes, gets firm hands on her shoulders. "Just calm down. Sit. I'm sure she'll be back soon." He sets her down at the table.

"Not unless someone returns her." The drunk slides past Muffin to lean against the wall behind the engineer. "Lolita said that our old friend Skin has 'the way and the interface'. Or is it the new wave kid that has them?"

"If C-corduroy's gentleman caller wasn't l-lying."

"I told you to stop calling him that." The drunk's protest is mere formality.

"So he has the boy too." The driver kicks himself for pushing the boy out the door. "Now what?"

Shoulders high. "The little miss seemed to know exactly where they are. She stormed out the door to get revenge and take over the world or something."

The engineer glares. "Well, where are they? Did you follow her?"

"Now, pet, does it look like I followed her?" He ignores the engineer's glare, continues when she opens her mouth to respond. "I thought maybe you would know where they are." Staring at Muffin intently.

"M-m-m-me?" Finger pushed against his nose. "W-why would I know? I d-don't know anything."

The drunk's head tilts to the side. "Aye, but you've been here with the kid and you're the only one who's read those flip-floppy books. And you did that thing before."

Wrinkles dug deep in Muffin's forehead. "W-what thing?" Eat? Run? Panic?

Dismissive hand twirling. "That thing with the kid when you were attacked and you just stood there. One minute, you were here." Index finger shoots out. "The next minute, you were there." The finger sweeps over to the other side of the room.

"That's impossible!" The engineer is on her feet before the driver can stop her. "You were obviously drunk. Or closed your eyes or something."

A large amount of air shoots out of his lungs. "Do we have to do this again now?" The drunk finds himself unable to have this conversation without a cigarette and is pleased to discover the pack he bought in the bottom of his pocket. Slightly worse for the wear, but he manages to pull a crumpled cigarette out, still in one piece. Lights it. "It. Does. Not. Matter if it's impossible, have you got that? I saw him with the kid. And our good friend, the 'gentleman caller'," Eyebrows raised at Muffin as he exhales. "was trying to stab one or both of them. And then the two of them were on the other side of the boy." He takes another drag, holds it in, lets it out. "I was not drunk, pet. It is impossible and it did happen, so can we please move on? Just accept that we've signed on for some insanity and let us get to dealing with it."

The engineer drops to her knees, head in hands, weeping.

The drunk drops his cigarette, stares. He broke the engineer.

Glad for the distraction, Muffin reaches down to pick the burning ember up off the floor and hands it back to the drunk, avoids looking at the engineer having a breakdown.

"I can't, I can't." Empty voice inside the tears.

The driver leans over to rub her back, questions in his eyes for the other two. "Can't what, honey?"

"I just can't." The intensity of the sobs increases. "It's all impossible. It's all..."

The drunk grabs Muffin's shirt collar and yanks him to his feet. "Well, we'll just be leaving the two of you alone then." Pushes the boy out the door quick quick.

Muffin winces, but keeps his protests in his head. He's willing to take a little pain to get away from the engineer's unexpected tears. In the room with Corduroy, he lets his breath out. "W-what was that?"

"I think our little miss finally snapped." The drunk settles down on the bed next to the kid. Spots the calico on the floor. "When did the cats get here? How did they get here?" He looks around for more and meets the vacant green eyes of an overweight Siamese. "Where are the others?"

"I d-don't know. There's just the two of them. They came after you l-left and made me get this out of Corduroy's pocket." Muffin opens his hand to show the drunk the compass.

Frowning, the drunk snatches it from the boy's palm. "'Up'? It's an 'up' compass?" He eyes the boy doubtfully.

Muffin snatches it back. "Y-yes, it's an 'up' c-compass."

"What does that mean?"

"I d-don't know. In the dream, it was p-pointing straight at up when we were in the temple." His own doubt on his face as he realizes that it's pointing in the opposite direction now. Even when he pulled it out of Corduroy's pocket, it wasn't straight down. Is that bad? He thinks that might be bad.

Eyebrows moving past his receded hairline. "In the dream?"

Chewing his lower lip. "I-I think I'm a little feverish maybe? When I p-picked up the compass, I was at the t-t-temple and C-corduroy was awake and we met Lolita."

The drunk folds his arms across his chest. "You met Lolita? Did you have a tea party?"

"Sh-shut up. It was w-weird. We were, we were in the temple and she went b-behind the Kannon and I f-followed her. I don't think I was really there, so i-it's okay for me to go b-back there." Quick to reaffirm this. Quick to let any of the gods hanging about know that he's not a heathen, no need to send him to any of the hells. "A-and she opened a, a little door."

The drunk was sure that he cleaned the stab wound well enough. It should not be getting infected badly enough to induce hallucinations. "A little door?" He doesn't even have to inject any sarcasm into the words. They sound ridiculous enough on their own. Someone in his head runs around to make the connections and turn on the lights and he sits up straight. "A little door!"

Taken aback by the drunk's religious fervour. "Uh, y-yeah. A little d-door. She just pulled it open and then um, sh-she made Corduroy go to sleep or something. I d-d-didn't really get it. She started doing something with th-the rabbit and then I was—"

"No, no!" The drunk leaps to his feet. "A little door! That's what she said when she left. She said, 'I'll close that little door' or something like that. I thought she was talking about finishing this whole disaster, but she really meant a little door." Stepping out into the narrow hall. "We've got to get back to the temple. That's where they are. Apparently, we've got to close a little door."

"W-w-what about Corduroy?" Muffin calls after him, but no response. He turns his gaze back to the sleeper. If he was going to get someone who was sleeping for no reason to wake up, what would he do? The same question he's been asking himself all afternoon and he still has no answers. He tried rubbing the compass all over Corduroy, but that didn't work. And in retrospect, he really shouldn't have expected it to. But the cats got it out for him, so there must be something. Pondering as he limps down the hall after the drunk.

Stopped by the sudden presence of the girl with pink hair who meets his eyes squarely. "This has all gone to hell." Somber.

Muffin tries to keep his balance, fails, tries to lean into the fall to keep the wound on his back closed. Tailbone connects sharply with the floor and he pulls air in through his teeth. "W-what?"

She offers him her hand. "It's all gone to hell. The whole thing. If he's the one behind this." For some reason, he knows she's talking about the boy with the funny hair. Takes the hand, lets himself be pulled off the floor. "I just knew something was off, you know? The old man works in cycles. For him to start so early, it just isn't his style. But I really never thought that their relationship would lead to this. I mean, she's just a kid. Sure, she has her rabbit and she's got dreams of big things, but she's still a kid. And him, he knows better." Muffin is distracted by hallucinations of the boy and the girl in the pink top hat. "I'll be damned if I know how the boy got so much control over all this."

"Y-y-you didn't know?"

Gum snapping furiously. "Of course I didn't know." She pushes him into the captain's room and shuts the door.

Muffin swallows his breath. Alone with Pink Hair.

"Um, okay, if you're going to be thinking like that, we need to set some things straight." Flopping backwards onto the sofa.

Defensive hands flying so fast in front of his face that he catches the tip of his nose. "N-n-no! No! I d-didn't—I mean, I was j-j-just—"

Her red lips stretch out with amusement. "Whatever." Arm dangles over the armrest to let nails drag against the thin beige carpet. "He's supposed to be with us. She's supposed to be with us. Sure, he likes to screw around with the old man, screw around with me, play us off each other sometimes, but there isn't supposed to be any issue with the succession of directions." She scratches the tip of her straight nose lightly, frowning. "Well, not now, anyway."

Muffin doesn't stop to question why he knows she's talking about New Wave and Lolita and he feels sure that the answer to "So when then?" would be meaningless to him, so he focuses on the present. "S-s-so what happened?"

Flamboyant hand twirling in the air above her. "Good question. I guess it was Little Miss Top Hat that called our mutual friend out." Muffin sees Corduroy behind the girl on the sofa. Shakes his head and the image is gone. "I mean, I knew she wanted more power, but I didn't think she would go this far."

"S-s-so her meeting C-corduroy Jacket at the, the t-t-t-temple was bad?"

She sits up abruptly. "Of course it was bad!" Glaring at him. "I don't know why you got picked. Your drunk friend seems a whole lot sharper."

He sighs. She's right. Except he's not sure if the drunk is his friend. "P-p-picked?"

"Yeah, I guess Sleeping Beauty thought you were the one." She crosses the room, picks up a black pack and tosses it to him.

He misses the catch and the pack hits the floor at his feet with a flat thump.

"Christ, you can't even catch." She retakes her seat across from him. "It's time for you to wake up the princess and save the directions." Eyes brightening at her perceived wit. Darkening when he doesn't laugh. "Fine, whatever. Just get your boss out of bed and moving, okay?"

"B-but I—" Should he tell her that he tried rubbing with the compass?

Only the whites of her eyes are visible. "Just look in the bag. Everything you need is in there. Your smarty-pants princess is a good pirate."

"The engineer?"

Eyes on her face in the mirror in her hand. "Is that what you call her?" Dragging a red stick across already red lips.

"How c-come you're telling me all this?"

Head coquettish against one shoulder. "He broke some rules. I can break some rules."

"Um, s-so could you tell me where we're supposed to g-g-go then?"

Audible exhalation of air. "Seriously, when you wake up the princess, ask why you." A fresh piece of gum pushed between renewed red lips.

He opens his mouth to protest, defend himself, but resigns himself to being the stupid choice when he notices that the girl with the short pink hair is turning into wavy heat lines. He picks up the bag at his feet when she is gone. Maybe he should just ask the engineer what to use. She's the one who stole all this when they were at the temple. He opens the door, bag in hand, ready to step out into the hall.

"Fuck you! Just fuck you! This isn't about you and your goddamn drunken idiocy!"

"Oh, that's lovely! Lovely! Everything is because I'm drunk, is it? Not a sober moment for this one, oh no!"

Muffin closes the door and shuts out the engineer's ear-splitting shrieks. He can figure this out by himself. Eases himself onto the sofa, dumps out the bag next to him.

Tiny candles, bigger candles, really big candle. Five yen coins; offerings to Kannon, he expects. He should probably return those. Pamphlets describing the giant golden Kannon. Pamphlets describing Buddhism. Pamphlets describing Hase temple. Does he need to look at every pamphlet or can he just put some aside? Surreptitious glances over each shoulder. She's definitely not here. He shoves the pamphlets aside. Kyohon. He opens it expectantly, but it's just a pilgrim's journal, pages still blank. Puts it aside. Countless charms to protect drivers, at least thirty to help students pass tests, one for mercy to all living creatures, five or six to help get over lost loves. Pursing his lips, he goes back to the charm for mercy for all living things. This isn't part of the standard list of temple charms. Flips it over and can't stop a dramatic gasp when he sees the character for 'direction'. 'Mercy in all directions'. He almost slaps his forehead vaudeville-style. Kannon is the goddess of mercy, the Kannon with eleven heads sheds mercy to all living creatures in all directions. How could he forget this? His mother was right, he doesn't visit the temple often enough. Glancing at the other pieces of the temple stolen by the engineer, but nothing grips him like the purple and gold mercy charm. Gripping it tightly, he slips out the door and down the hall to where Corduroy lays.

"Look, we just go and see. I know you've had some kind of 'breakdown', but if that's going to stop you from doing your job, maybe you need to take a nap while the big boys do the dirty work."

"What are you even talking about?" The engineer sounds ready to throw her fists or some broken glass in the drunk's face.

Muffin quickly pulls the door shut behind him and sets himself down on the floor next to Corduroy. Within seconds, the Siamese is weighing heavily on his lap.

"B-but right now, I have to—"

She pushes her head against his chest, forces another soundless meow out of her throat.

Giving in. A quick rub behind the ears. "Is that g-good?" He feels his bones shake as her purrs grow louder. "Okay, I'll pet you more, I p-promise, but right now, I-I have to just do this." Both hands back on the charm, eyes flicking between it and the inert body on the bed next to him. "Um, m-maybe I could just?" He places the charm on Corduroy's forehead, whose smooth respiration is unchanged. Eyebrows knitting a new eyebrow between them. "Okaaay. Maybeeee..." He waves the charm back and forth, feet to head. Nothing. Brings the charm to his own head as he scratches the back of his neck and meets the calico's eyes. "G-g-got any ideas? I'm pretty sure this is the right thing, but m-maybe it's one of the other ch-charms?"

The calico pushes out a flat almost-growl and jumps up on Corduroy's stomach. Gets out her claws like she is softening the belly up, sits down, looks up at Muffin expectantly.

"The s-stomach?" He moves forward to place the charm on Corduroy's stomach and is rewarded by the calico's hisses. Pulling back abruptly. "N-n-n-not the stomach?" Okay, he's thinking. Thinking, thinking. Suddenly, light bulbs. If Corduroy is supposed to be up, then maybe he should be getting this charm in some kind of up position. Laying it on the bed next to Corduroy's head yields nothing but a sigh from the calico, but laying it directly above leads to coughing and eyes flying open.

You're staring up at a ceiling you don't remember. Aren't you under attack? You throw yourself forward, but surprisingly, just your head inches forward.

"H-h-hey, um, hey." Muffin places a hand on Corduroy's shoulder and hopes it is somehow reassuring.

You let your head drop back down, slide your eyes to the side. The nervous kid. Did he kidnap you? Is he the one behind all this? No, wait. Salaryman is the one behind all this. So what are you doing here? Opening your mouth, but it's like that time in the hospital only worse since you're pretty sure that a glass of water is not going to make this better. You hope your eyes are questioning enough that the nervous boy will fill you in.

Should he do some hair-stroking? Maybe that would be creepy. "Um, yeah, s-so we're on the boat. We g-got away from that Salaryman, but um, I g-guess he c-cut you or something? Because you p-passed out or something. And I-I guess I woke you up now w-with this."

Nervous dangles something gold and purple over your head. Is it a temple charm? Could be a mobile phone strap. You set insistent eyes on him. You need more information than that.

Muffin folds his arms across his chest, stares at Corduroy. Eyes are open, that's good. But no voice and no moving, except for a little bit of wiggly head. That's bad. Maybe he didn't do it right?

The Siamese purrs thickly against his thigh, casting warm eyes up at him.

He reaches down to scratch behind her ears, then hangs the charm directly above Corduroy's head. If this doesn't work, he'll try the feet, he tells himself.

All the tightness is gone from your throat and you suppose it's got something to do with Nervous hanging that thing over your head. "That is much better. So where is Boy? Wasn't he attacking us?" You start to sit up, lose all muscle control without warning, flop back down.

The Siamese digs her claws into his leg, starts fluffing his thigh.

Making the connection, he is careful to keep the charm over his new friend's head all the way up into a sitting position.

You tilt your head back to look at this thing keeping you mobile. No weirder than a group of pirates chasing you around the city trying to blow you up. You guess. "So you got this at the temple?"

Muffin bobs his head up and down. "Y-yeah. I mean, the, the engineer did."

"Which one's the engineer?"

"She's the l-l-little one with short hair. She looks angry a, a lot."

Remembering the frowning girl walking in front of you with that other man. "Oh yeah, she seemed angry." You look around, careful not to move out from under the little charm Nervous is holding above your head. "So this is your boat, huh?"

"Well, it's n-not my boat. I m-mean, it's all of ours."

Raising an eyebrow in his direction. "That's what I meant."

On his feet and headed for the door to keep his red cheeks from being seen. "A-anyway, we should tell the others y-you're awake. We have to get you to the temple or s-something."

Hitting the bed with a crunch and you're forced to ask yourself who eats crackers in bed. Probably the man with the drinking problem. He seems like a cracker eater.

"Oh! I-I'm sorry! I j-just—I guess I wasn't—" Muffin races back to the bed, gets the charm dangling in the air again. Careful escorting Corduroy to the door this time.

The driver pushes each opponent into their corner. "Look." Sternest voice he can muster. It's not quite his pirate yell, but it usually commands the goodwill of luxury ship passengers and crew. "The captain's not here and that puts me in charge. We are going to the temple. That's it. Discussion over." He turns to his lover. "Get this baby moving as fast as you can. We need to be there two hours ago."

"But—" She is not ready to let this go. The shape of the drunk's neck still sits between her fingers.

"No." He turns away and peers out the porthole. "No. I said there's no more discussion. Go." Listens for her footsteps, lets out his breath when he hears them. He will pay for his assumption of authority when they finally get some time alone again. When the door shuts behind her, he turns to the drunk. "You get to the other end, help her get the boat to Kamakura without her knowing."

"Now—" He's supposed to help the woman who just tried to squeeze the life out of him?

Cut off. "No. Go. We'll get there faster with two of you on deck." He watches the drunk slink from the room, stays rigid for a few more seconds then slumps down into a chair. The shuffling in the doorway draws his eyes. The kid?

You try to trust Nervous, trust that he won't live up to the name you've stuck him with and get nervous and move that charm that is apparently the only thing keeping you on your feet. You'd like to believe that you won't feel the floor meet your head again, but he's proven too many times already that that's not how things are likely to go.

Muffin doesn't take his eyes off his unexpected charge while addressing the driver. "Um, we, we should go back to the t-temple, I think."

"Yeah, we're going. I just sent the engineer up to take care of it." Should he ask? Muffin is a pretty weird kid. Maybe he should just let it go. But this careful procession demands a reason. "So what are you doing?"

"Okay, I don't know what's—" All set to explain or get some explanations and your mouth snaps shut and you're on the floor. Again. Why is it this nervous kid who has this power over you? You'd curse if you could open your mouth.

"O-o-oh crap!" Muffin is on his knees, trying to get the charm above Corduroy's head the right way. This is harder than he thought it would be.

"No, seriously. What are you doing?" The driver grabs Muffin's hand, forces him to meet his eyes.

Shoulders greeting his ears. "I d-don't know. I just know that this thing m-makes Corduroy stand. W-watch." Gets the placement right.

You push yourself up on your elbows. Glare at the boy holding the charm. "This is getting ridiculous. Could you just hold your hand steady for five minutes? I have a serious headache from slamming into the floor every five seconds." Will you have to live your life like this? You prefer the situation where you are exploded on for the rest of your life and unable to hold down a job ever again.

"S-sorry." Eyes on the driver. "See?"

"Can't we go any faster?" Snapping turtle style. The engineer is tired of dodging cars, bicycles, pedestrians, small animals on the street leading to the temple. There are not enough sidewalks in this town.

"S-sorry." Muffin apologizes immediately. It's him slowing them up. If only he could master keeping Corduroy upright.

You glare at Nervous out of the corner of your eye as you shuffle forward. It's worse slamming into the ground when there is a multitude of touristy strangers watching you and whispering amongst themselves. But despite the humiliation of dropping to the ground every five minutes, you are glad these people are here. If a gaggle of tourists is watching, Salaryman can't stab you, right?

The driver clutches the engineer's hand more tightly. "Just try to be more touristy and less pirate-y." Hissing between clenched teeth. "It's bad enough it's the middle of the day."

"Stairs!" The drunk gives a potential hazard warning to Muffin and the kid, and pushes out a sigh. If it took this long on a straight road, how much longer will the stairs take? Maybe they should get the kid a helmet. "Alright then. We should be off."

The driver rests his eyes on his angry engineer. "Look, we can't send him alone. And you tried to kill him this afternoon."

Pulling free of him, she waves an uncaring hand in front of her face. "Yeah, whatever. Fine. Go. Clear the way. We'll be there sometime tonight." She glares at the boy with the charm. "Are you sure it only works with you?"

"Don't start. We all tried and every time, it was bam! Into the floor." The driver is terse.

"Fine. Just go already." She keeps her eyes fixed on the charm above the kid's head.

The driver leaps up the stairs with the drunk.

"So when we get there, then what?"

Corduroy's voice startles him after so much silence and Muffin almost jerks his arm back, catches himself, stays steady. But not steady enough to avoid a glare. "Um, there's a, a little d-door behind the Kannon. I think you j-j-just have to close it."

"That's it? We just have to close a door?" You're dumbfounded by the simplicity. Though not as simple as just touching the Kannon, which was your first guess, and that obviously did not work out.

Muffin starts to bring his shoulders up, stops himself. The charm wobbles but remains above Corduroy's head. "I g-guess. I mean, in the dream or, or whatever, that's all Lolita did and you k-kind of collapsed."

Chewing your bottom lip, you almost stop your mini shuffle steps. Remember in time that Muffin wouldn't stop and it would be your head against the rocks yet again. "I still don't get it. If that was real, why don't I remember it?" That day with Boy and he read the scroll and said that you were already there. And then you had sex with him. Was he already a robot then? Did you have sex with a robot? You're not sure if you should be grossed out or high-fiving yourself.

Concentrating as they take each step two feet at a time. "Uuuuh, I d-don't know. At the end of my dream, she kind of did s-something with the rabbit."

"That creepy red-eyed thing?" The engineer winces. Rabbits in general are creepy with those hyperspeed noses. But the red-eyed ones are some kind of crazy demon rabbits.

"Yeah, yeah. She got it out and o-on the floor and then she told you to, to forget the whole thing."

"So I forgot?" You thought you weren't susceptible to hypnosis. You always like to think there's something special about you.

He stops the upward movement of his shoulders again. "I g-guess. I mean, if you don't remember."

"You're sure it wasn't a dream?" Everyone can be hypnotized. You're not everyone.

Slow head from side to side. "I-I don't think so. I mean, it wasn't really h-happening, so like that, it was a d-dream. But I think what happened was real. The k-kyohon said you were at the temple before."

Twisting around to meet his eyes. "How did you—" Cursing your own stupidity as you crack your head against a cobbled stair.

"Crap, crap, crap." Muffin gets down on one knee to get the charm dangling over Corduroy's head. At least it wasn't his fault this time.

Slowly getting to your feet, ready to voice your question again. Feeling a little tail-chasing though. At this point, does it matter why they know you were there? Where they got the book? They're obviously into this up to their armpits with you. Salaryman has their captain and your Boy. But the angry girl cuts you short.

"I don't think this is going to work." She glares at the stones below her feet. "This is a crappy plan."

Muffin concentrates on raising his hand with Corduroy's head as they slowly ascend, gaining strange looks from tourists descending. "It's n-n-not so much a plan as a, a general guideline," he mutters. "I mean, we have to get to the image of K-kannon. S-s-so make sure we do."

Sudden shrieking and all heads fly up, face the top of the stairs.

Without the train doors, you have some trouble recognizing him, but then it hits you. Crazy Jumper. Crazy Jumper is hopping from one foot to the other on the top step and shrieking. Holding your breath, crossing your fingers that it is just an insane coincidence, that he has nothing to do with you being here.

"Soooo...?" The engineer tries to put together a sentence, but the man with the small backpack strapped to his chest hopping up and down mesmerizes her. She heard somewhere that some temples take in kids who have been abandoned because of disabilities. Maybe he's one of them?

Eyes back and forth between Corduroy and the crazy man at the top of the stairs. "Y-y-you know him, d-don't you?" He's stared at this face long enough to know when things are amiss.

Mutely shaking your head. "I..." How can you even explain this? "I don't really know him. I mean, I—"

Finally pulling words out of the shrieks, the engineer puzzle-pieces it that this is no random crazy guy. "He's saying something about the interface and the way."

"W-what?" Too focused on Corduroy's face, Muffin ignored the actual content of the loud voice.

"The way is marked! The interface awaits connection! Connection! Connection! Aaaah!" Hopping ceases without warning and Crazy Jumper meets your eyes with startling lucidity. "You're the connection." In a stage whisper. "You're the connection. You're up. You're up. You're up. You're up."

The engineer is tempted to run up the remaining steps and give him a whack on the back of the head, get him out of the loop, but she keeps her whacking hand firmly in her pocket. "Is he trying to warn us or attack us?"

You shrug. "The last time I saw him, he ran screaming away from me on the train." He told you you were wrong, that you didn't know which way was up. He was right. And now he says you're the connection. Are they going to try and plug you into Boy? You shudder at the thought that you have inadvertently become a part of a cheap sci-fi porno. Or worse, some kind of Japanese anime porn. "Maybe we should just ignore him?"

"He's n-n-not really doing anything now."

"Well, let's keep moving anyway." The engineer lifts her foot onto the next shallow step.

You try to watch Crazy Jumper as closely as you can, but navigating the stairs without moving out from under Nervous's nervous hand takes too much of your attention. You hear his constant whispered assertion that you're up and when you look up again, he's not there.

The engineer frowns. "He must have run off." But she was looking right at him and there was no running. He just wasn't there. She needs to get more sleep. Too much running around being chased by men in suits and protected by cats. "Come on, the guys are waiting."

You start counting out loud under your breath to help Nervous keep pace with you. Why didn't you think of this before? He seems to respond well to the structure and you inch your way up the stairs a little faster than before.

The driver tries to pretend that he did not see that dead rat, but no matter how much he tells himself that it was just a fuzzy old hat, he knows that a fuzzy old hat is unlikely to be tucked away on the ground under the temple floor. Pulls himself along on his belly after the drunk, who moves like a snake, forcing the driver to wonder just how often he has the opportunity to crawl along the ground on his belly.

He stops abruptly and the driver, still focused on the rat/hat, smashes his face into the drunk's boot, earning a scowl and a finger to his lips. The drunk gestures to his ear, raises questioning brows, gestures up with his thumb.

Listening carefully. The soft shh-shh disorients him. What could make that sound? Oh. A body being dragged. That would make that soft sound on a wooden floor. The captain? Silently apologizing to the kid with Muffin, the driver hopes that it's the boy. Soft voices rising above the soft shuffle.

"Yeah, totally, like there, that's uh good."

Every muscle in his body rigid. The driver wills himself to breathe. The drunk waves him forward. They need to get to the other side of the room.

Low, dry chortling from directly above his head. "The look on her face was really something to see." The driver wonders how Salaryman always manages to sound like he's casually inspecting his fingernails. "I take it she had no idea you were involved so heavily."

Stoner snickering. "Nah, like she uh totally thought it was uh you know the regular cycle only uh early or something. But like that guy, uh yeah right. As if he could you know get things uh started. Always me. But damn, you know? Totally not like uh cooperating with me, right?" Sneakers scuffing past him, towards the door. "Like if he would just you know uh do like what I said."

"Well, he can be quite stubborn. He seemed fairly certain that the usual way was best." Thud like a head hitting the floor over their heads.

"Totally, totally, And you know, like uh I can understand that, right? But like now is uh different. Gotta think different."

"I thought the costume was particularly inspired. Quite terrifying to see you stepping out of his skin in so spectacular a fashion."

"Hey, like uh thanks. It's like, can't get him to do what you uh need, like pretend to uh be him you know and like do it uh yourself, right?" The drunk can practically hear New Wave's smirk.

Hearing the muffled click of the lighter in the room above him, the drunk regrets not being able to get his own cigarettes from his pocket. Is he already as addicted as he was before? Crossing his fingers that the answer is no. It was hard enough to quit the last time. Gets back to crawling to take his mind off craving. Lessons from the Stop Smoking hotline. Although they just said to keep busy; they didn't actually specify crawling.

Waiting for the other two at the top of the stairs, stomach becoming tighter and tighter. All the tourists that were around, on the street, coming down the stairs, that's all of them. Casting her eyes about the temple grounds in the dimming afternoon, the engineer can't see anyone else. And even on the stairs, everyone is going down and getting there pretty fast. Only Muffin and the kid are coming up. She ignores the dread the empty grounds inspire in her and looks around for an alternate entrance to the building where they keep the Kannon. There was that hallway made of doors on the side, but that still leads square into the middle of the room. A little too far from the statue and a little too close to whoever's already there. Plus, they'll have to walk right in front of the main door across the gravel on the open grounds. She crosses that way off her list for the fiftieth time. But her list just has one option so she spends a moment cursing.

You heave a sigh of relief when your foot hits the top step. Then dread slaps you in the face. This is a million times worse than last time and last time, you almost died. There's no way you can do anything shuffling forward with this idiot holding a temple charm over your head. "You know, I agree with her. This is a crappy plan."

Tempted to put his hands on his hips and let the kid fall. "O-okay, we have to do this. It's n-not a question anymore. You can't stand up or move or, or do anything without me holding this stu-stupid thing up." He shakes the charm a little, watches the sudden panic in Corduroy's eyes. "They have our c-captain and we want her back. P-p-plus, isn't your boyfriend in there? Don't you even c-care about him?"

"I was actually thinking about breaking up with him," you

confess.

Muffin scowls. "Is this th-the way you break up with people? L-leave them to be maimed or k-killed or I don't know w-w-what they're going to do, but I bet it's bad. Did you hear that j-jumping man? They're going to use him for a connection."

"I thought I was the connection."

"I thought you were up." The engineer can't decide if a person could be both the connection and up, since it's completely ridiculous for a person to be either.

He stamps one foot on the gravel. "It, it doesn't matter. The fact is, w-we have to go in there and c-close that door."

"What if closing the door doesn't change anything?" You don't know why your heart is pounding like this.

He drops his eyes to his feet. "Then we're h-h-hopeless."

"You mean, we'll have no hope?" You try to say it so it doesn't sound like an English lesson, but you get a glare anyway.

"Y-y-y-yes, whatever. We'll be f-f-fucked. Is that the right English?" Not prone to cursing, but he has had enough of this and them standing on the top step is not changing anything and he just wants to get this over with because he feels like he might puke.

"Um, yeah." Somehow, you're always shocked when people who are not native to your language dig out the f-word. "So let's go." Start the count, get ready to shuffle forward with your new best friend, Nervous.

You're halted by the engineer's hand on your shoulder. "No. We can't cross the grounds and go in the front door."

"Then what?" You're pretty sure temples don't have back doors.

She jerks her head to the woods surrounding the complex. "We go through the woods, come up from behind. It's the only way." Relieved that she finally thought one up. She was starting to believe that the only way in was to walk into Mr. Skin's arms. Her own skin crawling at the thought.

"Okay, but how do we get in? There's just a wall on that side.

And it's not even a paper door wall." All this time, you've been annoyed with the paper door walls, having busted through many accidentally. And now when it would be useful, of course, there is a real wall made of wood.

The engineer raises her shoulders. "I don't know. The wall might be weak so we can slam through. Or maybe get under and come up through the floor. In any case, it's the only way we're not likely to be spotted. And we need all the camouflage we can get. You guys stick out." She steps towards the thicket at the edge of the outermost building. "Come on."

You combine your number chanting with curses, a curse for each number. Shit one, damn two, fuck three, crap four. Nervous raises his eyebrows but keeps pace. All the twigs and roots and general disarray of the wooded area are not working in your favour. You have trouble keeping this guy over your head on smooth, smooth concrete. These brambles will be the death of you. Your face is already almost entirely shredded. But you shuffle forward in silence. You're not interested in the abandon Boy speech again. It's not like you would abandon him, anyway. Just, maybe if you just didn't show up, they couldn't do whatever and then they wouldn't need Boy anymore and he would come home and you would have delicious Greek food again.

Tired of leaning against trees, waiting for the Muffin-Corduroy team to pass, the engineer moves forward, clearing a path for the balancing act behind her. Maybe this will help them move faster. Intent on kicking debris aside and bending back tree branches, she trips over a hairless cat, hits the ground. The cat glares at her, arches its back and steps briskly back the way the engineer came. Shortly followed by Muffin's muffled cry of surprise. Back on her feet in what she expects is the general direction of the main building. A final kick sends leaves and twigs shooting off to her side and then she is in a clearing. With a lot of cats. She reminds herself again that she will take some amnesia drugs when this is all over. Cats forming kitty towers and shredding the center of a wall does not sit well with her scientific training.

A meow at her feet gets her mouth closed and her eyes on the ground. The calico. The calico that was on the ship with them. Plugging her ears, chanting "La, la, la, la" in her mind at the question of how the calico got here before them.

The calico scratches her leg, lets out a growl meowl.

"Fine," the engineer snaps. "I'll take you seriously." She lets her eyes run over the careful towers of cats lined up in front of the wall, the top cat in each tower hard at work scratching furiously at the wall before them. "Is this where the Kannon is?"

Did the calico's eyeballs actually just roll back? Is she being mocked by a cat?

"Okay, fine. Obviously, this is where they keep the stupid statue. So how long is this going to take? Are you cats planning to dig right through the wall with your claws?"

Purring, the calico pushes herself up against the engineer's legs. Pushes until the engineer feels compelled to step backwards or fall over.

She crouches down to eye the multi-coloured cat at her feet suspiciously. Wanting to not understand what the cat is saying, but thinking she just might. "So we should push through?"

Rewarded with throaty rumbling and a sandpapery tongue on the back of her hand.

"Hehhhhhhhhh." Muffin drags the sound out, intonation rising the longer the sound lasts.

Eyes fixed on the ground at your feet, you want to punch him for that boringly standard reaction to something surprising. Is that all anyone is this country can say when presented with the unknown? You choke your own "hehhhh" down when you look up and see all the cats using the wall of the building in front of you as a scratching post. You have been in this country too long. "What is with all these cats?" Seems like years ago Pink Hair told you in a dream to pet a cat the next time you saw one. "What is going on with the cats? Seriously."

"W-well, they're kind of, um…" Muffin realizes he can't explain the cats, although he felt certain he could. Must not reveal his ignorance. Corduroy already thinks he's lame. "They're um our p-p-protectors or something."

The engineer almost laughs. "Our protectors?" If only she could be as optimistic as that. She would have said yes to the driver before he had even finished asking. "They're cats. They make an army and follow us. None of us knows why. And now they're apparently weakening a spot in the wall for us."

"How did they know we were coming?" You've always been a cat person so you're fine with an army of them. But an army of telepathic cats? You feel like there's a line being crossed there.

The engineer shakes her head, finger to her lips. "Shhh. No questions that can't be answered. Let's get in there and close that door." She steps towards the wall like she's not crazy.

Trusting your ability to move in a perfectly straight vertical line, you slowly crouch down, make it to your knees, give the redhead a good scrub behind the ears. Smile at the rumbles moving from the cat's throat through the bones in your knees. "Okay, honey," you whisper, as you massage the small head. "I gotta go now." Your ability to rise in a straight line is apparently not as great as your ability to descend and your face hits a pile of mulching leaves.

The edge of the floorboard catches his eye and the drunk snakes his way over. Loose! Ha! He grabs the edge and fiddles with it, until it pops out and falls to the dirt in front of his eyes. Eyes that turn back to the driver and urge him forward.

Together pulling enough of the floor free to squeeze a head through. The drunk's head. Up to his nose. Peering from side to side, getting his bearings. They are just in front of the doorway leading out to the hall with the paper doors. Not so far from the statue, far enough from the door. And close enough to see the body on the floor is not the captain. Squints for the fine detail of the boy's chest rising and falling.

"It's just in front of the hall door," he whispers when he drops back down next to the driver. "The boy is not more than four metres to our right."

"What about the captain?"

Head shaking from the drunk. "Just the boy."

"So I guess we should—"

"Run, Mr. Fluffles! Ruuuuuun!" Lolita's shrieking is accompanied by her heavy feet taking the stairs, thundering into the temple.

Followed by lighter feet and deeper voices.

"I'm certainly not doubting your judgement, but perhaps it might have been prudent to have taken care of her earlier. If he finds out she's involved, he'll cut her in two." Salaryman's shiny loafers take the steps two at a time. "And to be perfectly honest, it's been difficult to keep quiet on this. He does know how to question a man."

"Yeah, like, uh, okay. You like uh leave him to me, you know. Like uh, I know how that uh guy works." A quick laugh. "I'm like uh in his dangling skin, right? And anyway, there was uh like that and I you know, right?" New Wave trails behind.

The drunk holds in a laugh at what is clearly an uncomfortable silence from the man in the suit. Mirth ended by the realization that they are discussing Mr. Skin as if he were separate from the new wave kid. The boy said he saw New Wave come out of Mr. Skin's skin. A poke from the driver next to him. Looks and sees thumbs frantically gesturing up. Reluctantly, he peers over the edge of the hole in the floor, prays to any gods of drink that might be nearby.

The girl in the miniature hat is standing defiant, hands on decorated hips, between the drunk and the boy still unconscious on the floor. The drunk decides that between her petticoats and the boy's head, he's got good cover. Not likely that the man in the suit entering the room with nonchalant ease will spot the top of his head poking over the edge of a hole in the floor.

"Now, dear. There's no need for such a commotion. Why can't we just discuss this like adults?" Unnatural emphasis on the last word.

A platform boot slams into the ground and the drunk winces, hopes that foot didn't actually catch the boy in the head, that it was just a perspective thing. "Are you calling me a child? Just because you're older than me doesn't mean I'm a child! You're like a million years old! Everyone's younger than you! God!" And the foot stamps uncomfortably close to the boy's head for the second time.

Cold eyes on New Wave. "He's older than me."

"I think uh like the point is not you know who's older, right. Like you're mad and I totally uh get that. But uh, come on. This is you know." He stops speaking abruptly, lets his eyes slide away.

"What? What is it?" A menacing step forward. "Were you going to say 'stupid'? Were you? You totally were!" She drops to her knees, ruining white knee-high socks on the dusty temple floor, hooks an arm around the boy's neck, yanks him up towards her. The drunk hears airways close, wonders if now would be a good time for a fantastic rescue. Maybe the cats will step in. "That's it! You lied to me and now you call me stupid! You are such an ass! We are so totally broken up!" She tightens her grip. "Where's the way?"

Placating hands raised, New Wave steps forward, uses his thick black eyebrows to indicate that Salaryman should really be on his way. "Look, if you like uh kill him, then you you know get like uh."

"I don't get anything, but neither do you!"

He pushes both hands deep in his pockets, one side of his mouth turns up. "Yeah, but uh I've got no reason to care." Shoulders shrugging casually. "Like uh, he can get you know the whole uh set up again, you know. At the uh right time, right. But you like don't uh get another uh chance, right. I know what she'll uh do to you, okay."

Slowly rising to her feet, much to the drunk's relief. The driver pokes him in the gut again, but he waves a dismissive hand. This is better than the subtitled telly. If only it wasn't Corduroy's love monkey being strangled by the little princess in all the lace.

The princess in all the lace laughs, lower pitched than her usual giggle. "You think so? Why do you think I have the fashion patrol outside? If you don't give me the way, I'll be glad to break your stupid interface and have the fashion patrol rip you to pieces." The drunk can hear the sweet smile appear on her face. "After all, darling, I know how to destroy you. Even he doesn't know how, I bet." Gesturing towards the retreating Salaryman with her free hand.

Eyebrows raised with feigned indifference. "Oh, there is a way?" He steps back into the centre of the room. "Well, this is interesting."

"Okay, you like uh have someplace to be, right." New Wave turns his head in the direction of the man in the suit and the drunk watches that man shoot backwards as if punched in the gut by a torpedo, out the open temple doors. Hears him slam into the tree in the centre of the courtyard out front.

"Where. Is. The. Way?" The girl's voice is filled with swords. The driver shudders under the floorboards.

Slowly shaking his head, sending slightly greasy dark hair slapping into the sides of his face. "No way. Like, you totally don't uh get to you know."

"Then neither do you." She inches backward, pulling the boy along with her. "I think you don't realize that I totally have nothing to lose here." Turns her head to the rabbit resting on the boy's shoulder. "Mr. Fluffles, could you get the girls in here?"

Obediently hopping down to the floor, nose at hyperspeed, bouncing after Salaryman.

New Wave starts toward the rabbit, stops running-into-a-wall abruptly. Looks up at Lolita, astonished. "How did you like uh do that?"

Head tilted coquettishly to one shoulder. "Just a little something Mr. Fluffles and I worked out. We figured you might try to hurt him since you're such a total jerk."

The rabbit stops to take a bathroom break at New Wave's feet. Jumps out the door, down the stairs.

The driver feels the ground beneath his stomach rumble with the weight of hundreds of pairs of unnaturally tall shoes stomping rhythmically towards the temple doors.

The drunk can't keep his mouth shut at the sight of the solemn-faced lolitas armed old-school style. Where did those girls get all the swords? He's sure that many belong in museums. He thinks he's even seen some of them in museums. What would a lolita need an engraved, fifteenth-century katana for?

The girls come to an abrupt halt an arm's length in front of the boy with the asymmetrical hair. Raise swords.

"Okay, okay." New Wave raises his white flag hands. "I can uh see you like worked it all out, yeah. So here's the way." White flag hands fall back to his sides, well-worn sneakers move him to one side and there lies the captain. "There's just like one uh thing, you know? You have to like put that down to pick uh this up."

Crushes the boy's neck in her elbow. "And what? You're going to take it?" Small snort of laughter and her free hand flies to her face, eyes wide, cheeks blooming. "Oh my god. Did I just make that sound?"

"Quiet!" The engineer has had it with Muffin's grunting. Can't he just push without making that noise?

"I c-can't help it. This i-is hard." He allows himself to shoot some eye daggers at the cats clustered on the ground around them. "I thought they w-w-weakened this wall."

The whispered bickering of these two is making you yearn for a Phillips head screwdriver to shove through a few of their body parts. But even if you had such a weapon, you couldn't use it with Nervous over there and you flat on your back. Obviously, he can't push the wall in and keep you on your feet, but you can't open your mouth without that stupid charm hanging over your head. You can't even sigh out loud. Thinking about sighing apparently jiggles something and your head rolls off the rock Nervous was so careful to prop it up on so you could see the dull proceedings. Explosions and paralysis. This is pretty not much what you were hoping to get out of life.

"What the hell is that noise?" It's not just a noise, she can feel the rumbling in her boots. Like an earthquake getting ready to happen. Or a lot of really heavy people running by.

"Ow!" Unable to hear the engineer or any unbelievable noise. Too absorbed in sudden backside pain from his shoulders to his feet. Staggering backwards from the wall, he cranes his neck to peer over his own shoulder and looks down on hissing cats. "Ow! H-hey cats! W-what!"

"Get back here. Goddammit." She twists around with tiny fists prepared for penalty punches. The drunk was right; it is a good idea. She'll have to rename it though or he'll get all high and mighty. Maybe 'fists of vengeance'. That's better than penalty punches. Fists of vengeance unclenching at the sight of Muffin toppling from the weight of cats clinging to his back. Cats which scatter before he hits the ground.

"Ow!" There are too many rocks on the ground here. Several of them are lodged in his spine and he groans, turns his head to one side and sees Corduroy's awkwardly tilted face. "Hey, y-you okay?"

You try to make your eyes convey the extreme pain of your head being twisted against this stupid rock, your desire to punch him in the face. You're not sure if your eyes are capable of such extreme emotion.

He pushes himself up on one elbow, dislodging one of the vertebrae rocks. "Hold on." Muffin fumbles in his pocket for the charm. It's not there. His heart stops but he gets it beating again with the realization that he has two pockets.

Charm in position over your head, you drag those eyebrows down to scowl at Nervous above you. "Damn, don't balance my head on rocks. I almost broke my neck just now. Help me up." Enough of this lying idly by. They clearly are never going to push through the stupid wall without you and if this doesn't end soon, you may lose your mind. Cancer and insanity, that's all you need. Frowning suddenly. Wait, isn't it the cancer causing your insanity? Put it aside, accept the hand up the engineer is pushing at you.

"D-d-do you think the cats attacked me to make me h-help you?" He wishes for the millionth time that they could just go back to the boat and be pirates. Without cats. Somehow, stealing on the high seas seems so much safer than whatever they're doing now. Plus, he's pretty sure that fall reopened his stitches and he's not sure if he's bleeding again, but if he is, could he bleed to death before it gets stitched up again? Dying a non-pirate virgin is less consolation than he thought it would be.

You shrug. "How should I know what the cats do? I think they have their own agenda." Stare at the wall in front of you. "So, what? We just have to push?"

The engineer nods slowly, wonders how much pushing the kid can do while keeping a watchful eye on Muffin and the charm. "Yeah. I think so, anyway. It seems like that's what these cats were trying to communicate." If cats could communicate with people. The silent tag-on in her mind.

Mentally roll those sleeves up. You saw how hard they were pushing before. Nervous was even making some kind of crazy hard-work noises. But maybe that's just him 'doing his best'. "Stay with me," you instruct him sternly. It looks like some of the cats did a little too much hard work and there was no litterbox handy. Falling face first here would be worse than those mulching leaves from before.

Nodding. Why didn't he wipe his sweaty palms off on his pants before? He might drop the charm. Suddenly feeling like those dreams he used to have before entrance exams, where he would show up to the test and not know any of the answers because the questions were all in Persian.

You press against the wall, gently at first, then with increasing pressure. The engineer leans in next to you and for a moment, there is only the sound of the smallest cat chasing a ball of string amongst the leaves. You take a deep breath and think that this might be one of those times where you should be remembering which way up is, even though you've never really been too clear on it. You set those uncertainties aside, think about being in there rather than out here and damn, if you could just close that little door, if that's all it takes to be free of explosions and paralysis.

"You bastard!" In a voice that could and does shatter glass. The drunk is grateful for the solid wall behind him. Only the glass in the entryway flies out of its frame. "Just give it to me! It's totally your fault we're even here anyway! If you had just left everything alone, you know? I was happy until I met you!" A crescendo peaking on the last sentence.

The drunk wishes she would let go of the boy so they could rescue someone at least. A light bulb over his head and he drops back down beneath the floor. Answers the questions in the driver's eyes with a hand in the direction of New Wave. The captain is behind him and the lolita army seems intent on just that boy and his frilly shirt. If there are loose boards on this side, the chances are good for loose boards on the other side. Old temples, they're falling apart.

New Wave staggers back, hand on his heart. "You were happy uh like before me? How can you uh say that, right? I thought you uh like knew, it's you know."

Scurrying after the drunk, the driver raises his eyebrows at the sincerity in New Wave's voice. Does he really love Lolita? Abruptly understanding the drunk's love of the *dorama* filling the television in this country.

"Oh, you love me. Right, I totally forgot. That's why you totally lied to me! And pretended to be him, just so—what? Were you trying to, like, impress me? Or play some crazy joke on me? Or did you just want to show me for the millionth time how you can play every side and get away with it? Like 'ooh, look at me. I'm so strong.'" Dark eyes turn into perfect circles framed by raised eyebrows as she waggles her fingers next to her head mockingly.

Lolita army feet take a single step and set the floor shaking.

The driver ignores the trembling of the floor, reaches up, pushes fingers into cracks and tries to pry something loose. The drunk scrabbles about next to him and he hopes that the lovers upstairs are too absorbed in their drama to notice the mice in the floor beneath.

"See, like that is so uh unfair, right. I didn't like uh lie to you. I just you know didn't uh tell you." The drunk can practically hear him shoving his hands in his pockets and looking off to the side. "And whatever. As if I uh even try to like—I mean, like, I don't think uh I'm you know—"

"Fashion patrol!" Sharp bark showing drill sergeant promise.

The lolitas take a heavy step forward. The driver uses the thunder as cover to yank a piece of floor out.

"Now, boy, you mind tellin' me what's going on here?"

The two men under the floor let go of loose floorboards and press their faces to the ground. Remembering how easily he was found out earlier, the drunk tries to take fewer breaths.

"Oh, like uh, hey." A combination of sheepish and surprised.

"No 'hey', boy. Dammit, what the hell is she doing here? So she's the reason I don't have the book, I guess. You know without that book, this is about ten times more hard for me, right? You do know that, boy."

"Well, the thing uh is like well…"

Hands on hips, tossing her hair to one side. "He's been dressing up as you."

"Like, shut up." Hissed through clenched teeth.

"Now I did wonder if somethin' like that weren't goin' on." Slow shuffle steps stop directly above their heads and the drunk doesn't know how much longer he can go without a breath. "See, the timing just ain't right. Shouldn't be happening now and then suddenly, I'm hearin' that I done things that, quite frankly, I never did. And boy, I got a problem with that." Polar ice caps.

You fall forward as the wall unexpectedly gives way. You didn't think it would be so easy, not after all that grunting Nervous did. The dark-haired girl next to you hits the floor with her face and you take a moment to feel satisfied that you were pushing with your shoulder, head turned to the side. At least you won't lose a tooth. Although she can pull herself up again and you're stuck here, ear to the ground, at the mercy of the tall product of an overprotective mother.

His reflexes are good, if nothing else. "S-sorry, sorry, I d-didn't think you would get through s-so quickly."

You remove your ear from the floor, wish you had left it there when the shrieks of the girl in pink hit your eardrums. Freeze when the shriek dies out and the slacker voice of your good friend New Wave talks about not lying and really loving the girl in pink. The first time he showed up on your doorstep, you knew he would try to kill you in your sleep. And here you are. He's not trying to kill you in your sleep, but you're pretty sure he wants to kill you at some point. And the creepy southern voice? Who the hell is that? New players at this stage of the game do not fill you with confidence. Locking eyes with Nervous, you crawl through the hole in the wall together. Kneel on the floor in the narrow space between the wall and the giant statue directly in front of you. You look around frantically. Isn't there supposed to be a door here? "So?"

Muffin can't figure out what this question means. The door is right there. The weirdly tiny, arched-like-a-fairytale-cottage door. Looking at Corduroy, then the door at the base of the statue only centimetres from Corduroy's bent knees. Back to Corduroy's blank, preparing-to-be-angry face. "Y-you can't s-s-see it?"

Ready to send your eyeballs rolling back when terror squeezes out annoyance. Are you failing some kind of test? Is your tumour actually giving you hallucinations of abject failure? Is it really cancer? "See what?" It would be better if you sounded less squeaky.

"The, the door." Maybe Corduroy's going blind. Is it because of the way he's holding the charm? Tries to adjust without moving too much. "H-how about now?"

"Oh, for the—" The engineer is ready to jump through the hole and haul Muffin up by the collar. "Just point or something. We can't see this door you're seeing, okay?" She ignores the implication of her own words.

Stretching out a hesitant finger. "Th-there. It's right there."

You turn your eyes to follow his finger, but there's just wood. Just more shiny gold wood. Feeling like a giant ass as you raise a hand and reach towards the base of the statue. "Uh, is it a push door or a pull door?" You see the questions in his eyes and curse all English teachers everywhere. Why doesn't anyone ever teach what people really need to know? "I mean, is it a door you have to pull closed or push to close?"

Muffin lets out a tense breath. Looking at the regular knob-type door and seeing that it is in fact a 'pull door'. "Um, p-pull. You have t-to reach in and p-p-pull it shut."

You take a deep breath. In and out. Good. Reach forward, slam your hand into golden wood. Glare at Nervous who looks even more nervous, which you were pretty sure was not possible.

"A, a little t-to your l-left."

You move your hand a little to the left, ignoring the throbbing of your bruised knuckles and push forward, wincing. You slam into nothing. Opening your eyes and your hand is gone. Eaten by the statue up to your wrist. You resist the urge to yank it back. "Now what? Where is the knob?"

About to lean forward to grab the stupid thing on his own, but catching himself before the charm moves away from Corduroy's head and he earns another angry glare. "Uh, there's like a h-h-handle about three c-centimetres away from your l-littlest finger."

"My pinkie?" you ask as you waggle it.

Muffin nods. He's having trouble swallowing. "Y-y-yeah, that one. If you j-just kind of move it f-forward, you'll hit the handle."

Wiggling your pinkie, you start to understand how the blind people in the train station feel with their canes tapping forward looking for the end of the yellow Braille brick path on the floor. Jerking back in surprise when your finger hits something solid. Down you go.

Muffin is quick to get the charm back over Corduroy's head, but silently full of curses. How can he be expected to keep the charm in the right place with sudden movement like that? He is no mind reader. "So do you need me to tell you again?"

Rubbing your head, pushing yourself onto your knees again. "No, I remember. Just kind of freaked me out."

The engineer keeps her mouth shut behind them, still recovering from the heart attack induced by Corduroy's sudden leap backwards. But ready to yell at them, tell them to hurry up already, her fiancé is out there with the crazy girl and her crazy boyfriend with the speech impediment. Using the word 'fiancé' defiantly in her head. She may not have said 'yes' yet, but only because she hasn't had the chance. To hell with making her stupid list.

Hesitantly, but with less nervous tension, or at least you hope you're less nervous since the last thing you need is to jump back and slam your head into the floor again, you reach forward and feel for the door handle, ignoring your eyes telling you that your hand is surrounded by cedar. Is Kannon made of cedar? Maybe it's pine. Your hand bumps something cold. Feels like metal. Metal like a handle. Holding in the triumphant whoo-hoo as you wrap your fingers around it, pull the door until you hear a click and you can't pull it anymore. Lean back on your heels and wait for everything to change.

Mr. Skin stops his lecture, Lolita stops shrieking, her boy stops dodging the question, all turn to stare at the looming statue filling the room.

The edge of this new hole is ragged and the drunk tries to keep his face away from it as he pulls himself out. Last thing he needs is a splinter in his nose. He sees the lot floorside speechless, the army of lolitas dropping their weapons in a cacophonous unified movement, the inert body of Salaryman suddenly falling through the doorway behind the lolitas; ignores it all. The captain is tantalizingly close; all they need to do is crawl out of the hole, drag her into it and get the hell out of here. The crazies can do whatever they want.

Tiptoe movement towards their leader. The driver grabs an arm and tries to pretend that he is invisible. He heard that this works in cancer therapy, visualization or something. With the drunk grasping the other arm firmly, he gives a tug to get her moving, winces at the sudden squeak of her rubber-soled shoes dragging.

"What just happened?" Her tiny girl voice even tinier. Without turning away from the golden goddess of mercy, Lolita crouches down to let a shivering Mr. Fluffles crawl into her boxy handbag.

Slowly shaking his head, repeatedly revealing and hiding one eye. "Like uh, the door. The door." New Wave starts giggling to himself.

"Goddammit!" Mr. Skin would throw his hat to the floor if he was wearing one.

Cats jump on you, past you, over you, stream through the hole and make their way around the statue. Is this a good sign? Did everything change? Digging deep and finding a final bit of courage, you move out from under the charm. And your face slams into the floor again. Everything did not change.

Anxious. This shouldn't be. Muffin thought that closing the door would make things right, but here Corduroy is, face on the floor. Quick with the charm, but not quick enough.

You glare at him as you pull yourself upright yet again. "Goddammit."

The engineer frowns, pushes past the two idiots squatting on the floor in front of the hole. Something has to have changed. Things have to be different. They closed the door. That has to put an end to this whole ridiculous affair and she can focus her mind on forgetting.

Nervous starts to rise to go after the angry girl and you have no choice but to follow. This is it. This is your new life. It's so much worse than the explosion-filled life.

The driver drops an arm at the sight of his lover emerging from behind the golden giant in the centre of the room. What is she doing? He want to run over to her, but his criminal nature compels him to remain hidden behind New Wave and the guy with all the skin. Although that guy is mostly just gaping and not seeming too threatening.

"Ah, no, man." New Wave's laughter is languid. "You go uh give her like a hug or something, right? Gotta show the uh love."

The driver tries not to think about whether New Wave knew they were here the whole time. Either way, no point in pretending they're not here now. He gets a punch in the arm from the drunk as he steps forward, deliberately avoids wrapping his arms around his lover. He doesn't take orders from men who can't even give them properly. "What happened? What's going on?"

Cats surround New Wave, climb up his body to rest on his shoulders, his head. "Like uh, good question, you know." Staring pointedly at Lolita. "You like uh don't know, do you?"

Inching away from the cats pouring into the room. "You jerk. Of course I know. You know. God. We are so totally broken up."

"You already said that." Maybe it is not really so wise of the drunk to point it out.

"I know I did." Hissing and he can almost see the tongue reaching out across the room to give him a slap.

"Well, that's it. That's jes' great." No more shuffle stepping. Mr. Skin actually picks up his feet and thuds out of the room. "All the damned time I spend on this. I am sick to death of you, boy. Can't keep your own damned self out of things. I ever get the chance, boy..." Inaudible muttering as he kicks the unconscious Salaryman aside, pounds down the front steps out to the temple yard.

Slow, careful steps. No more curse-counting. Your anger is spent. You just want to find a comfortable bed, stop introducing your face to different types of surfaces. Too many kinds of wood are already imprinted on your cheeks. You still have dead leaves in your hair. You step out into the room, in front of the giant Kannon that you thought could save you, and the boy with the asymmetrical hair bursts out laughing. Great. Just great.

"You don't know!" He struggles to breathe between high-pitched giggles, tears forming the corners of his eyes. Turning to meet the eyes of cats on either shoulder. "See that? He's like still uh, in the game, doesn't even like uh know it. Old man uh always runnin' out too uh soon, right."

The tiny grey stray on his head casually draws claws across his forehead, pulling aside black hair to reveal both eyes for just a minute.

You stare at Lolita, the red-eyed rabbit, the giggling boy, the captain unconscious on the floor, Salaryman unconscious on the floor. Your heart leaps. You're doing something right. Or maybe these pirates are doing something right. Your heart sinks.

"Oh, come on." Laden with sarcasm and you turn your head upwards. Pink Hair is perched comfortably on Kannon's sloping left shoulder. Legs crossed and dangling over the edge to kick the goddess of mercy in the breast. "Do I have to spell this out for you?" She snaps her gum, runs lacquered nails through tangled hair.

"S-s-spell what out?" Muffin needs it spelled out.

Ignore Nervous. You're sure he's a nice guy, but he doesn't have much to offer in a crisis. You notice Boy on the floor, surrounded by Persians. Why does he get Persians and New Wave gets a gang of scraggly strays? Is that what Pink Hair has to spell out? Shake your head clear. Focus. The cats are not the issue here. What is the issue? The spelling out, the spelling out. What does she not have to spell out for you? Goddammit. You could think a lot better if you didn't have to worry about Mr. Needs to Get Out More moving accidentally and sending you toppling.

"All your uh hard work for like nothing, right." New Wave turns a wide grin up to the girl balanced on Kannon's shoulder.

"You should talk." She scoffs, pulls out a compact and lipstick, gets to work. "I thought you weren't going to do this again. I thought we had a deal. Bad enough I have to deal with him." Lets her eyes find the doorway, the man with the extra skin beyond it.

The drunk can hear the forced casual in her voice. He hopes it's not due to a failed past relationship. Did his pretty pixie used to date the boy with the bad hair?

She drops the eight metres from Kannon's shoulder to the floor to stand in front of him, red nails on boyish hips. "Look, I haven't said anything before, but you really have to stop thinking like that. It's getting a little old. He's not my boyfriend. He was never my boyfriend. You don't stand a chance with me. Okay? Got that?" Snaps her gum loudly, big finish.

Ignore them. Ignore the laughing asshole with a cat on his head. Ignore Boy on the floor, although you're really worried about him and regretting what you said before about breaking up with him. You can't just leave him like this. And then the train hits you. The busiest train in the city, the one all the suicides choose. The one that hits hard enough to send you flying. Up. You just have to remember which way is up. That's what she said before, right? Sudden concern that it's a trick question. You've always been so certain that up was that way (handy mental figure points to the natural wood ceiling); it seems too easy. Is that still up?

Lolita glares as New Wave collapses in laughter. "What is so funny, you jerk?"

Pink Hair clicks her tongue, slow side to side with her pink hair. "See, you should have just stayed out of it. You're not ready. If you were, you'd be laughing with him. Or concerned with me."

Both hands on hips, Mr. Fluffles swinging wildly on one wrist, she puts her tongue as far out as she can make it go. "You just have to better than me, don't you? You just think you're so great. Well, at least I have some creativity and maybe I want to try some new things. You're just rules, rules, rules."

"Hey! Those rules are important!" Gum cracking briskly, she crosses the room to push Lolita backwards. "Those rules keep this world right-side up."

"But why should it be right-side up?" Lower lip pushed way out. "Why can't it be some other way sometimes?"

"Because it can't be some other way sometimes, you idiot. God. Why do I have to explain this to you?" Turning on one heel to glare at New Wave still rolling around on the floor. "You started this. You should be telling her."

"I uh like—" New Wave meets your eyes and the laughter that was dying down takes off again. Clearly, you are the cause of his mirth.

"Fuck you." Growling, maybe not loud enough for him to hear, but loud enough to make you feel better and cause Nervous to raise his eyebrows slightly. Honestly, his mother has to be one of those horrible fifties nuclear war scare era moms, the ones that bake cookies when they hear that the bomb is on its way. Only such a mother could produce this oddly nervous and prudish son.

Muffin can see that Corduroy is sending angry eyes his way, but can't figure out why. He's done nothing this time. He's just standing here, making sure that everyone stays on their feet. Underappreciated. He is underappreciated. They'll probably get back out to sea and he'll be back to making coffee and going to the grocery store, even though it is so obvious that he is totally saving the day here. "F-fuck you." Adopting Corduroy's low-volume growl. He may keep it; this is the kind of cursing he is capable of.

You jerk your head back a little. Is he saying that to you? Follow his line of sight, figure it's more directed at his pirate friends and anyway, you have other things to think about. Like which way is up. Eeney-meeney-miney-moe it and you get left. You're not so comfortable with left. You're actually not comfortable with any up other than the one you're used to. Swallow your breath, hope Nervous stays steady. You point to the high, wood ceiling above your head.

"That way is up!"

Trying to be dramatic and declarative, but still feeling a little silly. Of course, that way is up. And if this is not the thing Pink Hair didn't want to spell out for you? Put that out of your head; that's tumour talk.

Pink Hair runs over and brings a hand up to high five the drunk, who gladly raises his own hand to meet hers. He's pretty sure the captain won't mind being dropped. She's unconscious. And he's touched the pixie. It's not the kind of touching he had hoped for, but at least it proves that she's real enough for that kind of touching.

New Wave pulls himself up off the floor, brushes the dust off his black slim-fit trousers. "Don't get too excited. We'll do this again."

Pink Hair sticks out her tongue, dances energetic circles around

Lolita. "Doesn't matter. You're oh for a million or something here. I always win. I make good choices. Look at my pirates here!" Swoops down on the driver, grabs his face, plants a red kiss on his cheek.

Lolita turns a sad face down at Mr. Fluffles, whose frantic twitching seems to slow. She runs a pale hand over white fur. "Oh, Mr. Fluffles. Don't be too disappointed." Turning slowly, she puts one pink boot in front of the other. Shuffles towards the open, glassless temple doors. "We just didn't think it all through this time, right? If we had just gotten Up to be here a little later, we could have gotten more time. It's a learning experience, Mr. Fluffles. And what else have we learned?" The army of lolitas move as one to pick up fallen weapons, turn as if commanded by a 'ten-hut' and follow their leader out into the open space in front of the temple. "That's right. We've learned that love is dangerous." Her voice is drowned out by the footsteps of her many legions moving across the gravel, down the stairs.

Groaning and rubbing her head, the captain wonders where she is this time.

"Captain!" Startled out of lurid dreams of Pink Hair and the kinds of touching possible with a pixie.

Your jaw drops. You are one smart cookie and the significance of the captain finding her way back to consciousness is not lost on you. If she's awake, you're free. But you thought that before and you've pretty much used up all the bravery and daring you have so you turn your face up to Nervous. "I'm going to go this way. If I fall, please catch me. My head hurts."

Muffin nods solemnly.

You step forward and remain standing. So this is it. You're standing without a nervous boy holding a thing over your head. Nothing is exploding. You're surrounded by pirates and people you can't begin to explain, but nothing is exploding.